A GAME OF SECRETS

D1493979

Thomas Wiseman

A Game of Secrets

Futura Publications Limited

A Futura Book

First published in Great Britain by
Jonathan Cape Limited in 1979
First Futura Publications edition 1980
Reprinted 1980

ISBN 0 7088 1777 7

Typeset, printed and bound in Great Britain by
Hazell Watson & Viney Ltd
Aylesbury, Bucks

Futura Publications Limited
110 Warner Road
Camberwell, London SE5

FOR MALOU

It will be apparent to the reader that not all the events depicted in these pages are pure invention, but this should not lead to the expectation of total historical accuracy. Whatever the author's borrowings from fact, this is a work of fiction and the characters are imaginary, even those who happen to be called 'President Truman' or 'Defence Secretary Forrestal' or 'Admiral Leahy'.

Of course, one's imagination is coloured by what is known to have happened, and in the matter of the secret actions of governments the Freedom of Information Act in the United States does now enable the patient researcher to see the tip of the iceberg. From this the writer of fiction can attempt to construe the rest.

T. W.

We had received some dozen reports referring to the source, who appeared in the documents under the code-name Homer, but little progress had been made towards identifying him. The FBI was still sending us reams about the Embassy charladies, and the enquiry into our menial personnel was spinning itself out endlessly. To me, this remains the most inexplicable feature of the whole affair. There was already evidence that the Foreign Office had been penetrated. Both Krivitsky and Volkov had said so. There was, of course, nothing to suggest that the three sources referred to the same man. There is still no basis for that supposition . . .

Kim Philby, *My Secret War*

'I should lay it down that the existence of secret agents should not be tolerated, as tending to augment the positive dangers of the evil against which they are used. That the spy will fabricate his information is a mere commonplace. But in the sphere of political and revolutionary action, relying on violence, the professional spy has every facility to fabricate the facts themselves, and will spread the double evil of emulation in one direction, and of panic, hasty legislation, unreflecting hate, in the other. However, this is an imperfect world . . .'

Joseph Conrad, *The Secret Agent*

PART ONE

I first got to know Bill Hardtman in Berlin at the end of the Second World War when we were both working in Intelligence. I liked him at once. He had the best manners of any American I have known. He had been partly educated in England, and came to like our way of doing things, and that was a bond between us.

This is Hardtman's story, not mine: I bring myself into it only by way of explaining how I know so much about him. His confidences were not all imparted at the time of these events – some things he told me about only much later. At one stage he showed me a manuscript he was working on. It was to have explained everything from his point of view, and in it he was extraordinarily frank – particularly about certain aspects of his private life – but in the end he decided that even the frankest account would not be believed, the waters had been too muddied by then, and he burned what he had written. However, I have a good, almost photographic, memory for details, and much of what he had put down on paper I am able to recall, and then I have my own sources, too.

I begin with the murder of Starkov, in Berlin, during the great snowfall of January 1948, though Hardtman was not there at the time, and had no idea that this faraway Cold War incident was going to affect his life.

It was a dreadful winter everywhere, but in Berlin it was worse than in most places. For the Germans there was not much to eat and it was hard to keep warm. A barbaric wind came through the bare branches of the trees and the empty window spaces of the bombed buildings. This wind came all the way from the Russian steppes, the Berliners told you. All the worst things that had befallen them were of Russian origin. But had the curses of the condemned ever brought down the gallows? They gave you their wry, dark, knowing smile while paying lip-service to our naïve belief that we would be able to find a way of getting on with the Russians. The Germans knew better. There would have to be another war to tie up the loose ends of Europe – I had heard them say this in '45, their deeply dazed faces lighting up in a moment of anticipated *Schadenfreude* (the worst had already happened to them, now it was our turn), and three years later they were able to add, 'I told you so'. By then there were plenty of people on our side, too, who thought another war was inevitable. Churchill, though out of office, was confidently expecting to be called upon again to save Europe – this time from the egregious embrace of Uncle Joe. Behind the scenes he was telling his good friend the American Ambassador in London that once the Soviets had developed the atom bomb, war would be a certainty, and now was the time to let the Russians know that we would raze their cities to the ground if they did not retire from Berlin, abandon Eastern Germany and withdraw to the Polish frontier.

Britain was in the middle of a severe fuel crisis and freezing, but there were those who warmed their hearts on Churchillian bravado and made believe we could still put our foot down if we chose. We would teach the Russians a lesson in international manners. Our imperial spirit was to have one or two other eccentric resurgences, even as it waned.

The Alexanderplatz was always the centre of the working-class section of Berlin. It had many high, workers' habitations of a kind of imposing plainness by comparison with the baroque excesses evident in other parts of the city. Behind the great avenue that leads up to the Platz there is a maze of little streets where, it was said, you could buy and sell anything that the heart desired and the law forbade. These streets at 6 o'clock at night became darker than during the wartime blackouts, for there was a nightly electricity cut that came into force then. It was a good time for the pursuit of a certain kind of trade. In dozens of doorways, the flames of cigarette lighters cast their feeble light upon the dealings of men in long overcoats and half-mittens, whose pockets were filled with bread slices, Hershey bars, PX nylons, Western currencies, cigarettes, and other saleable commodities. One of the other commodities sometimes sold in these streets was information, and so it was quite usual for Starkov to wander around here, talking to his spies, while pretending to be engaged in the black market.

On this particular evening in January 1948 there were not many people about because of the snowstorm that had been blowing intermittently for the past twenty-four hours, creating traffic havoc and causing the abandonment of many vehicles. Starkov seemed to be in a hurry. He was not stopping in his usual doorways. Instead, with head down, he was setting off in a westerly direction. He was a large man with a rather flat face. He wore a good overcoat with a fur collar. Also a broad-brimmed hat.

He was now heading in the direction of the Potsdamer Platz where the British, American and Russian sectors of the occupied city met. He did not pass many people – an old woman pushing a pram containing a few pieces of wood, another carrying a paraffin can. There was something almost romantic about the so-dark streets and the swirling snowfall and the melancholy-faced Russian hurrying to his appointment. You might have supposed that he had fallen in love with an English girl and was meeting her at the railway station. From behind a window covered up with cardboard and tar-paper came the sound of a dance tune, a foxtrot, scratchy and faint, being played on a gramophone.

The broad brim of Starkov's hat was becoming heavy with snow, and as if bothered by this extra weight he took off the hat and shook it, once or twice, at the same time looking around him. He seemed not entirely sure that he was in the right street, it was so dark. Taking out a small electric torch, he directed its narrow beam this way and that. The pencil of light showed two bulky forms a short distance behind him. *They* appeared to know exactly where they were and where they were going, but Starkov seemed reluctant to ask them for directions. They did not look the types who might be helpful – they were in too much of a hurry.

In his eagerness not to be late for his appointment, Starkov was virtually running, and once or twice came close to slipping – there was hard ice under the new snow. His hurry was somehow communicated to the men behind him, for whenever he broke into a run they did, too. His ballooning breathclouds, caught in the beams of their flashlights, gave them a trail to follow.

Starkov was sweating, and his normal expression of vague melancholy had changed to one of sudden – and specific – fear. He was quite white from head to toe. Turning a corner, he suddenly began to run all out, putting on an amazing turn of speed for someone of his size, and considering the slipperiness of the road. Running and slipping like some ice-skater gone berserk, he was making towards a gutted tenement that appeared intermittently through the snowstorm.

By the time his pursuers had turned the corner, too, also now running hard and sliding about, he was nowhere to be seen, his snow-piled form having merged into ruins and rubble as white as he.

They shone their flashlights in all directions. The beams showed doorways piled high with snow, making virtually flush surfaces with door jambs. Window embrasures had filled up, leaving only cracks of glass visible here and there. Retaining walls were buttressed by snow. Lampposts were grossly enlarged, like circus clowns with dangling false stomachs.

The sound of boots on iron made them direct their flashlights upward. High amid the bare girders of a fire-bombed building there was a sort of open bridgeway connecting the burnt-out part with a habitable section. They caught a glimpse of something moving along this bridge, and since there was no sign of their quarry anywhere else, they looked for some way of getting to this upper level. It was apparently reached by means of fire-escape ladders, which they at once began to mount. Their flashlights shining in

16

all directions marked their progress. When they reached the bridge of girders and wood planks that went right through the middle of the ruin, they began to run and continued until they came to a part of the building that was occupied. They beat with heavy fists upon a rough wooden door; it was opened after a long time and they were met by a solid wall of congealed bad breath. Overriding the protesting voices, they forced their way inside.

Below, in one of the dark doorways, the snow began to move and slowly, cautiously, Starkov emerged, shaking himself, leaving behind him the deep imprint of his body.

Despite the cold and the continuing snowfall, he took off his hat and coat, thereby transforming his sillhouette, and walking quickly, but with a different gait than before, retraced his steps, skirting the various checkpoints, until he found an unpatrolled section of the boundary where he was able to cross unnoticed into the British sector of the city.

He walked for some time in a seemingly aimless way, even taking a stroll in the Tiergarten, which once had been a wooded park but was now just a bare field. He kept looking round to see if he was being followed, and finally satisfied that he was not, made his way into the centre. Once past the Allied Control Authority Building, he turned into a side street and continued until he came to a newish-looking sign which said: British Welfare Committee, 5th floor. Room 607.

The lift at the end of the hallway was not working because of the electricty cut, and the stairs were dark. Shining his small electric torch, Starkov heaved himself up five flights of stairs, scattering snow like a wind-blown tree. By the time he had got to the top he seemed to have no breath left and looked on the verge of collapse.

When he found room 607 in his torch beam, he banged violently on the door. His knocking produced no response. His flat face began to heave with disbelief and panic and he proceeded to beat both fists against the door as if determined to batter it down.

After about two minutes of this, the door was finally

17

opened, and a slight, ginger-haired English corporal, very much wrapped up against the cold, holding a cigarette deep inside the hollow of one hand while finishing buttoning his fly with the other, gave the caller a perfunctory glance and informed him: 'Closed.' He started to shut the door, but something in the visitor's expression of disbelief made him go so far as to translate. '*Geschlossen* till tomorrow. *Come back tomorrow. Verstehen? Comprendo?*'

Starkov seemed to be shaking, whether from cold or emotion was not clear. A burst of very foreign sounds came from his lips, causing Corporal Brown to wince. 'Now *try* to understand, sir,' he said through the slightly open door. 'No bloody use you carrying on. Don't understand a bloody word you're saying. *Nicht verstehen*. You Russian or something?' he added, since the outpouring seemed quite foreign enough for that. 'Russe?' he demanded, pointing at him. 'You *Russe* – eh?'

Starkov nodded vigorously, and made a great many wild gesticulations, which Corporal Brown interpreted as expressing a desire to come in.

'O.K., mate, O.K., now take it easy, now,' he told him, opening the door a little further. 'You want to take it easy or you're going ter burst a bloody blood vessel, you are. O.K., go on then, let's 'ave you in. You *are* in a state.' He shook his head. 'Parla Italiano?' he demanded, to give himself time to think, and nodded with relief when the foreigner shook his head. 'Well, neither do I, mate, so that makes two of us, don't it? *Deutsch-sprechen?*' he tried next.

There now began an outpouring in German from which Corporal Brown made out little more than the recurring expression *Tod und Leben*, *Tod und Leben*, which, screwing up his brow, he translated as meaning life and death.

'What about a cup o' tea then?' he offered, pointing to the gas ring on which a kettle was steaming steadily.

The Russian was nodding continuously as Corporal Brown poured out the tea into tin mugs and shovelled three spoonsful of sugar into each one. ''Ere, 'ave a borrow of this,' he said offering his tin spoon. He was trying to work out what to do. These foreigners were an excitable lot. *Tod und Leben?*

'Now look 'ere, sir,' Corporal Brown said, offering the Russian one of his Woodbines. 'Officer that speaks your lingo went 'ome. *Schlafen gehen.* Shut-eye. *Comprendo?*' He began to snore to drive home his meaning, but without success. The Russian was becoming more and more confused. 'Is it something important then?' Corporal Brown inquired, and when this elicited a further outburst, he had an inspiration. 'Now tell you what,' he said. 'let's just 'ave a dekko 'ere . . .' And he began to rummage in desk drawers until he had found what he was looking for; a printed form, with a series of questions, in German, French, English and Russian.

At first Starkov could not make out what he was being asked to do, but when Corporal Brown kept pointing to the question 'Nature of business', an incredulous kind of comprehension at last came over the Russian's face, and taking out a pen he began to write rapidly.

'Leave your address where you can be reached,' Corporal Brown told him and took the form back and put it in a drawer, and with a sigh of relief steered the visitor out.

It continued to snow all night long, finally stopping at around 7 a.m. The storm had caused many vehicles to be abandoned in the streets, where some had become buried in snow drifts. In the morning, police and Control Authority personnel were supervising the clearing of the streets. Cars which blocked important traffic arteries were being dug out and towed clear.

Workers were digging out one car in the middle of the Kantstrasse. When the snow had been shovelled away, they could not see inside because windscreen and windows were iced-up and opaque. It was only when a small circle of ice had been scraped away that somebody looking inside saw that there was a figure in the back seat, upright, still as death. A thick woollen scarf was wound several times around his neck. There was no movement whatso-

19

ever in the flat face, the features of which seemed unrelated to each other, as if they had been thrown together accidentally.

'Must 'ave froze stiff, poor 'ole bugger,' one of the diggers said, peering into the car.

The door locks were frozen and it took some time to deice them and find a key that fitted. By then people were gathering around.

When, finally, the rear door was opened, a British patrol had arrived on the scene and a sergeant got into the car and took a look at the unmoving figure. He felt for the man's pulse and decided he was dead. Must have become stranded in the snowstorm and taken shelter in an abandoned car, the sergeant guessed. It was only as he was pulling the body out, dragging it by the armpits, that the thick woollen scarf began to unwind itself, revealing that Starkov's throat had been cut from ear to ear.

In Washington it had also snowed. Graham Forster, woken up at an unaccustomed hour by the phone's boringly persistent ring, lifted a corner of the curtains to see what sort of time it was (his watch not being luminous) and found himself looking out upon a gentle snow scene: white roofs, a row of high narrow houses, Georgian windows, wistaria thickening on brick and stucco, basement areas enclosed by iron railings – he might have been back in Chelsea.

'It's Christopher,' the voice on the phone said, when Forster finally lifted the receiver. An apologetic laugh followed. 'Know this is not your customary hour for rising . . . are you there, Graham?'

'More or less. Though I have the kind of head that makes me wish I weren't.'

Christopher Holbrook repeated his apologetic laugh, apologizing for the other man's hangover.

'Can you – uh – talk?' he asked.

'Only up to a point,' Forster said, shooting a glance at the deeply slumbering youth by his side, whose face in the morning light was of an even coarser mould than it had appeared to be last night.

'The fact is,' Holbrook said, 'the Yanks will have to be informed. So you had better come in on this.'

'How desperately urgent is it?'

'The telegram was marked Most Immediate.'

'Then it can wait until lunch,' Forster said. 'Town Club? My treat.'

'I think it had better not be the Town. We don't want to run into our American friends before I've had a chance to brief you.'

'The Mayflower? Half-past one?'

'Make it quarter-past,' Holbrook pleaded. 'I've got a lot on my plate.'

'I'll try,' Forster promised.

'I think I want another gin,' Graham Forster said, crooking his little finger at the waiter. The first couple of large drinks had begun to put him together again, but the process was not quite complete yet. 'Give me another moment, Chris, and you shall have the benefit of all my mental faculties, such as they are.'

'These oysters really are not at all bad,' Holbrook remarked. 'Last time I ate oysters as good as these was at Prunier's before the war.'

When the waiter's attention had been secured, and he had come to their table, Forster ordered another double gin, with a touch of tonic, no ice.

'And you, Chris? Will you have another one of those?' He was referring to the glass of California Chablis that Holbrook was sipping. 'How is that, by the way?'

'Apart from the metallurgic flavour – I find most things in America taste as if they have come out of a tin – or can, as they say – not at all bad. But I won't have another, thank you. One glass is enough for me at lunch time.'

Forster gave a tolerant smile. With another gin coming, he was beginning to feel a lot better. When, a few minutes later, the alcohol level in his blood had become sufficiently raised, a ruddy glow, that could have been mistaken for a sign of good health, spread over his face. There were moments – if the drink was working well but not too well

21

– when he could be charming: at such times he had the white head of a wicked and distinguished uncle.

'Remember the marvellous meal we had at that little place in Charlotte Street? Before the war. The days of our mis-spent youth. What was the name of the place? Full of Jews, but damned good. We had lobsters, partridge, plum pudding, sherry, mulled claret, and afterwards we went and drank chartreuse at Quags.'

'The Café Royal.'

'No, no, I do remember now, it was the Trocadero. And it wasn't chartreuse at all. It was white port. I remember we got absolutely stinking on white port.'

'Yes, I do seem to remember you did,' Holbrook said.

'All by myself? How damned unconvivial of you, Chris. I have noticed that puritan streak of abstemiousness in you.'

Holbrook looked tense; he had small features, there was something petty about the mouth, the nose, the ears. He gave the impression of being a man of small appetite. He had a wintery smile, and a continual air of faint embarrassment.

To follow the oysters, he chose lamb chops and peas, and asked the waiter to be a good fellow and find some mint sauce. Forster's appetite had not yet recovered, and he chose grilled bluefish.

'Well, what's the flap?' he now asked, drinking his gin.

Holbrook looked around. He had made it a habit always to refuse the first table offered to him at any restaurant: his security-consciousness thus satisfied, he felt free to talk. He double-checked by making sure nobody was seated within earshot, and then said with the air of someone continuing a light, lunch-time conversation.

'Chap got his throat cut. In Berlin. Our zone. Turns out he was Starkov, *Starkov of the MGB.*'

'Starkov,' Graham Forster said. 'So Starkov has bought it. Well, well, well. Or should one say good, good, good?'

'What makes it such a sod,' Christopher Holbrook said, 'is that he'd come to volunteer, and we let him slip through our fingers. Shown the door by some imbecile corporal minding the shop. Medlicott, the station head, bungled the whole thing – even with K there to hold his hand. Can you believe it!'

'Yes, I can, I *can*.'

'Well, there's a fearful stink about it. The idiot prole left at the desk, not a word of German let alone Russian to save his life, could only think of getting the fellow to fill in a form. You know, nature of business, et cetera. Which he did, and that's what makes it worse – because he was offering us treasure, Graham. Treasure.'

'Tell about the treasure, Chris.'

Graham Forster had finished his third gin and was signalling for another. From the way he was only picking at the fish, it seemed that his appetite had entirely left him.

'Well, understandably, he was only giving away just enough to hook us.'

'And how much is just enough?'

'To begin with he was offering to tell us the identity of Homer.'

'Was he now! Was he indeed! How substantial a hook was it exactly?'

'He corroborated everything that Krivitsky told us in '40. That Homer was recruited by the Russians when he was an undergraduate at Oxford. That he'd been to Eton. That he was an idealist. Very well connected. And working in the Foreign Office.'

'Nothing exactly new then in Starkov's bag?' Forster said.

'Fact that he got his throat cut does tend to validate our previous sources. There *is* one additional piece of information. According to our late informant, Homer now is working out of Washington, and a very prolific source indeed. Which, of course, does line up with what the Yanks have been saying. Looks as though it may be someone in the Embassy, I think. Graham, we are obliged to pass this on to the Americans. Which was why I called you this morning: I don't think we should delay – I'd rather we told them. If they find out from *their* sources, they'll accuse us of withholding . . .'

'They are not going to like this,' Forster mused. 'Someone in the Embassy – eh? My Gawd! That will make things cosy for us. Eton and Oxford, hmm? I suppose that means J. Edgar's Rover Boys will stop grilling our charladies and turn the heat on us.'

'I didn't go to Eton myself,' Holbrook said. 'It was Westminster, as a matter of fact.'

'You think that lets you out?' Forster gave a chortle. 'The Rover Boys leave no stone unturned, and as far as they are concerned Westminster is a mere stone's throw from Eton. As the Russian crow flies.'

Holbrook gave his faintly embarrassed smile. 'I suppose the Russians may have the idea that all upperclass Englishmen go to Eton, and that Westminster is just another name for it. Ah – you did go to Eton, Graham . . .'

'Yes, but not Oxford,' Forster said. 'It was Cambridge, actually.'

'That's right. Sculled for them, didn't you?'

'Yes, briefly.'

'You did rather a lot of things briefly at Cambridge.'

'I have to remember,' Forster said by way of warning himself, 'that one has no secrets from one's internal security officer. True, I was a bit of a gadabout at Cambridge. So many activities. So many temptations. The way of all flesh – eh? Well, nearly all flesh,' he hastily corrected himself. 'I believe *you*, Chris, kept your nose pretty much to the grindstone at Oxford. Got a First, didn't you?'

'Yes,' Holbrook admitted without relish.

'Well, from what I've been told, the temptations at Oxford were not nearly so great.'

'Be that as it may . . .' Holbrook began.

'You may also have been more single-minded in your objectives,' Forster said.

'I leave it to you,' Holbrook said, 'exactly how you tell the Americans. But I suggest you do it at once, and do make it clear we are not allowing any grass to grow under

24

our feet. We are double-checking everybody. From the highest to the lowest.'

'I'm sure they'll be very glad to hear that. The Yanks are so very possessive about their little secrets.'

2

At first sight the British Embassy in Washington has about it a faint air of Hampstead Garden Suburb, a sort of genteel grandeur. Nothing showy like the Iranian Embassy down the road, with its blue and white Persian ceramics; the British place, in red brick and limestone, looks more like a country house with well-wooded grounds all around.

At the time of which I write, the lines of Sir Edwin Lutyens's distinguished conception had been somewhat spoilt by the construction of additional office accommodation: extra storeys had been put on top of the Old Chancery and a whole new wing had been built that enclosed what had previously been an open forecourt, obscuring from view much of the front elevation of the original building, truncating the noble columns and the high domed central window. A visual offence undoubtedly – for the eye should have been drawn unresistingly to the high pediment with the royal crest, instead of being distracted by a brick wall that created the impression of the entablature resting on midget pillars. But the Embassy staff had swelled from a total of thirty-nine before the war to over four hundred, and all that additional pushing of pens had to be done somewhere.

The continuing growth of our staff in Washington was an indication of how much we now depended on the Americans. Too much, some of us thought. We were in danger of losing our own identity and becoming one of Uncle Sam's satellites.

Our parties, at any rate, were still in keeping with Britain's ostensible position in the world, and were usually grand affairs. There was one in January, shortly following the mishap in Berlin. I had just come back from there myself, after trying to salvage as much as I could from that mess. The fact that we might have had Homer on the reception line was not allowed to cramp our style. The ability not to panic is an aspect of our national character that has often stood us in good stead, and we called upon it on this occasion. Since Homer could have been any of a dozen or more highly placed individuals, everybody acted as if the possibility that you were he need not be entertained. Innocent until proved guilty – that was the British way.

The big American cars wound continuously between the lion and the unicorn mounted on the Embassy gateposts, and made their way across the forecourt and then alongside the Old Chancery to the *porte cochère* of the Residence. Footmen opened car doors and directed guests to the cloakrooms and up the twin staircases that rose past full-length portraits of the kings and queens of England.

There was a firm handshake and a calm, confident smile for each guest. Everything under control.

In former days it had been customary to agonize over the guest list with Social Register in one hand and a Congressional Directory in the other, but in 1948 everybody was asked. There were Congressmen from West Virginia and Utah, Presidents of the Railroad Brotherhoods, representatives of the Grange, the farm bureaux, the Boy Scouts, the Camp Fire Girls, the 4-H, the AFL, the CIO, the business associations, the veterans' groups, and of course the military, the State Department, the Treasury Department, and the other embassies.

The American women in their Dior copies from Bergdorf Goodman – the New Look had come in – were all sharply protruding shoulder blades that the backless gowns emphasized quite needlessly. All those thin sharp women, exposing their pale unappetizing flesh above hips as ruffled and flounced as any Victorian bronze's. The Russian women had no necks and huge bosoms contained in their usual sackcloth, which, for evening wear, had a kind of shine. The English women were all neck and no bosom. The French women lived up to their reputation and were chic.

And they were all very weary of parties. There were too many of them in Washington.

In the ballroom the band was playing a medley of Gilbert and Sullivan airs. And Peter Volniakov, the new Russian cultural attaché, was eating his way down the length of the buffet table, helping himself to everything. *Oeufs en gelée* were followed by smoked salmon in aspic and *pâté de foie gras* and hot shrimp puffs and bacon-wrapped oysters and cold turkey and cold roast beef and cold Scotch salmon. He was a large young man, visibly going to fat from party to party. He had only recently arrived in Washington and he could not get over the food – how plentiful it was, how tasty. While his eyes searched for other things to eat, he was also on the lookout for pretty women. The thin ones clutching their gold rope-weave purses were not to his taste. He had appetite for richer fare . . . and his eyes gleamed when he saw Laurene Hardtman. She had the sort of bold, dark, flashing good looks that owe as much to sheer animation as to actual bone structure . . . the nose was long but straight and delicately angled from the forehead, which was round and soft. She wore a Balenciaga, high at the front, plunging at the back into a deep and daring V that drew the eye as if by a directional sign to a most enticing rear. Volniakov clearly was enticed. He was looking around for some way of getting an introduction to her when he saw Christopher Holbrook.

'Something I can get you, Mr Volniakov?' he inquired, in response to the Russian's urgent summons.

'No, no; have plenty. Too much. Of everything is too much in America. Is your problem. Regret is not our problem in Rosha. If have to have problem, prefer yours.' He gave Holbrook a friendly dig in the ribs, and chuckled. He was a most amiable fellow. 'Tell to me,' he asked, 'who it is, this charr-ming woman? There.'

'Mrs Hardtman. She is the wife of one of the President's new assistants.'

'You can introduce me, please?'

'Yes, of course, if you wish.'

28

'You would make me a favour. Please.'

Holbrook led Volniakov over to Laurene Hardtman, and introduced him.

'I want to tell you, Mrs Hardtman,' he said, kissing her hand, 'that in one regard you have us beaten. Only one. Womans here is much more beautiful. No question.' He waved a large Russian finger at her. 'Including especially present company.'

'Well, thanks, Mr Volniakov. You are very gallant. I have heard that Russian women are very beautiful too.'

'Is also true,' Volniakov conceded, with a large gesture of his arms. 'But a little too much . . .' He drew a massive shape with his hands. 'Is better thin. Like you, Mrs Hardtman. For woman like you, I go crazy in my mind.'

'I can see you're a dangerous man, Mr Volniakov,' Laurene said, laughing.

Graham Forster, well oiled by now, was at the other end of the ballroom, by a set of leather screens depicting in gold leaf the defeat of the Spanish Armada. He was talking to Walter Cole, explaining to him about the British upper classes.

'You see,' he was saying, 'we may look silly cunts, we may even be silly cunts, but we do know what's first class and what isn't. We have an eye. Our inheritance – Even when some of us haven't got too much up here, we still have this eye, which tells us what's what. Generations of living with the best has given us taste. What you might call an instinct for the best. We may not know anything about art, but we know good paintings, you see, because after all we've had the stuff around us for centuries . . .'

'Pity,' his listener reflected confidentially, 'this great eye of yours doesn't help you stop Homer.'

'Well, the problem there is,' Forster confided in return, 'that he may be absolutely first rate, too, don't you see? I mean, he would have to be, wouldn't he? If he's been getting away with it this long.'

'You mean he also has got this instinct for the best?'

'Well, he'd be bound to have. With his background.'

'There has got to be something wrong with your instinct,'

29

Cole said with an easy chuckle, 'if it lets him choose the Commies. Instead of us.'

'We do tend to make somewhat eccentric choices at times,' Forster conceded, and added quickly: 'I think Christopher is absolutely first-rate. Be on to him in no time, I'll bet.'

'It's eight years since you people first heard of Homer's existence,' Cole pointed out.

'We're flying some kites; we'll see where the wind takes them, and draw the appropriate conclusions,' Forster said. 'Oh I'm the first to admit there has been tardiness in the past . . . but we are getting cracking on this now.'

Walter Cole, was officially on a leave of absence from his New York law firm to head a Committee advising the President on the reconstruction of American Intelligence.

He was a sociable man who looked like an old-fashioned banker; tall, thin, with steel-rimmed glasses, white hair, white moustache and deep pouches under his eyes. He laughed a good deal, and was often at parties. A jovial man, though not given to letting himself be contradicted, and sometimes you saw his banker's eyes light up at the prospect of a killing. His marriage was said not to be too happy. At any rate, he went everywhere by himself. He was, as the saying is, highly visible, perhaps on the theory that the best possible cover for someone heading a covert action is to be seen everywhere.

'I notice,' he now remarked, 'that our friend the new Soviet cultural attaché – who, I can tell you, knows nothing about the ballet; I've already tried him on that – has been talking to Laurene Hardtman for the past fifteen minutes. Looks quite bowled over by her. It is Laurene Hardtman, isn't it?'

'Yes, I believe it is.'

'She looks wonderful. I haven't seen her in – oh – must be fifteen years. And Bill Hardtman, is he here?'

'He's here somewhere.'

'We were at Yale together,' Cole said.

'Oh were you? You know him well, then?'

'Used to.' He chuckled reminiscently.

'Seems very pleasant,' Forster said. 'Met tonight, first time. I think he just got here two or three days ago.'

'He's a great guy,' Cole said. 'Like him a lot, must see if I can find him.'

'You'll be working with him, I take it?' Forster said.

'That would be most agreeable,' Cole said.

There were more than 800 people at the reception, and before he could find Hardtman Cole ran into somebody else he wanted to talk to.

Hardtman at this moment was with the Ambassador, by the high french windows; behind them the damp twilight was turning a washed-out blue over the white expanse of the rose garden. They appeared to be having a most cordial conversation.

And indeed they were. We were all very pleased about Bill Hardtman's appointment. He was known for his pro-British attitudes and the fact that he would be advising the President on national security questions was reassuring to us, especially at this time. Feeling at the Embassy was that the Americans were becoming just a little bit hysterical on the subject of spies, particularly our spy. Holbrook and his security staff, and the SIS boys in Washington, felt they should be left to close in on Homer in their own way. Since he was likely to be someone pretty high up, discreetness was called for. While the Americans could not be prevented from conducting their own inquiries in their own way, it was generally felt that their methods were a little crude. They thought *us* complacent. We hoped to have an ally in Bill Hardtman.

3

It was just before Christmas 1947 that Hardtman had received a phone call requesting him to come to Washington to see the President. The caller was Admiral Leahy, previously Roosevelt's and now Truman's chief of staff.

'What is it that the President wants to see me about?' Hardtman had inquired.

'I think he'd like to tell you that himself, Mr Hardtman. I'll just say – it's a matter of national importance.'

'When does he want to see me?'

'How about tomorrow, Mr Hardtman?'

'*Tomorrow.*'

'It *is* urgent.'

Hardtman was not above being flattered by such an urgent summons. But it was not exactly a good time to be going to Washington. The previous afternoon it had begun to snow, and it had not stopped since. Looking out of the top floor window of his house on East 69th Street, between Fifth and Madison, he couldn't see Madison at all, it was blanked out by the thick snowfall. Looking the other way, he could make out some movement along Fifth Avenue, but not very much. A heavy whiteness lay over Central Park. There had been announcements on the radio all morning about trains being cancelled, or delayed by up to three hours and the airports were closed.

'I don't know what it's like in Washington,' he told the Admiral, 'but here we're pretty well snowed under.'

'We've got some snow here, too,' the Admiral said, unimpressed.

'Well, I don't know if the trains are running . . .'

He did not like to give the impression of being put out by a little bad weather. '. . . if there is a train I can get on, I will certainly . . .'

'There's a train gets in to Union Station ten of three,' the Admiral said. 'If you were to catch that one I could provisionally put you down to see the President at three-thirty. I'll have someone check the railways, find out if the train's on time, and move your appointment accordingly. If you run into any problems, let me know.'

So that was that. When he had replaced the telephone, Hardtman wondered if he could not have put off the meeting for a day or so; he hated being rushed; looking out of the window at streets in which nothing was moving, it did seem rather optimistic of him to have promised to be in Washington tomorrow. He decided to wait and see what sort of day it would be.

It turned out to be exactly the same sort of day. The snow was still falling, and now the cars were just vague white humps in the road. Across the street, massive spikes of ice hung from parapets and cornices and balconies. An arched entrance looked like a portcullised gate. Laurene thought he was insane to go. But having checked with the station and learnt that trains to Washington were running, he decided that it ought not to be impossible to drive himself to Penn Station. At least there wouldn't be much traffic.

Theirs was one of the few houses in the area with its own garage and the Lincoln started smoothly enough. He found the drive to Penn Station rather exhilarating. The New York streets, virtually devoid of traffic, were a bizzare sight, and as he made steady progress downtown, he had a feeling of setting out on an adventure. He left the car right bang in front of the station, with a feeling of impunity, considering the weather and his mission.

The train was warm and comfortable – one of those new slicked-up trains with cocktail lounge and observation car – and it was spectacular riding high across the white countryside, with the freight yards of New Jersey resembling a vast plain of igloos, and all the fields and forests under snow and the lakes and ponds iced up, and at the Delaware the bridge making a soaring leap over the ice floes; like a great leap of the heart. Hardtman at this

33

moment was filled with all those high expectations that a Presidential summons can engender.

Washington being a few degrees warmer than New York, everybody had decided to act as if conditions were normal, and those who usually went by streetcar piled into streetcars, and those who usually took their cars went by car, with resultant chaos.

Outside Union Station the golden eagles atop the black columnar lamp-posts had extended wings of sheet ice. The dome of the Capitol, partly hidden, showed dully in the distance like a quarter moon seen through clouds. It was hard to find a taxi, and Hardtman had walked down Louisiana Avenue and turned into D Street before he was able to pick one up. It was now 3.10, sufficient time to get to the White House by 3.30 under normal circumstances, but circumstances were far from normal. Everywhere cars had become stuck in the snow and were spinning their wheels as drivers stepped furiously on the gas and dug themselves in deeper. Many cars had been abandoned where they were stuck. Some motorists had driven on to the pavement, horns sounding to force pedestrians out of their way. As the taxi came into a street with tramlines, conditions became even worse. The third rail of the streetcar system had frozen over, breaking the electrical contact and preventing the trams from picking up power, and they had come to a halt too.

Something in Hardtman's nature responded with horror to this vision of disorder.

The driver of the taxi, swinging his driving wheel around loosely, skidding in and out of narrow openings as they presented themselves, had several times slid to a halt inches from another car, and now, suddenly, his bumper was hooked almost casually over the bumper of a bulbous, orange four-door Nash sedan. It was not serious, but the owner of the Nash came out spoiling for a fight.

'Get this pile of crap off my car!' he said, examining his chromework with loving concern.

'Hey, what you call my cab? What you call my cab?

34

You better just move your fuckin' pink joy-ride outta my way, Mister.' And with that he leapt up on to the Nash's bumper and rocked it violently until it was clear of his cab.

'Now move, Mister.'

'Who you telling to move, Mac?'

'You, I'm telling *you* to move. You're blocking my way.'

'You're blocking *my* way, Mac. You move.'

'Since he won't move, I propose we do,' Hardtman suggested to his driver.

'I don't move. He moves . . .'

It seemed futile to go on trying to introduce a note of reason into this situation.

'Well, thank you for your helpfulness,' Hardtman told the cabby, paying him off. 'I wish you all the success you deserve.'

There was no sign of another free cab and he set off walking towards the White House. The freezing air made him numb. An icy drizzle pricked his skin with the deadening coldness of those cold showers that are recommended for curing the body of untoward appetites. He felt chastened after the exaltation of the train journey. He realized he was going to be late. On foot there was no way the distance could be covered in time. He could see the White House ahead of him: a long white lawn surmounted by a circular colonade. He hated to be late; and to be late for an appointment with the President, no matter how good your excuse, was an offence not easily dismissed.

The snowfall had become a small storm, Hardtman picked his way between the cars when he could; his trousers were becoming soaked. The White House, what he could see of it, kept disappearing into the surrounding whiteness.

By the time he got to the northwest gate he was fifteen minutes late. The cops checked their list, and when they found his name and had verified it against his driving licence, they showed him where to go: along a drive that wound round to the low west wing, past shrubs that had become squat snowmen. He followed their directions, found the basement entrance and went up a few steps into the lobby. There was a big White House cop at Reception, and Hardtman hurried over to him and said who he was and that he had an appointment with the President. The cop looked up from his clipboard to the wall clock, and Hardtman said, 'Yes, I know I'm late – the traffic.'

'O.K. – sir. Put your coat here. Right here, sir.' He pointed to a large table, with buffalo legs, heaped with dripping hats and coats.

Beyond the entrance lobby, there was a thick carpet underfoot, instead of marble, and it was like being in a private house, except for the obvious Secret Servicemen, their white nylon shirts faintly luminous, standing about at various points along the corridor.

'Admiral Leahy wanted to have a word with you first,' the cop/receptionist explained, giving little pass signals to men at desks or by wall telephone instruments.

A male aide, and a female secretary wearing earphones and transcribing from a Dictaphone, were the only people in the Admiral's outer office. The aide, on seeing Hardtman, looked at his wrist watch, nodded tightly and went through a door on his left. The Admiral was out in a moment, massive black eyebrows rising up a perturbed brow that continued wrinkled all the way up to the dome of his head, where there was a little white hair. Hardtman murmured something about the trouble he'd had getting a cab, and the Admiral nodded swiftly, not wasting words, and guided him along a corridor. Outside the President's office aides stood about, talking to each other: a Secret Serviceman was on the phone; a Filipino steward, in white jacket, waited to be called.

'Hoped we could have had a moment to get acquainted first,' the Admiral said tersely, 'but . . .' He put his head into the office of the President's Appointments Secretary, Matt Connolly. 'All right to go in, Matt?' Connolly looked at his clock, frowned, and said, 'Oh sure,' and the Admiral with the faintest of preliminary taps, and without waiting for any word from inside, took Hardtman into the Oval Room.

It was a large office, but gave an impression of being very filled with things, and the present incumbent was not immediately noticeable amid all the important portraits and the bric-à-brac of State. Harry S. Truman emerged from the objects that surrounded him rather like a form taking shape in a darkened cinema as your eyes became adjusted. And then there he was behind his large, carved desk, surrounded by family photographs in silver filigree frames, stacks of books, stacks of documents, telephones, a brass lamp, a chrome thermos jug, a vase of flowers, ashtrays. The room seemed too large, too formally imposing for the small dapper man with pink cheeks and bright eyes who sat with the rose garden behind him, beaming at his visitors, his expression saying that they were not to stand on ceremony, that sort of thing cut no ice with him. He bounded up from his chair, and came forward, both arms outstretched, to administer a vigorous handshake.

'Glad you could make it, Mr Hardtman. Know you're a busy man.'

'I apologize for my lateness, Mr President,' Hardtman said, 'but conditions out there were just chaotic.'

'Oh I know, I know. Amazing what a little snowfall can do to the nation's capital. Just amazing. Want to dry those out?' Harry Truman asked, pointing to Hardtman's soaked shoes.

Hardtman shook his head, amused – but not tempted – by the prospect of conducting his interview with the President in bare feet.

'No, thank you all the same, Mr President. It's most kind of you to suggest it, but they'll dry out all right.'

The Admiral was standing by dutifully. The President showed Hardtman to a sofa facing the fireplace, and seated himself in a chair on his right, motioning the Admiral to sit on the left.

'Mr Hardtman, you smoke? If you care to smoke, just go right ahead. There's some in that box. Just help yourself, when you want.' Seeing something, he shook his head remonstratingly. 'Now look at that, now look at that.' He indicated a burn in the rug. 'One of our friends of the

Press, shouldn't be surprised. Lazy cusses. Those fellows never heard of ashtrays. That's what comes of lettin' them smoke in here, see what they do. Burn holes in my rug. See that, Admiral. Fellow that comes along after me is going to say what kind of a horse's ass was this Harry Truman lettin' the Press burn holes in his rug.' His eyes shone good-humouredly, magnified behind the thick lenses of his steel-frame spectacles. 'I guess worse has been said of occupiers of this office, and I guess worse'll be said of me –'

'The penalty of office, Mr President.'

'The Admiral tell you what's on my mind?'

'There wasn't time,' the Admiral said.

'Oh there wasn't – well let him see directive NSC 1C. Let Mr Hardtman read it.'

From a buff folder, the Admiral extracted a single sheet of yellow flimsy and passed it across.

'You want me to read this right now, Mr President?'

'Yes, go ahead – it's short. And forget what you've read, when you leave this room.'

'I'll do my best,' Hardtman said, with the beginning of a smile. But Mr Truman's cherry pink face had gone serious.

'No, that's essential. Same applies to everything said in this room – to be treated as strictly between us.'

'I'll treat it as such.'

Hardtman began to read the directive.

The opaqueness of the language obliged him to read it twice to make sure he had understood it properly. Then he looked up. Harry Truman was watching him closely.

'Has this directive gone into effect?'

The President nodded. 'It has.'

'I take it,' Hardtman began, 'I would not have been called here had you not been familiar with certain views that I have expressed about the reorganization of Intelligence?'

'That's right, Mr Hardtman. I'm familiar with the views you hold.'

'You want my off-the-cuff reaction to this?' Hardtman asked, holding up the piece of yellow flimsy.

'Yes, sir,' Harry Truman said.

'Well, Mr President, since you are familiar with my general views, you will not wish me to be less than frank.'

'Be as outspoken as you like, Mr Hardtman.'

Hardtman thought for a moment, and then said:

'Well, my immediate thought, Mr President, is that this gives Central Intelligence carte blanche pretty well . . .'

'I have heard that point of view expressed,' Truman said. 'Go on, Mr Hardtman.'

'I can't help thinking that you may have created something here that neither you – nor anyone else – will be able to control. The wording is so . . . so open to whatever interpretation anyone might wish to give it.'

'Appreciate your frankness, Mr Hardtman, and let me say I understand your misgivings, but you know the President can never make a decision that some people won't have misgivings about. Sure, there's an inherent danger with any clandestine action that it's going to get out of hand. That's why I've said to the Agency that it's incumbent upon them to obtain policy approval for what they do. But can't ask them to come running for approval every move they want to make . . . that's no way to run anything. I believe in letting people get on with the job. Comes down to personalities in the end. Whom you entrust something to. In strict confidence, I'll tell you I've appointed Walter Cole to head the clandestine section. What's your reaction to that?'

'I know Walter Cole. We were at Yale together.'

'He's considered to be a pretty able fellow, isn't that so?'

'Oh very able. Though during the war, when he was with OSS, it was said of him that he not only took risks, but liked taking them.'

'You don't care to take too many risks, Mr Hardtman?'

Hardtman was staring into the fireplace, where logs were laid out, though no fire had been lit for a long time. Raising his eyes, he found himself looking at a portrait of Harry Truman's mother. He turned from her homely stern features to the President.

'I always remember something I was once told by a man I greatly admire, Oliver Wendell Holmes. He was a man who believed in the *via media*. He said that of course in times of high excitement this is not the most popular road to take, and once in a thousand the extremists do pull off something. But not too often. Usually they get themselves and the rest of us in a lot of hot water for very little gain. He, Holmes, didn't have too high an opinion of extremists, and neither do I, Mr President.'

'You telling me you disapprove of Walter Cole for the job?'

'I don't have enough facts, Mr President, to be in a position to give an opinion about that,' Hardtman said cautiously.

'Well, what I want you to do – what I've in mind, Mr Hardtman – is for you to get enough facts. Write me a report. A detailed report. Let me have all your recommendations as to how things ought to be done different. I'm sure you'll find a lot of things that you'll think ought to be done different, and I'd appreciate if you were to let me have the benefit of your thinking in this area, because I've read your articles, and I've got a high regard for your judgment.'

'Very kind of you to say that, Mr President, and naturally I will give your invitation very serious consideration. However, I would need to know more precisely what . . .'

'Same time,' Mr Truman interrupted, 'you can keep an eye on Walter Cole for me. Say you know him? Wild man, is he? Well, it's necessary to have that sort for some jobs – but I would feel a whole lot better about it if I knew you were keeping an eye on him. Like I keep having to tell the brass' – his eyes brightened at the memory – 'if anybody declares war on anybody, it's going to be me, not some dashing air force colonel with an itchy trigger finger. *Or* Walter Cole.'

'This – uh – role you want me to play, Mr President, could you tell me what you see my position as being, vis-à-vis yourself and Cole and the whole . . .'

'Want you to have executive authority to see whatever

you want to see – I don't want them to hide anything from you. Or, more to the point, *me*. I already have a committee looking into this whole Intelligence question, and I'd want you to liaise with them. Get the whole thing into fine focus for me. I don't want to go down in history as having set up an American peacetime Gestapo. I want to know the dangers. The whole area of Intelligence in this country is a caboodle of back-biting old women, I sometimes think. All with their vested interests. That's why I've come to you because I think I can rely on you, from all I've heard, and read, to keep out of the politicking, and come up with some honest, disinterested, answers.'

'I am sure that this is something that needs to be done. If I were to take it on . . .'

Harry Truman looked at his watch.

'Hell,' he said, rising. 'Matt is going to kill me. Wish we had more time, Mr Hardtman, but I've already cut twenty minutes out of my next appointment . . .' He stuck out a firm hand. 'Hope to have you with me,' he said. 'Thank you for coming. 'Specially on a day like this. Hope your shoes are drying out. What size do you take? Maybe the Admiral could fix you up with a pair of his. Mine'd be too big for you.' He chuckled.

The Admiral had got up and was going to the door. Hardtman followed, since there was seemingly no way of extending the interview. Together they walked down the short corridor, past the lounging Secret Servicemen, to the chief of staff's office.

'Let me tell you how the Boss works,' the Admiral said when they were seated. 'Now I worked for Mr Roosevelt, too, and the difference is that whereas Roosevelt took personal charge of certain kinds of action, because he didn't have a lot of confidence in some of his executive departments, Mr Truman leaves people to get on with the task he's given them. That means, very often, that what a particular job amounts to is what somebody makes it amount to.'

'Yes, I see. But in practice, how would I be expected to operate?'

'Well, we'll give you an office, and put you down as a Presidential assistant and issue an executive order to say you are conducting a Presidential inquiry into security questions, and that you're to be given full co-operation. And, from there on in, it's up to you. If you find something about which the President should know immediately, you just let me know. I see him every morning, and I will tell him right away. The Boss'd want to have your full report on his desk in – let's say – three months' time?'

'And after that?'

'Who knows, Mr Hardtman. Who can say? I can tell you this – I'm going to be retiring pretty soon. The Boss – if he's re-elected – is going to need all the good men he can get.'

The National Security Act of 1947 establishing the Central Intelligence Agency had not included specific authority to conduct covert operations. It had, however, created the National Security Council and given that body authority to direct the CIA to 'perform such other functions and duties related to Intelligence affecting national security as the National Security Council may from time to time direct'.

It had become known to some of us that the National Security Council at its first meeting in December 1947 had issued a top secret directive granting CIA authority to conduct covert operations. This was directive NSC 1C that Truman had shown to Hardtman.

The directive gave the go-ahead for CIA to engage 'in such actions and acts as may be required, including covert actions and acts, to counter, reduce and discredit International Communism throughout the world'. Covert operations were defined as covert activities related to propaganda, economic warfare, political action, and included sabotage, psychological warfare, demolition, and assistance to resistance movements, and other 'actions and acts compatible with the directive'. It was the responsibility of the Director of CIA, or of his duly designed deputy, to obtain policy approval for all actions. But the procedure for obtaining such approval was not spelled out, and in practice the amiable sailors appointed by Truman to advise him on national security were not up to dealing with someone as smart and devious as Walter Cole.

Truman was aware of this. He had been warned by, among others, Dean Acheson, then Under Secretary of State, of the danger of giving such vague general powers to an agency whose activities, by their very nature, could not be too closely scrutinized.

The National Security Council, which Congress had placed in the position of overseeing CIA, had the function of advising the President. As created, it had no executive powers, but from its first meeting Defence Secretary Forrestal attempted to turn it into a decision-making body on the model of the British Cabinet. He wanted to give it an executive staff that would be empowered to direct other governmental agencies.

Truman had seen this as an attempt to usurp some of his Presidential powers. Though he had not been elected to the Presidency, and was not thought to stand much chance in the elections due to be held later that year, he was the President under the Constitution and he was not going to give up one iota of his power to anyone.

However, he was obliged to move carefully. Congress was controlled by the Republicans. His popularity in the country was at a low point, and from all sides there were calls for him to step down and let someone better qualified assume the Presidency. He could not afford to make any mistakes. Having scared Congress into passing the National Security Act (if he had not scared the Congressmen they would have gone fishing, it was said) he could not now curtail its effectiveness by imposing too many restrictions on the Agency he had set up. That would seem namby-pamby, or suggest that the dangers from world Communism were not as great as he had made out.

Appointing Hardtman to his national security staff, with the task of keeping an eye on covert actions, was a way of keeping some of the Agency's wilder men under some control. At the same time, since Hardtman's official role was simply to report back to the President – liaison rather than control – it could not be said that the President was being soft on Communism and hamstringing his own agencies with excessive restrictions.

It was a difficult and delicate job, calling for the exercise of tacit authority rather than direct power, and Hardtman looked like the right man for it. He had a good war record with OSS, and later had worked with Army Intelligence and the War Crimes Commission. He had spent many hours interrogating Nazi war criminals and had become highly knowledgeable about how the Nazi security services had functioned. Based on what he had learnt, he had in 1946 given a series of lectures at Yale in which he discussed the problem of creating an effective security service within a democratic system; and he showed himself aware of the moral issues. The Gestapo had probably been the most effective state security service ever devised, he said in his lectures. But at what cost! Because our own system was less efficient, he said, we must not be panicked into creating an efficient one on the Nazi model. Better to be a little inefficient. There was a point up to which we could – and should – improve our security; but there was also a point at which we should accept our system, with all its short-comings, as being the best we could do without sacrificing the individual's freedom. It was, he cautioned, even more necessary to protect ourselves against our protectors than against spies and subversives.

He justified this view on the following basis. He did not believe that there was a need for more input, meaning more and better spies and sources. On the contrary, we already had more input than our services could usefully digest. We were flooded with Intelligence and our main problem was to be able to evaluate it correctly. He used Pearl Harbour as an illustration. A perfect example of Intelligence functioning brilliantly and providing all the data to indicate the imminence of the strike – the crucial message was in the hands of the President, the Chief of the General Staff, the Army Secretary and the Navy Secretary hours before the attack – and not being acted upon because of organizational defects and the problems of communication and evaluation. 'We were pretty damn sure on the highest levels that the Japanese were going to attack at one p.m., Sunday, December 7th. But we were not able to translate that knowledge fast enough into a defensive plan of action, simply because our procedures for doing so were too slow and haphazard.'

It was Hardtman's overall theme that it was not only morally wrong to increase the secret powers of American Intelligence, but also unnecessary, and confusing. We did not need more inflow. The more there was, the easier it became for an enemy to plant misinformation on us. What we needed instead was a deeply worked out and highly sophisticated 'image of the enemy', which should be a composite picture consisting of everything known about him, historically, psychologically, politically, militarily. This image was the matrix into which raw intelligence should be poured: only if the two jelled did you have a commodity of any use. Again he gave Pearl Harbour as an example. The Japanese had acted in strict accordance with their principles, national self-interests and psychology, and anyone possessing a correct image of the enemy in December 1941, would have been able to foretell, even on the basis of half the raw intelligence at hand, that a Japanese attack was coming. What nations could contrive to keep secret – troop movements, war plans, orders, weapons – was of far less significance than what they could not keep secret: their national historical needs, and their collective psychology which would lead them to seek to satisfy those needs in a particular manner. Nations did not act uncharacteristically. It was a mistake to base national policy on information obtained from a spy – at best such information could only be corroborative of political analysis. And so he was in favour of demoting the spies of both sides to lesser roles, and relying more on understanding the forces of national and historical needs.

The lectures had been published in *Foreign Affairs*, and had produced some favourable comments. They had been brought to Truman's attention, and while he had not accepted the whole argument, he had come to the conclusion that in the balancing game of politics Hardtman was just the man to put on the opposite side of the scales to Walter Cole.

Immediately after seeing the President, Hardtman telephoned his wife in New York and told her the news.

'If you want to do it,' she said immediately, 'I want you to do it.'

'It means living in Washington. I don't know how you are going to take to that.'

'Oh I can live anywhere, if it's with you,' she replied loyally.

'Debbie is going to be a lot further away from us. I don't know when we'll see her.'

'Darling, Debbie's nearly sixteen, she's getting to be pretty independent. And Washington isn't exactly the ends of the earth. By train it's going to be four or five hours, no more.'

'You wouldn't want to move her to a school nearer Washington?'

'No; that'd be unfair to her. She's doing so well at Bay House, and it's such a good school . . . she'd miss all her friends . . .'

'And us. How about missing us?'

'There's the summer and weekends. At that age the social activity is awfully important. Debbie's so involved in everything going on at Bay House it'd be really tough on her to pull her out and make her start again somewhere else. Besides, let's be realistic, we don't know how long we'll be in Washington. With the election coming up in November . . . Bill, let's see how it all goes before making any major switch . . .'

On the train journey back to New York Hardtman thought about the job. He was troubled, because he was a man who liked to have things clear cut, and this invitation to come to Washington was by no means clear cut. Normally he would not have embarked upon a new undertaking without a great deal more detailed information about what

46

was expected of him, what his area of responsibility would be exactly, how he would operate; but he could see that the nature of this job was such that it could not be clearly defined in advance. That was the challenge of it. He would have to play it by ear. Well, he thought, the worst that could happen was that he might have to resign. There was no way of finding out what this job was going to amount to, except by doing it. The President had appeared to be genuinely eager to have him along. No point in asking a lot of questions. That would just seem pernickerty. In something like this, you had to take a chance. Might not work out, but having been asked, how could he refuse? He was forty-five; he had gone as far as he could go in his profession; nothing new was going to happen to him if he did not make it happen. Did he want something new to happen? It had not occurred to him that he did – for he was really quite contented with things as they were – until that moment crossing the Delaware when his heart had taken an unexpected leap.

I should say something more about the sort of man Hardtman was.

In manner you could have taken him for an Englishman. He had a fondness for certain English ways of putting things and a taste for irony. Americans, I have found, tend to say what they mean – this is sometimes considered naïve of them, or else rude. With us, or some of us, anyway, meaning is often conveyed not so much in what we say as in how we say it. We can, of course, be just as rude, if we wish, but we will rely more on tone of voice, in capacity to express disdain, mockery, contempt, superiority, rather than on bluntness. Americans will quickly tell you what they think and feel; we are more concealed, and in this respect Hardtman resembled us more than his own countrymen.

His appearance suggested orderliness. He was clean-shaven, his light brown hair was brushed down flat and neatly parted on the left; he wore a gold tie pin in his collar and one-colour ties and suits of a conservative cut. He

47

looked a solid man. The overall impression he gave was of carefulness; carefulness of dress, of manner, of speech, of thought – and, if this is not a contradiction in terms, which in his case it was not, carefulness of feeling. Not the sort of man to be ruled by sudden impulse or one who might resort to hasty or extravagant action.

Yet he was not a pedant: his blue-grey eyes, though rather more grey than blue, prevented him from being that; they had the grace to permit unconventionality in others, whatever they did or did not permit himself. I always felt that he was like a sportsman in training for some big event, and his reserve and his prudence were in the service of his larger aspirations. Also, he was new to Washington, and it behove him to go carefully. And then he did not need to make an impact; that had already been done for him a long time ago – by all the Hardtmans before him. So he could afford to remain quiet and let louder men dominate the scene – it was usually not for long; his very quietness compelled attention, made people want to draw him out. And this he would sometimes respond to, but in a manner that left you thinking there was much more he could tell if he chose.

So: a careful man, but not – in his formal political affiliations, at least – a conservative. At Yale he had been categorized as a radical, even a rather dangerous one. He had been known for his condemnation of the 'malefactors of great wealth' and 'the vested interests' – actually he was using Teddy Roosevelt's phraseology, but there is no reason to suppose he was insincere, for he continued to maintain, in politics, a position that was well left of centre. That he went into Wall Street and made money is neither here nor there; anyway, he did not make that much, not enough to be condemned for – though it was enough to live on very well.

If there was any contradiction between his professed beliefs and his style of living, he dealt with this by saying that, yes, he believed in the more equitable sharing out of wealth; but this had to come about in an orderly fashion – it could not happen overnight without causing the destruction of all that was valuable in our present society. Progress could best be achieved from within. He was not in favour of storming the walls. Let change come from the realization in men's hearts that such change was called for and just. For the time being the instruments of power were monetary, and this meant that any man who wished to be effective in the world had to have money. Hence he had set out, quite calculatingly, to make money. Not for his personal glory, or to be able to lord it over others, but simply to be effective in the world. The fact that he had also married a rich girl – one of the Blum girls of the Howard & Blum departments store chain – was fortuitous. He had not set out to marry an heiress, nor did he have any need of her money. He had quite enough of his own by the time he was twenty-nine to maintain the life style he wished to have, and on a day-to-day basis he and Laurene lived largely on his income. She used her money (he carefully separated it in his mind from 'their' money, which consisted of what *he* made) to pursue her own objectives, and occasionally for the purchase of a painting or other valuable object that he would not have been able to afford; but he would not permit himself to become *dependent* on her wealth.

In practice, Hardtman's radical views were accepted by his rich conservative friends as an excusable form of personal eccentricity; whilst among his radical friends, his wealth was not held against him, since he had the good manners not to flaunt it and since, too, he was supporting causes that were against his own financial interests. Of course, he was not 'one of them'. But they were practical men, too, and he was a useful ally to have.

It has to be said, however, that his radicalism had been diminishing as he got older. It was not that he had changed his views, but he seemed to become more and more attached, sentimentally, to those aspects of his childhood and youth that were the product of privilege and class. He had fond memories of the Promenade des Anglais at the height of Edwardian English affluence: the wealthy Englishmen in their white ducks, the women in white muslin, their children tended by nannies. Ah – the graciousness of those days. He remembered the cake shops. You could spend more on one cake than some families had to live on all week, and what splendid cakes they were! Masterpieces of French confectionary art. And the food, generally, of course, was so good. He had been spoilt by his years in France, where eating was concerned. He remembered the Atlantic crossings on the *France*, the *Queen Elizabeth*, the *Aquitania*, the *Normandie*. The impeccable service on those great ocean liners, the perfect orderliness of the arrangements. He travelled first class, though in theory he was against the perpetuation of class divisions, nowhere more immediately evident than on a large ocean liner – with physical barriers everywhere and notices prohibiting third class passengers from entering the second class, and second class passengers from entering the first class. These restrictions, moreover, were treated with the utmost seriousness. It was a legal as well as a social offence to step outside your class; to use a first class toilet if you had a second class ticket. He found these divisions absurd, and even wicked, but at the same time he felt it would achieve nothing for him to travel second class. It would be making a meaningless gesture, and he was not given to that.

He could be hard on people, including himself. One heard him say that such and such a person wasn't up to it. Simply not up to it, though a decent enough man. There were many who came into that category. The way such verdicts were delivered – casually, mildly, but with the tone of voice making his point – created an impression of arrogance, of passing judgment from a position of superiority. He made enemies in this way, and later there would be people who would take satisfaction in his downfall. Of course, he had loyal friends who considered him to have been a sacrificial victim, but there was a streak of arrogance in his nature that alienated some people. He admitted as much himself, in his characteristically unrepentant manner.

I remember a lunch I had with him soon after all the

scandal. We went to one of the little French restaurants that he favoured, close to the East river. Though he had gone through a crushing series of events, there was still the faint air of superiority in his manner. He couldn't help that, I suppose. He really was a rather superior man. He sat up very straight, looking thinner and greyer and wiser, eating his omelette *fines herbs* and sipping a glass of Montrachet.

'Do you know,' he said to me, his bland blue-grey eyes icing up a little around the edges, 'that Truman insists upon introducing the visiting VIPs to the servants? One of those little democratic gestures dear to his Democratic heart. Ah . . .' He gave his slightly (but only slightly) self-deprecating smile, and added, 'I suppose that is snobbish of me. I have been accused of being a snob, though that must be the least of the accusations they make.' He shrugged, took another sip of Montrachet. 'I don't give a damn, frankly, what people think of me. But I intend to get to the bottom of that whole business; the fact that I resigned doesn't mean I accept the crass construction "they" put on things. No, I intend to find out . . . And you can be of help, you have a very logical mind, and you know everything that's going on . . . more than I ever knew.'

4

Hardtman had arrived in Washington in January, and was given an office in the Old State Department Building, adjoining the White House. A great baroque pile, like a many-tiered wedding cake, the building had earned the nickname of 'the squirrel cage', perhaps because of the way in which its inmates tended to multiply heedlessly. Its corridors were seemingly endless and there was usually somebody moving in or out.

He had been given an office on the third floor with a connecting outer office for a secretary, but no secretary. And no telephone. At any rate, no connected phone. There were several instruments of different colours sitting on desks and tables but the lines were dead. He spent an hour getting himself reconnected, and after that he waited for the telephone to ring – sure that people must have been waiting impatiently to get through to him. But there were no calls.

It was a handsome office with high ceiling, elaborately decorated with plasterwork that was an example of the plasterer's art carried to unnecessary extremes. Along one wall there was a Victorian mahogany bookcase filled with the Navy Lists going back a century and with the annual editions of Foreign Relations of the United States. The desk was large and intricately carved and had, in addition to the usual drawers, a cupboard on the other side of the leg niche. This cupboard had a small brass key in its brass lock, and when he unlocked it Hardtman found several glasses inside and an almost empty bottle of Harvey's Fine Tawny Hunting Port. He looked around, rather expecting to find copper pneumatic tubes for the rapid conveyance of inter-departmental memoranda, but some recent endeavour at modernization had evidently dispensed with them. Modernization had also closed up the reddish marble fireplace, and replaced it with a three-bar electric heater. There was a desk chair that swivelled *and* tilted. The pictures on the walls were all of ships and admirals.

He went to the window: the glass was of the pebbled kind used in lavatories, and he could not see out. The sash catch had rusted in the shut position and it took some effort to slide it open; when he finally succeeded he discovered that the effort was not worth it – the view was of row upon row of air-conditioning units in the windows opposite, and of an asphalt parking lot where delivery vans were drawn up.

While waiting for someone to call, he opened drawers and cupboards. They were all quite empty. He opened the mahogany bookcase and took down a copy of the Navy List for 1878. As he turned its pages a sheet of paper fell out. He picked it up. It was White House notepaper, headed with the room number of the room he was now in, and underneath was printed

THE MAKING OF A COPY OF THIS MESSAGE
IS STRICTLY PROHIBITED

Written on the paper, in hand, were a series of names, which must have been, Hardtman quickly realized, the names of horses, for there were the times of races alongside, and the odds being offered. At the bottom of the list in a larger hand, there appeared the words

ZLOT TROT/CANTER/GALLOP – STAMPEDE!

Hardtman returned the sheet of paper to the Navy List of 1878, and lifted the telephone to make sure it had not been disconnected again. The Admiral hadn't even phoned to say welcome aboard. Well, his arrival was certainly being handled in a low-key fashion. No danger of drawing undue attention to the President's new assistant for security. He waited half an hour and then called the Admiral's office, and announced that he had arrived. This evoked only the mildest response from the aide on the telephone. He would inform the Admiral when he returned.

'Meanwhile,' Hardtman said, 'I'd be very grateful if it

could be arranged for me to have a directory of government department telephone numbers, including the unlisted ones. And a secretary. And a typewriter. And notepaper. You think that could be done – right away?'

'Well, Mr Hardtman, I'm afraid I don't . . .'

'No need to be afraid,' Hardtman told him. 'I don't bite. If I don't have to.'

Stepping out of his office to go to the men's room, Hardtman almost bumped into a large young man with bulging cheeks headed for the same destination. Both apologizing for the near collision, they went on together, and then stood side by side at the urinals.

'I'm Bill Hardtman, I have an office right along here . . .'

'Myers,' the other man said. 'Sidney Myers. You have an office along here? . . .'

'Yes.'

'I thought they'd closed up this part . . .'

'Oh – Why?'

'Some rumour. People say it's falling down. They say the White House is falling down too. I believe them. It's quite feasible. Quite feasible, if you think about it.'

'And you do?'

'Yeah,' he admitted. 'See, I'm a pessimist.'

Buttoning himself up, Sidney added. 'So long. Be seeing you, I expect,' and waddled off down the corridor.

In the course of the morning Sidney Myers paid several more visits to the men's room, and Hardtman, having left his door slightly ajar, took the opportunity on one of these occasions to renew the acquaintanceship, since his phone still had not rung. Sidling up to the adjacent urinal, he was recognized.

'Hardtman? Right?'

'That's right.'

Hardtman allowed a decent pause for the sake of establishing the right degree of casualness. Then gathering that Sidney Myers was close to finishing his natural function, he said : 'Are you State Department?'

'No – you?'

'No. What sort of area? – uh . . .'

'I'm on contract,' Sidney Myers said, 'to advise the President. And you?'

'Same sort of thing,' Hardtman said.

'There's a lot of us,' Sidney said, buttoning up.

'A lot of . . . ?'

'Presidential advisers. Tell you the truth, this place is lousy with them.'

'Oh is that so?'

'What office you in?'

'708.'

'Oh yeah – that was Professor Mittleweiss's office. He was advising the President too.'

'What happened to Professor Mittleweiss?'

'No idea. People come and go all the time.'

'What was his field?'

'An economist. I have an idea he was working on German monetary reform. Or reparations. One or the other. This place is full of professors. The Boss likes to push professors around, being an autodidact like he is. He'll hire a professor at the drop of a hat. We've had several history professors, one psychology professor, a chemistry professor . . . there was even a music professor.'

'What was the music professor doing here?'

'The Boss is very musical. What's your field, Hardtman?'

'Security.'

'*Ah-hah!*' Sidney said with heavy meaning. '*Ah-hah!* One of those guys.'

'Advisory rather than executive,' he pointed out. 'And you Sidney? What's your field?'

'I'm sort of in a special category . . . I range over a whole lot of topics.'

'But your special responsibility?'

'I think things through – I think things through to their logical conclusion.'

'What sort of things?'

'Sort of things other people don't want to think about.'

Returning to his office, Hardtman occupied the rest of the morning trying to reach various people, but without success. The messages he left for them to phone him back produced no return calls. He began to suspect that people didn't know who he was or what he was doing here. Perhaps the news of his appointment had not yet reached them. Perhaps it was being kept a little too hush-hush. He phoned through to Leahy's office again, and was told the Admiral was not back yet. Hardtman left word that people did not seem to have been informed of his position and that they did not know he was supposed to be receiving their full co-operation.

'I'm sure the Admiral will be in touch with you shortly,' the aide said.

Shortly. Marvellous word. How short – or long – was shortly? A real bureaucratic all-purpose, fob-off word. Not this morning, not this afternoon. Not tomorrow. Not next week. Not next year. But shortly.

Well, I shall shortly go out and have lunch, he told himself, and then made one more attempt at establishing contact with somebody. He tried to get through to Walter Cole.

A secretary took his name, position, and extension number, and told him that Mr Cole would be phoning him back. Shortly.

Giving up, Hardtman put through an inter-departmental call to Sidney Myers, and suggested lunch. He was fearful that he would get another negative response, but no, Sidney was delighted to have lunch.

They went to the Occidental, next to the Willard Hotel. Sidney had a robust appetite, and no problem eating and speaking at the same time. Perfect co-ordination enabled him to put away food at a terrific rate, without slowing down the flow of his words. His large spherical face was suffused by a deep flush that darkened different features at different times, sometimes his upper cheek, sometimes his swelling jowl, giving him as many phases as the moon. He ate as if working against time, as if needing to stockpile nourishment. A considerable reserve had already been laid down as evinced by his bulging waistline and multiple chins.

'You say you think things through,' Hardtman picked

up on a remark of Sidney's. 'If it's not indiscreet to ask, what sort of things?'

'Well, things like what happens,' Sidney said with mouth full of fish, 'if there's a war between us and the Soviets and we drop the bomb on each other and wipe each other out.'

'Sounds as though there isn't much to think about in such a case.'

'Well, that's where you're wrong, that's where everybody's wrong. That's why it's such an under-developed field. I'm practically alone . . . No, supposing we are wiped out – supposing half the country is gone. What's that mean? It means there's half the country left. And they also have got half their country left. The question then is, on present data, who can regenerate faster, and most quickly to reach a stage of war-readiness again? This has to be thought through, and nobody has done it till now.'

'And who can get there first?'

'We can.'

'How come we can?'

Sidney put a boiled potato in his mouth and mashed it with one bite.

'Our industrial growth rate, based on our superior and more general level of mechanization, enables us to regenerate much faster than they can, so we could reach the stage of having the A-bomb – and a better A-bomb – in operational numbers long before them. But they'd catch up while we were readying ourselves for another war . . . which'd take us a certain amount of time, psychologically.'

'What's the outcome of that war?'

'We win it too. We win the next eleven wars. I've projected it out.'

'Why not the twelfth?'

'The twelfth is doubtful. I don't think we win that one.'

'Gee, what went wrong?'

'Well, while we can regenerate our industry faster than they can, they procreate faster than we do – 'specially under those sort of conditions, when our birth rate'd just

57

plummet, but their people expect less and so are readier to bring children into the world even under the worst conditions. In the end, despite the fact our industrial capacity is greater, their procreative capacity starts weighing things in their favour round about the twelfth all-out war.'

'You mean at that point we are going to have to be Red rather than dead?'

'It could happen,' Sidney conceded.

Walking back to the 'squirrel cage', Hardtman had a sense of artificiality about himself, no doubt produced by the conversation with Sidney. He saw quite clearly the jostling crowds of shoppers and government workers spread out along the pavements, by store windows, looking at the movie posters, dragging their feet through the thick slush that still remained on the ground, and yet they were at a distance from him. Half would live, half would die, given a certain set of circumstances.

As they walked back across the Ellipse, Hardtman said: 'Did you know my predecessor in Room 708?'

'He was a crazy character,' Sidney said.

'That so?'

'Once told me a crazy scheme of his. Wow! Was it wild! He was trying to sell the Boss on the idea of flooding Eastern bloc countries with dough forged by the United States Treasury. He said, should be easy. Piece of cake for the Treasury to print money. It's their business. Idea behind it was – give the Red a taste of filthy lucre. Bomb 'em with money. Push it under their doors. Rig lotteries so that everybody gets to win. He swears it'd undermine their whole economy. Cause riots and uprisings. Export the capitalist disease, he says. Make 'em all money-mad, he says. Drive 'em nuts, he says. That'll show 'em.'

Hardtman laughed. 'That is what he was working on?'

'I tell you he had pages and pages of figures, mathematical proofs of what it'd do to their economy, and how once contaminated by the money bug the Commies'd have to quarantine themselves from the victims, i.e., draw back within their own borders for self-protection . . .'

'Didn't realize the groves of Academe produced such lethal thinkers,' Hardtman said.

'Oh you have no idea – they're all lethal thinkers, those guys.'

That night, a little after midnight, when Hardtman had just fallen asleep, the phone rang.

'You called me.' A high-pitched, quick voice insisted.

'Who is this?'

A laugh followed, ascending the scales. 'Who d'you think? Now who do you think? I wake you?'

'You did, Walter.'

'Early to bed, early to rise . . .' The laugh got higher.

'It's not that early.'

'It isn't? Couldn't get back to you before, Bill. All sorts of things, all sorts. I've been ordered to let you see all our "Magic". We're going to be working together, is that right? Well, I look forward to that, Bill. We ought to get together soon.'

'That's what I had in mind. How about lunch sometime this week?'

'This week is bad for me, Bill . . .'

'Well, if you can't make lunch, what about you coming to my office – or I'll come to yours – I don't want to delay this.'

'Let me see what I can cancel. Call you right back.'

Five minutes later he was back on the line.

'I fixed it,' he said.

'You always make your business appointments at night?'

'You know my problem?'

'No.'

'I can't sleep. I'm a night person so I wake everybody up. I can make Friday.'

'All right. Where?'

'Why don't we just say I'll pick you up at the gate. Twelve forty-five? I'll book a table. O.K.?'

'Put myself in your hands.'

'Wise decision. Take care, Bill. My best to the lovely Laurene. How's *Rebecca*?'

'Deborah. At boarding-school.'

'Good God, Bill, last time I saw you she was crawling on the floor.'

'That's right.'

'It's a conspiracy . . .'

'What?'

'Time! Time, Bill. The greatest conspiracy is time.'

'No wonder you're an insomniac, with weighty thoughts like that on your mind.'

'See you Friday, Bill.'

5

Walter Cole. That high-pitched voice becoming higher with the excitement of certainty. Always looking for an argument, Walter. Thrived on it. Always proclaiming his irrefutable knowledge, his unshakable certitude. There were so many things about which Walter *knew* – knew with a bright-eyed knowingness that permitted no opposition. There really was no arguing with him, in the end. 'I guarantee you,' was a favourite gambit of his for shutting you up. Oh: 'What d'you want to bet . . . ?' This was not just a figure of speech. At the height of an intricate argument, he would suddenly come out with: 'I bet you fifty bucks I'm right . . . and you're wrong . . .' Out would come the calfskin wallet, from which ten five-dollar bills would be extracted and put on the table, his eyes challenging you to do likewise, or else climb down, concede that he was right. It was a technique that could infuriate: up to a point he would argue with you, step by step, adhering to recognized principles of debate, but then, suddenly, all that would be abandoned in favour of the bullying power of the dare. O.K., if you're so sure, put your money on it. And if one was unwilling to do so, this was of course made to seem an admission of the weakness of one's argument. Endless circular arguments. About politics. About life. About who was going to win the Ladies' Singles at Wimbledon. Or the elections in Germany. Or drop dead next. Walter had an opinion on everything, and it was extremely rare for him to be less than certain. When asked, how come you know so much more than everybody else, he'd say: 'I hear things. I've got my sources.' Which was assumed to be a reference to the Cole family network. 'Also, I'm smart. Haven't you heard – the geneticists in California have proved, scientifically, that some people just have got more brains. Just are brighter, as a race, as a class . . .'

An argument might start quite casually, for no particular reason, with Walter coming up to you, placing a hand on your shoulder, and demanding, 'Well, what's new?' And if you had nothing new to tell him, he would tell you something. 'You know there's going to be a coup d'état in at least *two* Balkan States, within the next month? I bet you . . .'

'How d'you know.'

'I know. Sources of mine.'

'You can't possibly know. If *you* know, those governments would know too, wouldn't they? And presumably take the appropriate counter-measures.'

'Wait and see. Remember that I told you.' And sometimes he was right, and he never omitted to rub it in when he was. Nor did he hesitate to use having been right in the past to prop up some shaky current conjecture . . . He did have a source of private information; all those highly placed cousins and uncles. From infancy he had been in touch with what was 'really going on'. And it was this which perhaps gave him the air of always knowing better than you.

A lot of people got quite angry in the face of his implacable assertions about anything and everything, and could have punched him. But here there was a difficulty. He was so tall, almost 6 ft 3 in., with very long arms, and anyone contemplating taking a swing at him had to reckon with the sheer distance that needed to be traversed to make contact with that remote jaw.

Towards women, young and old alike, he was always very polite. With them he was gallantly ready to admit that they could possibly be right. He did not take the views of women seriously enough to argue with them. His combativeness was reserved for men . . .

Sometimes his statements could be very wild, and though everyone calmed down again later, there were moments at the height of an argument when if his words could have killed, you would have been dead . . . notwithstanding his ho-ho-ho laugh.

This was Walter Cole, the fair-haired, opinionated youth Hardtman had known twenty-five years ago at Yale.

On the Friday Cole's taxi was at the northwest gate five minutes after the appointed time, and as the rear door swung open Hardtman saw the long body crammed into the shabby damp-smelling interior like a jack-in-the-box, and experienced a mild shock as he saw the white hair, neat as a freshly pressed shirt, on the high head. There was a silvery moustache to match. The smile was as sure as it had always been. The totally white hair was unexpected.

'Well, Walter,' he said, getting into the cab, 'how's it all going?'

'Oh all right, Bill. Good, good.'

'Neither of us is as young as we were.'

'That's true enough . . .'

Hardtman was about to remark on the oddness of their being thrown together like this – after all these years, but Cole stopped him with a cautioning expression, indicating the taxi-driver's back. For the duration of the cab ride they confined themselves to social chat about wives, children, friends, and how they all had fared. So and so had died. So and so was divorced for the second time. Somebody else was doing well.

Coatless and hatless and tall, Cole paid off the cab in a sudden light snow flurry, and a doorman from the Town Club came forward with his large umbrella. They went in, moving from the dimness of the winter streets to the greater dimness of the Club's wood-panelled lobby, to which daylight descended in dribs and drabs from high leaded windows. In the middle of the marble floor of the lobby there was a circular sofa, with cylindrical back piece, where a couple of white-haired men sat waiting. The majority of the club members and their guests treated it as something to walk around.

'Sorry I stopped you talking in the cab,' Cole said,

shaking the sprinkling of snow off himself, as if brushing off a hero's welcome. 'But I thought it unwise to talk – there. You never know.' He chuckled. 'A measure of paranoia *is* necessary for this job.'

'Well, I guess one's own car is more private.'

'Don't own one,' Cole said. He had taken Hardtman by the elbow and was steering him round the leather sofa. 'Now that may be *unnecessarily* paranoid of me, but driving around in your own car does make it damn easy for everybody to know where you are all the time.'

'Which you would rather they didn't, I gather, from the fact that you have five different telephone numbers at none of which you are to be found.'

Cole chuckled. 'Don't want to get known for your haunts, do you? Helps not to be in one and the same place all the time – huh? Wouldn't you say?'

Cole had never liked staying still. That was something Hardtman now recalled. Those long – endless – arguments at Yale had always been conducted in motion, walking around the quadrangle and the gardens, and the squares and the streets of New Haven.

Cole also walked up and down corridors, in and out of doors, around rose gardens and libraries and croquet lawns and the decks of ocean liners; he was very happy in rotundas of all kinds, where he could go in circles to his heart's content. It was Cole's style also to go all round any given subject and rarely come to the point. Even his categorical predictions and assertions, about which he challenged you to prove him wrong, upon close examination turned out to be less definite than they at first seemed. He had a fortune-teller's knack of covering himself. 'God, you're like the witches in Macbeth,' Hardtman had once hotly accused him, at Yale, out of his own passion for clarity. 'You always turn out to have been right because what you state is so equivocal, so hedged about, you can twist it around to make it fit whatever happens. You're an equivocating old hag, Walter. It's the technique of witch-doctors and demagogues. Make a categorical prediction, in a vague enough context, and of course you usually can show you were right. Same system as astrology and palmistry.'

Hardtman smiled to himself at the recollection of his vehemence. He said: 'Well, Walter. You haven't changed much. Except for the white hair.'

'Neither have you, Bill.'

'What are you up to?'

'Oh this and that.'

'Shall we go in and eat?'

Cole led the way into the dining room. On the way to their table several stops were made, and introductions effected. The talk made Hardtman feel he was in a country whose language he did not yet speak.

When they were seated and glancing at that day's menu, Cole said: 'Fill me in, Bill, on what exactly you are going to be doing.'

'I'm writing a report for the President.'

'There's a committee doing the same thing. I am on it. As you know.'

'That's like being judge and jury at your own trial, isn't it?'

'Oh, is it going to be a trial?'

'I was speaking metaphorically. I think the Boss wants somebody to correlate all the differing advice he's been getting, somebody without any vested interests.'

'That's the way to do it,' Cole agreed. 'So you'll be talking to people expressing all sides of the question?'

'Yes, but I'm not interested in theories. I want to hear about what you are actually doing – I think that's much more to the point.'

'Well, of course, I'll help all I can.'

'Let me ask you, Walter, so we know where we stand. What are *you* pushing for – in your report?'

'In a nutshell?'

'For the moment.'

'I want autonomy. Complete independence of the three services, and the FBI. Responsibility to the President alone. A secret budget.'

'That's clear enough. And – what safeguards? For Congress.'

'Someone like you – to keep an eye on things.'

'You're a difficult man to keep an eye on, Walter. Can't even get you on the phone.'

'*You* can always get me, Bill. I always ring back within twelve hours.'

'A lot can happen in twelve hours.'

'Other safeguards can be devised . . . that's what we'd have to work out, you and I. We're talking about my little neck of the woods. The other part can of course be a lot more visible.'

The arrival of the waiter obliged them to consider the menu, which was not inspiring.

'The cold chicken is probably the safest bet,' Cole advised. 'We can get them to give us a decent bottle of wine with it. They have a Château Neuf du Pape that's not at all bad.'

'I'll be guided by you, Walter.'

Cole gave the order, and when the waiter had gone, Hardtman tried to get down to business.

'Let me ask you something, Walter. What are your main areas of interest right now?'

'These are very early stages, Bill,' Cole said. 'Basically I'm trying to get a team together. At the moment what we have are the leftovers of Central Intelligence Group – and, of course, the Herr General Gehlen. Except *we* haven't got Gehlen. The Army has got him, and though they occasionally let us take a peek at what he gives them, we don't have charge of the material or any role in assessing it.'

'You must have some activity going. I can't believe you are idling your engine . . .'

'We're feeling our way still.'

'Where exactly . . . ?'

'Wherever we find a helping hand or a welcoming smile.'

'Hah?'

'Bill, we are sounding out. Sounding out, that's all.'

'What form does this sounding out take?'

'Well, wherever we have known friends we try to establish if we'd be welcome. Don't like to force our way in where we're not wanted.'

'No, I am sure. How do you decide – if you're wanted?'

'We come bearing modest gifts to test the friendliness of the natives.'

'Where have you encountered the greatest friendliness so far?'

'We have good friends in Italy. Unfortunately, the other side has got good friends there too. We come with our little trinkets, they with theirs.'

'And whose are most highly esteemed will, I expect, be shown by the outcome of next month's elections.'

'We're keeping our fingers crossed.'

'And apart from that?'

'The Pope of course is an asset. He's putting it over most forcibly, most forcibly, that voting Communist is contrary to the teachings of Christ.'

'What else?'

'Americans with family connections in Italy have been encouraged to write letters home, pointing out how awkward it would be for all of us if the Communists were to win, and end up straddling our lines of communication in the Mediterranean.'

'And over and above that?'

'Over and above that – I hope and pray . . .'

'Any results . . . ?'

'A word in the right ear never comes amiss . . .' He laughed. Ho-ho-ho. The chicken had arrived, and so had the Château Neuf du Pape. He gave his full attention to the waiter opening the wine, and when some had been poured out for tasting Cole took his time, and only after a long moment of suspense allowed 'Yes, yes, *yes*. It's all right.'

Hardtman drank a glass of wine and ate a little of his cold chicken before returning to the subject under discussion.

'How about Berlin?'

'*How* about Berlin?' Cole reiterated.

'You must have something going there – Dick Helm's old beat? He's not one to leave empty-handed.'

'The answer to your question is, Bill, we are going easy, very easy . . . oh planting a few seeds here and there, in the hope they may grow into some sturdy young plants one day . . .'

'As answers go,' Hardtman said, 'yours aren't what I'd call models of explicitness, Walter.'

'Well, Bill, starting a garden where little or nothing has grown before is a slow business.'

'There are times, Walter, when you promise as much as a veiled belly-dancer; and actually deliver as little.'

'I'll tell you something, Bill. So you can't say I don't give you the stuff. Something is going to happen in Berlin. How much d'you want to bet?'

'Couched like that, not much.'

'No, but I *know*. I can't tell you, but I've got information. Things are brewing there. Berlin is going to blow up, any time. They're going to start by interfering with our access to the city . . . You'll see I'm right. I can't tell you everything – I really can't – Lives are at stake. Worse, the sources will start drying up, if things get around. But I guarantee you, I am right about this – the whole Berlin thing is just going to blow up in our face.'

'It's a reasonable guess.'

'Not a *guess*, Bill. Not a guess. A certainty – I got it from an absolutely unquestionable source.'

'All your white hairs have not made you any less sure Walter.'

'I leave it to you liberals to indulge in doubt.'

'O.K., what's on the cards in Berlin, and what are you doing about it?'

'I am trying to work something out. It's too early to talk about, but if the worst comes to the worst – *and it's going to* – I hope to have got something to fall back on.'

At the end of the meal, Cole suggested they go upstairs for a *digestif*. It was past three o'clock and the Club was fast emptying. Cole walked ahead, up the wide stairs, along a deep landing, and into another darkly panelled room. There was nobody else there. The bar was un-attended. Cole went behind it and picked up various bottles and held them up to the grey light.

'Courvoisier? Rémy Martin? Cointreau? Maraschino?'
'Courvoisier.'

Cole poured out ample drinks, and then signed for them in the 'honours' book.

'I think I had better call these doubles, don't you?' he said, writing.

Glasses in hand the two men ambled across the room to a window bay where there were a couple of leather wing chairs. The sky had got darker. Through the high window senior bureaucrats could be seen returning to their great pillared work places, a little unsteadily, some of them, after their long lunches.

Cole offered Hardtman a cigar and the two men had some moments of close accord as they lit up, and sipped their brandies.

An eighteenth-century longcase clock chimed the quarter hour with a pretty little melody.

Hardtman smiled, drew thoughtfully on his cigar. Then he said, 'Look, Walter, I know your style is: behind the scenes, the unseen hand . . . et cetera. I know that's how you make it come together, and that you don't like to be asked too many questions. But I am here to ask questions, that's my job as I understand it. So level with me, Walter. It will be easier, for both of us, if we can proceed on the basis of mutual trust than if I have to get an executive order very time I want to know something.'

'Bill,' Cole said, 'the reason I'm not telling you much is because there isn't much to tell at this stage. Look – the first task of my Intelligence outfit is its own internal security. My concern is that we are clean from top to bottom, and I will be honest with you: I am not sure of that yet. The Reds have had a long-term world plan that includes the penetration of the highest levels of govern-ment in every Western country in the world. Communism is a religion, and there is no level of which I would be able to say confidently: they can't get in there. And I don't even exclude the White House. I know one very rich woman, came into three-and-a-half million on her thirtieth birthday, and she is one of them, without question. Finances their *apparat*, pays for their publications. Working to destroy the very privileges she so abundantly enjoys. So you can see, Bill, that I am not able to exclude anyone.'

'I take it you are satisfied I am in the clear?'

'Yes. I went over your FBI security clearance, naturally. They did a very thorough job on you.'

'Well?'

'Nothing – nothing significant.'

'What does that mean?'

'You were considered quite a radical at Yale, something of a pinko. But that doesn't worry me. The man who is not a Socialist in his youth has no heart, et cetera.'

'Does that mean you have no heart, Walter? As far as I can remember you were always a reactionary.'

Cole laughed his ho-ho-ho laugh.

'No, I'm perfectly satisfied that you and Laurene are O.K.'

'Laurene as well. She comes into the check too?'

'Naturally. She's your wife, and some things even the most careful man is unable to keep from his wife.'

'Oh you'd be surprised. No – I'm joking. I agree. Anyway, you're happy about Laurene?'

'Laurene, with her background, would have to be crazy to be a Communist.'

'Agreed. Well now that we've got that out of the way, let me ask you something. And look, Walter, stop uhming and ahing for Christ's sake and give me a straight answer. I'm not going to press you for details at this point – though I will want details later. Just let me in on your general thinking.'

'My thinking?' He deliberated, sipped his cognac, puffed on his cigar, looked out. Snow flakes were adhering to the window panes in thick blobs. 'My thinking, Bill, is this. The coming half-century will be characterized by

70

over-population. Far too many people in the world, not enough food, not enough raw materials to go around. One of the things I've done is I've initiated a long-term study of the prospects. We know some of it already. We know, for example, that if the world's climate were to return to what it was between 100 and 400 years ago, it'd result in a general cooling of the globe that would have catastrophic consequences. For example, India would have a major drought every four years and could only support three-quarters of her population. The rest of the world would have to supply 30 to 50 million metric tons of grain each year to prevent the deaths of 150 million Indians. China would have a major famine every five years ... The Soviet Union would lose Kazakhstan for grain ...'

'Why are you projecting a hypothetical cooling of the earth when ... ?'

'I just want to point out to you that under certain distant, but feasible circumstances, we'd have to say to more than half the world: "Tough luck, fellows. It's a life raft situation. There's no more room on our raft.'

'That's if *we* were on the life raft.'

'Whichever way. If they were on it, and we weren't, we'd have to make damn sure that we had the means of getting on.'

'By pushing them off?'

'If need be. Of course that's what we would do. We'd have to. We'd wrap it up, naturally, say it was our raft in the first place. And they stole it. We have a duty to see that our own civilization goes on, don't we? Now it doesn't matter where the threat comes from – whether it's some great natural disaster, or the Soviet Union. Or some little tinpot State sitting on a natural resource that we need and they are denying us ... whatever the source of the threat, there are certain things that we have got to do ...' Cole's face retained its magisterial calm, but his voice betrayed his mounting excitement as he warmed to his theme: his voice rose and quickened as he aroused himself to an ecstasy of irrefutability. Nobody could deny what he was

71

saying. It was self-evident. What did you want to bet?

'Well, Walter . . .' Hardtman began to say. But Cole would not be stopped now.

'. . . and those things, Bill, that we know have got to be done, have got to be done secretly, have got to be done clandestinely. You asked me about the general line of my thinking, and because we have known each other such a long time . . .'

'I agree, Walter, that there are some things that have to be done secretly. I accept that need, or I could not have taken this job. At the same time, I think the need for secrecy is a cloak of many patches that can be made to cover a multitude of sins . . .'

'Surely,' Walter Cole beamed across his brandy. He was a little flushed. 'I accept completely that some control of our activities is necessary and desirable in a democracy, and I welcome the fact that you are going to be the liaison with the White House. Because . . .' He made a very elegant gesture of his hand that was like some private signal between them, dispensing with the need for language. 'You know, Bill, you and I have had certain advantages in life: education, background, upbringing. I wouldn't say that makes us better than other people, but it means we know our way around better. We know what's done and what isn't. That's my answer to you concerning your worry about things done in secret. I think you and I know what'll wash and what won't. I think we have the groundplan of a mutual understanding. Bill, you and I, which should prove very useful. There won't be any mistakes. I think you and I will always know what we are talking about . . .'

'I sincerely hope so . . .'

'What I'm saying, is that people who speak the same language, between themselves don't need to say *everything* . . . All you'd have to say to me, is: Walter, it won't wash, the Boss wouldn't go for that, or: the timing is wrong. And I'd heed that. I'd take all the guidance you can give me. Conversely, if you said to me, Walter, it's felt that what'd need to happen there *is* . . . say no more. It'll be done.'

The delicately chiming clock drew Hardtman's attention to the time. He looked round. It was a quarter past four.

'Well,' he said, standing up. 'I'm certainly glad we're going to get on so well. You make it sound like Siamese twins. But now I think I should let you get back to one of the several telephone numbers that you call home.'

6

The Hardtmans had rented a row house in Georgetown, on the lower part of N Street, below Wisconsin Avenue. It was a pleasant street with red brick pavements, trees, cobblestone drives and some small front gardens.

Theirs was not one of the grander houses to be found on N Street, but it was a handsome example of Federal architecture, and had a rather fine stoop with a curving iron handrail going up to the entrance, a white door with an arched fanlight prettily divided by curved glazing bars that followed the curve of the arch. Pilasters, on which bronze coach lamps were mounted, supported a nominal triangular pediment. There were green louvre shutters to the windows, and the upper ones had shallow wrought iron balconies.

The narrowness of the front elevation was deceptive, for inside the house was quite spacious. You came in through a small hallway, where there was a small bronze bust of Roosevelt on a pedestal; the first room on the left was the library, the second was the drawing room and the third the dining room. All these rooms had french windows giving on to a small, cobbled patio with a high enclosing wall.

In March the patio was still under snow. It had been the coldest march in weather history. In North Dakota the mercury had reached 38 below zero.

When Hardtman came home, he would usually spend an hour or so in the library, reading papers that he had not been able to get through at the office. If Laurene was in, she would have a cocktail with him and chat about the evening's social engagement. There was some social engagement almost every night.

This particular cold evening in March when Hardtman handed his coat to the maid and asked if Mrs Hardtman was in the library, he was told:

'No – sir, she isn't.'

'She's not in?'

'Oh she's in all right, Mr Hardtman, but she isn't in the library and she isn't resting upstairs either, she's outside in the backyard, sir, havin' an exercise treatment with that doctor man, Dr Blake.'

'Outside in the backyard? In this cold?'

'Yes, sir, she is . . .'

'Oh surely not. In this weather?'

'Yes, sir,' the maid said full of disapproval, and added in a lower voice of shocked incredulity: '. . . and not wearin' any shoes or stockin's either . . .'

'You surely are wrong about that, Louella.'

'You just go an' see for yourself, sir.'

He went into the library, crossed to the french windows and drew the curtains back. Laurene, in white fox coat, was walking barefoot through the powdery fresh snow. The one lantern in the pergola had been switched on, and in its feeble light Laurene and Dr Blake looked like figures out of a dark Victorian woodcarving, poised for some unimaginable task.

Julian Blake, without overcoat, but with a long red football scarf wound around his neck, and trailing almost to the ground, was coaching and encouraging Laurene as she performed – that was the only word to describe the deliberate, almost theatrical manner in which it was done – her snow walk. The entire back area was marked by the criss-cross pattern of her dainty bare feet. She walked with the deliberation of someone learning how to walk, starting well back on her heels and then progressively moving her weight forward. At a certain point, she rose up like a ballet dancer, holding herself high. Then she walked stiff-legged, at the same time spreading her hands and flapping them, and shaking the loose fingers, as if she were about to attempt to fly.

Opening the french windows, Hardtman felt the shock of cold air.

'Dear, what are you doing?' he called.

'Snow-walking,' she called back.

'She's going to get pneumonia,' he told Julian Blake.

'On the contrary,' Dr Blake retorted unabashed. 'It will fortify her, make her feel fantastic. Snow-walking tones up the whole system. Kneipp, you know.'

'Kneipp . . . ?'

'Pfarrer Kneipp. Walk bare-foot in new-fallen snow for five minutes,' he counselled. 'It will cure toothache, relieve the lungs, expel noxious gases from the stomach and assist the venous return of the blood to heart and brain. I have a lot of time for these old Bavarian peasant remedies . . . as you know, Bill. You should try it, too, Bill. You'll feel marvellous, you'll see.'

Hardtman shivered. 'No thank you, Julian. I'm going to resort to an even older remedy. I'm going to have a Scotch. Come and join me when you're through.'

'With you in two minutes,' Laurene called back, head high, stretching her spine. As he closed the windows, re-lieved to be back in the warm, he saw her draw the frosty air deeply into her lungs, and then breathe out slowly, in a chain of little frothy breath clouds.

Laurene was always game to try something new, if it made an appeal to her imagination. Last year it had been pottery, arising out of a suddenly discovered passion for making things with her hands. This too was supposed to have a beneficial effect on health. 'We've all gotten to be much too cerebral,' she had asserted. 'No wonder every-body's crazy. Doing things with your hands is wonderfully restorative . . .' A top floor room in the New York house had been turned into a studio, and a pottery furnace in-stalled in the basement garage. Her teacher came three times a week; in the end she had so many pots and vases she did not know what to do with them all, and since she did not want to sell them there seemed little point in going on making still more. But she was glad to have learned pottery. She felt it was such a plus in life to be able to use your hands, and to know that, in an emergency, she could always make her own pots.

Now, as she came in, her teeth were chattering violently. 'Her teeth are chattering,' Hardtman said, with a frown.

'Good for the jaw,' Julian pointed out, 'it prevents tightness around the mouth, which creates such bad lines in the face . . .'

'You'd better have a vodka,' Hardtman, unconvinced, told her.

'Oh, I'd love a vodka, yes.'

'Julian?'

'Well, if Louella could be induced to rustle up a cup of strong black coffee . . .' Hardtman went to the door and called to Louella to bring Dr Blake a coffee; he made Laurene's drink and gave it to her.

'How you feeling?' he asked her.

'G-r-r-reat,' she said through chattering teeth. She sipped the vodka. 'No, really, Bill. It's *great*. Snow-walking. I don't know what it does, but it does something – makes you feel *alive*.'

'You sure you don't want a drink?' Hardtman asked Julian.

'No. I'll stick to coffee. Caffeine's my drug.'

'Yes, so I've noticed. You never take a drink?'

'I drink wine. And a gin and tonic occasionally. Any more and I become dull . . .'

'And we can't have that,' Laurene said.

'Whereas coffee . . . it was Voltaire's drug . . . he used to drink bucketsful, fifty cups a day. Hones the mind, sharp as sharp . . .'

'How can you ever sleep?' Hardtman asked.

'Ahh –' Julian said, 'I've been teaching Laurene that, in class – how to quieten the mind.'

'He's remarkable,' Laurene said. 'He really is.'

'Well, thank you. You *are* kind to say that.'

'Why don't you stay for dinner, Julian?' Laurene suggested.

Julian Blake had a way, if he wanted to know you, of making you like him. He made himself useful to you. From him you learned which were the best restaurants, and the cheapest, and where to go for the weekend. He could give you detailed road instructions for getting into or out of the city at the fastest possible speed at different times of the day and week. He knew taxi services nobody else knew about that could furnish you with a cab when all the other services were busy. And he could tell you where to go, and at what time, in order to pick up a girl.

In short, Julian was the type of man who knew his way around and was willing to share his knowledge.

He was a kind of doctor – I say 'kind of' because the form of unorthodox medicine that he practised was considered slightly disreputable by many people. His speciality was something he called 'the therapy of the nerves', but he used other techniques too, and was a qualified osteopath.

People said he was a genius with his fingers, and he was reputed to have cured many prominent Washingtonians of a wide range of ailments – best back man in the country, Senator Gilchrist, who was given to categorical statements, called him. In addition, Julian gave Yoga classes for people who wished to become more fully attuned to their own bodies. His method was eclectic and he drew upon a wide variety of disciplines; he did not have the narrow outlook of the traditional Yoga teacher, but took from Yoga what it suited him to take, and left the rest. Likewise, he took some water cures from Kneipp, while leaving others, sometimes prescribing warm baths and sometimes cold, and sometimes alternations of the two. In certain instances the sitz-bath was employed (either hot or cold), whereas at other times the treatment was confined to the feet. Vapour baths, too, were highly efficacious, in some cases. Though not all. His principle was to treat the patient rather than the illness, and no two people were alike, and a form of treatment that might be ideal for one might not suit somebody else. He was not doctrinaire. Some patients found cold water beneficial, others preferred warm. The water-cure did not suit everyone. Sometimes Yoga was more appropriate. Or the therapy of the nerves. He maintained that no one culture had a monopoly of cures, and while bran bread, recommended by Kneipp, was effective in some cases of digestive troubles, it was not effective where the digestive disturbances were due to emotional factors. In such cases the psychosomatic connection needed to be fully understood, and in this respect he drew a great deal on the teachings of Wilhelm Reich.

Wise beyond his years was what people said of Julian, for he was only in his mid-thirties, and rather dashing, with long untidy hair, heavy-lidded eyes, sensuous lips and a most accommodating smile. People said that there was no reason why a healer should not also have charm. Julian knew his stuff; the range of his knowledge was amazing – he knew so much about so many things, which must have been due to his extraordinarily varied background and education. He had very rapidly stepped beyond the confines of the conventional English school system. While still at Oxford, it was said, he used to spend summers in Amsterdam, studying under Felix Kersten, the originator of the massage of the nerves. Kersten's own teacher was Dr Ko, the great Chinese specialist in manual therapy, and Julian also made a pilgrimage to Berlin, where Ko was then practising, and had learned much from him too. Ko had shown him the efficacy of little-known Eastern techniques, and in pursuit of further elucidation Julian had gone to Japan, where he had studied under Master Kodo Sawaki, originator of the Japanese Zen renaissance. He had also gone to Peking and Shanghai and Nanking to immerse himself in Yoga and its variants. But he did not limit himself to Eastern techniques. In America he became a follower of Wilhelm Reich, whose theories of bio-energy, and the way mental states could impede or enhance its flow, fitted in with Julian's practical experience of being able to release energy – and 'good flow' – by means of massage.

If some people found the theories a little too arcane for their taste, there was no denying the powers that he possessed in his fingers, his ability to soothe away pain, to find the tension knots deep in the body and untie them; people went away from one of his treatments not only rid of specific pains and aches but feeling wonderfully restored and somehow lighter. Some of his cures had become quite legendary around Washington. There were gout sufferers

79

whose feet burned perpetually, whom he had cured, and people with inexplicable allergies, who could not eat garlic or onions without suffering the intestinal tortures of the damned, and they had been cured, too. A Catholic priest afflicted with a most embarrassing tic of the eyebrow (which gave the unfortunate impression that he was pro-positioning the young couples he was marrying, the old men to whom he was administering the last rites, and the maiden ladies to whose dull confessions he was so often obliged to listen) also had been cured by Julian, by a com-bination of acupuncture in the groin, and deep massage of the forehead, and one or two sessions of hypnotism. But his most famous cure, the one that had established his repu-tation and got him taken up by lots of prominent people, was of Arnold Leussenhoep, the newspaper magnate.

Luessenhoep was one of those larger than life characters that America has been so prodigal in producing. Not wish-ing to do anything by halves, he overdid everything. In-cluding his appearance. He was a huge man in height and in breadth, and he lived on an appropriately large scale. His house off Connecticut Avenue was decorated with exotic marbles, mother-of-pearl, coloured glass, gold and bronze. Alabaster statues abounded. It was not possible to go to the bathroom without passing between Doric columns. There was an indoor and an outdoor swimming pool, and the indoor one, modelled upon the swimming pool on the *Queen Mary*, was of golden quartzite beneath a domed ceiling of mother-of-pearl. Blackamoors in gold turbans and gold slippers and gold earrings and gold sashes stood in marble niches outside the den. The open-air swimming pool had a changing pavilion based on a Palladian original. There was a sunken garden, with fountains.

In addition to owning newspapers and magazines, Luessenhoep was a prominent figure in the Republican Party, a man whose opinions, backed up by substantial monetary contributions, carried considerable weight.

Luessenhoep was a manic depressive. This was well known. In his manic phases he would endorse outsiders for the Presidential nomination, endow Luessenhoep rooms in museums, engage new editors at enormous salaries, buy unprofitable art magazines, construct elaborate games and rides in children's playgrounds (he had commissioned bronze statues of Tarzan, Jane, Boy and assorted chimpanzees for one playground), buy foreign cars, motor yachts – he was passionate about the sea – and private airplanes, go without sleep for days, drink inordinately, eat inordinately, give huge parties every night, and indulge his suddenly insatiable sexual appetite with squads of call girls. The only way his wife, Dolly, had been able to deal with him when he was in the grip of his manias was to have him certified. In the private sanatorium where he was confined he would slowly, sometimes after weeks, sometimes only after months, quieten down. The trouble was that as soon as he was well enough to be discharged, he would get depressed. In his depressive phase he would become obsessively stingy, fire the hot-shot editors he had previously hired; sell the art magazines; institute stringent economies in all his households. The telephones in guest rooms were replaced by pay-phones, and the servants' accounts subjected to an audit. Also, he was impotent, and apt to fall asleep all the time. While a lot of people preferred him in this phase of his swings, it was no fun for him, and sooner or later he would return again to his manias.

All kinds of treatments had been attempted, but the psychiatrists had no success – they were hired in the depressive phase, and fired in the manic. The trouble was, they said, that his delusions were all so readily enactable that it was difficult to demonstrate to him that they were delusions. 'You think you are Le Roi Soleil,' a soon-to-be-fired psychiatrist had interpreted once, having learned that Luessenhoep was seeking to re-create Versailles on one of his country estates.

'But I don't *think* I am, I am,' he had replied with little-boy glee. 'King of the *Eastern Morning Star* and the *Western Evening Sun*.'

His wife, Dolly, had called in Julian to treat Luessenhoep for a back condition. In the course of regular deep massage, Julian had discovered that his patient's energy flow was badly impeded by armouring. This was during one of the depressive phases. The massages helped the flow of what the ancient Chinese called Qi, and what Reich called bio-energy. Excessive armouring, fostered by pleasure-anxiety, had produced energy blocks.

Like others, Luessenhoep found that after a nerve massage, he felt lifted and more energetic. Julian gave him back his vitality, without pushing him in the direction of over-excitement and mania. The surges of energy released by the treatment were controllable by Yoga-type meditation. The improvement in his condition was so dramatic that Luessenhoep, in a fit of generosity, said he wished to endow an Institute of Physio-Neural Therapy for the development of this form of treatment. This was the beginning of Julian's great fashionability in Washington.

It helped, of course, that he had the gift of making himself agreeable, and that he knew many people in different walks of life. He knew millionaires like Luessenhoep, and Senators and members of the Administration and Embassy officials and newspaper editors and famous football players, but he also knew reporters and models and small-part actresses and the owners of bars, and charter boat captains and artists and nightclub singers and jazz musicians, and other individuals of whom it was not known what business they were in.

He had a great interest in photography. He would sometimes spend hours creeping around in areas like Glen Falls, telephoto lens on his camera, waiting for the opportunity to capture some rare bird on film. Camera in hand, he would go into ghetto neighbourhoods where street fights were common; here drunks and derelicts and prostitutes and crooks became his subjects and companions. He had the gift of being able to get on with anyone. And his photos were rather good and some were published in the *Illustrated London News* and in the *Tatler and Bystander*.

Moving easily between these different strata, he brought a touch of Bohemianism to the somewhat staid social rounds of Washington.

He was not universally approved of; some people thought that a physician (even a practitioner of unorthodx medicine) ought to get more sleep and not be seen in jazz clubs with Negro girls, or go quite so often to receptions at the Polish Embassy, and if he did, not stay until practically everybody else had left. But apparently he needed little sleep, could replenish himself in a few moments of deep relaxation. His frequent late nights did not show in his face: fingers combing the long black hair over his ears, eyes getting brighter – instead of duller – as the night wore on, he appeared to thrive on a life style that would have prostrated anyone else. It did seem to prove the efficacy of his system that he stood up so well to the wear and tear, though perhaps the fact that he hardly ever drank alcohol, just endless cups of black coffee, helped keep him in such good shape.

Inevitably, there were people who called him a quack – he did so himself sometimes. He would say, 'I'm just an old quack, but you know, that's what medicine *is*, all of it, sheer bloody quackery, I sometimes think we'd be better off if we left it all alone . . . What I can't stand are people who lay down the law, think they have got *the* answer. I despise all orthodoxies, but the medical orthodoxies most of all. If I've learned anything, it's that all cures work at the beginning, and fail in the end.'

To the Hardtmans, his unconventionality was one of his attractions. On the whole they had found Washington rather stuffy, and the parties they were obliged to go to pretty wearisome. It was such a relief when Julian was there; with his unconventional attitudes to everything – which he was permitted to have, since he was a practitioner of strange and even exotic cures, and it was to be expected that someone who believed in breathing properly would also have unconventional opinions about world affairs and their solutions, and about sex and morality and Christianity.

The Hardtmans had rather taken to him, and you often saw him at their house. He was a very useful standby for any hostess, since he was single and not offended to be asked at the last moment; and he could be relied upon to enliven any evening. He was entertaining and attentive and had a fund of good stories.

One night he'd tell of some scoundrel who had made a fortune by buying up bomb sites during the London Blitz. Another night he'd be talking of Trobriand Islanders of Melanesia, who had no Oedipus complex, no sexual repression, and a sex-economy far superior to our own. He was always telling about simple or savage peoples who, in some respects, were superior to us. He seemed to enjoy the implicit mockery of our civilized values. 'We like to pretend to ourselves,' he said, 'that we invented order. That nature is chaos on which we have imposed our order. But anarchy in nature is virtually unknown, and when it does occur it doesn't last long. Order reasserts itself as part of the natural process. It's not our doing.'

The great and famous, many of whom he apparently knew, were favourite targets of his raillery. Mr Churchill, in particular. He could do a wicked imitation of him.

'Used to ring me up in the middle of the night. Voice thick as brandy sauce . . .' Julian's own voice would become slurred, richly boozy, as he mimicked the rumbling Churchill: ' "Can't sleep. Bloody annoying people been getting my goat all day long. How soon can you get over here and do your jiggerypokery, young fellow? Damned annoying people. Want to sleep, do they? Well, I wake them up . . ." ' And now the Churchill voice had a malicious resonance to it. ' "I wake 'em up, all right. And if they have the temerity to complain – I remind them that *I* am responsible for winning the war and therefore *my* well-being is a damned sight more important than theirs." '

Julian sometimes raised eyebrows; but he could usually sense the mood of the company to perfection, and adapt his position accordingly. If encouraged, he could go on to greater ribaldry. But if not, he could neatly withdraw, remarking that 'hagiography is not one of my talents'. And indeed it wasn't. One rarely heard him sing the praises of anyone. Unless they were Trobriand Islanders or Red Indians of the Nez Perce tribe, or the Osage ('fantastic horse-riders, totally unspoilt by white civilization'). His ironic sallies were made acceptable by the humour in his eyes, and by his equivocal manner. You could never be sure if he was kidding or not.

'Well, Reich, of course is mad. That's obvious. But it's a very creative form of madness.' A big wide smile invested the paradox with a whole range of unascertainable meanings. 'There are certain leaps that the human mind is only capable of making when it has rid itself of the anchorage of common sense. Common sense is, let's face it, very common. Not Reich. *He takes off*. While others go humbly uhming and ahing around the great mysteries, he has actually discovered the life-energy, and put it in a box. I say splendid! If you can put chocolates in a box, why not life-energy?' He was quite a card, Julian.

'The Russians,' Luessenhoep said one evening, 'have a quite different attitude to human life. You know, they didn't even keep records of their war dead. Did you know that? It's the Oriental mind, and the Oriental mind . . . it's well known . . .' Here he seemed to go somewhat adrift, and Julian chimed in. Luessenhoep was ready to let himself be relieved from completing his thoughts on the subject. 'Yes,' Julian continued, 'he was a cousin of the King's, you know. Matter of fact, the King was very fond of Arthur. Oh cool as anything, Arthur, Viscount Freemantle. He'd walk along the front line, tapping backsides with his thumb stick. "Better get your bum down, corporal, if you don't want it shot off." He wasn't even stooping himself. Walking straight. Just before they were due to attack, he found somebody smoking, and tore him off a strip. "Put out that cigarette, Jones. Where do you think you are? Don't you realize you're on parade?" Might Lave been Horseguards' Parade, the way old Arthur was acting. Went over the top, first man over. Tackled a Jerry machine-gun nest. Wiped it out with a grenade. And, of course, bought it. Posthumous VC, all that, buried at Westminster Abbey. HM at the funeral . . . "In-credib-b-b-ly brave man, Arthur," declares the King. But, I suppose, it might be said . . . foolhardy,' added Julian.

It was not quite clear what this was meant to illustrate –

unless it was English pluck as against Oriental indifference – but the story was appreciated, Julian told it so well, getting all the voices right, including the King's – even getting the King's erratic pauses to control his stutter, so that you felt sure Julian knew the King, too.

If you did see wicked mockery behind some of the things he said, Julian could quickly deny any such intention; putting on a very serious look, forehead ruffling becomingly, he'd say something like, 'A good Red Indian, Arthur,' leaving you not knowing quite how to take this.

For some time now, doom talk had been a commonplace with the *petit fours* and the brandy. How many million dead did you say? And that was only the A-bomb. The super-bomb, said those with inside knowledge, would be a thousand times more destructive.

Forrestal, the Defence Secretary, who came one evening, said he put the chances of war about one in four. With his broken nose and tight, difficult mouth, he looked like a better class of criminal. There was about him, all the time, the possibility of violence. In his presence, you felt that war was by no means unlikely. He told Walter Cole: 'Did you know that in 1914 Thomas Mann wrote a defence of the German Kaiser, justifying Germany's aggression? I am having that checked? He's an American resident now, Mann. We must know who stands with us and who opposes us.'

One such evening the term 'preventive war' cropped up.

'Ah yes,' Julian said, 'if you cannot stop war, start it. Logical, isn't it?'

Hardtman said, 'I always thought it was rather civilized of the English to spare the ladies the unpleasantness of having to inhale the men's cigar smoke.' And he suggested that the men withdraw to one of the other rooms. Laurene would not have this.

'But I like the smell of cigars. Oh no, I'm not buying *that*.'

'Join us by all means, if you wish, dear,' he said, in a manner meant to discourage her.

In the library, when the cigars were going, he asked the weaponry man Waldo Peters:

'Where'd you hear that term "preventive war"?'

'A lot of people talk about it.'

'And what do people say?'

'Don't you know, Bill? I thought this was your field.'

'I like to hear what other people are saying . . .'

'Well, naturally, nobody *likes* the idea. But I've heard it said that in certain circumstances we might be obliged – compelled – to resort to it.'

'Compelled to resort to preventive war?'

'The Russians don't understand anything else,' Luessenhoep interjected. 'See what happened in Czechoslovakia. Gone down the drain without even a murmur from the Left. Did you hear the garbage Henry Wallace talks? Says the Communist coup was to forestall an American-inspired takeover. That man's a Stalinist agent.'

'Do you happen to recall, Waldo, where you first heard the term preventive war? Sounds like Pentagon jargon to me,' Hardtman said.

'That's right,' Waldo said. 'Also called a pre-emptive first strike.'

'What we called a sneak attack, when the Japs did it,' Hardtman said.

'Completely different circumstances, Bill. Now you tell us, Bill. *Come on*. Let's have it from the horse's mouth. What is the likelihood?'

7

On April 1st, Hardtman was invited to attend a general Army Intelligence briefing.

He drove there himself, over the 14th Street Bridge, and on the other side of the Potomac turned off the highway and took one of the curving feed roads down to the Pentagon.

After being checked through at the entrance, he found he was in the outer of five concentric rings. He started to walk round this ring, trying to get his bearings. What possibilities for endless circumambulations, he thought. Perfect for Walter Cole. Hardtman, however, was not in a mood to go in circles, and after a while he had to acknowledge that he was in the wrong ring, or it was the wrong level. How to get to the right level in this curious building? No lifts. Only ramps. Spoke-like corridors connecting the rings. If he made his way along one of the spokes, that should bring him to a central point . . . He was testing this theory when he saw a familiar bulk ambling away from him down the corridor.

'Hey!' he called. 'Hey, Sidney!' and ran to catch up with him. 'Well, we do meet in the weirdest corridors,' he said when he had got level with the far-ranging thinker. 'What are you doing here? Lecturing the brass again?'

'No, this time we are supposed to listen. Are you going to the Defence briefing?'

'If I can find where it is.'

'Follow me. This place is laid out in a very logical way, it's easy.'

'Yeah, maybe for the military mind. Isn't mine.'

With Sidney leading, they made their way down the spoke that cut through B ring, C ring and D ring, until they came to the heart of the building: a great concourse, dim as the underworld, but very lively, lively as an airport

... with bookstalls and a bank and a drugstore and a florist and a travel agency.

Messengers and repairmen pedalled by on tricycles. Everyone else walked. They went up a ramp. A guard was on duty by a floor stand that said: Defence Department. Restricted Area. They showed their special passes and were waved through.

The conference room was full, with about fifty people seated on stacking chairs. The briefing was under way.

Sidney had seen someone he knew and gone to sit down next to him, Hardtman looked around for an empty place, and spotting Walter Cole towards the back of the room, close by the door, went and joined him.

'Keeping in the background as usual, Walter?'

'I like to be close to the door. Makes walking out simpler.'

'So – you're a claustrophobic. That's your secret, hmm?'

'Just phobic about wasting my time.'

On a dais, an army spokesman was saying that as of April 1st, which was today, the Russians were instituting a new system of inspection of personnel entering or leaving their zone in Berlin. General Clay considered this move to have very serious implications, and was asking for authorization to double the guards on American trains. He proposed to give orders that any attempts by Russians to board American trains should be repulsed, and to tell his troops to shoot if necessary. Next a telegram from the Political Adviser for Germany, Robert Murphy, was read out:

Charge that western powers have destroyed Control Council constitutes important element in Soviet plan force all three western powers out of Berlin, in order liquidate this remaining quote centre of reaction unquote east of Iron Curtain.

Murphy went on to give his interpretation of the meaning and end purpose of these new Soviet moves. He concluded that:

current Soviet-Communist propaganda campaign regarding alleged invasion of Soviet zone by organized bandits and refugee workers from western zones (reference my A238, March 25 and A247, March 29 and Moscow's telegram 75, March 30) suggests Soviet may be forced, in order to safeguard economic order north-eastern Germany, to ensure quote proper regulation and control unquote of railways and highways connecting Berlin and western Germany, which pass through Soviet zone.

Hardtman looked at Cole questioningly.

'I told you something was brewing in Berlin,' Cole said.

'Yes.'

'Why look at me?'

'I know how you like to stir things up, Walter.'

'Only if it's in a good cause.' He put his finger to his lips. 'I want to hear this.'

The army spokesman was giving a résumé of General Clay's case for meeting Russian intimidation with force. The presence of the western occupants in Berlin, Clay was asserting, had become a symbol of resistance to eastern expansionism, and was unquestionably an index of prestige in Central and Eastern Europe. Conversely, withdrawal would involve great loss of prestige. A docile submission to pressure would suggest to the Germans that our withdrawal from the rest of Germany would just be a question of time. Clay was said to be in favour of sending in a convoy with troop protection to ensure that it would reach Berlin. He fully realized the danger of such action, but felt that on balance it was more likely to prevent war than cause it.

Forrestal spoke next. He looked grey as a rock. Above his mouth an arid upper lip of stubbled flesh called for a moustache – once, indeed, he had had a moustache, a rather jaunty affair, but that was in gayer times. Now he was sombre. From time to time, as he spoke, he unconsciously fingered the empty space over his mouth, as if missing the moustache. A nervous habit, evidently. Another nervous habit was dipping his finger tips in a glass of water and moistening his lips. He did this several times. He also picked or scratched at certain points of his scalp, without appearing to realize he was doing this. He had a lot of nervous habits.

As he spoke, he made a number of slips of the tongue, and mixed up people's names. He called Robert Murphy 'Robert Hardy', and he called the Director of Central Intelligence, Admiral Hillenkoetter, 'Holly' instead of 'Hilly'. Giving the President's decision on the recommendations of the Joint Chiefs of Staff and the Defence Department, he could not keep the disapproval out of his voice. The President, he said, had decided against calling in congressional leaders as being too productive of war hysteria. He had also rejected the proposal to send a personal warning to Stalin, on the grounds that this would blow up the incident to disproportionate size. 'Disproportionate size,' he repeated sardonically. 'I guess he doesn't consider it enough they kick us in the balls. Wants 'em cut off before we react.' This got some grim laughs. He continued, with a distant smile. The President had ordered Clay to keep exactly the same number of guards on the trains as before, and while they were to prevent the Russians from coming aboard, they were to do so without the use of arms, and only to shoot if they were shot at. 'That is the President's decision,' Forrestal said, once more dipping his fingers in water. He turned to Admiral Hillenkoetter.

'Well, Holly . . . what odds are you giving us now, Hilly?' It sounded like an intentional pun and there was some laughter.

Hillenkoetter said, 'We say there's no likelihood of war within the next sixty days. Ourselves, we'd be ready to extend that period a little, but the air force is not prepared to go along with us there. So we're saying sixty days to the Boss, at the moment.'

The question of what defence resources could be mustered by the West in that period of time was then discussed. The conclusions were disturbing. There were reserves of only two and one-third divisions. Of these, only one could be committed immediately. At least twenty divisions would be needed to hold the Russians even as far west as the Rhine. That was if the atomic bomb was left out of the picture.

'We have to have military custody of the bomb,' somebody said.

'The Boss won't hear of it,' Forrestal said. 'I've talked to him about it several times. He's adamant on the question of civilian custody. Says he's not going to let any dashing air force colonel press the button for him. If it's got to be, he'll do it. He doesn't pass the buck, he likes it.'

The question of Britain's possession of atomic weapons was raised, and Graham Forster said that in order to put an end to rumours he was authorized to say there would shortly be a statement in the House of Commons to the effect that the Government was proceeding with rearmament and the construction of modern weapons, including guided missiles, atomic weapons, etc. The British Press would be sent a 'D' Notice, and would be asked not to emphasize the atomic weapons unduly, and full co-operation was expected. He was also able to say, off the record, that a request by America to base more B29s – the atom bomb carriers – in Britain would be looked upon sympathetically by His Majesty's Government, though a considerable measure of opposition could be expected in the country at large.

A CIA Intelligence summary came next. It dealt mainly with the date by which the Russians could be expected to have an operational atom bomb. An atom bomb had been made at a secret factory in Sterlitamak in the Urals, and a test had been carried out last year. But the bomb had failed to explode. It was not believed that the Soviets had a functioning atomic weapon at present. Latest intelligence indicated that they would not have such a weapon in operational numbers before 1955. By then they could have between twenty and fifty such bombs. Meanwhile, it could not be ruled out that they might have smaller numbers of such weapons by as early as next year, and by 1952 they would almost certainly have them. In the field of guided missiles the Soviets were ahead of the US and they would keep their lead for at least five years.

'I have to go,' Cole said, getting up. 'I have a meeting. This must be about over. They can't go on much longer repeating the same stale old facts.'

'Naturally, you would know all this.'

'Naturally. They're wrong about one thing – the Russians will explode an atomic bomb next year. What you want to bet?'

'Why don't you tell them? Isn't that your job?'

'In good time.'

They slipped out quietly and made their way through the rings and into the car park, where they remained talking by Hardtman's Lincoln. Cole had refused a lift. He was waiting for his taxi.

They were joined by a stone-cold sober and statesman-like Graham Forster.

'You know the cleverest move Truman could make?' he said. 'Order Forrestal to take a long holiday. He's so jumpy right now, he'd reach for the draw at the sight of his own unshaven face in the mirror. And I do not speak metaphorically. I hear he has bought himself a Smith & Wesson.'

Hardtman said, 'It has been made clear to him that Gary Cooper never draws first.'

'Maybe Forrestal isn't a Cooper fan,' Forster said. 'A holiday would be safer.'

'Safety is not the sole consideration,' Cole said.

'No?' Forster asked.

'If we are compelled to pull out of Berlin,' Cole said, 'it will be the beginning of World War III.'

'You are completely misreading the situation,' Forster said a little tetchily. 'Really you should get somebody in who knows something about the Russians. This business is just their reaction to our moves to create a separate West German government, and maybe,' he added looking at Cole, 'to one or two other things that we are doing. What they are doing is strictly in accordance with their usual practice. An act of *reversible* belligerence, designed to create the maximum discomfort to us without committing themselves to any action. I don't think they have the slightest intention of provoking a war over Berlin, but if we over-react we could get into one by accident.'

'Is that the official British view?' Cole asked.

'The British view,' Forster said, 'is that we should keep cool.'

'That,' Cole said, 'seems to be the British response to most situations.'

Back at the Old State Department Building, Hardtman found moving men taking equipment and filing cabinets out of Sidney Myer's office. The long-range thinker was supervising the move in person.

'What's happening?' Hardtman asked him.

'Moving office.'

'Where you going?'

'Just over the other side of the corridor.'

'Glad to hear we're not losing you.'

Sidney frowned.

'Frankly, this – here – is the crummy side. You've got no view, this side.'

'I noticed that. Your new office has a view?'

'I've got a *suite* of offices on the other side, with windows and balcony overlooking the White House south lawn.'

'That sounds pretty good.'

A workman passed carrying rolls of wallpaper. Sidney stopped him to check the colours and design.

'This one,' he said, 'is for the ante-room. You got that? And the other one goes in the inner sanctum. Don't make any mistakes, huh?'

'Anyway you want it,' the workman said.

'You need to have a restful outlook,' Sidney Myers said.

'I would imagine,' Hardtman agreed.

'Speaking of that, what are you doing about the summer?'

'The summer?'

'Summer here is murder.'

'Haven't had time to give that too much thought.'

'Well, you should. Most people take places out in the

country. Warrenton is a good area. Nice crowd of people go there. From Warrenton you can commute. You should look into it. Best places get snapped up by early spring.'

'That's a good piece of advice, Sidney. I'll follow it up.'

'Good horse-riding country, Warrenton. You have kids?'

'One. A girl – she's at Bay School . . .'

'She like riding?'

'I don't really know.'

'If she likes riding, it's a good place. Golf too. Anyway, you should look into it. Nobody in his right mind stays in Washington in July/August. And I can tell you anybody who does, isn't in his right mind by the end of it . . .'

It was still cold and wet, and difficult, therefore, to imagine the great August heat that everybody spoke of with such awe.

Hardtman's office was slowly getting filled up with the papers that were pouring down on him from all sides. He had been listed for 'D/3' distribution, which meant that in addition to receiving Walter Cole's traffic, which was the hardest to obtain, he also got a good deal of material from the Army, the State Department, the Treasury, the Air Force and the FBI. Each of these government agencies had its own Intelligence division, generating mountains of papers. Hardtman also had the right to ask for something that had not been sent to him. Should the department concerned refuse to comply with his request, he could get an executive order compelling it to show him what he wanted to see. So far he had used this special power only once: to compel the Army to let him see its reports on the dismantling of the German war armaments industries. The Russians had charged that many of the biggest concerns were continuing in operation under the control of their former Nazi bosses.

The executive order when issued had resulted in twelve large cases of files being brought to his office. The material was dense, full of charts and statistics, and no key was provided to enable an outsider to get to the guts fast. It would have taken five men a week to go through everything. Hardtman had to content himself with some rapid sampling. However, if what he found out about German war industries was not very much, he had learned that the alternative to withholding information was to flood him with more than he could handle.

After this experience, he saw how impossible it was going to be for one man to do the job he had been given. It required a department. Perhaps he was not meant to be too successful in finding things out. Well, if so, they had not calculated with his stubborn determination to do what he assumed to be his job. There were other ways of doing it. What was not to be gathered by direct questioning or patient ploughing could sometimes be inferred from listening for nuances and watching for signs. And so he made many phone calls, and talked to a great many people, and ate lots of lunches, and was amiable and unpressing, and listening hard all the time.

'Oh let's indulge ourselves in a decent claret,' one of Cole's boys remarked one lunchtime, and at the end insisted on being allowed to pick up the bill. 'No, no, I insist. It was my idea, the wine.' When Hardtman however persisted in taking the bill, the other man said in a tone of exasperation. 'Oh don't be a fool, Bill. It goes on the unvouchered funds.'

Next time he saw Cole, Hardtman asked casually: 'What's the size of your budget, Walter?'

'I don't deal with that.'

'Who does?'

'There's a comptroller . . .'

'He tells you what you can spend?'

'Doesn't work like that. Our kind of operation, you have to spend what it costs.'

'Where's it come from?'

'There's a fund.'

'An unvouchered fund?'

'Not every bottle of vintage claret is recorded,' he said, 'but I have to account for every penny spent – to my own conscience.'

96

'What sort of figure is your conscience letting you spend in Berlin right now?'

'It's not broken down geographically.'

Such answers, if not exactly informative, at any rate indicated that Cole had a secret budget, and presumably he was using it for some purpose.

One afternoon, going through his notes, Hardtman found a jotting that said, 'March 25 A238 and March 29 A247.' These, he recalled, were references to two of Robert Murphy's telegrams. At the Pentagon briefing Hardtman had scribbled a reminder to himself: 'Western bandits, currency dealers, etc. Murphy's telegr.'

He checked through his files. He did receive some of Murphy's telegrams under 'D/3' distribution. These particular ones, though, had not been sent to him, and so he rang his contact in the State Department and requested copies. Half an hour later the man rang back to say that these particular telegrams were not being distributed.

'What's in them?'

'Nothing very interesting. Maybe they are thought to contain too little of interest outside of the Department.'

'Still, I'd like to see them.'

'I don't see how I can let you have them. It's red tape but ...'

'I can get an executive order if need be.'

'Let me check, see if we can get round the red tape. Ring you back.'

But it was towards the end of the afternoon and by the time Hardtman left his office he had not yet heard from the State Department.

A thin mist adhered to the surface of the Tidal Basin; the sky was a meshwork of gunmetal clouds; the air had a chill dampness – one breathed it with misgiving. It was not good air. It made nose and throat tighten, and the chest wheeze. Hardtman turned up his coat collar, which was not high enough to cover more than his adam's apple. The cold air was around his throat. Rising vapour gave the impression that the Jefferson Memorial was floating on the water. The Tidal Basin was ringed by stark, bare trees.

There was plenty of parking space. It was not a day for sightseers. Hardtman got out of his car and walked towards the wide steps of the monument. There was a strong wind. It made the brownish water of the Tidal Basin quite choppy and drove sharp needles of rain beneath the downturned brim of his hat and on to his face. He started up the marble steps. There was a guard just inside the Memorial, all buttoned up against the cold. Hardtman went in, and stood looking up at the high bronze figure on the black granite pedestal. In this big empty inner space, open on all four sides, you had to hang on to your hat on a windy day such as this. He stood there, windblown, and read the inscriptions on the walls. He was quite alone here. He read first the familiar quotation, the one about the truths that were self-evident, and then he read other words, less well known, embodying truths less readily bandied about.

He felt mysteriously stirred. It was for him a moment of personal dedication. He began to turn away, and was just about to leave when he saw someone come through one of the open spaces between the high columns. He, too, was muffled up against the wind; he appeared to be coming straight towards Hardtman. A few steps away he suddenly stopped, and a somewhat embarrassed smile appeared on his face.

'Good heavens, it's you, Hardtman.'

'Come to read the self-evident truths, Holbrook?'

Holbrook, as if caught doing something improper, said sheepishly: 'I've never seen it before. And I thought I ought to.'

'Impressive, isn't it?' Hardtman said regarding the massive bronze figure of Jefferson.

Holbrook was looking all around. His eyes lighting on the famous quotation, he began to read it out loud, determinedly, in his precise, cold English voice: '. . . hold these truths to be self-evident: that all men are created equal, that they are endowed by their Creator with certain inalienable rights, among these are life, liberty, and the pursuit of happiness, that to secure these . . .'

'Yes, yes, it does bear repeating,' Hardtman said. He began to move away. Holbrook seemed set on reading the entire quotation, and after that one there were three others. 'We must see you soon.'

'Yes, indeed. My best regards to Mrs Hardtman.'

8

Early in April General Lucius Clay decided to test the new Russian order. A military train was sent in. Upon first entering the Soviet zone, it was not stopped or hindered. There were no signs of Russian troops, and no obstacles had been placed across the tracks. Then, after having covered a short distance, the train was without warning shunted off the main line, into a siding.

The manoeuvre was effected by electrical switching of points from a railway control box. No one came to explain or to question. The train was simply left there, in the siding, as if forgotten. The American commander on the train could clearly see the control box from which the switching had been effected. There were only two men in the box. No armed guards. An exhaustive examination of the surrounding terrain through field glasses failed to reveal any sign of Soviet troops – which of course did not mean that there weren't any in the vicinity. Everything was quiet.

It would have been simple for the Americans to send half a dozen men to the box and have the train shunted back on to the main line so that it could continue into Berlin. Provided there was no interference from the Russians. They could even have dealt with interference from the Russians, according to Clay and Murphy. A team of army engineers capable of overcoming any 'technical difficulties' that the train might encounter was on board. And enough armed personnel to repel anything short of a full-scale military attack.

But the Americans on the train made no moves. They sought instructions by radio and were told to sit tight. While they were doing this, Clay was having long emotional discussions with Washington; he was demanding permission to send in an armoured division to ensure that the train got through. In this he was backed by the Political

Adviser, Robert Murphy. Both argued that a resolute show of force would make the Russians climb down. But among the President's military advisers, General Wedemeyer, in particular, strongly opposed such actions. The President refused to sanction them. For the umpteenth time, Clay offered his resignation. For the umpteenth time he was induced to calm down, and persuaded to stay on.

After remaining several days in the siding, the American train withdrew ignominiously. By this retreat, according to Murphy, perpetuating the Berlin problem. Others took a different view. Dean Acheson conceded that the Russians could be bluffing; but war was too high a price for finding out that they were not.

About the time of the train incident, Hardtman received a phone call from the State Department to say they could let him have the gist of the Murphy telegrams he had wanted to see.

'O.K., shoot.'

'Well,' the State Department man said, 'I am paraphrasing, but basically Murphy refers to Russian charges that we are sending quote organized bandits and saboteurs into their zone to take away foodstuff and industrial plant, carry out economic and industrial sabotage, and engage in illegal currency dealings to weaken and undermine the stability and security of their sector. That kind of stuff. He is repeating these allegations as the basis for his conclusion that they are going to do something like clamp down on the road and rail traffic into their zone. As they have now done.'

Hardtman replaced the phone, thought for a while, and then decided he had better go and see Walter Cole.

The buildings were not old enough to have anything that could be thought of as a style, but they were pre-war, and the functional sprawl suggested a time when the more charming flamboyances of 1920s and 1930s architecture – Aztec temple shapes, sunrise effects, et cetera – had already been discarded for something plainer, shorn of the decorative. There was a drive that wound past an outer complex of institutional buildings, and then a large convex mirror indicating a blind corner, and having negotiated this Hardtman drove into a forecourt around which a number of red brick buildings were grouped. Leaving his car parked in a Reserved space, he counted the entrances from the left – since they were not numbered – and went into the fourth one, as Cole had instructed.

Inside he looked in vain for any listing of offices. He was in an empty foyer with glass doors at the end. A young man in a blue suit stood on the other side of the glass, as if he had nothing better to do. When Hardtman had come close enough to be clearly seen, the young man smiled, and at the same time, as if there were some casual connection between these two events, the glass doors slid open.

'Hi, Mr Hardtman,' the young man said. He had clear blue eyes, and was sporting a triangle of white handkerchief in his upper pocket. His white voile shirt had four-button cuffs. The glass doors had slid closed again as soon as Hardtman was in.

'Somebody will be right along to take you in, sir. Meanwhile could I ask you to wear this, Mr Hardtman? All the time, please, while you're in the building.'

He took out of his pocket a plastic clip-on badge, with Hardtman's photograph and the words SPECIAL VISITOR CAT. A1. *William C. Hardtman.*

'In the old days one wore carnations, now it's one's own police photograph,' Hardtman observed.

'A carnation would be handsomer, I agree,' the young man said, 'but less secure.' He smiled agreeably.

The young man also was wearing a plastic buttonhole with his photograph. He was identified as: STAFF CAT. K2. *Kadowski.*

The plain steel doors of the lift were opening and an attractive young woman in a moulded suit of blue gross-grain appeared. She had gorgeous legs in sheer nylons, and in defiance of the New Look the skirt went barely to her knees.

'I'll look after you, Mr Hardtman,' she said giving him a smile. She had blue eyes too. She signed for him and took him to the lift, and continued to smile at him, warmly, up to the first floor. Here another young man, the spitting image of the one downstairs, was waiting. His plastic buttonhole seemed to be of an altogether grander order. He was STAFF CAT. A3. *DeMoto*.

'I'm Mr Cole's personal assistant, Frank DeMoto,' he introduced himself. 'Nice to meet you, Mr Hardtman.'

'Nice to meet you, Mr DeMoto.'

There were more glass doors of the sliding variety at both sides of the corridor. That was one way of looking at it. The other way of looking at it was that as you stepped out of the lift you were in a glass cage from which you could not emerge until somebody had approved your release. There was a wait now. Then the lift doors closed and the glass doors opened.

The personal assistant led the way down a narrow corridor, Hardtman came next, and the young woman with the good legs followed. They went by a succession of doors without any names or numbers on them.

'How do you find anybody here?' Hardtman asked the personal assistant.

'Anybody you need to find, you know where to find him.'

'Conversely, anyone you don't need to find, you don't know where to find?'

'That's right.'

Some way along the corridor, the personal assitant stopped before one of several identical doors, and said, 'Go right on in, Mr Hardtman.'

'I'll say goodbye to you here,' the young woman with the good legs said.

'Well, been nice knowing you,' Hardtman said. Walter Cole's assistant signed the three-ply slip the young woman handed him; and she took her copy and left.

There was the usual outer office with a secretary and beyond it an inner office, the door of which was open, and Walter Cole was coming forward, with extended hand.

He said, 'Thank you, Frank. I'll sign for Mr Hardtman.

You don't need to hang around.' He gave Frank a signature.

'I'm beginning to feel like a parcel,' Hardtman said.

'Just so we know where everybody is. In case they got lost.'

'Which it can't be hard to get in this place,' Hardtman ventured to suggest.

'Well, goodbye, Mr Hardtman,' the personal assistant said. 'Be seeing you, I guess.'

'Right.'

'You want to take a look around before we sit down?' Cole offered.

'Not too much.'

'Let me just show you one thing.'

'All right.'

He followed Walter Cole along the corridor for a while until they came to a door that gave on to a large room divided up into many small glass cubicles in which young men and women were seated at work, their tense expressions indicating the examination room.

'What are they doing?' Hardtman asked.

'Tests,' Cole said. 'This is how we select our people.'

'What sort of tests?'

'Oh the usual. Rorschach – ink blot. Apperception. The Higgins . . .'

'The Higgins?'

'Make a self-inventory based on a 566 item-questionnaire.'

'Umm –'

'Also, the Spitz.'

'I don't know that one either.'

'A personal preference schedule based on 255 pairs of self-descriptive statements.'

'That would give anyone away.'

'We also ask them to answer the question: Who are you?'

'Do many of them know?'

'They take a crack at it. Finally, there's a tough one. The question just says: Why? We fail a lot on that.'

'You do? What's the correct answer?'

'I don't know. Each applicant has to find his own. But we fail quite a few who give long self-justifying answers as to why they want to work in the CIA. Which is what they think the question is about. I guess they protest too much, and that weeds them out.'

'What *is* the question about, or is my asking that a sign of *my* essential ineligibility?'

'It's calculated to reveal character. I don't know what the answer ought to be in each case, but I can only say I accepted an applicant who answered the question *Why?* with *Why not?*, and walked out of the examination room.'

'There's your taste for risk again, Walter.'

'Is that what it is? You want to see the laboratories, Bill?'

'No thanks, Walter. I have things to discuss with you.'

'The Technical Section is beginning to shape up. You should really see it sometime. We have a guy there who is working on a way of monitoring conversations in a closed room, from the outside of the building. By electronically interpreting the vibrations of the voices on the window panes.'

'Fantastic,' Hardtman said.

'You and I would call it gibberish, but he says he is getting the beginnings of comprehensive sounds. Now what vistas that opens up.'

'Quite incredible.'

'All right, let's go back to my office.'

It was an office like any other, lacking any personal touches.

'This where you've been hanging out all the time, Walter?'

'It's one of my places.' This was as near as Cole ever came to giving a definite answer. 'Man with many hats has to have many places to hang them, huh? And you, Bill? You comfortably settled in?'

'View is not the greatest – asphalt parking lot. Previous occupier whiled away the time playing the horses. Found a piece of White House notepaper, marked Top Secret/Eyes Only, with half a dozen hot tips.'

'That must have been the *inestimable* Professor Mittleweiss. I know about his hot tips. All dogs.'

'You know Mittleweiss?'

'Oh sure.'

'Apparently he had some crazy scheme?'

'You know about his scheme?'

'I heard something.'

'What a leaking barrel that guy is.'

'His scheme, from what I heard, is the kind we ought to let leak out. Down the drain.'

'Well, it has some appeal, you know. If, as they claim, capitalism contains the seeds of its own destruction, there's something to be said for planting a few of the seeds in *their* garden. Extra insurance. Trouble is Mittleweiss can't keep his mouth shut. Tells everybody. Wants all the credit beforehand. I wouldn't have him under my roof. You can see what he's after. Glory and fame. I told him, "When people tell me I'm doing a good job, I tell them that if they know what a good job I'm doing, I can't be doing such a good job." Sherry?'

'Thanks, yes. Conversely, if you're doing a bad job, and it's not known how bad a job you're doing, you're not doing such a bad job.'

'I do enjoy your sardonic sense of humour, Bill.'

'I'm glad.'

Cole had got out the sherry bottle, and was pouring.

'Well, what do you think of our place?'

'No numbers on the doors, no names – finding somebody must be like playing blind man's buff.'

'It's not as much of a labyrinth as it seems. Once you know your way around.'

They both sipped their sherries, and Hardtman let a brief silence develop.

'Well, Bill, what was the urgent matter?' Cole asked finally.

'I want to know what you're doing in Berlin.'

Cole considered this seriously. His face became open and frank.

'Let me answer you this way, Bill. The Communists are using their extensive funds, and influence, with the labour unions, the publishing companies, the women's organizations, and all sorts of other front organizations to gain control of the key elements of power all over Europe, and we cannot combat that without supporting those elements we can find who are friendly to us.'

'I believe that principle has been accepted. What I want to know is what *exactly* you are doing. Let's take Berlin. What have you got going there?'

'IOUs, Bill, IOUs.'

'Payable when?'

'In due course.'

'Whenever that is. Time notes with no date on them?'

'These things cannot be specified so exactly.'

'Who are they? These people who now owe us something?'

'There has been a very good response from the police force. I think we can rely on 40 per cent of the entire German police force in Berlin.'

'Impressive, if you really can count on them.'

'If we give them the quid they'll give us the quo.'

'The quid meaning arms, money, training – and an attractive option scheme in the company's future?'

'It means whatever is needed to keep up their morale.'

'So we are building up a paramilitary . . . force – ?'

'We're making friends . . . And of course you can't abandon friends in times of adversity. If it becomes necessary for us to pull out of Berlin . . .'

'What basis do you have for believing that these people are reliable, that we can count on them, and, most important of all, that we can control them?'

'We have a man there who is a born military leader, a Yugoslav whose training was in the Hapsburg Military Academy. He is brilliant. He is gathering a nucleus together for the day when the forces of oppression in Europe will

107

begin to roll back and there will be vast uprising in the East.'

'Meanwhile, are his people engaging in black marketeering, illegal currency dealings, sabotage, smuggling ... ?'

'That's not policy. But, as you know, in all Intelligence operations, the details to some extent have to be left to the agent in the field to decide on in the light of the prevailing local circumstances.'

'You saying *you* don't know of such things being done?'

'I don't.'

'Is that because you don't need to know?'

'It's unfair of you to imply that I'm keeping anything from you. I answer all your questions, don't I?'

'Yes, in a way. But the system is a self-serving closed circuit. I don't know *what* it is that I don't know. Therefore I don't know if I need to know or not. And so, not knowing, I can continue to assume I don't need to know ...'

'I wouldn't see it that way.'

'How would you see it?'

Walter Cole hesitated, and a frown appeared on his high handsome brow. He got up suddenly and went to the window. He had been sitting still for what was rather a long stretch of time for him. Now he looked down on to an internal courtyard. There was a view of tubbed trees, a modern fountain that made modern patterns with its spray, cast-iron benches on which company workers sat waiting for their dates; the company encouraged dating within the organization in preference to outside, and in certain cases actually prohibited unsanctioned intercourse with unvetted outsiders. The frown on Cole's face deepened. He touched the wired glass; perhaps he was suddenly beset by the disturbing thought that the other side might have already perfected ways of deciphering conversations from the vibrations of the window panes. But here he was doubly secure, since his office gave on an inner courtyard, into which people were not allowed unless they could answer the questions *Who are you?* and *Why?* correctly.

'You know something, Bill?' Walter Cole said. 'The

clandestine section was offered to the State Department, and they wouldn't touch it. The Army was asked to handle it, and they didn't want to know. So they came to me. Because they know that I know that in those grey areas where the use of force is both too risky and impracticable, and where diplomacy is helpless, covert action has to be the answer. And they know that I know that the public expects certain things to be done – to protect their interests – but that it doesn't necessarily want to know *what* is being done. I am not one of those who believe in the doctor telling the patient everything. I don't think the patient wants it either.'

With his white hair he sometimes had the appearance of a trusted family friend, rich in knowledge of the ways of the world, a man who knew what was good for you.

Hardtman said: 'I accept that there are things that have to be done that have to be done in secret. But keeping things secret from the other side is not the same as keeping them secret from yourself – and your own side. Sometimes you scare me, Walter. Can't you see that you are starting things that nobody knows about, and the Russians are reacting to your moves, and we are reacting to their moves, and so on, and we are setting up a chain of reactions with possibly disastrous consequences, and are obscuring from ourselves the knowledge of who started what? That's what I am worried about.'

'And I agree with you,' Cole said. It was always suspicious when Walter Cole agreed with you, it was so unlike him. 'But I tell you, the reason we have to be so careful ... why I'm not as open maybe as I'd like to be, the reason is that every move we make the Commies get to know about. For instance, what made them so confident that we were not going to do anything in Berlin? That we were just going to take it when they shunted our train off the tracks ... ?'

'Maybe they've also figured it out that Gary Cooper never draws first.'

'I think that's a hell of a lot for them to count on without specific information.'

'You think they knew Clay had orders not to resort to

force? How could they know that? Nobody knew until the last moment. Clay and Murphy were all the time pushing for an armoured division to go in and force the train through . . .'

'Which means they know of decisions taken on the very highest levels in Washington.'

'That is pretty high.'

'Bill, there's a leak in the British Embassy. We've suspected it for a long time, and there has been recent confirmation. Of couse, the British, since they act jointly with us, are informed of every move, and so if the Soviets have got an agent in there . . .'

'On that sort of level?'

'On that sort of level, yes.'

'It's difficult to believe.'

'The British have had information in their possession since 1940 that there was a Russian agent in their Foreign Office.'

'Since '40! They can't have been doing much about it.'

'Not much. Trouble is, he's one of their very own. Eton and Oxford. Upper class. An idealistic bolshie. That was the tip off. And now he's in Washington.'

'Any ideas who it could be?'

'You know I am prohibited by statute from engaging in domestic activity.'

'I would like to see the statute that could prohibit you, Walter.'

This time Cole did not laugh.

'It's handled by the FBI. And of course the British have their own – leisurely – way of doing things. They think that catching spies is like solving *The Times* crossword puzzle. Holbrook gave me *his* favourite the other day.'

'Who was it?'

'Graham Forster.'

'Forster!'

'He has the right sort of background. Not Oxford, true, but Eton and Cambridge. Foreign Office.'

'That's hardly conclusive.'

'Holbrook has dug up the fascinating fact that Forster's middle name is Gore.'

'Yes.'

'He has an interesting theory about that.'

'About the name Gore?'

'Yes. Apparently the Russian for Homer is Gomer . . .'

'I wouldn't have believed it, but if you tell me so . . .'

'And Gore is a near anagram of Gomer.'

'A *near* anagram! You think the Russians would be so sporting as to provide us with clues.'

'Maybe not the Russians. But Homer himself might. Might appeal to his peculiar sense of humour. Another thing. Forster was at that Defence briefing, so he knew that Clay had been ordered not to resort to armed force.'

'There must have been fifty others at that briefing.'

'Not that many Englishmen who'd been to Eton and worked in the Foreign Office: process of elimination.'

'I would have thought Forster a pretty unlikely bet.'

'You may be right. I talked to him, tried out one or two things. You know who *he* thinks it is? Holbrook.'

'Well, that sort of returns the compliment. But why Holbrook? What is his name an anagram of?'

'He says Holbrook always looks guilty, and since he has no secret sex life to be guilty about, or any sex life for that matter, Forster concludes that his perpetual sheepish expression has to be due to the fact that he's a spy. Also says he wanders around peculiar places. The Lincoln Memorial. The National Gallery. The Smithsonian.'

'I didn't know they were peculiar places. I've been to them myself. As a matter of fact, I recently ran into Holbrook at the Jefferson.'

'Could he have been making a drop?'

'Well, I suppose he could. He said he had come to read the self-evident truths.'

'Sounds suspicious to me, Bill.'

'I suppose *my* being there might have seemed suspicious to him.'

'Why *were* you there?'

'To read the self-evident truths.'

'I'd have thought a man like you wouldn't need to read them.'

'They bear re-reading. You should try it sometimes, Walter.' He paused. 'Who are you putting your money on?'

'I only like to bet on certs, Bill. Oh, I have one or two favourites, but for the moment no certainties. I can tell you this, though. If it were up to me I wouldn't go about it the way the FBI are doing – amassing huge dossiers on the cleaning women. *Or* the way the British are doing. Anagrams.' He shook his head disgustedly.

'How then, Walter?'

'Tell me,' Cole said abruptly, 'what's your opinion of Dolly Luessenhoep? I know she and Laurene are good friends . . .'

'Dolly? You mean apropos what we're discussing?'

'Working-class background. Made her way up in a spectacular, if questionable manner. Committing her husband to insane asylums, and taking charge of his money and business interests.'

'I don't see how your process of elmination gets to her.'

'Her campaigns against the big pharmaceutical industries . . . smacks pretty much of the party line. Of course, *she* can't be Homer, I'll give you that. None of the sources describes Homer as a woman. And she couldn't have penetrated the British Foreign Office. But don't forget, Bill, even Homer has to have a support organization. She does contribute to a lot of causes.'

'My impression is that Dolly acts like a rich woman to her little finger, including bossing everybody around.'

'*They* can boss people too. You know she's contributed $5,000 to the Washington Labour School, and $10,000 to the American-Soviet Friendship League. She's been to Russia, was given an interview with Stalin.'

'Printed in the Luessenhoep papers. I remember it.'

'Not unfriendly to the Soviet regime.'

'She's not Walter Winchell. That's why she got the interview. Journalists tend not to bite the hand that feeds them exclusives. That can be left to the editorialists, who don't have to sit across a desk from their subject matter. Her editorials are pretty tough on the Communists.'

'They're Arnold's doing. Supposing all those causes she contributes to are just a cover, supposing some of them are fronts, for channelling the money . . . what a deep penetration scheme that would be! Dolly Luessenhoep, taking over one of America's richest and most powerful men, running him in accordance with party orders . . .'

'Walter, at this rate pretty soon you're going to be the only one left on our side.'

'You make the same mistake as the British. You say it couldn't possibly be so-and-so, I went to school with him. The point is Homer did go to school with them.'

'Tell me how you'd go about finding him.'

Cole was silent for a moment, thinking; then he said: 'Well, I assume, first, that if he's lasted out, undetected, since the 1930s, he's smart, and his cover has got to be near perfect. Now the question is how does he keep it up, without giving himself away? Hell, he's probably somebody I have lunch with twice a month. If he has a sense of cause, there must be a touch of fanaticism in him somewhere, how does he keep that hidden all the time? Well, I tell you. I don't know what he looks like, but I've heard his laugh. I bet he's got that sort of bitchy British laugh. Because I'm sure of this, the way he keeps it up is by being an oddball and a sarcastic bastard. You know what I mean? The sort you never know how to take what they are saying – are they kidding you, are they serious? I've got his *tone* of voice in my mind, I know the way he phrases things, sitting on both sides of the fence at the same time.'

'I'm impressed,' Hardtman said, 'I think you may be on to him.'

'The thing is, Bill, that's why I have to be so damn careful, because not only do I have lunch with him twice a month, but I bet I meet him for cocktails at your house.'

As a matter of fact, Walter Cole's own household was not immune to leaks either. His wife suffered from serious psychological disturbances, and was seeing a psychiatrist three times a week. Of course, the man had been thoroughly checked, and cleared. All the same, it was not perfect security for the wife of the head of the covert section to be lying on a couch telling her dreams and free associating. She may even have been given drugs to help her unburden herself, since the man she saw was not a strict Freudian. A lot of her trouble had to do with the personality of her husband, and so he was bound to come up in the treatment.

The psychiatrist made notes after seeing each patient, and these were locked away in an ordinary filing cabinet. There is no record of his office ever having been burgled, but there are other ways of getting hold of the contents of confidential reports. The notes on Mrs Cole were extensive, and much of the material concerned her feelings towards her husband. Though Cole, naturally, did not tell her the details of secret actions that he was planning, or instituting, she was a very instinctive woman and always seemed to be able to sense when he was up to no good.

PART TWO

9

Julian Blake's International Institute of Psycho-Organic Medicine and Physio-Neural Treatment was situated in a red brick Victorian house with bay windows and one or two somewhat half-hearted onion-shaped black cupolas that you really didn't notice too much, if you didn't want to. It was on a small tree-lined street, off Connecticut Avenue, not far from the Mayflower Hotel. A middling sort of street that had known worse days – and better. The houses were of varying styles, and in varying condition, but mostly old, four or five storeys high; there were some with stoops, some with front doors on street level, and some even had minute patches of front garden.

Though there were one or two small apartment buildings and residential hotels in the street, most of the houses were used as offices. There was the Appalachian Trail Club at the beginning of the street, and a little further on there was the headquarters of the Federation of Ladies' Clubs; after that you passed an Association of the Defenders of Wild Life, a Cathedral Club, a School of Ballroom Dancing, an engineering institute, the College of Advanced Governmental Studies (which offered a correspondence course in government), and then came Julian's place.

If the name of Arnold Luessenhoep on the notepaper led people to expect something in keeping with the newspaper tycoon's grandiose style, they would have been disappointed by the entrance to the Institute, which was modest, not to say shabby.

Having cured Luessenhoep of his spells of manic generosity Julian had been obliged to reconcile himself to his patron's resultant carefulness with money. A spontaneous surge of inexpressible gratitude had led the tycoon to set up the Institute, but in a later mood of more controlled gratefulness he had reduced his contributions to a bare minimum.

Julian would explain, without making it sound at all like an apology, quite the contrary in fact, that the forms of therapy practised and taught by him had no need of lavish appurtenances, or for that matter, even though he was on the top floor, a lift. Walking up four flights of stairs helped the Pranayama, the wind, which was also the vital breath of life.

Julian occupied only the top floor of the building: below him there was a publisher of Episcopalian texts; then on the first floor there was the Anna Burovna School of Russian Ballet, and on the ground floor the Marco Polo Travel Co., which specialized in cut-rate exotic tours.

Having found their way to the top floor, and passed through the slightly sleazy confusion of the vestibule, where there was a different girl on duty practically every day (each as pretty as the next), the patients or class members usually felt very *avant garde*! – and quite ready to benefit from the unorthodox brilliance of their physician and teacher. If they entertained any doubts about the treatment, the name of Arnold Luessenhoep on the notepaper reassured them. The story was well known that he had himself been cured by Julian.

If there remained any vestige of unease in their minds, this was disposed of by the signed photographs in the vestibule. They covered the walls. The eminent patients included Winston Churchill, Prince Hendrik of the Netherlands, ex-King Peter of Yugoslavia, the Emperor Haile Selassie, the Duke of Windsor, Joe di Maggio, Jeanne Crain, looking just as pretty and sweet as in *State Fair*, the Duchess of Argyll, the young Lord Montagu, Lord Nuffield, Don Greenwood of the Cleveland Browns; and while some had merely signed their photos, others had written a warm message of appreciation as well.

There was a constant flow of pretty girls through the offices of the Institute. Some of these were secretaries or relief secretaries or replacement secretaries; others were models or dancers who came to Julian for Yoga lessons to

118

improve their posture and litheness and stamina. Perhaps there was some ailment from which these exceptionally pretty girls suffered, but it seemed unlikely, considering how full of life they were.

Julian would continue with whatever he was doing while the class assembled. He discouraged chatting, and was terse in answering questions. Even when he knew somebody quite well, he did not say much. Needless talking dissipated vital energy, he taught. Instead, he sat quietly waiting, if he had nothing specific to do, creating a sense of complete peacefulness around himself by his totally unhurried manner. This was in contrast to other doctors who always seemed to be in such a rush; not Julian. He did not feel the need – indeed he taught this – to fill every moment of spare time with some activity. Being still was an activity too. And so the immediate effect of entering his rooms was calming, after the bustle of the city outside, and the aspirants at once felt a slower quieter rhythm pervade their beings.

Once or twice, when she was leaving after a class, Laurene passed a large old black woman on the stairs, climbing slowly and painfully and with much effort and self-coercion. Pausing, panting, she would address herself in round scolding terms. 'Now you jus' get yerself up them stairs, you old lazybones you.'

'Can I help you?' Laurene had offered.

'Well, that's real nice of you, but there ain't no call. I can manage by mahself now, now the doctor give me the magic needles.'

With one arm she was pushing herself up on a crutch, while with the other she hung on to the banisters, and in this way, step by step, she moved her considerable weight up the stairs.

'Would you like to put your weight on my shoulder?' Laurene asked.

'Wouldna' wanna do that – ah'd crush you ah would, ah weighs a ton.'

'Well, let me see you to the top anyway.'

'It's mah hip,' she said. 'It's the art-ritiss. Ah got old

119

bones and ah guess they is jus' wearin' out like everythin' do. Nothin' lasts forever.'

She stopped talking while getting herself up the next flight, and then, when resting once more, she continued:

'Oh that Dr Blake, ah love him, he's a real gentleman. A real fine man. He is jus' beautiful. A lovely person, and a mos' pleasant man. Givin' me them magic needles, stickin' them all over me, and twiddlin' 'em about like he's playin' the devil's own instrument, and it sure do hurt sometimes but he say that's when it's doin' the most benefit to me, when it hurt, because that's when he's hittin' de point dead on. And he is so right about that. Because ah's feelin' so much better since he been givin' me the miracle cure of the needles.'

The Negro woman was among those treated free of charge; another was a small child of about six or seven, who was sometimes sitting in the waiting room when Laurene came out of class. She said hello to him, but he never replied, and kept his eyes downcast. He seemed always on the verge of bursting into tears, and his lower lip trembled all the time.

Laurene sometimes wondered about the proportion of non-paying to paying patients; even though the Luessenhoeps were providing some financial support, she had the impression that the Institute was run on a shoestring. Despite having all those pretty secretaries floating around, Julian seemed to do everything himself: often it was he who answered the phone and made the appointments. The Institute's hours were highly flexible. You could arrive there on a weekday at 11 a.m. and find it closed; on the other hand, treatments were sometimes going on past midnight, or on a Sunday afternoon.

The Yoga class was held in a large bare room with Indonesian rush mats on the wooden floor. There was also a smaller office, with a doctor's couch, where Julian gave treatments; nerve massage, Shiatzu, acupuncture.

The Yoga class that Laurene attended was on Tuesdays and Thursdays. Dolly went the same day and she was all

120

the time urging friends and acquaintances to come with her. 'He is just incredible,' she promised, 'a genius with his fingers, and not at all expensive.'

It was she who had brought Laurene, and lately she had been bringing Senator Keever's wife. A pinched-looking woman with dark harassed eyes, Helen Keever had difficulties with some of the exercises, suffering as she did from extensive armouring, which stopped her from breathing out properly and from achieving the position of giving in. In relaxation periods she couldn't relax. Julian was very attentive to her: he showed her how to roll her head in a relaxed way, he gently moved her limbs into the positions for doing the Cat, and squashed her cheeks in to show her how to form her lips to kiss the sky.

Speaking to the class, Julian's voice was dry and soft and insistent, never bullying.

'Shall we do something about those dead pelvises, ladies? Hmm? Let's try, shall we? ...'

While the class sat cross-legged on the floor, or cat-like on the heels, both being good positions, Julian gave one of his little homilies.

'What we are trying to achieve, remember, is bodily *harmony* that will give rise to TOTAL BODILY HEALTH. If a person is mobile in every other way, but inhibits mobility in the pelvis, his *entire* mobility is blocked. Take the example of a worm. A worm shows uniform wave-like rhythmical movement involving the whole body. If one part of his body were immobilized, so it could not participate in the rhythmic motion, then the *whole* body would be impeded by this block. That is the problem of dead areas. If there is deadness of the pelvis it is not only the pelvic area that is affected – it's the whole body rhythm, as in the case of the worm.'

(At one of her evenings Laurene gently teased Julian: 'Far be it from me to throw cold water on your sexy worm, but aren't worms different from humans? I mean, if you cut their heads off, don't they grow another? Can you really say what goes for the worm goes for us?' To which

Julian had replied that, according to Reich, the basic life flow was perceivable in a worm or a plant as much as in more complex cell structures such as humans.)

Sometimes after a class they were all invited next door to Julian's private rooms for camomile tea (which he made and served himself) and questions. These were rather special occasions, because Julian did not allow questions in class. If anyone questioned a particular exercise or what it was intended to achieve, Julian simply said: 'You have entrusted yourself to me. If you question the process, it will not work for you. Questions are an expression of armouring, which is what we are trying to get rid of. You have to learn the giving in position. Believe me, it's essential. So no quibbling questions, please.'

Julian's own apartment was furnished as simply, and in much the same style, as other rooms in the Institute. There were the same sort of rush mats scattered about the floors, but here there were cushions and bolsters too. It was a little more comfortable than the treatment rooms, but not much.

When one of the pretty models asked what she should do when she couldn't sleep at night, and was it all right to take sleeping pills, he told her:

'Sweetie, I would rather you didn't. Try doing a Sirsasana, and cycle numbers 122 or 187 on your exercise chart. Or, if you prefer, I will give you a tisane. It's one I make myself from the roots, seeds and leaves of *Angelica silvestris* – Angelica. A very lovely name, isn't it, for a very beneficial and too-little-known natural medicament?'

Other members of the class asked about other conditions, and sometimes Julian recommended an exercise or a tisane or an alteration in life style, whilst in other cases, he said: 'You would benefit from nerve massage. Ring up in the morning and make an appointment.'

After these practical questions, the Senator's wife Mrs Keever, asked:

'Why is there so much emphasis on the giving in position? I have not found that in other forms of Yoga.'

Julian's response to challenge was to smile; it was a good

122

expedient, for his smile was one of his most attractive features.

'Well, Mrs Keever,' he said, 'I don't teach pure Yoga, you know. I mix the most ancient knowledge with the newest. Para-Yoga you might call what I do, except that I hate labels, don't you? They pin you down, while what we are trying to achieve is free movement. But you are quite right that the emphasis on the giving in position derives from Reich rather than Yoga. Though Yoga also promotes the idea of letting yourself experience your own body rhythms, without resistance. The reason why so much importance is attached to the giving in position? Well, Reich says that sex pleasure *is* the life process *per se,* not just a sort of bribe from God to introduce procreation. In experiments Reich has shown that pelvic armouring impedes the movement of bio-electrical energy from the centre to the periphery: out of the self, toward the world – which is the movement of life.'

Mrs Keever continued to look down at the ground in her cross-legged position. She was clearly not satisfied by the answer she had been given.

'Going on what I've read,' she said, 'Yoga teaches that the path of the senses – or, of sensual desire – leads to, to . . . the destruction of the self of those who follow it. Whereas, Dr Reich, it looks to me, preaches the freeing of the senses for indulgence. Wouldn't you say that's a contradiction?'

Julian appeared to enter a period of brief meditation. His face was blank. Finally, he said: 'Yes, yes, it is a contradiction. But, you know, that shouldn't worry you. The *modus vivendi* of the unconscious – of the life forces within us – is the reconciliation of opposites. In Reich and Yoga we find a striking instance of such a reconciliation.'

Mrs Keever was opening her mouth; she clearly wished to say something more, she had got her argumentativeness from her husband, the Senator, but Julian stopped her, looking at his watch.

'I'm afraid that ends our time for today, ladies.'

*

In April, with spring in the mind, if not yet in the air, the class rode high on a surge of expectancy.

'Release fingers,' Julian urged, 'spread the wrist and rest the forearm on the floor, fingers pointing to the feet.'

He moved among the class members, correcting postures.

'Exhale strongly, raising the head slowly off the floor and extending the neck towards the legs. Josie, love, do try to breathe, sweetie. Yes, yes, that's the whole idea. *Breathe*. Now everybody: both feet closer to hands. Try, *try*. You'll get there. Good, very good. Now relax everyone ... Take a rest. Empty the body of all tension. Feel it flow out of you ... can you? *Can you?*'

As the class, breathing strongly, began to relax, Julian went on talking in his precise English manner. 'What we have been doing is called Chakra Bandhasana Thirty-one. Chakra is a nerve centre. And Bandha is a sort of fetter or bond. You find the chakras within the spinal column where the nadis cross. When you've mastered this exercise you'll be bending over backwards, grasping yourselves by the ankles.' There were gasps of disbelief at this. 'Oh it's very good for you,' Julian said, 'stimulates parts of the body that you didn't know you had. I promise you. Now five minutes of complete relaxation before you leave.'

As the class was leaving, he asked Laurene, 'You have time for a drink?'

'Well, just one.'

'That's all it can be. I have to be at the Luessenhoeps at six.'

'Professional call? I see Dolly wasn't here today.'

'Arnold hasn't been too well. One has to keep an eye on him. He is apt to backslide. I'm also taking some photographs of Dolly. I do it for the *Illustrated London News*. They've given me a sort of roving commission. The pictures do come out rather well, I think. I must do you sometime, Laurene. Washington's prettiest hostess. Will you sit for me?'

She nodded non-commitally.

'Would you?' he insisted, as they came into his living

124

quarters. 'You have a – a remarkable face.' He looked at her closely, professionally. 'It's a very beautiful face,' he said in the judicious manner of someone expressing the plain and indisputable truth.

'Well, maybe one day, sure . . .' Laurene agreed vaguely.

They had entered one of the private rooms; it had only low furniture, and cushions on the floor. 'Hey, which way is Mecca?' she was tempted to ask.

Out of habit she sat down in the cross-legged position on what looked like a prayer mat. As soon as she had done this she began to feel uncomfortable. All very well sitting like that in class, but here she felt silly, and conscious of the fact that from the sitting to the giving in position was just one movement. Dispensing with chairs did away with some of those formal distances that furniture imposes upon social relationships. But sometimes those distances were necessary. She began to get up.

'You are not comfortable?' he asked, handing her the drink and at the same time beginning to lower his body to the floor.

'Ice,' she said, rising as he sat.

'Stupid of me,' he said. 'Let me get it for you . . .' He was beginning to rise; despite the speed of all his movements, she was already on her feet and motioning him to remain seated.

'Just tell me where. I like snooping around other people's apartments. Where's your ice box?'

'Kitchen is through there,' he said, pointing with his head to the bead curtains.

It was obviously little used. Some unwashed cups and saucers in the sink. By the wall telephone shopping lists had been scrawled, with items ticked off. There was a big Westinghouse fridge. She opened it and found it contained, for all its cubic feet of space, only a can of Van Camp's beans with wieners.

She had a job getting the ice out of the freezer compartment, it was so solidly frozen in. She dropped a couple of cubes in her bourbon and rejoined him. He was drinking Vichy water. She sat next to him, cat-like on her haunches.

125

'Do you never drink at all?'

'I have a gin sometimes.' She was about to try to persuade him to have one now, since otherwise this was a very one-sided drink (she felt at a disadvantage if she was drinking and he wasn't) but a quick glance showed that there was only a little Fernet Branca left, and perhaps a thimbleful of gin.

'You really are getting on terribly well, in class. You're taking to it. You're far and away the best.'

'I'm your best pupil? Better than Dolly?'

'Oh yes. She is very determined, and she's further on than you, having been at it longer. But your aptitude is so much greater. You have a natural gracefulness. You don't have to think about it too much. It comes naturally to you. You must be a very good dancer.'

'Oh quite good.'

'You get the hang of new movements very quickly. As if you knew them already and are just re-learning them . . .'

'And you're wonderful too,' she said with a faint touch of sharpness, and a slight frown.

'If I may still be your teacher, for a moment. Don't frown. It will make lines on that pretty brow . . .'

'Julian, I'm forty.'

'You look ten years younger, Laurene.'

'I've been feeling younger since coming to the classes. What d'you put in those tisanes?'

'You look wonderful, Laurene. You have the body of a young girl.'

'Of which you have seen a fair number – bodies of young girls, I mean. In the course of your work.'

'You have genuine youthfulness,' he said unruffled. It was difficult with Julian to know exactly what he meant. She had noticed that people often missed when he was being ironical. Was he now being ironical with her? Mocking the vanity of women wishing to remain looking young.

She began to look about the room, picking up books and glancing at them and putting them down again. Opening Kneipp's *My Water Cure*, she found herself looking at drawings of Victorian gentlemen in sitz baths, and others standing under various watering devices. It was comical. At times she felt as if a huge practical joke were being played on her.

'Really, Julian,' she said, 'all . . . this . . . how can you go along with all this?'

'Water can be very beneficial,' he assured her seriously. 'Just think how much better you feel sometimes after a hot bath, or a cold shower. Or a swim in a mountain lake. It's not nonsense.'

'But as a cure for . . . for . . . smallpox . . . for insanity?'

'There is no need to believe it all,' he told her, 'in order to find value in some of it.'

'Oh you're so wise,' she said with a touch of irritation. 'Damn you.' And laughed.

He laughed too. She continued glancing through his books. Hildegard of Bingen and Albert Magnus and Hieronymus Bock and Priessnitz and Reich and Gurdjieff.

'Over my head,' she said, after a brief glance through some of the pages.

'What nonsense,' he protested. 'Not at all. Merely *new to you*. You have a very good mind.'

He had not moved. That was one of the striking things about him; his capacity for stillness – proof of the efficacy of what he taught. For he never used up nervous energy in distracted useless actions. He took out a cigarette and inserted it in the Dunhill De-Nicotea holder. The way he smoked his cigarette through the holder made her think of someone smoking an opium pipe – it had that kind of deliberate calm. Not at all the way she smoked – puffing away with a vast expenditure of nervous energy.

'Laurene,' he said with the suddenness of inspiration, 'would you like to join the Institute . . . as a governor?'

'What would that involve?'

'Oh – lending your name. Speaking from time to time on behalf of some of the principles we believe in here. You know, the sort of things we've often talked about. The dangers from chemical additives in foods. The need to return to more natural ways of living.'

'That's Dolly's line. I'm sure she does all that sort of thing much better than I ever could.'

'Of course Dolly is a great asset. But she is rather well-known for her unconventional views on the subject of medicine, so there is an unfortunate tendency to discount what she says. Besides, she's not as pretty as you. You would get more attention.'

'I'd be happy to endorse the work . . .'

'The other thing is, the Luessenhoeps give us grants. Enables me to enlarge the scope of what we are doing, and to take on patients who couldn't afford to pay.'

Before she could say anything, he went on, quickly: 'It's valuable work, Laurene. What *you* see is only the side of it that helps people to look and feel better, younger. But it's not just that. There is a connection between the present day scourges of mankind: cancer, the cardiovascular diseases, ulcers, pulmonary emphysema – and the fact that people can't breathe. Can't breathe because they can't let go . . . can't surrender themselves.'

'You mean if I stayed in the sack all the time I'd get to be a hundred? Promise?'

He laughed – a most worldly laugh – and she thought of the reconciliation of opposites, the *modus vivendi* of the unconscious; Julian *was* those opposites reconciled, with his capacity for spirituality and for coming down to earth again almost indecently fast.

'You think I have a *breathing* problem?' she asked.

'I should think you are one of those children of nature for whom the message came across a long time ago . . .'

'What makes you think that?'

'I'll tell you, if you like.'

'Better not,' she said. 'Not now. We both have got to be somewhere. And perhaps this sort of discussion ought to take place in your consulting room, not here.'

'Yes, perhaps,' he agreed, and in the same breath asked, '*Would* you like to be a governor?'

'More to the point, would I like to contribute to the Institute's finances?'

'That too – we need the money. But that would be up to you. There's no price tag on being a governor.'

'Well, you know,' she said, starting around the room, as a preliminary to leaving, 'if you are thinking of the Blum Foundation, I don't myself control the donations . . . there is a Board of Trustees . . . I really don't have a lot to say as far as choosing the recipients is concerned. My own personal finances are handled by my lawyers. I have no idea if we are in a position at present to undertake any fresh commitments . . . I would have to ask them. There are so many deserving causes . . . there has to be some system of priorities . . .'

'Of course.'

While speaking she had been idly examining the wall decorations – Chinese charts of the human body, showing the meridians and acupuncture points. Illustrations from old pharmaceutical books. Framed photographs. A wedding picture.

'Your parents?'

'Yes . . .'

'Where are they . . . ?'

'They're dead.'

'Oh dear.'

'Oh dear indeed . . .' He offered no further information and she did not press, not liking to probe into personal sorrows.

'And this,' she asked, 'is this . . . ?' He was smiling mysteriously as she examined the English schoolboys in their top hats, tailcoats and Eton collars. 'Let me see if I can pick you out?' She pointed to a schoolboy with a cherubic face.

'What a good eye you have,' he said, and she smiled delightedly, pleased to have been able to spot him among all the other little Eton boys, who all looked so much alike.

'We really do have to go, both of us,' she said.

'Oh my God, yes,' he said, seeing the time.

They rushed out together. He did not take a coat – he was in a Harris tweed sports jacket and grey flannels.

'Can I drop you off?' he offered pointing to his car. It was a yellow pre-war Bentley convertible, with the hood folded down, despite the bad weather.

'It would take you out of your way,' she said, 'if you are going to the Luessenhoeps, and you're late already. Dolly doesn't like people being late. I can get a cab.'

'Oh damnation!' he cried, suddenly fumbling furiously in his pockets. 'Come out without a penny. Damn! You don't happen to have ten bucks you could loan me? Or I'll have to go all the way back.'

Laurene looked in her bag and found two fives to give him.

'Oh that *is* sweet of you. I shan't forget. I'm very punctilious about that sort of thing . . .' And with a cheery wave, turning up his jacket collar against the cold wind, he dashed to his ear. Sitting up high behind the almost perpendicular windscreen, he started the engine and there came a sweet roar of power. A semaphore-type traffic indicator shot out as he was moving off. 'Say hello to Dolly for me,' she called to him. He gave her another wave, his long hair blowing about his ears, and then accelerated abruptly.

Dolly Luessenhoep, as a young girl, had discovered that the turbulences and eruptions characterized as spring fevers could be cured by drinking elder-root tea. It cleansed the blood of impurities, and calmed the spirit. From that time on, she had believed in nature cures, and when she began to run her husband's newspapers she threw the whole weight of the Luessenhoep press behind nature, at the same time seizing every opportunity to attack the pharmaceutical industry. She was always, through the newspapers, warning of the danger to health of eating chemically treated foods. Julian's remarkable cures – especially his cure of her husband – lent new force to what Dolly had been preaching for years. Julian used no artificial medicaments, only what nature itself provided: plants, water, his own hands. And his patients got better.

Dolly had made rapid progress with Yoga; had graduated from asanas to pranayamas and pratyharasa and now, after a mere eighteen months was at the threshold of the Sixth Stage, dharana. She was a determined and energetic woman and applied to the achievement of peace of mind and bodily relaxation the huge drive that she brought to all her many other activities. Somehow she managed to pack two Yoga classes a week into her hectic schedule. In addition, she spent time and effort on promoting the Institute's work.

She was a country girl, by origin, and she knew about the healing properties of danewort and cowslip, and how beneficial bran bread was, and aniseed, and how good mead was for you, and all the uses of oil of cloves and oak bark. Her closeness to Julian was to some extent due to her often avowed belief in such remedies and the fact that he agreed with her about most things.

And, of course, like other very rich women, she did enjoy the power of whispering a word in the right ear. It had involved no great endeavour on her part to get Julian taken up by important people. When she said to them, 'You have got to meet Julian, he's a genius,' they were willing enough: on some other occasion they might want something from her.

There existed a point of view that hers was the kind of helpfulness which places the helped at the mercy of the helper. I have heard it said that dear old Dolly derived almost sadistic pleasure from helping others. Be that as it may, she was a source of funds for many a worthy cause and quite a few more or less worthy individuals. I would not want to look too closely into her motives. Such analysis can render most impulses questionable. For whatever reasons, Dolly was a helper, and she helped Julian.

She had got where she was by making herself so helpful to people that finally they could not do without her. This was how she had come to marry Arnold Luessenhoep and to run his businesses. In the first place she had been his secretary, and what a secretary! Soon she was indispensable. He was a large, untidy man, moody, and extraordinarily absent-minded: and he needed her to hold his life together. Realizing this, he smartly married her, whereupon his business prospered, and a degree of order came into his existence. She became the manager of his money and his life, and contrived to fulfil her role while allowing him to have the illusion that he was making all the important decisions, and she was merely carrying them out.

She was in her early forties, thin, tough in body and mind, sporting: a good skier, swimmer, tennis-player, and an excellent rifle shot. Much of the responsibility for running her husband's newspaper and publishing enterprises was now in her hands. And she kept a firm watch on his other business interests as well, though these occupied her less, since they interested her less. (They were to do with food canning, coal, real estate and shipping.) Her main concern was the papers, which she ran toughly and brilliantly.

While Arnold retained overall editorial control and decided whom to support for President, what the American position on Berlin should be, by how much taxes should be lowered, and what to do about crime, she brought out the kind of popular newspapers that people wanted to read. She had taught herself the newspaper business until she knew it inside out, and she never missed a trick. She developed those pages which advised and instructed on matters ranging from personal health to income tax. Believing that what Americans were most interested in was bettering themselves, as she had bettered herself, she told them how to do it, how others had done it, how she herself had done it. She proclaimed the message of health, beauty, knowledge, self-knowledge and financial wisdom.

While her readers did not thrive noticeably, her newspapers did. Under Dolly's guidance, their circulations more than doubled.

There was nothing cynical about the way she appealed to the needs of the readers; she was genuinely concerned to improve their lot, and believed that her popular papers, crammed with self-help tips, contributed something to the betterment of their lives.

In addition, Dolly gave money to various groups and

organizations and foundations concerned with improving the conditions of the ordinary man. Some people said that this was mere window-dressing, carefully calculated to gain the working man's sympathy, since he formed a large part of the readership of the Luessenhoep press, and that at heart Mrs Luessenhoep was just as exploitive of the masses as any other millionaire. But nobody said this to her face. They did not dare to. She was known to flare up at any such suggestion, and once in her bad books you could remain in them forever. Even the President was careful how he handled her. Speaking to others he often called her 'that bitch Mrs Luessenhoep', but when they played poker together he called her Dolly and she reciprocated by calling him Harry.

Laurene was fascinated by Dolly's capacity for ruthless decision and rough language. She had once seen her attack a Congressman who had somehow incurred her displeasure. It had happened at the Luessenhoep mansion on Connecticut Avenue, between Versailles-style facing mirrors that multiplied the chandeliers and elongated the hall into an endless corridor.

As she tore into him, the Congressman's smile collapsed on his face as if his puppet's strings had been cut. He tried to push up the lips by sheer will power, but produced only a kind of snarl. Dolly was lashing into him, and he was taking it, with that instinctive politician's knowledge that it did not matter how much you were humiliated and denigrated, how much you sweated with uncertainty, and farted with fear, as long as you came out the winner in the end it made no difference that you had only won with a single vote. A single vote was enough. And so he took it all, and tried to smile.

'Next time you're aiming to get yourself elected,' Dolly told him, 'don't count on me as a friend. If I've helped somebody, I expect some loyalty in return. Anyone forgets that, he's dead with me, and you just died, Dick, you just died. Know your trouble? You want it too much, and you want it all, and you want it all the time, and at any price. You've got shifty eyes, Dick. I don't trust you, and I don't

133

think the people are going to trust you long, because they're wise to that look. Don't underrate the people, they have a nose for what you are. They may be awful slow, but finally they catch on.'

'*Dear* Dolly,' the Congressman said, meanwhile desperately hauling up the fallen smile. 'I wouldn't take that from anyone except you, and from you only because I love you and you know you don't mean it, and even if you did mean it you'd give me a chance to explain, and I'm confident that given that chance by you I *could* explain, I could explain everything.'

Being famed for her bluntness, Dolly rather cultivated it: she enjoyed being able to shock and startle. And just to confuse everyone, she could be equally extreme in singing praises. Of course, she was careful to be rude only to those people she could afford to be rude to, people in some way dependent on her for money, support or favours. To those she considered on her own level – that is, equally capable of dispensing favours – she was charming. She was charming to Laurene. Also she liked Laurene, even admired her. Dolly was not unattractive to the kind of men who find aggressive women a sexual challenge, but she was not a beauty as Laurene was. Moreover, Laurene had something else: subtle and feminine ways of asserting herself, and the classiness of old money. What Dolly had had to get by force, by ruthless self-assertion, and by beating somebody else down, Laurene had been given as her birthright. She belonged to the secret élite that really ran America: by word-of-mouth, with hints and nudges, and without raising their voices.

10

It was not true that Laurene's lawyers handled her financial affairs and that she had no idea what additional commitments she would be able to take on. Nor was it true that she had little say in the dispensation of Blum Foundation funds. But she had long ago learned how to protect herself from the importunings of strangers and friends. Part of her rich girl's education.

To prevent her being exploited by adventurers and swindlers her money had been tied up in trusts, each of them run by a different group of trustees, whose consent had to be obtained for any major expenditure. But there was also provision for her to fire the trustees, and although this required twelve months to become effective – enough time for the most romantically inclined girl to regain her senses – in practice, when the trustees discovered how sensible Laurene was about her money, they never interfered with her wishes. They might *advise* against something, but if she proved to be adamant, they did not insist.

Laurene could have dispensed with the entire trustee arrangement on her thirtieth birthday but she had chosen to maintain it. It was a convenience. It ensured that no one could get control of her fortune, on any pretext; if she were to go mad, or disappear, or commit a crime, or fall into a permanent coma, or if she were to be sued for countless millions, or blackmailed, or to have ransoms demanded of her, or vast alimony, or suffer any other of the mishaps to which the very rich are exposed, her money would still be safe, locked away in a maze of foundations and trusts that nobody could unlock without years of litigation. This meant that when she wished it to be so, her money was tied-up and unavailable to her; but when she did not wish it to be tied-up, a phone call from her was enough to untie it.

The people charged with administering Laurene's money had come to have considerable respect for her financial acumen, and if anything tended to regret what they sometimes considered her excessive carefulness. She was not one to throw her money around, and did not care for any form of investment that smelled even remotely of risk. Her money was mostly in real estate, insurance companies and government bonds. Her charities, grants and benefactions were limited to such amounts as could be set against her tax liability in a particular year.

The founder of the Blum fortune, Adolph Blum, had come to the United States before the Civil War. He came from Vienna. There his business was making buttons, braiding and tassels for the Hapsburg armies. The revolt in Vienna in March 1848 (coming after the February Revolution in Paris) had impressed upon Adolph Blum that the old order was changing, and at such times a business dependent on government patronage (and military styles that were liable to become outmoded overnight) was in a highly vulnerable position. He was a realist, and this compelled him to recognize that when major upheavals occurred, whatever the benefits and reforms they brought, the Jew's position usually became worse. Taking his lead from Prince Metternich (whose statesmanship and realism he held in high regard), Adolph Blum decided to get out while the going was good.

He settled in Boston where the small tight German-Jewish community kept itself apart not only from the traditionally anti-Semitic gentiles but also from the Eastern European Jews, to whom the Germanic Jews considered themselves superior. He had been able to bring out enough money to set himself up in the button business. He expanded it to include costume jewellery, and after two years he was able to bring over most of his family, his wife, their five children, and two brothers and their wives and children. All these Blums set to work expanding the business; they supplied buttons and trimmings for ladies' dresses, ostrich feathers and boa feathers for hats and fans, gold braiding for uniforms, beaten silver and tortoiseshell for combs and hairbrushes, sequins and diamanté and mother-of-pearl for evening dresses, silver and brass buckles for shoes and belts and harnesses. They made much of the fact that they had formerly been suppliers of sword tassels to the Hapsburg armies, and they prospered in Boston.

They were wholesale merchants, and they bought a great deal in Europe, from the same craftsmen and manufacturers they had used formerly. The branch of the family that had stayed behind (headed by Adolph's two brothers, Leo and Erwin) acted as agents in Vienna and Berlin. On this basis, the business expanded, and began to deal in a broad range of luxury goods, supplying the rich not only with mother-of-pearl buttons but also with cut glass chandeliers copied from the French, chinoiserie, Venetian glass, Persian and Turkish carpets, chinaware, silverware and silverplate, damask table cloths, Irish linen napkins. Chantilly lace and Duchesse lace.

After the Civil War, Adolph Blum started to look around for a retail outlet of his own and found an established drygoods store in New York at Sixth Avenue and Fifteenth Street that was in need of capital for expansion. Blum supplied the capital, became a partner of the owner, Arthur Howard, and so Howard and Blum came into being. Blum opened a basement in the store where he sold, first, trimmings and buttons, and later also silverware and china and carpets and curtains.

It was one of the earliest department stores, and when Blum saw how well it was doing he started to look for other sites in other cities where this success could be duplicated, for there was no reason why something that worked in New York should not also work in Kansas City and San Francisco and Baltimore and Boston and Washington.

By the time Adolph Blum died at the age of 88, the Howard and Blum empire had also become enlarged through the marriages of his sons. One son, Motz, married a Grant girl of the Grant chain of shoe shops; another, Paul, married the daughter of Frederick Cowper, a partner in the respected Wall Street firm of investment brokers,

Cowper, Copley and Lievenstock. In this way, the family interests proliferated; by the turn of the century a division had taken place whereby one branch of the family tended to be principally involved in wholesale, another in retail, and another in finance. This was a practical division that did not, however, destroy the homogeneity of the family business, which in overall direction of its affairs acted as a single entity in the general interest of the whole.

Laurene's father, Max, the grandson of the founder of the business, was on the retail side, and ran the stores, which by 1908 numbered twelve, of which five were the largest or second largest in their towns.

By the time Laurene was born, the Boston Blums were long-established merchant princes. Laurene's father, Max, was a large man with a scimitar of a nose, white hair dating from early manhood, and a taste for philosophy. He had gone to Harvard, but left before graduating, and then worked his way up in the stores (as was customary among the Blums), starting as a floor assistant. He was perversely proud (as far as Laurene was concerned) of this phase of his career and somewhat to her embarrassment would tell funny stories of incidents with customers. Laurene, when she was younger, would protest: 'Oh, Papa, people are going to think you're a shopkeeper.' To which he would reply, 'But I am, sweetheart, that's what I am.'

That Laurene grew up a bit of a snob was perhaps understandable, since Max had married a Boston girl of good family, one of the Campbells, a gentile, who never entirely succeeded in adapting herself to the family's ways. Coming into the Fifth Avenue store one day, she had been shocked to find her husband attempting to cater to a customer's impossible demands. The woman finally stormed out, saying she was going to speak to the President of the company, to which Max had replied, 'Madam, you have already done so.'

Lucille Blum (or Campbell Blum as she signed herself) had found her marriage to Max a continuing series of shocks. For he kept bringing up his Jewishness. She could not fathom why. He told stories that reminded people of it, even used Yiddish expressions, in quotation marks, it was true, pronouncing them in his impeccable New England accent, but Yiddish all the same.

Lucy Campbell Blum had her redeeming features (she was beautiful, and strong in times of crisis and loved her husband and supported him), but she did pass on to Laurene a disdain for shopkeeping, and a sense of being intended for 'better things'. Laurene was their only child, and Lucy used all her skills and influence to make her more than 'just' a merchant's daughter. That was something only to be achieved through marriage. So, from childhood, Laurene learned that she was a privileged and special person who would always be able to have the best, and that her principal task in life was to learn to distinguish the best from the second-rate; especially where suitors were concerned.

Graduating from Smith College she had listened to a speech by a prominent industrialist to the effect that women were the guardians of the nation's moral tone. It was their role in life to maintain high standards 'because it is you girls who keep us men up to scratch'. The whole moral tone of any civilization, this speaker maintained, was set by the women. Men, weaker moral creatures, measured themselves against the standards imposed by women. If women, by their behaviour and actions, lowered the moral tone, men would quickly follow them down the slippery slope. Girls who had enjoyed the privilege of a fine education, such as they had had, were obligated to encourage and promote what was best in men, to pick out the truly valuable and discard the dross.

There was a lot of dross to discard, Laurene had soon found. And with her finely educated nose for such things, she discarded it smartly. She was not one to let passion rule her.

Her mother thought that while an American education was second to none, Laurene ought to have her mind broadened by other cultures and took her on a grand tour of Europe. America was in the grip of Depression, and a miserable place. Other countries might be simarly afflicted,

139

but you did not notice it so much staying at the Hôtel des Bains on the Venice Lido, or at the Schweizerhof in Lucerne or the Trois Couronnes in Vevey. No matter its internal troubles, a visit to Austria, birthplace of the founder of the Blum fortune, was called for and they found the Hotel Sacher truly impeccable, with service on a scale and of an excellence unknown back home. Likewise, at the Vierjahreszeiten in Munich and the Ritz in Madrid. They loved the French Riviera and stayed for a time at a rented villa at Beaulieu, and at a party given by Mrs Frank Jay Gould met André Gide. There were rose petals in the fingerbowls and gold lamé place mats. Lucy may have hoped that in addition to improving her French accent, Laurene was going to meet a count or a prince, or an English lord at least, but though there were one or two promising flirtations, nothing permanent came of them, and at the end of the year, seeing the way things were going in Europe, they decided to return home. Europe, Lucy said, was about to go down the drain yet again, and was clearly no place for a Blum, even a Campbell Blum.

In New York, Laurene continued to pursue the best of everything, as she had been brought up to do. Beaus took her to the St Regis Roof to dine and dance, or to the Drake Room for more intimate dinners, or to '21' or, on splashier occasions, such as New Years, to the Stork Room or El Morocco. She wore veiled hats, used a silver and enamel compact, plucked her eyebrows, smoked in public, wore silver fox around her neck, and drank bootleg gin. She remembered the graduation day exhortation to maintain the moral tone of the country but did not see what she could do about it, except avoid being taken in by second-raters.

She was well on her way down the slippery slope of which she had been warned, when she met Bill Hardtman and was told by her educated nose that here at last was a man worth keeping up to scratch. Like someone discovering a vocation, she now saw in Bill a man she could influence towards a truly purposeful life. He was not yet thirty and already had made a large amount of money – and a reputation – as a Wall Street corporation lawyer, and at the same time was active in many fields, speaking out against Fascism, pointing to the dangers that the National Socialist Party of Herr Hitler posed in Germany, condemning 'the malefactors of profit', those men who in their greed brought the creative aspects of capitalism into disrepute. He was at that time publicly and privately postulating two categories of capitalism, one admirable and indeed necessary for progress, the other iniquitous and damaging. The admirable form of capitalism was expressed in the creativity of the entrepreneur who, by his bold and imaginative use of money, fulfilled the role of engendering new discoveries essential to civilization. The iniquitous form of capitalism, against which the Marxists rightly inveighed, was rentier-capitalism, living off interest.

Although she might have been considered something of a rentier herself, Laurene loved it when Bill talked in this way. It indicated how honest he was that he did not exempt close friends from the obloquy which the pursuit of money had earned them. He made it clear of course that it was the obsessive (and, therefore, socially unproductive) pursuit of money to which he was opposed; *he* had rational and sound reasons for wishing to make money. He was twenty-nine years old, and much under the influence of Bernard Shaw, H. L. Mencken, Sinclair Lewis and Theodore Dreiser. People who were too fond of making money, he was apt to say in the presence of pretty girls, used up in that pursuit much of their libidinal drive. And that wasn't good. He was also under the influence of Freud at this time, in particular of a Freudian-Marxist historian who had taught him at Yale, and who perceived in the organization of American capitalist society a scheme to suppress the orgiastic potency of the individual, which capitalism was bound to see as a threat to the status quo.

His own tastes were expensive, he was accustomed to good things, and he saw no reason why he should have to do without them, and so these lectures on the enervating effect of money-making were usually delivered in places like '21' or Delmonico's, where such strictures had at least the charm of paradox.

Laurene had met Bill at a party; he had invited her to lunch, which lasted so long that he suggested they have dinner, and after that it seemed pointless for her to go home. She did not give herself to any Tom, Dick or Harry, did not throw herself around any more than her money; but in Bill Hardtman's case she hadn't hesitated. She loved him, and believed in him, and wanted to make something of him. Where his efforts had formerly been dispersed in a number of different directions, she canalized them, and took charge of everything that need not concern him, leaving him free to concentrate on the main thrust of his career. He could never have worked so well, or taken on so much, without her. And they were a good combination, they seemed made for each other, people said.

Prior to meeting Bill, she had had only two other real affairs. The rest of her beaus had all been kept within certain limits. She took the attitude that she was not going to become a notch on anybody's score-board. Having a sensual nature, this was a vow not easily kept, but she solved the problem by making a rule for herself. No penetration. Other delights, yes, but not *that*. To prevent herself being carried away, she made it a practice that if one of her beaus was disposed to take his clothes off, she would keep hers on; conversely, if she undressed, he had to remain clothed.

When finally she gave herself freely to Bill Hardtman – only the third man with whom that line had been crossed – the moment had for her a nuptial significance. Of course, he did not know this at the time, since he did not know that he was being admitted to what had been so elaborately withheld from her previous lovers, but there was something in her eyes, a new sort of daring, a commitment to what is unknowable, that affected him, made the occasion one of implicit vows. The light of love shone in her eyes, and she had a mystical sense that this was the man with whom she was going to spend her life; he was the person that her inheritance, her upbringing, her elaborate and expensive education, her foreign travel and her cautious search had brought her to, and he seemed perfect in every way. As a man, as a lover, as a guide. But then perhaps her rule was due to be set aside and any man for whom she finally abandoned it would have been elevated in this way.

If Bill Hardtman was not everything that Laurene imagined, he came nearer than anyone else she had met. She saw him as a man of strength and courage and wisdom and honour. If he was sometimes inclined to moralize, and to lecture, this was because he was concerned with ideas and principles, and naturally he had to express them. The sort of men who were never pompous were the sort who never had a difficult thought that required formulation.

They were married in 1932, and continued to live in his bachelor apartment on Fifth Avenue and 61st Street, overlooking Central Park, until the seventh month of her pregnancy, when they moved to a larger place further uptown on Park Avenue, in the low Eighties. She missed the swirling excitement of living right in the centre of things, with all the constant coming and goings – now that she was at least twenty minutes' walk from the centre – but the new address was more appropriate for a mother-to-be.

The first nine years of their marriage appear to have been extremely happy.

When America entered the war, Bill Hardtman was sent to London to work in Intelligence, liaising between the Americans and the British, and after D-day he was given a secret job in France, of which he never spoke, except in the most general terms.

To Laurene the war years were a dirty trick of time, taking her out of her belle époque and dumping her brutally at the brink of her forties. She was as attractive as ever in her late thirties; maturity gave her a special sexual glow, but the milestones were now flashing by with increasing rapidity, and the rest was going to be all downhill. During the war years, the slow surreptitious passage of time was scarcely noticed, there was so much else to worry about, and then the war was over and there was an abrupt leap into another era, and everybody seemed to have become so much older all of a sudden.

A sure sign of impending middle-age was the way she

indulged her nostalgia for the past, in particular, the magical year of her grand tour with mother, when she had kissed an Hungarian count in the moonlight, on the beach of the Venice Lido.

Being married, and raising a child had given her a sense of purpose and quiet satisfaction, and it was satisfying, too, to see that she had not been wrong about Bill, that he had grown in stature. He was cut out for something of importance, people always said. So the call from the President had not been altogether unexpected. Something like that had been due to him. And Laurene had derived almost as much satisfaction from the summons as Bill, for in accordance with her education she identified totally with her husband's achievements.

Only occasionally did she allow herself to think that perhaps her own life had been wasted; that if she had only had enough drive, she could have used her inheritance more directly to make something of herself. But that had not been the way in the Blum family; the men went into the stores, and the women married: marriage (to someone like Bill Hardtman) had seemed to her infinitely preferable to being a shopkeeper, on however grand a scale. But later she sometimes thought, as she approached forty, that there *could* have been something else . . . that she, with all her great advantages in life, had missed out on something.

It was this faint sense of dissatisfaction that, perhaps, made her go to Julian and take up Yoga. With him, she had an awareness of Something Else that she did not yet know about.

Laurene quickly established herself in Washington. She had always been good at giving parties, and making herself sought after, and here, in addition, she could feel she was doing something purposeful in filling her house with politicians and officials and members of the Administration: helping her husband in his work. She set out to give the best damned dinners in Washington. And succeeded to a large extent. She had a flair for entertaining, an instinct for choosing the right combination of people to make an evening go. No dead wood around her dinner table! To be asked you had to be brilliant, or beautiful, or important, or amusing, or at least married to someone in one or other of those categories, Bill Hardtman used to say that Laurene's dinner parties were made up of such distinguished people that *he'd* never be asked if he weren't married to the hostess.

She was herself one of the undoubted attractions of those evenings. Nobody carried off the fashion for the long bare back line better than Laurene, and the sudden busy bustle of materials around the hips made the back seem even barer, even more enticing. She had kept her figure, dieting rigorously, whenever she put on a pound or two, going off to health farms if a more drastic remedy was called for. And then, of course, when she consented to show herself again, her new self required some tribute to justify the ordeals it had undergone in the cause of beauty, and she was apt to flirt. Whether she went further was not known and on the whole people supposed not, because there were no scandalous stories about her. But then she was very discreet.

There was the time she and Bill went to the Swiss mountains to ski. After her morning's lesson with the instructor, she was left to her own devices. She had taken the téléphérique to the top of what appeared to be an easy slope. But when she began to negotiate the descent it became apparent that it was both longer and more difficult than she had realized. She tried to sideslip down the steeper inclines, as she had been taught to do, but this was slower going, and she had also misjudged the speed with which darkness falls in the mountains at that time of year.

As the light began to fade rapidly, she panicked, tried to speed up the descent by abandoning the slow but safe side-slip, and restored instead to the snowplough. She could do this quite well on the nursery slopes, but here there were big bumps to contend with and whenever she hit one it sent her spinning off out of control, and she kept falling: a ski came off and it took her precious minutes, with the sky getting darker all the time, to put it on again, and then she realized that she could not see down, had no sense of direction any more (after all the twisting and turning to get her ski back on), and all around her the horizon was the same. She was lost. Once or twice she caught glimpses of other skiers flashing by in the distance but they appeared not to hear her shouts or to see her frantically waving arms. She did not know, or had forgotten, that you were supposed to place crossed skis upright in the snow to signal distress. To make things worse, it had begun to snow, reducing visibility still more, and adding to her confusion and panic. Her body was covered with bruises from her falls, she hurt all over, and had lost the last remnant of her confidence – she couldn't go another ten metres on her skies, and just sat down in the snow and cried. They would come looking for her, in due course, with flares and ski ambulances, and would find her frozen to death. Yet there were people not far from her, going down all the time, for whom it was all seemingly easy, only she could not catch their attention. And then, when she had despaired of being found, except dead, someone did see her. This skier passed her, as all the others had passed her, but then he swung in a large loop and came round to where she was stuck in the snow. He spoke no English, and in her frantic attempt to communicate her plight, she forgot what German she knew. But he understood she was in trouble, that she was a beginner, and could not get down by herself.

Making signs to her, and skiing alongside, he tried to escort her down; but she was altogether too exhausted and frightened now, and kept falling badly. Her eyes had lost all ability to interpret the darkness; to her it was like trying to find her way across the moon. Thereupon he took charge of her, with great firmness, holding her like a child between his skis. He was tall and she came only up to his chin and he took her poles and showed her how to support herself upon his arms as if they were practice bars in a gymnasium, and she felt suddenly safe and snug within the concave of his body as he skied down with her, very slowly at first, with her skis inside his; she was gaining in confidence every moment, and as this happened they were able to go faster and she felt the glorious sensation of smoothness and speed and perfect balance, with no danger of falling between his solid arms, his knees gently nudging her as he guided her down: she could not question anything, but had to respond automatically to his smallest nudge, let herself go, give herself up entirely to the earth's pull. He moved her for the turns with a pressure of knees and thighs, making her body go into the correct slips and slides. She kept thinking she would fall, but didn't, though it often took all his skill to prevent them both falling. He saved the situation again and again, and she began to feel the exhilaration of this descent, coming down in the dark – there was hardly any light now, and she did not know how he was able to see anything – and this gave her a sense of floating, her skis seemed not to touch the ground, and she felt free and agile (though it was his agility and his skill transfused into her by the marvel of his coaxing knees and thighs.) Suddenly she had got it, and was moving correctly and freely and enjoying her dramatic escape from death.

It was when they had reached the point where the ground became less steep, and she could see the lights of Davos below, and her sense of security had returned, that she became aware of all the intimate ways that his body was making contact with hers as he jockeyed her down, how her whole body was contained by his and as he bent his knees, and she did too, for the final schuss down, she was virtually sitting in his lap.

Naturally, after all this, there was a sense of closeness between them as they stopped for her to catch her breath. There was an open shelter at the rim of the slope above the village, and she began to thank him profusely, speaking in a mixture of English, German and French. He replied severely in German, lecturing her – evidently – about adhering to the rules of the piste; showing her that she must cross her skis to signal for help, and warning her about undertaking such a descent on her own in failing light. He also showed her that she must lean out from the mountainside, not cling to it, as she tended to do, and all the time he was demonstrating these things he was touching her with the permitted familiarity of the teacher, showing her

147

how she must dispose of her weight, lean out, lean out, not be afraid of falling, and she became aware that his hands were touching her in a way that was extraneous to the instruction being given. It seemed churlish after he had saved her life to protest at such liberties; besides, she did wish to express her gratitude to him, and also was thrilled by his great skill, and in the dark his face and age and other characteristics did not matter. He was handling her freely, dealing with the zips and catches and buttons of her ski pants; fortunately she was wearing long johns underneath and she was grateful that he did not seek to remove these – it really was like in the days of her youth again and exciting for that reason. His skis outside hers, he was kissing her and doing things to her that seemed quite unbelievable here in this cold mountain shelter.

When she met Bill and their party at the hotel and explained her lateness by saying she had got lost on the mountain, and might have died of exposure had not someone come along, a man, an expert skier, who saw her down, they said, Ah, so that was what wives got up to on the nursery slopes, and she laughed along with them.

There may have been other adventures; she was often seen lunching with men at the Mayflower and the Occidental and Harveys. All very open places, and the handling of her money did involve her with a variety of people. For those business lunches she wore stunning hats – hats were the mode and suited her. She wore large, floppy-brimmed hats of velours as thin as felt from Lilly Daché, or something from Braagaard with a crushed crown and a brim descending over one eye. Veils were being worn then, of long mesh dotted with wool specks; Laurene, hatted and veiled, could look, despite all she was wearing, amazingly naked. Did she dress in this fashion to talk about stocks and shares, and what real estate values were going up or down, and to discuss cocoa futures? Perhaps, perhaps.

11

Hardtman had begun work on his report. It was a tricky business deciding what to put in and what to leave out. He made a succession of first drafts, all of which he burned in the end, because what he had put down amounted to no more than suspicions. And it was not right to burden the President with suspicions. That would be doing exactly what Clay had done in sending a cable that talked of *'feeling we may be on the brink of war'*, without providing a single piece of hard evidence for this. Hardtman had seen signs, and he knew that signs always mean *something*, and he had his suspicions about what these particular signs meant, but so far he had no real evidence.

Hardtman was thinking along these lines, and getting nowhere, when the phone rang. It was Laurene to say that Debbie was not coming home that weekend.

'Why not this time?'

'She says she has things to do. Well, it *is* a bit far.'

'It's not that far. What does she have to do that's so important? Seems she can never find time to see us these days.'

'At that age some things do seem more pressing than others and, I guess, parents are always there, so they come last.'

'It's the third weekend in a row that she cancelled out. What's going on?'

'I am sure nothing is going on, Bill.'

'It's a sign. Signs mean *something*.'

'I would know. She's O.K.'

'You're sure?'

'Yes.'

'Well, I'm not so sure. I don't feel happy about it.'

'She's growing up. She's going to be sixteen in a few months.'

'That's still a little early to be given carte blanche to do whatever she likes.'

'You have a suspicious mind, Bill.'

'We'll talk about it. I want to see Debbie this weekend.'

When he got home, he returned to the subject immediately.

'Look,' he said, 'this is the third time. I just happen to believe that is no way to conduct your life, making arrangements and breaking them so cavalierly. She hasn't been to see us for ten weeks, and last time she came she just sat talking to Julian all the time.'

'Why don't you tell her she has *got* to come home?'

'I would like her to come of her own free will. Because she wants to.'

'You can't make her want to come home if what she wants to do is stay with her friends.'

'What do you suppose they do, she and her friends?'

'I don't know. Talk politics? Pet? Maybe both. Are you worried that your little girl may be having some fun?'

'Oh come on, Laurene. You get an edge in your voice whenever we talk about Debbie.'

'Do I?'

'Yes.'

'Because you're over-protective towards her.'

'What kind of smarty-pants talk is that? *Over*-protective.'

'What is it you're worried about? I've talked to her on the phone. She's perfectly all right, bubbling, happy. Are you afraid she may be too happy, is that what you're afraid of? That she may have something going for her ...'

'Oh come on, Laurene. She is a little young for that still.'

'You want to keep her your little girl all her life ...'

'Oh come on ...'

'Well, she won't be. Much as she loves her wonderful Daddy, and she does, I know, I know she adores you, and that you adore her, she has got to be permitted to grow away from you, from us. She's going to be sixteen ... I love her just as much as you do, Bill. But I don't want to cling to her because I know what that does.'

'Oh for Christ's sake, that's your night school Freud showing.'

'I think you should pick up the phone, Bill, and tell her she has got to come home. That's what I think you should do.'

Her lips were tight with stubbornness, producing ugly lines to her chin. There were times when something got into Laurene, when they were set on a collision course, and nothing he said or did was able to divert her. Something about his feelings for Debbie made Laurene furious. You would almost have thought that she was jealous. The way her face got that suddenly distant, ironic look whenever he made a big fuss about Deb. As if to say: how men do go on about little slips of girls.

The way Hardtman dealt with this kind of situation was to disengage, which infuriated her even more, his unwillingness to quarrel. But there was nothing she could do except fume to herself. Whenever something in their life seemed to be building towards a showdown, he would somehow avoid it, as he did now.

He said, 'If she doesn't have time to come and see us, I'll go and see her.'

'We can never talk, can we?'

'Isn't that what we've been doing?'

'If you think this is *talking* . . .'

When Laurene had left the room, Hardtman called the school. The operator put him through to Deborah's house and to the extension on her floor. Another girl answered and began acting cute when she heard a man's voice. 'I'll see if I can find her,' she said, making a siren song of it. 'Hang on.'

A girl's voice, a voice of vibrant girlhood. At the same time very exact.

'This is Deborah Hardtman. Who is this, please?'

'It's Daddy.'

'Oh Daddy . . . Daddy!' The young adult's voice had in a moment become transformed by a childlike delight. 'Oh I'm sorry I'm not seeing you this weekend, Daddy. I feel terrible about it, but . . .'

151

'You don't have to feel terrible about it, sweetheart, because you are seeing me.'

'Oh?' The 'oh' was equivocal, halfway between obedience and rebellion.

'I'm coming to see you . . . I'll take the train up on Saturday. If that doesn't interfere with your plans.'

'When would you be here?' The voice was non-committal.

'Suppose I take you out to dinner Saturday night. I'll stay in New York. At the Plaza. Go back Sunday. How's that sound?'

'That sounds lovely, Daddy. But really I hate to put you to all this inconvenience, just to see me . . .'

'Seeing you is no inconvenience to me, Debbie. I want to see you.'

'Sounds wonderful, Daddy. When would you get in? Saturday?'

'Let's say I'll see you in the plaza around four o'clock? All right?'

'All right. How's Mummy?'

'She's fine. O.K., sweetheart? See you Saturday. Work well.'

'And you.'

On Saturday, Hardtman took a morning train to New York and arrived at Penn Station at 2 p.m. He had a late lunch alone and then went to pick up the hire-car. Getting out was slow, but once across the East river and on the Long Island Expressway, he began to make better time, and in under an hour was off the highway and in the country. Soon he saw Little Neck projecting into the Sound, and a little later he was crossing the base of Great Neck and heading towards the bay.

The approach to Bay House was by way of a long narrow tree-lined drive; the branches met and tangled overhead, creating a permanent bower, a leafy cool passage in summer, now a tunnel of flashing overhead lights. At the end of the drive, the school was an unexpected sight. It was not the usual white clapboard Colonial construction typical of the area, but a neo-Gothic seat of learning, with turrets and steeples and spires and arched quadrangles, that made it look more like an old English university than a girls' boarding school.

Leaving the car in the drive, Hardtman passed through high iron gates into a central plaza, around which the residential houses were grouped. Girls in school uniforms, white blouses and blue box-pleated skirts, went by him, ranging in age from obvious children to equally obvious young woman. He stood outside Debbie's house, waiting for her to come down. It was 4.15. She should have been waiting for him, instead of making him wait . . . Such discourtesies made him cross. Already acquiring her mother's grand habits. *Well.* He strolled around the plaza looking at the statues . . . formidable ladies in formidable cloaks. On the steps of the fountain a fat girl was eating a creamy sponge cake out of a box. As the minutes went by, he became more annoyed at being kept waiting. Although he did not like to do it, for some reason, he thought he had better go up to her dormitary and find out what the hell she was doing. At the foot of the narrow circular stone steps he was passed by a tall girl coming down. Seeing his uncertain expression, she asked, 'Can I help you?'

'Well, yes,' he said, 'yes . . . Do you know Deborah . . . Deborah Hardtman?'

'Yes, yes, sure I know Debbie.'

'Do you know where I could find her?'

The school colleague must have been a year or so older than Debbie, because she had the poise and the self-awareness and the faint knowingness of someone not entirely unaccustomed to men's attentions. 'Well,' she said, 'gee, I'm sorry – but Debbie isn't here. She's seeing her father today.'

'I'm her father,' Hardtman said, and saw the girl's whole manner change; she had suddenly dropped a couple of years of sophistication.

'Oh gee – *you're* her father. Oh gee! Oh – well! But she's meeting you at the Plaza. That's what she told me.'

'Oh no,' he said in dismay. 'I meant the plaza here. What a mix-up.' He sighed. 'I said I was going to stay the night at the Plaza Hotel, so she must have thought I meant there.

But, my goodness, she should have realized I would come and fetch her. Do you girls just go up to New York by yourselves? Is that permitted?'

'Sometimes,' the schoolfriend said. 'Not too often.'

He frowned and smiled alternately. She looked like a very nice girl, and he was glad she was Debbie's friend. Pretty too. How fast they grew up these days.

'Is there a phone I can use?' he asked, and she took him to it and waited while he phoned the Plaza and had Debbie paged.

'Better wait where you are,' he told her when she had finally been found and brought to the phone. 'You'll be all right there, won't you?'

'Yes, Daddy,' she said with what he thought was faint amusement in her voice. The girlfriend asked to speak to her. Half turning away, she said something quick and secret that he did not catch. While she was listening to what Debbie was saying, she smiled at Hardtman. She was nodding her head. She had full lips and bright excitable eyes. Again she said something secret that he was evidently not meant to hear, and he heard Debbie giggle. He made a gesture indicating he had to go and Debbie's friend immediately concluded her conversation. When he thanked her, she said. 'You're most welcome, sir.' The father being now fully authenticated she had become less flirty around the eyes.

Debbie was sitting reading in the Palm Court when he arrived at the Plaza an hour and a half later.

'What's the book?' he asked as he sat down by her, and she showed it him. 'Is it good?'

'It's a scream,' she said. 'Oh it's *so* funny.'

'I read the reviews.'

'It's killingly funny,' she said.

'I must read it,' Hardtman promised.

'I don't know if you would like it,' she added as a kind of second thought. 'Maybe you wouldn't. It's very outré. The humour. You know?'

'Outré. Hum. Well, I don't mind outré humour.'

'Well, perhaps it isn't exactly outré, what I mean is it isn't, well, you know – conventional. I'm sorry about the mix-up,' she added quickly. 'I was sure you meant me to meet you at the Plaza.'

'If you stopped to think, Debbie – would I have made you come to New York by yourself? How did you come?'

'Oh – I – I got a lift.'

'A lift? You don't mean you hitch-hiked?'

'No, somebody from the school was going up to New York. One of the teachers. She gave me a lift.'

'Oh I see. Well, Debbie –' he leaned across the small square pink marble table and kissed her fondly. 'So you've been doing things behind my back, hmm?'

'*I* have, Daddy?' She was a little put out.

'Growing up. You're – a young lady, practically. A lovely young lady.'

She smiled back at him with a degree of self-composure that rather surprised him. It was evident that she was not entirely unused to such compliments.

He looked around. It was quarter to seven now and the Palm Court was packed with people meeting.

'A place of romantic assignations, I see,' Hardtman said.

'Yes,' she began, as if about to say more, but then changed her mind.

'You are obviously very busy,' he said, 'since you don't have time to come and see us.'

'There are lots of activities at school,' she agreed. 'They believe in that. We have these debating societies and all these other societies. There's the school paper, which takes up a lot of time. And there's the sailing now.'

'Sailing? You sail?'

'I love it.'

'I didn't know . . . Is there somebody properly qualified with you . . . ?'

'Yes, there is, Daddy.'

'Shouldn't we have been asked first, if you could go sailing?'

'You *were* asked. Mummy said yes.'

'She didn't tell me.'

'Daddy, they are not going to let us drown and give the school a bad name and lose all their business. You can bet they are not going to let us drown. They take every precaution.'

'I see. And what other dangerous pastimes have you been pursuing . . . ?'

She laughed. At an adjoining table a middle-aged balding man who had been waiting, reading a paper, now stood up to greet a young woman whose bare arms showed whitely through chiffony sleeves. She was dark and very dolled up; shiny crimson lips, false eyelashes, plucked eyebrows. Debbie was looking her over out of the corner of her eyes. Eager-to-please eyes met those of the waiting man briefly, intimately, and then turned away, and he said, 'Well, how nice, well how nice . . .' and pushed in the chair for her, and she looked up at him and flashed him a big private smile together with her formal, 'Oh thank you.' The man asked, 'Would you like some champagne?' and she said, 'Oh I'd love champagne,' and he called the waitress and, after studying the menu, said: 'Bring us a half bottle of the Louis Rodier, darling. Well chilled.'

'I'll bring it in an ice bucket, sir,' she informed him.

'Thank you, dear.'

'How's your work been going, Daddy?'

'New beginnings are always tough, one makes so many false starts. But I am beginning to see the light of day. I think. *I think*,' he emphasized for exactitude.

'But you're enjoying it?'

'I don't know that I'd say that exactly – enjoying is not perhaps the right word. But you're right in this respect, I like to work.'

The waitress came, and Hardtman ordered a dry martini for himself, and asked Debbie if she would like Coke or Seven-Up or something.

'I'd like a cocktail,' Debbie said, 'I'd like . . .'

He laughed. 'You might *like* a cocktail but you're not having one. You're under age, for Heaven's sake. You want to get me arrested? At home I don't mind you having a glass of wine occasionally. But I am not going to allow you to drink in bars at your age.' This lecture was delivered in front of the waitress. Debbie's face had gone a deep red.

'Nothing for me,' she said.

Hardtman looked at her, and repented if not of the content, then of the tone of what he had said.

'Well, I also drank before I was allowed to,' he said. 'But what do you expect me to do? Collude with you? You can't expect that.'

She nodded, looking down.

'Are you ready for food, young lady?'

She nodded again.

'Shall we eat here?'

She said all right, and he stood up, signed the bill, and led her across the pillared lobby to a dark dining room, panelled in oak. It was not yet seven o'clock and there were only a few people eating this early. The maître d'hôtel took them to a window table where they could see the hansom cabs drawn up on the other side of the street, by the park.

Menus were brought and Debbie, who had said little since having been put in her place on the subject of the illicit cocktail, immersed herself in studying the bill of fare.

When the waiter came to take their order, Hardtman asked her if she had decided, and she said yes, she wanted the Rock Cornish Hen, and to start with, caviar.

'The Beluga, malpassol,' she told the waiter.

When the waiter had gone away, Hardtman said with a smile, 'Well, I see you have acquired some expensive tastes. Since when have you been eating caviar?'

'I like it, I really like it a lot,' she said.

He laughed. 'Hmm,' he said, 'hmmm. And where did you acquire a taste for caviar? I don't suppose they serve it in the school canteen.'

'I buy it,' she said. 'And we eat it in the dorm with sour cream and matzohs.'

'Well,' he said, 'if you can afford that out of your . . .'

'If I can't afford it, who can?' she said and looked at him directly, defiantly, face red, Laurene's stubborn chin. Of course, what she said was true. On paper, his little girl was already twenty times richer than he would ever be, and

157

although her money was tied up in trusts that she was not supposed to be able to get at until later stages in her life, she obviously had discovered ways of obtaining credit on the basis of her expectations. Must be that, because he was strict about the amount of money he allowed her. Unless Laurene had been giving her money . . . But he did not want to be rebuking her all the time, so he let pass the question of how she was getting money to buy caviar, and turned the conversation to himself.

'Now, if you want to know *my* vice,' he said, 'it's work. And it is a vice. I'm not just being cute about that. Sad to say, somewhere along the line I seem to have lost my capacity for play. I never had the time, and so I got out of it. I regret that. Person ought to be able to play too. May amaze you to hear it, but I used to be an O.K. cricketer . . .'

'No! When was that?'

'Oh when I was in England. At Oxford University. I was in my college second XI. I was considered a pretty good spin bowler. As a batsman,' he chuckled, 'well, I was *reliable*. That meant I could be sent in last man and be unlikely to get myself bowled out or run out while our best batsman was bashing the bowling about. Now some people can't do that . . . let the other fellow score all the runs, while they play a cautious defensive game. So it's considered an asset for any team to have somebody who can.'

'And that was you, Daddy?'

He didn't have the feeling that he had impressed her very much with his cricketing skills. 'You know,' he said, 'sometimes that's the hardest thing to do: sit tight, wait, wait and see what happens. All sorts of situations that you can't resolve immediately, and you have to be able to wait, let others make the running. See what comes out of it. It's called living with uncertainty, and it's what you've got to get good at because, as you are going to find out – nothing is certain in this life, and the people who come out best are those who can live with that, and have fun at the same time. Some people, they try to get to a safe place – a position of security – or stability – and *then* they'll enjoy themselves. But that's foolishness. There is no safe place

158

in this world, so you might as well make the best of what there is.'

'Oh I agree,' she said sagely. 'I believe in living for now.'

'Well, I didn't quite mean that,' he said smiling. 'That's often an excuse for just living selfishly, which is not what I meant. I meant that you have to live with your heart in your mouth and *hope* you're doing what's right – and commit yourself on the basis of that hope – while acknowledging that you may all be wrong. Being apprehensive is not such a bad thing. I think it was Goethe who said that the unquiet is the best in man. No, no – not Goethe, Anatole France. "A mind that is not uneasy, irritates and bores me," he said somewhere. That's right, that's right. It was Anatole France, though Goethe said something similar.'

'Things are pretty serious, aren't they?' she said, following his line of thought at once.

'Well, *well*. They could be. I don't really know, that's the truth of it. I don't think anybody knows. When you're on the outside of things, you imagine there must be somebody in there in the middle of it all who knows, who really knows. But there isn't. We're all in the dark. Some are more accustomed to seeing in the dark than others, but that's a long way from saying anything is really clear.'

'You mean even you, Daddy, being so close to the President and all? . . .'

'Well, I'm not *so* close to the President, honey. He doesn't take me into his confidence. I don't know that there's anyone he takes into his confidence. He's pretty much his own man. He listens to advice, I'm told, and then acts in accordance with his own judgment . . .'

'Do you think there is going to be a war between us and the Russians?'

'Now what gives you that idea? There is a lot of talk, I know. But that's just talk. This is not a country that believes in solving its problems by going to war . . .'

'That's what some of the parents of the kids at school say we ought to do.'

'Go to war?'

'They say we ought to get it over with while we're ahead.'

'And what do you think, Debbie?'

'We debated it in the current affairs society, and I spoke in favour of moderation and keeping a cool head.'

'Good for you.'

'I lost. I got accused of being a pinko . . .'

'Well, they were wrong, and you were right. Now, of course, the Western nations have got to organize themselves in a defensive union, that has become clear. And that is what we are doing. But it's with the purpose of *averting* war. The Russians don't like what we're doing, and they are making a lot of noise and flexing their muscles, but I don't think they are going to start a war, unless we make some terrible mistake. Provoke them in some way that they cannot afford to let pass. Then it could happen. But I hope – and believe – we're too smart to do anything like that. So I don't think you need worry yourself. I really don't think it's going to happen, despite all the talk.'

He thought she looked a shade disappointed, as if she would have preferred to be able to go back to her schoolfriends with inside news of impending catastrophe. It worried him, seeing in his own child this sort of half-yearning for the worst. Something in the human psyche was all the time flirting with self-destruction.

'Going to extremes, in anything,' he told her, 'always has some element of excitement about it, but really it's a dumb thing to do, in international affairs, and in your own private life, too.'

'Is that meant as a piece of *cautionary advice*, Daddy? For me? You think I may be going too far where caviar is concerned?' Her face was full of teases and dares, and seeing how pretty she was, and full of prankishness and games, he thought: she must be a lot of fun to be with, if you were not her father. Her heavy father.

'Mayn't I advise you, Debbie?'

'Of course you may, in fact I like you to. I'll let you into a big secret.' She gave him a devastating smile. 'I don't know about other girls, but *I* like you being concerned about me. I'm flattered. The girls at school thought it was just slightly terrific that my Dad, who is an adviser to the President, should come all the way to New York just to check what his little girl is up to. I do know that's why you came. But the truth is . . . I'm very careful. I really am. I take after you – I am very un-extreme. Oh I have dates, sure. All the girls at school date, but believe me I'm careful – to a fault!'

'Is that what you think I am?'

'Isn't that what you said?'

'Well, not quite . . . sometimes you have to take a risk when it's for something important. I just don't want you to risk yourself needlessly.'

'Well, I don't. So you can worry about something else now. O.K.?' and she leaned across the table, smiling, and gave him a daughterly kiss. 'But I do like it that you're so concerned about me. Makes me feel good. So there you are. I've found *my* safe place – it's you. You mustn't think if I don't come home every weekend that I'm not *with* you, because you're with me – you and Mummy – always, and I couldn't be happier about you both. I'm not getting up to all sorts of big deal unmentionable things, and I'm not about to, I'm just, carefully, finding out about me. What my place is on this soil. Trust me, Daddy. Please?'

'Of course I trust you,' he said.

He was reassured. The warmth that had always existed between them was till there. Perhaps she had been a tiny bit ironical about his middle-of-the-road position, but then he felt fairly ironical about that himself. There were moments when extreme actions had an appeal for him, too. He had been seventeen when he first went to England with his father, an impressionable age, and it was there that he learned of the virtue of moderation. If asked what had appealed to him so much about the English, he would have had to say – their manners. At one time he would have said this jokingly, but lately he had come to the conclusion that manners counted for more than was usually allowed. Underneath, the English were probably no better than anyone else. He did not believe that fundamental human nature differed greatly from place to place. This was why manners were so important. What had saved the English from the kind of moral collapse to which other nations – such as the Germans – had succumbed, was their sense of what was and what wasn't done. Manners. There were certain things that the English simply did not do. Put Jews in gas ovens, the English did not do that sort of thing. Which was why the spy Homer was so distressing to them, because what he was doing was not done either.

Doubtless, Hardtman had a somewhat romantic view of English manners. He was a tremendous Anglophile. Heaven help him, he even loved our climate, since it did not tend to extremes, being rarely either too hot or too cold, and that must have appealed to his sense of moderation in all things.

Looking around, he saw that the champagne-drinkers from the Palm Court had been put at an adjacent table – early eaters, too. Debbie also noticed them and smiled behind her hands. Hardtman watched romance burgeon. It was clear to see who they were. He was the sales director of a Hoboken furniture manufacturer: forty-eight, comfortably married, with grown-up children, and something lacking in his life. She was a secretary, thirty-six, trying to look twenty-seven: the see-through sleeves, the cute expressions, the elaborate pretence of not having much experience of this sort of thing, being taken out by a married man. Ah! What about those eager-to-please smiles. What about that! She wanted this furniture salesman. Her over-careful expressions concealed keenness, desire even. Her waist under all the chiffony folds was on the verge of thickening; the carefully displayed flesh of her neck and bosom was pale and used and in need of adornment. She wore a cultured pearl necklace and a diamanté brooch in the form of a Scots terrier, and snake bracelets, and her perfume was a little too strong.

He wore square-cut rimless spectacles; he was virtually bald down the centre of his head, from front to back. There was a kind of pass between the fluffy peaks of hair on either side. Though not vastly prepossessing, he was experienced in such affairs, and very much in charge.

'They gave me a room with two single beds,' he told her. 'So I told them I wanted the room changed to one with a King-size.' She looked in his eyes, just for a moment, tried to blush, and failing, assumed an unconvicing expression of modesty, looking down; he studied her bare arms through the see-through sleeves, picking his teeth with a silver toothpick, and she looked up again as if impelled to meet his eyes after all, and he gripped her knee briefly under the tablecloth.

Debbie was suppressing giggles behind her hand. Hardtman was faintly embarrassed at witnessing this seduction scene in his daughter's company. He ended the meal rather abruptly and led Debbie out.

'I don't greatly fancy driving all the way back to Great Neck tonight,' he told her. 'I think you had better stay here.'

Together they went to the desk, and Hardtman said, 'I'd like my daughter to stay over for the night. Do you have a room for her?'

'See what I can do for you, Mr Hardtman, the clerk said, his eyes lighting for an expressionless instant on Debbie. He consulted his booking charts, lips pursing. Eventually he looked up at Hardtman and said, 'I could let you have 415. That's adjoining your room, Mr Hardtman. If that would – uh – suit your daughter.'

'That'd be fine,' Hardtman said. It might have been his imagination but he thought he detected in the clerk's excessively blank features a hint of complicity, a too ready acceptance of the daughter story. Ah well – let him think what he damn well liked.

The elevator boy had the same blankly collusive look, not batting an eyelid all the way up to the fourth floor. Debbie was conspicuously suppressing a giggling fit.

'What is the big joke you are not letting me in on?' he asked her as they walked down the corridor to their rooms.

163

'Oh nothing, nothing, Daddy.'

'It's evidently not nothing, unless you've started regressing to infancy.'

'It's just . . . nothing, nothing really.'

He stared at her blankly.

'I don't think they believed that I'm your daughter, that's all.'

'I think you are sometimes *over*-imaginative, Debbie,' he said. He sounded cross.

In his room he put a call through to the school and explained that Debbie was spending the night with him in New York. He read the *New York Times*, the *Wall Street Journal*, the *Herald Tribune*. He glanced through one or two memorandums that he had brought with him. He was feeling quite sleepy and ready to go to bed when he heard a faint tap on the connecting door between his room and the adjoining one.

'Can I come in, Daddy?'

'Sure, Debbie.'

He heard a key being turned and then saw her in the doorway knotted inside a white hotel bathrobe, her face shiny after her bath, and he felt the sudden pang of separation: she was not going to be his baby girl much longer.

'Had a nice bath, sweetheart?'

'Yes. I wanted to come and give you a goodnight kiss.'

He opened his arms to her and she came and gave him a big hug.

'I don't like you to be cross with me,' she said. 'I can't sleep if you're cross with me.'

'I'm not cross with you. Why would I be?'

'Oh I thought . . .'

'No,' he said rocking her fondly. 'You know you're becoming a very lovely young girl.'

'Oh, baloney!'

'It's not baloney,' he said, 'but I don't intend to argue the point with you. Now go to bed. I don't know about you, but I'm beat.'

'Can I leave the door open?' she asked as she returned to her room.

'You're not still scared of the dark?'

'I don't like the feeling of . . . being alone. Just a crack?'

'O.K.'

Later, as he was on the point of falling asleep, he heard her call out to him in a wide-awake voice. 'Daddy, daddy, are you asleep . . . ? Isn't it a laugh, this . . . adjoining rooms?'

'Yes,' he said, and thought: I've lost her.

PART THREE

12

The capital had undergone an abrupt change of season while he was away. Getting out of the air-conditioned Pullman at Union Station, Hardtman felt as if he had suddenly been wrapped from head to toe in hot towels. The hot weather had come in a rush, everything happening at once, a quick and drastic change-over that caught Hardtman ill-prepared. Suddenly Washington had become a Southern city. The magnolias were in ostentatious bloom, great spreads of rose and white, and purple: around the Tidal Basin the Japanese cherry trees were now frothy pinks and whites, and throughout the city you became aware of trees – American elms, sycamores, oaks and limes and willows and spruce and redwood. The maze had ostensibly turned into a pleasure garden. Along the wide grassed banks of the Potomac, schoolboys played football, and there were busloads of tourists outside the White House, and under striped marquees on the Ellipse, and long lines of sight-seers making their way around the Reflecting Pool to the monuments. Hardtman saw these pleasure activities with the ironic hindsight of history: and so while the world played . . .

At this time there came into Hardtman's hands a confidential memorandum summarizing a conversation between Defence Secretary Forrestal and the President's aide, Clark Clifford.

For some time there had been rumours that wild men in the Pentagon were talking of launching a preventive war. An official British request was made asking for a statement of American intentions. The State Department's reply was unclear. The Foreign Office sought clarification with its usual exaggerated air of calm. Did the last sentence mean that the US was preparing to go to war in the event that the Soviets did not, by their actions, recognize our asserted rights? The Foreign Office went on to 'wonder whether this was precisely what the note meant, and secondly if it was altogether a wise decision for us to take'. Britain, said the FO, 'would not wish to add the scorpion's sting to the assertion of our rights'. The State Department's reply was that it 'did not believe the British interpretation was warranted'.

It was in the light of this diplomatic pussyfooting that the Clark Clifford memorandum was so significant. For it expressed, in far more direct language, what was in the mind of the American Defence Secretary.

Forrestal was quoted as having said: 'There is in my opinion an extraordinary, immediate and grave threat to the continued existence of this country. This country cannot afford the deceptive luxury of waging defensive warfare. As in the war of 1941–5 our survival depends on how and where *we* attack.'

There was also a quotation from an Army Intelligence group survey assessing the comparative military capabilities of the Soviet Union and the Western powers. This survey came to the conclusion that: 'Naturally the side which strikes first will have an advantage, especially if surprise is achieved.'

Hardtman was deeply disturbed by what he had read and at once made inquiries to determine how far Forrestal's thoughts had been put into action. There were, he found, contingency plans for virtually any eventuality. All sorts of military moves had been 'tried out' in the form of war games. But nobody he spoke to had heard of the existence of a pre-emptive strike programme.

The Hardtmans were entertaining a great deal. One often saw Graham Forster at their house, and Holbrook, and Arnold and Dolly Luessenhoep, and Walter Cole, and Julian Blake.

Leahy was there one evening and after dinner, when the conversation had become concerned with world catastrophe again, the Admiral remarked, '*I* would not have dropped the bomb.'

'Did you oppose it, Admiral?' Graham Forster asked, a wholly inappropriate grin on his face, explicable only in terms of how plastered he was.

'I did not know what it would do,' the Admiral said, 'I grew up in the days of ballistics – I understand explosives. I did not know what this was. Had I known, I would have opposed it. I remember telling your King, Forster – King George – who asked me about the bomb, I remember telling him it wouldn't work. I didn't understand nuclear watchermecallit. I understand explosives. I did not know. I was brought up to believe you do not make war on women and children. I would not have done it if it had been my decision, that's all I can say.'

'Does Truman regret it?' Forster asked, still grinning irrelevantly.

'The Boss regrets nothing. Once he has made a decision, he does not torture himself with regrets.'

'Why torture yourself when you can torture others,' Forster said, nodding mordantly.

'He took the decision in the belief that it would save the lives of tens of thousands of our men . . .'

'Balls,' Forster said. 'Sorry. Sorry, I'm a bit pissed. You'll have to excuse me, Admiral, but it is balls. What you've just said. It was to warn the Russians. Give 'em a whiff of grapeshot. This is what we can do to you. An illustration of our might. A demonstration explosion in Tokyo Bay would have been enough to make the Japs cave in. But he wanted to show the full lethal power of the bomb – to show the Commies who's boss in the post-war world.'

'That's a cynical interpretation that I reject completely,' the Admiral said, becoming rather red in the face.

Walter Cole, who had been listening quietly, observed in an aside to Hardtman, 'Our friend Forster does seem to get Lefter and Lefter as he gets drunker and drunker.'

Things were getting very tense. There was a growing feeling of unsafeness and impending calamity. Defence Secretary Forrestal had been found wandering in the streets at night in his pyjamas, gesticulating up at the sky and shouting, 'The Russians are coming, the Russians are coming.' People were talking of a 'nuclear Pearl Harbour' – even though the Russians were not thought to have the atom bomb yet. Molotov had been talking as if they did have it – and supposing he was not boasting? They were ahead in the field of guided missiles; suddenly the sky might darken with the mechanical horror birds.

Was it hysterical to think this way, or realistic? Millionaires were building deep fall-out shelters in their country estates, and laying in supplies of frozen chickens and small arms. It could all happen. Sometimes the worst did come to pass. Intelligence surveys spoke in precise cold language of the development of biological and chemical warfare against the U.S. Methods of introduction would probably include infection of food and water supplies, detonation of small bombs at predetermined times, use of natural vectors such as fleas and lice, contamination of the air, either directly or by ventilating systems, smearing agents on equipment, counters, and handrails. Animals, crops, and humans could be subjected to biological or chemical agents by saboteurs. Unassembled atomic bombs could be clandestinely introduced into the United States prior to a general attack, assembled, and then detonated in accordance with a preconceived plan. Sneak air attacks by one-way missions could be expected. Likeliest targets: New York, Washington, Detroit, Pittsburgh, Chicago, Akron, Duluth, San Francisco, Los Angeles and Puget Sound.

And at the same time as these great dangers were being spelled out, the extent of the penetration of the highest levels of the American Government by foreign agents was being revealed in the hearings of the House Un-American Activities Committee. There were Red agents in the White House, in the Treasury, in the State Department: the country was rotten with them. Elizabeth Bentley, a self-confessed Russian agent, had named thirty-two government officials who had supplied her with secret documents to pass on to her Communist bosses in the underground. A Communist agent had approached the father of the atom bomb, J. Robert Oppenheimer, in his own kitchen, as he was about to go in for dinner. The devils were everywhere.

In New York, John Foster Dulles, the most likely next Secretary of State, told the present Secretary, General Marshall: 'The American people would execute you if you did not use the atom bomb in the event of war.' In Berlin, General Clay, reportedly close to breakdown, said he would not hesitate to use the atomic bomb 'and I would hit Moscow and Leningrad first'.

Around this time Hardtman began to experience certain bizarre sensations, and to keep a kind of log of his recurring symptoms.

At the beginning of June he wrote in his pocket diary: 'Bizarre feeling again. Sense of being . . . underwater. Other times as if surrounded by thick protective glass. Things distant, far away, unreachable.' A few days later, another entry said, 'Feel as if not inside my own body sometimes.' And then a week or so later: 'I watch myself, as if from the outside. My centre has shifted. It does not seem to be inside me. Weird, weird.'

All this time he was working strenuously, meeting all sorts of people in different sections of the Intelligence community, studying organizational structures, complex divisions of authority. And working on the draft of his report to the President. He was able to work, even though, in some respects, he was not fully there.

Towards the end of May he was recording in his personal log: 'Falling feeling. Suddenly, out of the blue. As if ground is giving way under me.'

He was supposedly at the centre of things, with access to the most secret information, and yet he could not get things clear. His report to the President was constantly re-drafted because statements sounded too unspecific, but when he sought to put things more definitely he ran into the problem that he lacked the hard facts to back up categorical assertions. Still, signs had to be heeded, they always meant something – but what exactly? He was becoming dizzy from trying to work out what anything meant in this city.

At a cocktail party at the Hardtmans, Julian Blake was heard to ask Walter Cole, 'Is there a preventive war plan?'

To which Cole had replied with a chuckle. 'Oh, I expect those guys have a contingency plan for dealing with an invasion from Mars.'

'Dizziness. Feelings of unreality. Under glass. Under water,' Hardtman wrote in his pocket diary in June.

He mentioned these symptoms to Julian Blake one evening. Casually.

'Dizziness?' Julian said, ejecting a cigarette butt from his De-Nicotea holder.

'Yes. The room goes round – and I don't mean after I've had a few.'

'Could be you are not yet accustomed to the climate here,' Julian said. 'But if you like, I'll take a look at you.'

'As you say, probably the climate,' Hardtman agreed. 'I tend to agree with my old English doctor who used to say, "You either get better or you get worse" ...'

'True enough. But no harm in taking a look at you, Bill. I can do it right now.'

The fact that there was no need to make an appointment, go to an office, and submit to contraptions, made the examination seem sufficiently painless for Hardtman to agree to it. Julian did not even use a stethoscope. Just his fingers – those extraordinarily sensitive fingers that people were always talking about.

It was early evening, before dinner, and the other guests had not yet arrived.

'Why don't we go in the libarary where we won't be disturbed,' Julian suggested. This was where Hardtman worked on his papers in the evenings, and it was established that nobody came in uninvited.

In the privacy of the library, Julian sat down next to Hardtman and took his pulse. I say 'took his pulse', but it was not done quite in the way that the pulse is normally taken. Julian lightly touched the radial artery of Hardtman's left hand, first using just one finger, a moment later bringing two other fingers into play somewhat further up the wrist; and now, in a way that suggested the fingering of an accomplished violinist, his fingers moved up and down with varying rhythms and pressures, one pressing lightly, the others deeply, then reversing this and pressing more deeply where before his touch had been feather light, and lightly where his touch had been deep, in this way performing a whole range of light-to-deep palpations. This procedure lasted close on five minutes, and Julian had a very concentrated expression all the time.

When the examination of the left pulse was completed, Hardtman asked. 'Well, will I live?'

Julian ignored the remark, made a faint head movement demanding silence, and turned his attention to the other pulse. The same procedure was repeated. At the end of this, his serious – doctoring – expression relaxed somewhat, and he said, answering the question of five minutes before: 'You'll live. However . . .'

'There's always a catch,' Hardtman said.

'The deep pulse in the second position of the right hand . . .' His brow crumpled into an expression of concern.

'Misbehaving?'

'It's like wet blotting paper.'

'Which a good pulse ought not to be?' Hardtman queried.

'Have you had hepatitis, Bill?'

'Yes,' Hardtman said, astonished. 'How on earth did you know that? About eighteen years ago.'

'I could tell from the pulse,' Julian said. 'Apart from the legacy of that,' Julian said, 'you are in *pretty* good shape. Over-tired, of course. Under considerable stress. And, of course, very armoured . . .'

'Is that bad, being armoured?'

'It's the devil.'

'Why is it so devilish?'

'Causes blocks in the energy flow. When you're as armoured as you are you breathe less deeply, take in less oxygen, which means you burn energy less efficiently, and consequently have less of it available, become tired sooner, have to resort to artificial stimulants to get additional adrenalin flow to liberate more energy . . . Well, you see. That's also why you feel giddy.'

'It is?'

'Breathing is the problem, you are not breathing, are you?'

'I foolishly believed I was.'

Julian placed a hand on Hardtman's chest and shook his head at the feebleness of his respiration.

'You sip the air like a dowager Duchess sipping tea.'

'What do you do about that?'

'I would have to teach you to breathe. Believe me, very few people know how to. They have to be taught. There's also an indication to ease up on the hard stuff. If you could limit yourself to an occasional glass of wine . . .'

'As I think you've guessed – diagnosed – I need the hard stuff to give me a shot of energy . . .'

'Yes, I know,' Julian agreed. 'But – I am not being moralistic – it's not good for *you*. Your liver, Bill. The hepatitis has left scars . . . I'm afraid. I think we can do something about the drinking. You don't have an alcohol problem as such. You have an energy problem, especially at the moment, when there is such pressure on you. We can improve your energy flow in other ways.'

'How would you go about that, Julian?' Hardtman asked cautiously.

'Well, I think we would have to start with some deep massage, to relax you, overcome some of that deep-seated armouring, enable you to sleep – you are not sleeping well, are you?'

'Evidently I have no secrets from you, Julian. You know that from the pulse, too?'

Julian nodded.

'Now, once you are sleeping well you won't feel so tired and that will reduce your need for a shot of something to pick you up. We could try some Sirsasana for the liver. And there are other . . .'

'I'll bear in mind what you've said. We'd better join the others now, or Laurene will hunt us out. She doesn't approve of little secret cliques at her parties.'

He might have forgotten about Julian's diagnosis were it not for an experience a few days later. At the end of a tiring day, he had stood up and suddenly had the feeling of being at the same time behind his desk and up against the wall. It was the kind of sensation of disorientation in space one sometimes experiences waking up in total darkness in a strange room, but his office was well lit and everything was clearly visible. There was a loss – for a moment –of the basic perceptions of up and down, left and right. It was strange and frightening, and he had recourse to the hospitality cupboard in his pedestal desk, where he kept a bottle of whisky. Two large drinks straightened him out – restored his sense of up and down.

It was obviously tiredness, some mysterious form of work exhaustion, due to wading endlessly through reams of documents . . . There was no time for the present to seek deeper answers.

13

The whole of Washington had become a grey area: a meshwork of clouds obscured the sun, but the heat came through. One went about covered by a permanent film of moisture. It was not difficult now to imagine this place as the Indian swamp it once had been ...

It was clear to Hardtman that for his report to carry weight, it was useless just to express his opinion. That he had already done. It was now for him to prove his case. But the problem lay in the system's built-in capacity to cover it's own tracks. Every Congressional Committee was a leaking barrel according to Cole. You told something to a Committee in strictest secrecy and next day you read every word in the Washington press. The State Department wasn't secure. The White House wasn't. That was the case for secretiveness.

Hardtman told himself that he must go on digging, until he found something. At the same time, he admitted to himself that he might be over-interpreting. He did not think so, but it was necessary to reserve judgment until he had the facts. He would, while ruminating on these questions, wander the streets, sometimes going into dubious areas that not many whites visited. He would end up in strange parts of town. The Negroes here were different from those who served the whites, as houseboys or porters or shoeshine boys or chauffeurs – they did not have the yessuhboss talk. They stood about, endlessly it seemed, at street corners and in dingy doorways, and he had never seen people stand so still for so long, doing nothing at all, staring – biding their time. Their stillness, like the stillness of the earth, was surely deceptive. They were all, surely, even as they stepped out of the white man's way, biding their time ... They all were emitting signs, even the stillest of them. Ah, Hardtman thought, if the unquiet is the best in man, then I must be a champion among men.

It was not surprising that he should turn to Julian for some relief from his hard-to-define unease. He would not have known how to describe what he felt to an ordinary doctor. He did not greatly trust doctors. There were certain questions best left unasked, in case you got answers you did not care for. He had things to do, and his health would have to hold up until he had more time. If, meanwhile, Julian could make things easier for him: well, why not? He could depend on Julian's directness. So the treatments began. After a brief period of bristly resistance had been overcome – Hardtman felt there were some things best kept to oneself, which included one's own odours and also the deep workings of one's body and soul – he relaxed. All sorts of knots in him were being loosened as Julian's hands moved with swift assurance, in mysterious sequence. One moment it was the skull that was being pressed and squeezed and moulded, then it was a systematic pulling of the hair and the ear lobes and the toes, and a stretching open of the mouth. He massaged the points at the back of the neck known in Oriental medicine as the Pillars of Heaven; at the top of the pillars there is a place at the base of the skull known as the Silent Gate, and here he applied twenty pound pressure for three seconds. He found, and applied pressure to, the ditches between the tendons. His fingers traced a straight line along the inner arm to find the Depth of the Pond in the armpit. Such techniques are said to unlock the floodgates where energy is liable to become dammed up. He manipulated the bones, working to correct unnatural curvatures, to click slipped discs back into place, and to restructure the weight distribution upon badly fallen arches.

Above all, he taught Hardtman to breathe – to breathe out in one breath, unjerkily, totally, emptying the lungs: out of the self, towards the world.

Who can say what is the basis of any care? Some amazing successes are attributed to the herbalists of the Middle Ages. Hildegard of Bingen is said to have achieved successful cures of many diseases by means of immersions in straw. In the late nineteenth century, Kneipp treated epileptics by making them walk barefoot.

Julian's immediate and undeniable achievement was that he enabled Hardtman to sleep. And perhaps it was from this that the other benefits derived. After one week he was much improved. He had more energy. His daze had lifted. He drank less – only wine – and after the third day of treatment the falling sensations that had formerly beset him at periodic intervals, ceased.

Julian came every night, for half an hour or so. The regularity of the treatment was essential to maintain the rhythm of recovery. To this end he was prepared to fit in with his patients' arrangements. He would leave a dinner party in order to go and administer a treatment to someone, and return when he was through. He would sometimes excuse himself on such grounds when he was dining with the Hardtmans. Similarly, he would leave somebody else's house to come and see Hardtman at nine, at eleven, at midnight, or even at 2 a.m. It appeared that he needed little sleep. At any rate, he was usually out and about at night and reachable – his answering service could always find him.

'Must be all the coffee you drink that keeps you awake,' Hardtman said.

Julian had a theory about coffee. He maintained that French civilization owed a tremendous amount to the widespread introduction of the coffeehouse throughout France in the eighteenth century. At a time when the British were getting soused in their inns and public houses, the French in their cafés were cultivating the virtues of wit and reason.

As the summer wore on, Hardtman found himself placing increasing reliance upon Julian's treatments. With the reimposition of the Berlin blockade by the Russians at the end of June, the world appeared to be moving towards a major conflict. Returning home, after a confusing and exhausting day of running around Washington, Hardtman found Julian's nerve massage miraculously restorative.

180

Given in the early evening, it relaxed him and stimulated him at the same time, putting him in good form for whatever social engagement he was going to. Given late at night, the massage was profoundly relaxing, allowing him to fall into an untroubled sleep.

People marvelled at Hardtman's energy, at his capacity for long working days followed by a succession of late nights.

'I'm going to have to stop the treatment for a couple of days,' he mentioned to Julian one evening. 'I have to go to New York at the beginning of September. It's to speak at a dinner of the New York Press Club. Might have to have recourse to a couple of stiff whiskies to get me up.' He laughed uneasily.

'I wouldn't want you to fall back on that, Bill. Perhaps it won't be necessary. I'm jealous of my work, and you've done so well . . . When did you say the dinner was?' He had taken out a pocket diary and was checking through it.

'September 7th.'

'Well, I could do that.'

'What do you mean?'

'I could come with you.'

'You could? What about your other patients?'

'My patients tend to take long summer vacations. Come back second week in September. I give classes and seminars in the summer and I'll be doing some in New York. I could arrange to be there on September 7th.'

'Well, that'd be great, if you could,' Hardtman said.

He had come to be so attached to the nightly treatments that the prospect of missing two or three sessions had been bothering him. 'You really think you can make it?'

'With a little re-arrangement, it can be done. In any case, it will be pleasant to go together to New York.'

There was an occasion when Laurene remarked to Hardtman, 'You are getting very involved with Julian. Is that smart?'

'Well, you put me on to him.'

'Yes.'

181

'Yes – but what?'

'He – he gets in with people. Haven't you noticed?'

'Yes, of course. Sort of necessary, I would say, in his profession. On the whole, he does it more inoffensively than most.'

'I agree he has charm. That's the trouble.'

'Why trouble?'

Laurene hesitated, until Hardtman was looking quite concerned.

'He borrows money,' she said.

'Is that so?' He had to laugh at the solemn way she said this.

'For me that's a warning light.'

'Oh, come on, Laurene – When you say he borrows money, what do you mean? How much?'

She hesitated. 'Five dollars here, five dollars there. He never seems to have any money on him. He's a pocket-fumbler. Never as much as buys a cup of coffee, always discovers he's come out without his billfold . . .'

'His mind is on other things. I know some very rich men like that. Never have a penny in their pocket. Borrow from the chauffeur for matches . . .'

'He really has no money.'

'I'm not surprised. He never sends a bill. Has he sent you one? I have told him several times he has got to bill me. He always says he'll get around to it.'

She smiled with the knowingness of the rich.

'That's his technique. The soft sell.'

'Do I detect a note of . . . disenchantment with Julian?'

'No, no. I think he's brilliant. And fun. I just think you ought to be careful. He does float around a lot.'

'What is that supposed to imply? You want him all to yourself? He could hardly make a living just giving you and Dolly Yoga lessons and me massages. He does have to have some other patients as well.'

'Have you been to the Institute?'

'No. He always comes here.'

'Well (a) it's a dump, and (b) the walls of his waiting room are covered with signed photographs of famous patients he's treated . . . kings, dukes, film stars, Winston Churchill . . . you'd think you were at an astrologer's . . . framed letters, all that.'

'Maybe he takes the view that when in Rome . . .'

'You like him, don't you? You don't want to hear anything said against him?'

'Darling, you found him, and you always find the best. Don't you?'

'I found *you*,' she said.

'With your good nose. Don't tell me that delicate instrument for sorting the wheat from the chaff can sometimes be deceived.'

'It's been known.' She laughed.

'Well, in the case of Julian, I think you made one of your better choices. I think he's really extraordinarily gifted and at the same time – agreeable. He's enabled me to sleep. Given me more energy. The fact that he borrows small change and maybe is something of a Bohemian where the gals are concerned – oh I'm sure of *that* – is not anything *we* need hold against him.'

'I never know what he's really thinking,' Laurene persisted.

'Well, that's preferable, in my book, to people who are always telling you what's on their mind, and turns out it's not much . . .'

Laurene refused to let go of her line of thought. 'You know, even when he's giving out all that apple-sauce, he's got kind of a funny expression in his eyes, which unsays everything he's saying . . . like as kids when we used to swear an oath – cross your heart and hope to die – but kept our legs crossed under the table, so God wouldn't hold us to it.'

'I don't mind people keeping things to themselves,' Hardtman said. 'I don't think you need to come out with everything you feel. I'm a little bored with all that American directness. There's something to be said for hiding your feelings *à l'anglaise* – Some feelings ought to be hidden!'

'Something you're pretty good at.'

If there was a faint note of personal criticism in this, Hardtman chose not to see it.

'Well, hilarious as I know that does seem to you, governments are obliged to keep some things secret.'

'I wasn't talking about those sort of things.'

'Can't imagine what you were talking about then.'

'What really goes on in your mind and heart. We almost never talk any more. Or,' she added, 'anything else either ... come to that.'

Apart from a flick of an eyelid, Hardtman chose to ignore that remark too. But there was a line of determination in Laurene's face: she was not going to let him get away with such evasions.

'You know one of the things Julian says. When he's a bit gone on his fifth cup of coffee. Quoting the prophet Reich. Every marriage, he says, sickens as a result of an ever-increasing conflict between sex and economics. Sex, he says, only works with the same partner for a limited period – according to Reich it's four years – he's German and very precise. After that, what keeps couples together is economics, the moral demands of bourgeois capitalist society, and habit ... *habit.*'

'How about love?' Hardtman said. 'Hasn't he left that out?'

'Well, that's what I thought.'

'There maybe is something in what he says – if there's no love.'

'That's why, I guess, people need to be told, or shown, they're loved.'

'Oh I agree.'

'Any need to make a big secret of that?'

'No,' he said smiling and went to her and put his arm around her. 'How insecure you are,' he said, 'for someone who's got everything.'

'Have I, Bill? Have I?'

'Well, haven't you?' He touched her head. 'It's a heck of a job buying you a Christmas present.' His eyes had filled with playfulness, which made them bluer and more boyish, something they had not been for some time.

184

'I like it when you laugh, and play a little . . . instead of always . . .'

'It's a difficult time, Laurene. Be patient. You wouldn't want me to louse up this job, would you? Don't want to let your nose down, such a fine, clever, pretty nose . . .'

One day early in August, Sidney Myers put his head in at Hardtman's door. He had come back from Warrenton, he said, and was going to work through August at the office. He had a somewhat chastened look. Hardtman suggested lunch. He had become quite fond of the catastrophist.

'You don't look your usual cheerful self, Sidney,' Hardtman said when they were in the restaurant, and seated.

'I've been investigated,' Sidney said. He blushed blotchily all down one side of his large globular face. The other side remained pale, giving him a day and night aspect. He was, for once, not very concerned with the menu, usually his first interest when he sat down. He looked at it almost indifferently, and using it as a combination of mask and fan spoke through and over it. 'My name came up,' he said. '*Among the wrong sort of people.* I don't even know who they are. I've been racking my brains who I know who might be, you know, the "wrong sort".' He fanned himself violently with the menu. 'Anyway, it's all right now. They told me today I'm in the clear, Jesus, I don't mind telling you, though, I've had a lousy couple of weeks. For Christ's sake, if I'd had my security-clearance revoked, I couldn't work. What kind of work could I do? Who would give me a job, in my speciality?'

'The Russians?' Hardtman suggested, but Sidney did not laugh; he looked around quickly to see if anyone might have overheard, and then shot a rebuking look over his menu at Hardtman.

'Don't *joke* about things like that, Bill. Anyway, it's past history now. *The investigation cleared me so it's all right.* Right?'

'Yes.'

'You're in security. If they cleared me, it's all right?'

'Must be.'

'I'm outspoken. I put things in strong language, because I think you have got to. To get across. They're all so up to here in jargon, they don't get what anything means if you don't bang it across to them. Maybe I overdo that sometimes. Lay it on too strong. You think that could be it? I'm thinking back what else it could be. I was thinking . . .' He paused, looked assessingly at Hardtman. 'I was thinking, now you tell me. Little while back, I was giving a briefing to some of the brass, and I was trying to get something over to them, and so I said, "You fellas, you don't have a war plan. Hell, what you've got is a war-gasm. The other side presses your button and you go into an orgasm of destruction." What I was trying to say to them was they need a more *controllable* response capability. Not a tit for tat bang-bang-you're-all-dead approach.' He lowered his voice suddenly, realizing he was letting himself get carried away again. 'You think that might've offended them, you think they might have thought it wasn't loyal, to say that?'

'Oh, I don't know. It doesn't sound disloyal to me.'

'I was just trying to put it in a way that'd grab 'em.'

'You think they might have misunderstood? Thought you were against war?'

'I'm not *against* war,' Sidney protested hotly. 'I mean, if it has got to be. I'm no parlour pink pacifist, hell. What I was saying was we have got to get more sophisticated strategically.'

'I wouldn't have thought they'd hold that against you.'

'What else could it be? I'm just totally a-political. I'm a pragmatist. I don't have any doctrinal position. I go by what works.'

'Well, with this whole Hiss business going on, and the Bentley woman making her wild accusations – anybody could come under suspicion, Sidney. I wouldn't worry about it. If you say they've cleared you, they must be satisfied that you're in the clear.'

'Yuh,' Sidney agreed, looking like some overgrown sulking schoolboy who has been wrongly punished. 'What gets me mad is that I know I'm totally in the clear, I love this country, I don't have a disloyal feeling in my bones . . .'

'There's a lot of nervousness,' Hardtman said, and with that changed the subject, since it clearly was putting Sidney off his food. The conversation changed to Warrenton, horse-riding, kids and the weather – which had been very unusual: storms, floods, continuous rain, and very low temperatures for August. What had happened to Washington's unendurable summer, the sort of heat that drove men mad?

'It will come,' Sidney predicted.

At any rate, his appetite had returned, and he was spiritedly tucking into the Crab Lumps Occidental.

When they left the restaurant, it was raining heavily again. Sidney had brought an umbrella. They shared it back to the Old State Department Buildings, and took the lift together. As Hardtman was about to say goodbye, Sidney said, 'Why don't you come in my office a minute. Something I want to show you.'

He started to go in through his outer office. A secretary was typing there. 'Walk with me down the corridor, I got to go somewhere,' he suggested abruptly. Hardtman accompanied him to the men's room. Sidney checked the booths to make sure they were unoccupied, and then motioned to Hardtman to come closer.

'I want to ask you something, Bill. I've been open with you, haven't I? I mean I've been very direct with you. Will you tell me something? Oh c'mmon. Don't just stand looking on. It looks suspicious you just *standing* there. O.K., maybe you don't *need* to, but you can try. I'm trying.'

Hardtman, feeling foolishly conspiratorial, went and stood next to Sidney and unbuttoned. Nothing came.

'Bill,' Sidney said staring straight ahead at the white tile wall. 'I've heard that sometimes the security people tell you you've been cleared in order to give you a false sense of security, and meanwhile they are getting the goods on you, and waiting for you to drop your guard. Out of sheer relief people, you know, get talking and let out certain things, certain . . . You, Bill, today, you getting me to talk like that, now that wasn't . . . ?'

'Of course it wasn't. I'm not on that side of it, Sidney. I don't have anything to do with those investigations.'

'But you're to do with national security.'

'If anything we said was indiscreet, I've been just as indiscreet as you.'

'Well, you never know,' Sidney said. 'Half of the people around here, I don't know what they do.' He seemed marginally reassured as he buttoned up.

'O.K.?' Hardtman asked.

'Yes, I guess so.' He hesitated, and then placed a hand on the men's room door, stopping Hardtman from going out. 'But tell me, is it true they do that? Tell somebody he's cleared when he isn't ... ?'

'I wouldn't know, Sidney. But you must know if you're in the clear or not. They are not going to manufacture evidence.'

'How the fuck can *I* know. Can I remember every person I ever knew? Can I remember every lunch I ever had with some guy, like you, who pumps me a little about this or that? For all I know you could be a Commie agent and I've told you things I shouldn't. Like about Mittleweiss. They kept asking me who I'd talked to about Mittleweiss's scheme.'

'I don't think they are interested in just casual indiscretions.'

'Maybe I have the wrong sort of friends. How do I know who they all are, what they do? I'm not with them twenty-four hours of the day.'

'Relax, Sidney,' Hardtman advised. 'I should think that if they let you continue working, somebody in your position, and let you continue to have access to classified material, it's safe to assume they must be satisfied you're in the clear.'

'That's what I figured, too,' Sidney said, his big face breaking into a relieved grin, removing his hand from the men's room door.

Back in his office Hardtman decided to test the famed ability of the White House telephonists to track someone down, wherever he might be. He asked them to get him Professor Mittleweiss. No problem. The Professor was on the line in less than a minute.

'Professor Mittleweiss? You probably don't know me . . .'

'They have said who is calling, or I would not have taken the call.'

'O.K. Well, I'm occupying your former office at Old State.'

'Yes, Mr Hardtman.'

'Now I don't know if this is of any importance at all, but I thought I ought to check. Took out a volume of the Navy List and a sheet of your notepaper fell out, with a lot of names on it. It was marked Top Secret. Looks like a code of some sort. Now, of course, if this relates to something dead and past, we needn't worry – I was just concerned in case it related to an active project.'

'This could be most serious,' the Professor said with evident concern.

'Should I destroy the sheet of paper?'

'It might be best. Tell me, could anyone, apart from you, have seen this sheet of paper?'

'I doubt it. Nobody has occupied this office between your moving out, and my moving in.'

'One cannot be sure,' the Professor said. 'I do not like to ask you this on the telephone, but you understand my concern. Can you give me an indication of what appears on the sheet of paper, so that I can identify the – uh – subject to which it relates.'

'O.K.' Hardtman began to read out from the Professor's sheet of paper, 'UGLY AUNTIE 5–1 SPRING IN BERLIN 3–1 PEACOCK'S PLUMES 20–1 I LOVE YOU 6–1 . . .'

'Mr Hardtman, Mr Hardtman,' the Professor's voice was cutting in with some exasperation.

'Yes, Professor Mittleweiss?'

'Those are the names of horses, Mr Hardtman.'

'Oh, I see. Oh well, that's good to know. Then there's nothing to worry about. I just wanted to check to make sure. You can't be too careful.'

189

When he'd hung up, Hardtman called the operator and commended her for the speed with which she had found the Professor.

'Where did you find him, as a matter of interest?'

'Professor Mittleweiss? Oh, he's over at CIA, sir.'

'Thank you. Perhaps you could now try and find Walter Cole for me. That won't be so easy, I suspect.'

Cole was not to be found in the same place twice. You rang one telephone number, which referred you to another, and that one to a third, and so on.

On this occasion, it took three-and-a-half hours for the call to be returned.

'Walter,' Hardtman said, 'you're like that damned philosopher's river that nobody can bathe in twice.'

'Or even once,' Cole said. 'What's the problem, Bill?'

'I want to see you . . .'

'Could do lunch on . . .'

'No, not lunch. I want to see you latest tomorrow. I'll come round to wherever you are. Just stop the river long enough . . .'

'All right. Make it 10 a.m. tomorrow.'

He gave Hardtman an address not more than ten minutes from the Old State Department Building.

'Been meaning to call you. Wanted you to see our new place,' Cole said. 'And raise a celebratory glass . . .'

'You mean you have at last got a permanent roof over your head?'

'To tell you the truth, I don't know if the roof is on yet, but we do have a little more space . . .'

It was a nondescript office building in the post-war style, without embellishments.

A couple of guards were checking the identifications of everyone coming in. Cole was there to pass Hardtman through and give him his plastic badge.

'It's pretty chaotic,' Cole confided.

'I can see.'

Although final work was still going on, some offices were already functioning.

Of the four lifts, only one had so far descended and that had filled up with people ahead of them. The next lift did not arrive for another four minutes, and turned out to be already so full of construction workers and equipment that it was impossible for one extra person to get in. There was a wait of another five minutes before the next lift arrived, and that, too, was full.

'This is impossible,' Cole said. 'I apologize, Bill. There is going to be an express lift – eventually – for VIP use. But, as you see, not yet. We are going to be here all day.'

He looked around with the urgency of a man not accustomed to being kept waiting. Spotting the construction foreman, he went over to him, and said: 'Look, this is Mr. Hardtman. He's one of the President's aides. Can't you do something? I can't keep him waiting here . . .'

'Nothing I can do about it,' the foreman said. 'I can't kick the people out of the elevators, can I?'

'How do you go up?'

'If you want to ride up with me, you're welcome. It's an open elevator, huh?'

'We're never going to get up there otherwise. All right, Bill?'

Hardtman nodded. The foreman led the way out of the building, and it was only then that Hardtman realized what he was expected to do. They scrambled over mounds of earth until they came to a narrow shaft at the side of the building, a structure of four vertical rails, inside with a wooden platform was descending. When it reached the ground, half a dozen hard-hats got out and the foreman signalled to Cole and Hardtman to take their places. Hardtman looked at Cole and then up the windowless espanse of brickwork. 'You bothered by heights?' Cole asked.

'Mountaineering is your sport, not mine,' Hardtman said.

'It's perfectly safe, I should think,' Cole said.

'I think I prefer to wait for the conventional elevator,' Hardtman said. He was not going to be drawn into a schoolboyish dare. And then seeing on Cole's face the expression of having won a point, Hardtman said, 'Well, O.K., Walter. If you want to go up on that thing.' He could not afford to give away points to Cole. Three hard-hats got in with them. The foreman attached a chain across the open side of the cage, and gave the signal for the lift to ascend. Hardtman felt the ground fall away, and with the others tightly pressing around him, he saw the horizon descend and felt all anchorage go, felt his human base loosened from its earth fastening as the open platform rose uncertainly, shaking inside its minimal housing – he had become a fly crawling up a wall, but without the fly's confidence in the perpendicular. He saw Cole light a cigarette, cupping his hands around the match, and then letting the wind extinguish it. He tossed out the match and watched it fall. The sun was directly on them. A builder's canvas sheet had become dislodged from part of the construction and gone adrift, and to Hardtman it seemed as if his own shifty soul, so prone to displacement of late, was flapping about out there. There was the river to one side and on the other the city was becoming a plan, a gridiron system, an abstraction. They were only half-way up; the platform upon which he stood gave glimpses of receding ground between its wooden planks. He looked up and saw, even more unnerving than this contraption he was in, a kind of rickety platform hugging the side wall of the building, a most perilous structure, consisting of scaffolding and wooden planks, sagging in the middle like a clothes line. To believe that this infirm platform could support the weight of half a dozen hefty men required a belief in human handiwork that, at this moment, Hardtman could not readily muster. Only an act of blind faith could make him step on that thing. He looked at Cole, who was standing close to the swaying chain, swaying with it, not holding on to anything. Even the foreman was uneasy, for he put one arm up to the roofing and the other in front of Cole's swaying form to grip the side of the cage.

'Well, Walter,' Hardtman said, 'is this your way of making sure I don't pay you too many visits?'

Cole's silvery moustache twitched above his teeth. The sky had the stillness of a painting. Hardtman, becoming remote from everything, felt a bluish green bloom cover his eyes.

'After you, Bill.' Cole was motioning him to go ahead. Hardtman put his last shirt on the human enterprise and stepped out on to wooden planks that moved beneath his feet. He held on to the scaffolding, and for a moment his eye was drawn downwards, against his will, to the canvas sheet on the ground, spread out like a fallen body, and then he stumbled on. When his feet touched the solid floor inside the building, he said, 'Well, I enjoyed that, Walter. Better than a roller-coaster ride.' He wanted a cigarette, but decided not to light one now, in case his hand trembled and Cole saw this. He could not give away points.

Cole led the way along an antiseptic corridor and down side stairs to a lower floor. Doors had to be unbolted here, for them to be let in, and this was done only after Cole had shown first his pass and then his face at a small window, protected on the inside by fine steel mesh.

'Show you our bag of tricks, Bill.'

There was a flush of excitement on Cole's face as he took Hardtman from room to room, showing him what the Technical Section was working on. Ingenious new ways of picking locks, of disguising oneself, of opening and resealing letters, of photographing people without their being aware of it, of analysing handwriting, of identifying people by means of saliva tests, of listening in on private conversations . . . 'This here is a beaut, Bill. Look at this. Booby trap. The charge is detonated by smell. By smell, Bill. Just ordinary body smell will set it off.'

'Now there's an argument against B.O. for you.'

'It'll go off even if you're wearing Prince Gourielli.'

'You mean it can't tell the difference? Now I'm disappointed in you there, Walter. That sounds like a very crude device to me. If it can't distinguish between a stinking Commie and a decent American boy smelling of the great open spaces.'

'Dr Smith is the resident genius in this area. Come in and meet him.'

He was taken into a laboratory that smelled like a barber's shop. Dr Smith turned out to be a German, re-christened for the post-war era, and from his accent he was evidently not long in the United States.

'A brilliant man,' Cole said in an undertone. 'We were lucky to get him. The Soviets grabbed all the best brains for themselves.'

'What's his speciality?' Hardtman asked sniffing the air. 'Is he going to give us Prussian haircuts?'

Dr Smith's domain not only smelled like a barber's shop, it even looked like one. There were bottles of bay rum, and oil of rose, and friction rubs for the scalp, and Eau de Cologne, and lavender water, and attar of roses and Balm of Gilead. Tubes of shaving cream, both of the brushless and the lather type. Shaving brushes of finest badger bristle. Talcum powders. Hair sprays. Skin tonics.

'Let Dr Smith tell you about it, it's his project,' Cole said.

'To cut a long story short,' Dr Smith began, 'vat is ze purpose of zis? Please to consider. Ze image of a man isst Haar.'

'He means hair,' Cole put in.

'Yes, haar. Is vat I say.'

'I'm all ears,' Hardtman told him.

'Consider, for example, Lenin vizout beard, Stalin viz-out moustache. Imagine zem haarless. Ze difference zat make. Hum?'

'What sort of a difference?' Hardtman asked.

'Ze haar is ze man.'

'What's the project?'

'I discover way to make all haars fall out,' Dr Smith said beaming. 'You can imagine vot zis do. You can imagine . . .'

'Hitler without his moustache . . . yes, what a blow for freedom that might have been.'

At the mention of Hitler, Dr Smith frowned slightly as if Hardtman had been guilty of some indelicacy.

'What are all these lotions for?' Hardtman asked.

'Vot I make up to now stinks.'

'Try, try and try again – hmm?'

'He means the depilatory has a powerful smell, he's trying to disguise the smell . . .' Cole said.

'Oh I see.'

'So I mix viz attar of roses, Balm of Gilead, to giff beautiful smell.'

'Guy puts it on, and all his hair falls out. How about that!' Cole said.

Dr Smith beamed again.

Hardtman having declined the offer of a more extended tour, they went now to Cole's newest office. The sherry was got out, and a toast drunk.

'To invisibility – and hairlessness,' Hardtman proposed.

Cole drank to that, after which they both drank to a secret budget, and being responsible only to the President of the United States.

'And uprisings in the East,' Cole added.

Through the windows there was a view of the river and of Virginia beyond.

'What d'you make of that story about Jim Forrestal? Is he cracking up?' Hardtman asked.

'The pyjama incident?'

'I heard he was running around naked.'

'No, it was in his pyjamas. According to the version I heard.'

'What is the version you heard?'

'Police siren. He thought it was a general alarm.'

'The country's Defence Secretary ought to know the difference.'

'Should, I agree.'

'My impression is that he's right on the edge – he's going to break.'

'Could be.'

'Doesn't worry you?'

'You want to know what I think?'

'I always want to know what you think, Walter. I'm not always told, though.'

'Well, what I think is this. If the Russians get the idea they're dealing with a crazy Defence Secretary, it gives us the Madman's Advantage.'

'What's the Madman's Advantage?'

'Theory of mine. If the Russians think they're dealing with somebody who's completely rational, they can go right up to the edge, because they can calculate exactly at what point a rational person is going to react. Now that gives *them* an advantage, because a rational person does not over-react. But if they think they're dealing with a madman, they realize they have to be a lot more careful, because he might not react so rationally. That's why Jim's state of mind could be an advantage to us. Gets it over that we can't be *counted on* to act rationally always . . .'

'Whereas in reality we *can* be counted on to act rationally? There's a danger in that sort of bluffing. You may think you are pretending to be crazier than you are, when the truth is you're crazier than you think.'

'Ho ho ho. You know, Bill, I enjoy your wry sense of humour.'

'The demon barber, Herr Doktor Schmidt,' Hardtman said. 'Where've you been trying out his stink bombs?'

But Walter Cole was not to be caught off-guard.

'Everything you've seen, Bill, is towards developing various capabilities. For use in future circumstances. None of the devices is yet operational – as far as I know.'

'As far as you need to know.'

'Ho ho ho.'

Hardtman cut into the laugh. 'Walter, I thought you were having nothing to do with Professor Mittleweiss and his crazy schemes . . . wouldn't have him under your roof, you said.'

'That's right, Bill.'

'He's at CIA.'

'Not under *my* roof,' Cole said vaguely. 'Though I do believe that he got himself some sort of contract, on a free-lance basis, with PSS.'

'What's PSS?'

'Psychological Strategy Section.'

'That's not part of your outfit?'

'Oh no.'

'The White House operators have him listed under CIA.'

'That's probably for the convenience of their listing system.'

'Come on, Walter. Don't stall.'

'They – PSS – are consultants that we use from time to time. They advise us . . . on psychological strategy.'

'Walter, you're playing your usual game of going all around the point. We are talking about a question of good faith. You gave me to understand you were having nothing to do with that crackpot scheme of the Professor's. From my conversation with him I do not get the impression that his OPERATION ZLOT TROT, the stampede of the Western currencies, is as dead as you made me believe. What I want to know is why you misled me?'

He shrugged. 'Helps muddy the water.'

'It sure does. Is that your answer?'

'Bill, this is very tricky stuff. The Prof. is a blabbermouth, and it was necessary, as a matter of security, to be able to deny all knowledge of that scheme. I didn't think you would have wanted to know about it.'

'But I asked you.'

'I took that to be just conversation.'

'I have an official government function, Walter. When I ask you something it's not just conversation.'

'Bill, it's just inconceivable that a secret agency of government should have to comply with all the overt orders of the Government.'

'It's inconceivable, is it? Well, let me tell you. When I ask something, I expect an answer, and I expect to be told the truth.'

'If I'd known that was what you wanted, Bill, of course I would have told you.'

'All right. Let's put an end to all this gobbledegook. I want an answer now. All right? I want to know now what the Professor is up to.'

'You're sure you want to pursue this?'

'Yes, Walter.'

'Well, the theory is that reducing the real buying power of the other side's currency is to our advantage, and it is something that comes generally within the area of economic warfare as defined by the NSC directive. The Professor has some intricate economic theories, and calculations. I'm not sure I understand all the mumbo-jumbo. But what it amounts to is that if the East German Deutsche-mark becomes worth less and less in relation to the Westmark, it suggests to the Germans which side they might prefer to be on. It was happening anyway. The Professor's scheme just accelerates the process.'

'By pumping forged old Deutsche-marks into the Eastern sector, and so driving their value down still further . . .'

'I don't know that *that* has been done.'

'That was his scheme. Planting the seeds of destruction . . . remember?'

'Economic action is not my department, strictly speaking, so about that part I couldn't say . . .'

'About what part could you say?'

'Since there was going to be currency reform, involving the surrender of the old currency . . .'

'Ten per cent to be converted, ten per cent blocked and eighty per cent cancelled . . . The old currency becomes worth very little.'

'Yes.'

'And even less if it suddenly turns up in massive quantities in the Eastern sector where it remains legal tender.'

'That could well be.'

'Therefore if the natural seepage of devalued Deutsche-marks into the Eastern sector were to be supplemented by artifiical means such as organized smuggling of the old currency . . . drives up the Westmark, causes the Deutsche-mark to buy less and less. The currency dealers become rich. All helps to sew rancour and fan the flame of mutual animosity . . . the seeds of destruction, right?'

'Yes,' Walter Cole agreed, 'you see, the scheme has merit.'

'You imagined the Russians would just take that, without introducing countermeasures? One of the reasons they give for imposing the blockade is because we are going into their zone, committing acts of sabotage, engaging in black marketeering, currency manipulations . . . If that's your doing . . .'

Cole laughed. 'Oh I wouldn't want to claim credit for all of it. A good deal of that sort of thing goes on anyway.'

'Walter, you realize what you're doing? You know where it could lead?'

'Yes.'

'That's what I was afraid of.'

14

Until this time Hardtman had seen the President maybe half-a-dozen times, always with others present. But now he decided to request a private meeting, and he called Matt Connolly, the Appointments Secretary, and asked him to set this up.

It was arranged for three in the afternoon. Hardtman was in Connolly's office five minutes beforehand.

'Am I going to be alone with him?'

'That's the way you wanted it, Mr Hardtman.'

'How long have I got?'

Connolly looked in his book. 'Oh it's flexible.'

Harry Truman had gotten to fill the room more, Hardtman thought as he went in. He had grown more impressive somehow. But not solemn. He was still cordial and pink and snappy and sharp.

'How are you, Bill? How you putting up with this weather? It gets worse. You haven't seen anything yet.'

Hardtman smiled, and said, 'I guess I'll survive it. You seem to be standing up to it exceptionally well, Mr President. Looking very fit, if I may say so.'

'Oh I had a couple of days on the yacht. Got me some sunshine and good sleep. Man's got to sleep well to be fit. Have a sailor boy give me a rub-down before I turn in. He's very good. Wonderfully relaxing, a massage before you go to sleep.' He got up from behind his desk and came over to where Hardtman was sitting and pulled up a chair. 'Hate talking across a desk. All that paraphernalia gets in the way. Can't see the man for papers. Well, Bill. What have you got to tell me?'

'I am in the course of preparing the comprehensive report that you asked for, but there is something I felt should be brought to your attention right away, Mr President.'

'Go ahead.'

'There are some covert operations that we have got going in Berlin that do sort of fit the bill of what the Soviets are charging us with.'

'What operations are they?'

'I believe you brought a Professor Mittleweiss out here to advise on measures of economic warfare?'

'Mittleweiss, yes. That fella. Met him fishing. A while back. Interested in history, like I am. We had quite a talk. Strange cove. A little cuckoo maybe. Smart enough. I had him here for a while, but he left before you came. He had some crazy scheme.'

'Well, the thing is, he hasn't left. He's with CIA. PSS.'

'What's that?'

'Psychological Strategy Section.'

Harry Truman shook his head. 'The things they do dream up. Psychological strategy –hah? I thought Mittleweiss's field was economics. Is he advising them?'

'I think it's more than advising. I have pretty good reason to think that a revised version of this crazy scheme is actually being put into effect in Germany.'

'Is that so? I didn't think his scheme had much to be said for it. As I recall . . .' He paused, thinking, and took off his glasses, which made his eyes small and clear. He stared blankly at a portrait of Benjamin Franklin on the wall. '. . . wasn't it something to do with producing a money stampede in Eastern Europe, creating a great, new, German-style inflation that would ruin their economy . . . using Eastern European currencies, which he wanted me to get the US Treasury to forge on a massive scale . . .'

'That's right. It had been given the code name ZLOT TROT.'

'You telling me ZLOT TROT has been put into action?'

'An amended form. They don't need to forge the currencies. They can use surrendered old Deutsche-marks . . .'

'Well, well, well. Isn't that something. I didn't think it'd work. What exactly is the point you want to make, Bill?'

'The danger of undertaking a covert action whose consequences are unassessable, and which, once under way, becomes hard to control. I am talking about the use of organized bandits, smugglers, criminal elements for the attainment of questionable objectives . . .'

'Bill, do you need to tell me all this?'

'Well, I think, Mr President . . .' Hardtman began.

Harry Truman got up, walked over to the portrait of Benjamin Franklin, put his eyeglasses back on, examined the painting closely.

'I love this picture,' he said. 'It's one of the great portraits. I love beautiful pictures, landscapes, and portaits that look like people. We see enough of squalor. I think art is intended to lift the ideals of the people, not pull them down. Have you seen the statue of Lincoln in the Lincoln Memorial? You should. I think it's wonderful. It's interesting how much history you can learn just by studying statues and buildings . . .'

'I'm sure that's true.'

'Bill, why don't you put what you've just said to me in a memo. Boil it down to what I need to know. Keep it to half a page, if you can. I'll take a real good look at it. And let me say, I'm very glad you're keeping such a sharp eye on things.'

Afterwards, Hardtman could not be sure if the President had meant: 'Do you need to tell me *all* this?' or 'Do you need to *tell* me all this?' If the former, it was merely a rebuke for being a little long-winded. But if it was the other meaning . . . if the emphasis was on the word *tell* . . . No, that couldn't have been what he meant. The President was a busy man: he wanted it all boiled down to half a page. And then he would act.

For the next few days Hardtman worked all-out to finish his report. He wanted to present all his conclusions and to give the detailed factual evidence, such as it was, on which he based his opinions. He called it an Interim Report, to make it clear that all the facts were not yet in his possession. But it seemed to him that waiting for the whole picture to emerge might become an endlessly protracted business, and that it was better to set down what he now knew, or had reason to suspect, rather than wait until the final proof was in his hands. The report ran to more than

20,000 words and gave a detailed analysis of the way the clandestine section of CIA was functioning, and of the problems resulting from compartmentalization, and from the lack of clear overall policy-direction of its activities.

Bearing in mind what the President had told him about 'boiling it down to half a page', he also provided a summary of the salient points in his report. And he took care that this ran to exactly half a foolscap page.

When he had finished, he took the report to the Admiral and asked him to give it to the President as a matter of urgency.

Leahy promised he would read it that night and have it on the Boss's desk in the morning.

Now there followed a period of waiting. Several days went by without word from the Admiral or the Boss. Hardtman kept bearing in his head the words, 'Do you need to tell me all this?' and 'Boil it down to what I need to know.'

The summer had finally arrived, the unendurable Washington summer, with temperatures rising into the upper nineties. The heat wilted flower boxes, made the asphalt in the road ooze, and turned the armies of bureaucrats into limp men in crumpled seersucker suits and sodden shirts. There was no relief at night either. Often at midnight the temperature was in the eighties.

It was like being sick with a fever. You were not in your right mind half the time. And you became prone to strange ideas.

Waiting for the President's response, a deep-seated anger was building up in Hardtman. Supposing the Boss had simply chosen to ignore the report – decided to put it aside. Something he did not need to know about. Wild notions began to form in Hardtman's head. He would speak out publicly about the dangers, warn the nation. This was a time when he was at his sharpest with people, dropping the carefulness of manner he had previously adopted, telling them bluntly that they 'were inadequately informed' or 'didn't know what they were talking about'.

He wondered sometimes if he was succumbing to the

Washington disease. It was said that everybody went down with it sooner or later. It could produce in the most reasonably minded individuals the sense of being men of destiny, with the role of saving the world. Something in him rebelled against the position of adviser. In common with others, he had come to feel the impotence of proffering advice that was not heeded. He wished to enforce his views, since he was sure he was right. There it was, the well-known malady of *knowing* you were right, from which half of Washington suffered. Did such omniscience come out of the general over-excitement that affected men when they found themselves close to power? Was there something about having the President's ear that made people crazy? The knowledge of what the right word at the right moment could achieve. But you never knew if you had the President's ear, or not. And if you didn't, who did. The President's ear was a whore.

The silence was deeply disturbing to Hardtman. He had marked his report Most Urgent, and more than a week had gone by, and still there was no response. When he rang the Admiral's office to find out what was happening he was told that the report had been put before the Boss and no doubt he was studying it, and Hardtman would hear shortly. That word again, shortly.

Well, perhaps there were dozens of other equally urgent reports on the President's desk, all demanding attention and action.

Julian's treatments kept Hardtman sane. The agile fingers moved knowingly, bringing oxygen to the nerves, dispersing unwanted blood, pressing good blood and lymphatic fluid in the vessels towards the heart, and producing a corresponding suction effect that drew away needless blood. With his highly developed sense of touch, Julian could instantly find the Silent Gate at the base of the skull where congestion produces clouding of the brain. Sometimes Julian's treatments were so relaxing that Hardtman fell asleep on the sofa, and waking up had no awareness of how long he had slept, whether it was a matter of seconds, or half an hour. There was a sense of total relaxation that

204

Julian could induce, and, at this time, especially, Hardtman needed him.

If when they came back from the New York trip there was still no positive response from the President, Hardtman decided he would hand in his resignation.

The day before he was due to leave, he received a message that the President wanted to see him. He was to report to the Oval Room at 12.30.

It was almost one as people started coming out of the room: seemed like half the Pentagon's top brass had been in there. They had the tight air of men who had been obliged to restrain themselves. And they didn't look too pleased about it. Hardtman stood in the corridor waiting to go in. There was still somebody in there, Matt Connolly said. It was two or three minutes before the last man came out. It was Forrestal, face grey, but eyes strangely bright. Feverish? Connolly went in for a moment, and when he came out said, 'O.K., Mr Hardtman. You can go in.'

Harry Truman was walking about the Oval Room with springy steps; to say he was bouncing would not have been too wide of the mark.

'Bill,' he said before Hardtman could utter a word. 'I've had a terrific morning, I've had 'em in here and I've told 'em. Go on, sit down, Bill.' He gestured forcefully, and seeing that Hardtman was remaining standing, said, 'Don't mind me, I can't sit. I'm like a jumping bean . . .'

Hardtman remained standing, hands folded in front of him, waiting.

'I called 'em in,' Harry Truman said, 'and I told 'em. Told 'em Clay is an impulsive hot-tempered Southerner, quick to take offence as a Southern belle and jumpy as a school kid with the shit-runs, and that I'm not accepting his resignation however many times he offers it, and that he's going to carry out my orders or I'll have him busted out of the army and I don't care how many stars he's got on his collar . . .'

Harry Truman paused and beamed. Hardtman grinned.

'Well, that was telling 'em, Mr President.'

'Then I told 'em this.' A single finger poked out into the thick air, as if it was still full of delinquent generals, and for a moment Hardtman had the fancy that Harry Truman had made the entire Military Establishment go up in their own cigar smoke. 'I told 'em I been hearing a whole bunch of bullshit talked about a certain matter. "I expect you heard the same talk," I said. I said, "Sometimes I think that there must be more damn fools in the Pentagon than just about anyplace else, because what I've heard said around is that some of these fellas with more stars on their collars than brains in their heads want a war to straighten out the present world situation. A preventive war, they call it."' The President paused to savour the moment in recapitulation. 'You should have seen the faces of those birds, Bill. They were just seething inside to beat hell, but they weren't saying anything. So I went on to tell them. "Gentlemen," I said, "these people I'm talking about, and I'm sure none of them is in this room right now, because I don't believe anyone in this room would be such a damn fool – these people have got the cockeyed notion that you can combat world Communism by dropping a bomb on it. An atomic bomb, Gentlemen," I said, "it won't work, even if we could bring ourselves to do such a low-down mean wicked thing. Now don't go making any mistake, any of you. I will not shrink from doing what's necessary, if it becomes necessary, but it'll be my decision. The A-bomb will remain in civilian custody. What we need to combat Communism is not a war, it's ideas. There's no Communism in the Soviet Union, because it won't work, and that's a fact. What they have got is totalitarianism. Whenever you have thought control and subservience to a man or a group of men with no civilian checks on their powers, then you have totalitarianism. And that's not our way in this country." That's what I told them, Bill.'

'Bravo, Mr President. How'd they take it? Judging by the long faces I saw as they came out, they weren't too happy.'

'Oh, they bellyached some. Said we couldn't defend ourselves in Europe with what we've got at the moment.

Said the more planes we put in the air-lift the more it takes out of our strategic defence system. I told them I was aware of the problem . . . but my decision was to stay in Berlin.'

All of a sudden Harry Truman quietened down, the bounce went out of him and he sat down behind his desk, the family pictures all around him in their filigree silver frames. His eyes had gone dull. He played with a pencil in silence. When he spoke again, the jauntiness had quite gone from his voice. 'Bill,' he said very quietly, 'I have a feeling we're very close to war. Hope I'm wrong.'

Hardtman said, 'There is a thing that was written by Montaigne. He wrote: Fancy oft begets the event.'

Harry Truman nodded in agreement. 'Wrongdoers have no house with me,' he said.

'Clay with his sudden feelings of war,' Hardtman said. 'It's dangerous. We have to be damned careful we don't get into a situation of self-fulfilling prophecy.'

'Couldn't agree with you more. That's why I called you in, so you know I read your memo, your whole report, in fact, and I am convinced you are mostly right in what you say, and that steps should be taken to curb any more of this foolishness that is being planned. I wanted you to know that.'

'Well, I'm really glad you've told me that, Mr President, it's encouraging to hear.'

That day Hardtman left the Oval Room feeling for the first time since his arrival in Washington that he had achieved something positive.

PART FOUR

15

Coming out of the cathedral-like dimness of Union Station, they were subjected to a sudden flare of light. Hardtman adjusted the blinds. Julian, paisley silk scarf knotted inside an open-neck shirt, blazer draped around his shoulders, wearing grey flannels and old, scuffed suede shoes, had a weekend air about him.

Hardtman felt light-hearted, unusually so for him. Longish train journeys tended to relax him. They reminded him of the past – of times, as a boy, when he had accompanied his father on those European *wagon-lit* cars, with their rosewood panelling and mysterious switches and hidden reading lights. You could read and sleep and read and sleep and watch out for the snow lying on the roofs of railway stations, and whitening the steeples of village churches. A consular officer's tour of duty in any one place tends to be not excessively long. One day he is dealing with the problems of American sailors in Hamburg, and the next with the financial embarrassment of an American light opera company in Geneva, and then with would-be immigrants to the USA in Riga . . .

Hardtman had known much movement in his childhood and youth, and each new city and country had held fresh promise for him, as if the finding of oneself were a matter of place. He remembered the long twilight of Europe's northernmost seashores in the weeks of the summer solstice – white nights stretching from sunset to sunrise in rebuttal of darkness. Ah! It was out of elation that he had not slept in those days.

'Shall we stretch our legs as far as the lounge car?' Hardtman proposed. 'A drink before lunch? How about it, Julian?'

Hardtman had two dry Martinis before his lunch and a half bottle of well-chilled Montrachet with it. Even so, he felt wide-awake afterwards, with a progressive tightening-up inside himself that always preceded occasions such as speech-making.

The express train was a cooled and sealed container spiriting them through the heat, whose oppressiveness was confined to the other side of the glass. On their side they were not bothered by it. The few people who could be seen from time to time, on a bridge, in a station, in an open field, seemed weighted down by the heat outside, so difficult to imagine in the almost chilly Pullman car, as it was invariably difficult to imagine a condition or state other than one's own. Who could imagine the heat at the centre of an atomic explosion? A human being in the path of such heat left nothing of himself except the faint imprint of his silhouette upon rock. Could America have used the atom bomb against a country that had not committed the treacherous crime of Pearl Harbour? Beyond the rational militaristic arguments, had there been a more primitive motive force for the dropping of the bomb – an eye for an eye?

Julian had been telling a story to which Hardtman was only half paying attention.

'Frankly she was a bit of a baggage ...'

'What?'

'A broad.'

'Who was?'

'Old Babs.'

'And who is Old Babs – I've lost you somewhere. Babs?'

'Barbara Castlemaine.'

'Do I know her?'

'Hardly likely, Bill, since she's been dead three hundred years.'

'Why exactly are we talking about this dead broad?'

'She was a Villiers,' Julian said. 'Remarkable family. Historians speak of their vivacious personalities, combined with their errant and profligate natures. Of course, the Duke of Marlborough and his sister Arabella Churchill were Villiers on the distaff side.'

'Oh is that so?'

'The Churchills had nothing in their stock – before the

Villiers, that is – to account for their later brilliance. The Villiers would seem to have been the catalytic element in the blood. Barbara, of course, was the mistress of Charles II and became Countess Castlemaine and later Duchess of Cleveland...'

'I can see she must have been quite a gal,' Hardtman said, 'but refresh my memory, will you, as to how we got to talking about her.'

'We were talking, were we not, about the extent to which one is a free agent or affected by one's blood. And I happened to mention this ancestor of mine, Barbara Castlemaine...'

'She's an ancestor of yours?'

'So it would appear. I had my tree done – of course, it had been said before, but this confirmed it.'

'Well, well, well. Is that what accounts for the brilliance in your blood?'

'In view of some of the others in the direct line of descent,' he said, 'I am not sure one wishes to advertise the connection.'

Hardtman decided to go over his speech. It was an updated version of ideas he had expressed before, and there had been no objections from the State Department's Unofficial Publications Section, to which, as a matter of routine, he had sent the speech for approval. It had come back without comment, stamped NO OBJECTION TO PUBLICATION.

The title of his lecture was, 'The Intelligence Lesson of Pearl Harbour'. It was a subject on which he had made himself something of an authority. He maintained that Pearl Harbour had been clearly foreseeable, and that a properly organized Intelligence service would have foreseen it in time to alert the nation to the danger. Hardtman believed in the predictability of human responses, in the laws of probability, and had little time for the astonishing, which to him represented no more of human behaviour than can be encompassed with a statistical margin of error. Hardtman had faith in the assessability of all things, and no patience with a surrender to guesswork. He thought that Intelligence was too much a matter of opinion, of conjecture and fanciful flights of the imagination, with everybody learning as he went along. Hardtman wanted to impose rules on the game. He wished to protect the world and himself against unpleasant surprises.

Now he looked up at Julian.

'Would it interest you to read what I'm going to say?'

'Very much.'

Hardtman gave him the text of the speech, and then closed his eyes and dozed while Julian read.

'It's good,' he said when he had finished. 'Excellent, in fact. A brilliant analysis. And a logical presentation of what should be done.'

'No criticisms?'

'None at all. None. Unless – well, if you press me to make a critique, it could perhaps be said that – oh – you could afford to be a tiny bit more colourful.'

'Colourful?' Hardtman weighed this word upon the fine scales of his exact mind. 'In what way?'

'Well, it is an achievement to be quite as unsensational as you have managed to be. You do have a way of treating it all in – in your characteristically dry way.'

'I didn't want to be sensational,' Hardtman pointed out, 'because such treatment does count against you, with, well, people of consequence.'

'I absolutely agree,' Julian said, 'I am sure on balance you've done it exactly the right way.'

New York was just as hot as Washington, and a lot dirtier.

While Julian was running around trying to find a taxi, Hardtman went to buy a paper. Unfolding it, his attention was caught by a headline that read:

ATOM BOMB CUSTODY
SITUATION IS 'IMPROVED'
IN MILITARY EYES

He was starting to read this story when he heard Julian call out. He had found a taxi. Hardtman hurried to get in, and they set off joltingly. He tried to read the newspaper

214

story, but the ride was too bumpy and the print jumped before his eyes.

Getting out at the Plaza Hotel, he told Julian, who was keeping the cab on: 'Meet here at 6.30. In the Park bar.'

Up in his room, he called room service and ordered a large dry Martini: then with a sigh of misgiving, picked up the *Herald Tribune* and turned to the atom bomb story on the front page. He read with mounting dismay:

Military men reported yesterday that there had been recent improvements in conditions surrounding custody of America's stockpile of atomic weapons and their ready availability for possible use in a war emergency. The armed forces had been urging a change in the custody of the Nation's completed A-bombs. They want to ensure that military commanders would have immediate and unobstructed access to them so that they could retaliate instantly in the event of foreign attack. Non-military agencies have opposed transfer of atomic bombs from the civilian Atomic Energy Commission to the military services. Military has asserted in the past that the AEC would not have the bomb ready for use in an emergency. But recent developments have calmed the military's worst misgivings, and the question of access is now no longer considered as much of a problem as it once was. This is a result of recent easing of procedural mechanisms.

By the time he had read the story twice, the waiter had come with the dry Martini. Hardtman drank it down fast, after which he put a call into Washington, to a contact of his who was usually well-informed about Defence matters.

The call came through as Hardtman was shaving. Had he seen the *Herald Tribune* story, he asked his friend. He had not seen that particular paper, but a similar story had appeared in the *Washington Post*. Yes, he said, he thought it was accurate.

'What's behind it? What are the military so damn happy about?'

After giving a dressing down to the generals, the contact said, Truman had asked Forrestal to stay behind. They had a brief conversation in which Truman said that the policy of keeping the bomb in civilian custody must prevail for the time being, but it could be reviewed after the November elections. 'Forrestal seems to have taken it as a strong hint. He's given instructions for two sets of war plans to be drawn up, one based on the assumption that the bomb would not be used, the other on the assumption that it would be used.'

Oh the trickiness of politicians in general and Presidents in particular! What foolish conceit for any man to suppose he had the President's ear.

When he had put down the phone, Hardtman continued shaving with an outer air of calm. But something was brewing in him. Suddenly he paused, recalling Julian's only criticism of the speech – that it could perhaps be more colourful. Was that Julian's polite way of saying it was dull? Surely it was not dull. Exact, yes. He had a distaste for all forms of imprecision – for the reckless use of language. He was not given to exaggeration for effect. That was not his style. But, on the other hand, he was not dull, surely. What he had to say was important. That one had to keep a plurality of options open to one's own side and to the other side too. That the stages of a crisis could be measured in terms of the loss of options. That good Intelligence depended largely on possessing a correct image of the enemy, which in turn depended on the capacity to put oneself in his shoes.

By the time he had finished dressing, it was just before 6.30. He took the lift down. Julian was not in the bar yet. Hardtman seated himself in a leather alcove where it was already dim as night. He ordered a dry Martini and watched the evening crowd begin to assemble. There was a touch of raffishness about hotel life – even in the grandest of hotels – that was not unentertaining; people *de passage* – transients – were different from settled citizens close to home. You could tell this from their expressions as they entered a strange bar-room: they had an air of expectancy. He watched a succession of pretty young women arrive at the entrance of the bar and look around for the person they were to meet. They had the special self-confidence of New York girls, the conviction they were at the undisputed centre of things. Large hats made bare shoulders look barer. Deep decolletage normally associated with parties was now being worn in bars too. And their sensuous perfumes! How long it was since he had been in New York by himself. Grimy it might be, but it was electric too. All that free-floating energy to plug in to. He felt a need of it. Washington he had found enervating – he was wearied by endless circumlocution. Washington was as roundabout as an Egyptian diplomat, whereas New York was as direct as a pretty girl. So it seemed to Hardtman after his second Martini, noticing the revival of ostrich feathers as an adornment of women's hats and how the fashion had gone back towards the Edwardian, a period for which he felt an uneasy nostalgia. The period of his childhood . . . an unfairer world, no doubt, but to a child growing up in it and enjoying its privilages, it had had its attractions.

Julian had come in. There was a girl with him.

'Sorry we're late,' he said.

'We still have time for a drink,' Hardtman said, easily. He signalled the waiter.

'I hope you don't mind my bringing Joannie,' Julian said. 'She was going anyway.'

'Are you a journalist?' Hardtman asked. She nodded.

Julian, for once, wanted something alcoholic: brandy and soda. The girl – Joannie Fontanez – asked for Black Label on the rocks, emphasizing the amount of ice with two raised fingers.

'What paper are you with?' Hardtman asked her.

'I'm a freelance.'

She was wearing a creased long white linen skirt, and an open bolero jacket of the same material, worn over a shirt-waist, and she carried a voluminous handbag with outside zip pockets. Cigarette smoke clung to her face as if part of her. Her hair, which was brown and long, tended to fall across her face, partially obscuring it. Her eyes were

217

warm and interested. About 28, 29. Attractive. Tired eyes.

When the Scotch came she knocked it back smartly; it gave her an immediate lift and made her sparkle.

'Well,' Hardtman said to her, 'so you are interested in the problem of rationalizing Intelligence structures . . .'

'Yes, I am,' she said, not allowing herself to be teased on account of being a woman in a man's world.

'I'm glad to hear that. I wouldn't want to be dull copy for you.' He shot a quick look at Julian.

'You couldn't be that, Mr Hardtman,' she said politely.

'How do you know?'

'I know about you.'

'You do? How's that?'

'I looked you up.'

'What did you find out about me?' he asked playfully.

'You want to know?'

'Sure.'

She began to reel off the facts. 'Forty-five years old. Married. Once. To one of the Howard & Blum girls. One daughter. Fifteen. At Bay School. Father a consular official. Educated abroad – Europe. England. Yale, later. Successful lawyer. OSS during the war. Interrogated war criminals, including Kaltenbrunner and other top SS. Expert on Intelligence questions. Special ideas on subject developed in lectures and *Foreign Affairs* article. Working on Report to President on re-organization of Intelligence services.'

'You've done your homework, Miss Fontanez,' Hardtman said.

'Oh no, not really.' She laughed.

'You've put me in a nut-shell very neatly. Now tell me – you can give me some professional advice about something. Julian read my speech. And he liked it – I *think*, but he was hinting I could afford to be more colourful. Now in your survey of my . . . past . . .'

'I just looked you up in the morgue – that's all.'

'What I wanted to ask was – had you noticed a . . . lack of colour?'

'I wouldn't say that.'

218

'Ah! What would you say, Miss Fontanez? What would be your impression?'

'A Conservative . . . I guess.'

'Is that so, is that so? You know I used to be considered a bit of a Red. At Yale.'

She laughed, she had a most attractive laugh.

'Fontanez, is that Spanish?'

'Swiss. Helvetian. That's what I was told. It's the old – original – Switzerland. Way back. I don't really know, though. I've never been outside America myself.'

'Yes, time of the Romans, wasn't it? Helvetia.' He looked at his watch. 'Better not keep your colleagues waiting.'

'What I didn't get from the clippings,' she said, getting up, 'is what you're . . . well, about.'

'That might take rather longer than we have right now,' he said, as they started to walk out. 'What exactly do you mean?'

'I mean what are you committed to – if anything?'

'Yes, that would take longer than we have. But you may have a better idea, Miss Fontanez, after you've heard me speak. If you still don't know, you must ask me. I believe there will be time for questions.'

'I'll ask you,' she promised.

The taxi ride to mid-town Manhattan – the dinner was being held at the Commodore Hotel – took longer than expected and the lady Vice-President of the Press Club could not entirely suppress the tone of crossness from her words of welcome. Her name was Hettie Cooper, she was in her fifties, of large build, with an intimidating presence. Having spent thirty years suppressing all vestiges of feminine squeamishness, in order to be accepted as one of the boys, she had become tougher than most of her male colleagues.

'Well,' she said when she – at last – saw Hardtman coming towards her. 'We're here. I was starting to fret. But all's well, et cetera. Allow me to extend my welcome on behalf of the Committee and members, and since we are now running *more* than twenty minutes late, I propose we go straight on in. All right, Mr Hardtman? No need of the bathroom? If you'll just come along with me, Mr Hardtman, I can brief you as we run.' And she wasn't kidding – she had the stride of a trooper, and was halfway down the hall before Hardtman had taken his hat off. When he had caught up with her, she said in reporter's *sotto voce*: 'Who are those people?'

'They're my guests,' Hardtman said. 'My wife couldn't come, and so I took the liberty of . . .'

'We had only made allowance for two of you.'

'I believe Miss Fontanez is a member of the Press Club.'

'Did she book? I don't think she could have booked. Well, we'll see what we can do. And the guy with her?'

'He's a distinguished Washington physician, Dr Julian Blake.'

'We'll find someplace for them. Now – the arrangement is this. First, you meet the boys and girls for an informal chat. You answer any questions they may have . . .'

'I do?'

'That's the usual way we do it. The members appreciate the personal contact.'

'Uhm.'

'We'll have to keep it down. Fifteen minutes, maximum twenty. After that we go in to dinner. Guest of honour – you – sits at top table with myself – I'll be introducing you – and senior members. After I've made a few remarks on Club matters, you'll speak for 30–40 minutes. That's about the limit of their attention span after wine and liqueurs . . .'

'I'll bear it in mind . . .'

'Well, here we are.'

They had come to the Taft Room, which was a long oak-panelled dining room with a reception area as you came in.

Immediately Hardtman found himself in a crush of predominantly male, predominantly bald, excessively smoking, excessively drinking journalists. Without offering him a drink, or even a salted peanut, they introduced themselves, adding the names of their newspapers to their own: Whittaker – *Journal-American*; Silverstein – *Daily News*; Fulton – *Post*; Hudson – *Mirror* . . . And began to question him. Did he believe that more spies were going to be found in the White House, in the State Department, in the Treasury? The room was hot and Hardtman felt hemmed in. 'Well, now,' he said, after having parried the first few questions of this type as inoffensively as possible, 'I should remind you, gentlemen, that I am here to talk about Pearl Harbour, not to discuss the latest Washington rumours.'

'Rumours, Mr Hardtman?' Silverstein – *News* said with the air of a man familiar with all the tricks and evasions of officialdom. 'Elizabeth Bentley named thirty-two government officials who supplied her with secret documents to pass on to her Communist bosses in the underground . . .'

'Yes, I read that, too,' Hardtman said mildly.

'As a member of the President's national security staff, can you tell us, Mr Hardtman, what is being done to prevent further disastrous security failures . . . ?'

'Well, you know,' Hardtman said smiling, 'there is some room for doubt about Miss Bentley's general reliability.'

Hardtman had thought that he would be able to turn the questioning back to the subject he was there to talk about, but these reporters seemed unwilling to let go; they had got him there, a person connected in some way with national security, a Presidential adviser, and though he had only held his appointment since the beginning of the year, they were holding him personally responsible for the infiltration of the government by spies and subversives. Were there more? There were stories that the government was lousy with spies and homosexuals. What measures were being taken? Were our atom secrets safe? Was anything safe?

'Really, this is not my area. You should ask Mr Hoover about all this.'

'Mr Hoover is not here. You are, Mr Hardtman.'

'I am beginning to regret it. Look – I just got here, let me catch my breath, gentlemen. You think somebody might get me a drink?' Nobody moved. The faces around him were set. This was just another trick of officialdom for avoiding their questions. Looking around for some way to get out of this . . . no sign of the Vice-President Hettie –

nobody to help him – he suddenly spotted Joannie Fontanez and signalled to her.

'Get me a drink, will you?' he called to her. Her eyes were the first friendly eyes he had seen for ten minutes.

'Dry Martini?' she mimed back, and he nodded.

As she pushed her way through the other journalists to bring him the drink, the tight circle around him was eased a little. Taking the dry Martini from her, he said, 'How about getting me out of this?' He had hardly expected her to act so fast or so effectively. Before anyone else could speak, she said, 'Mr Hardtman, your home-town is New York, isn't it? I'm sure we all want to hear from you how you are finding life in the capital?'

Amid the groans and disgusted murmurs of the other journalists – what a woman's question! – Hardtman shot Joannie Fontanez a look of gratitude and began to answer. He took his time, elaborating on the advantages and disadvantages of life in the two cities, and whenever any of the other journalists sought to cut him short he ignored the interruption and just carried on. When he seemed to be running out of things to say, the heaven-sent Miss Fontanez was ready with another question.

'Mr Hardtman, how would you rate the way women dress in Washington, compared with New York?' 'And speaking as the husband of one of Washington's foremost hostesses . . .' And did he think . . . ? In this way she lightly and laughingly spun out the remainder of the time before dinner, not letting any of her male colleagues get a word in edgeways. When they tried to interrupt her, she said so charmingly, and with such a lovely smile, 'Could I finish, please?' that they hadn't the heart to persist: they were in their tuxedos and this was a social occasion, and so Hardtman got by until the guests were asked to be seated.

'You were just wonderful,' he told Miss Fontanez as the circle around him broke up.

'So were you,' she said. Everybody was moving towards where the seating plan was displayed on an easel.

'Don't leave me,' he told her, 'I might need you again.'

She smiled back at him, and waited. Julian had re-joined

them, and now Hettie Cooper came over and said in her bossy way, 'Dr Blake . . . and you –' she addressed Joannie Fontanez in the manner of an officer handing out marching orders to an enlisted man, 'are at table "F". Mr Hardtman, you are over here . . .'

'I think it might be better,' Hardtman said, 'if you put my guests at the same table as me.'

This suggestion appeared to dismay Hettie Cooper; her face which normally sagged in many places, under the eyes, below the chin, and around the nostrils, fell still further, and she seemed to be quietly choking.

Regaining control over herself, she said with an abrasive little laugh: 'We only calculated on your bringing one guest, Mr Hardtman. And since Dr Blake and Miss . . . Miss . . . this young woman appear to be together, I figured they would prefer to sit together.'

'Well, you can seat them together, *with me*,' Hardtman said. 'What's your problem, Miss Cooper?'

'There isn't room, at the top table, for an extra person,' she said hoarsely. 'The seating arrangements have all been made . . .' There was one long top table, facing a dozen or so smaller round tables.

'It looks a long enough table,' Hardtman said, 'I am sure you can squeeze in one more person.'

'It is not only a question of that,' Hettie Cooper hissed.

'No?' Something about Hettie Cooper annoyed Hardtman, made him dig his heels in. 'Then what is it a question of, may I ask?'

'Of seniority, Mr Hardtman,' Hettie Cooper said. 'This young woman . . .'

'Her name is Miss Fontanez . . .'

'Well, Miss Fontanez does not have the seniority to sit at the top table.'

Hardtman looked at the top table where senior members of the Press Club were now taking their places, and then looked at Hettie Cooper, and said: 'From what I can see, the people you've put at the table with me have got a little too much seniority. I would appreciate it if you would seat Dr Blake and Miss Fontanez with me . . .' And with-

223

out waiting for her concurrence he motioned to Julian and Miss Fontanez to be seated on his left. There was consternation at this, but Hardtman chose not to let himself become aware of the muttered conference behind his back. It went on for some time, without being resolved, and then out of the corner of his eye he saw Hettie Cooper bending down and speaking sternly in Joannie Fontanez's ear. No question, she was asking her to leave the table. This infuriated Hardtman. It seemed to him that from the moment of his arrival he had received nothing but rudeness. He was a man who, while remaining icily calm on the surface, could take deep offence at some small discourtesy. And seeing what was happening, that Miss Cooper could dare to go counter to his expressed wishes – the wishes of the guest of honour – he began to rise and said with a smile, in a voice loud enough for everyone in the immediate vicinity to hear: 'Since I see you are having problems seating my guests, I think they and I had better go and have dinner somewhere else.' He remained standing while Hettie Cooper's face fell as far as it could fall. For a long moment she called Hardtman's bluff and only when he began to move back his chair did she accept the *fait accompli*.

Realizing the position he had put her in, Hardtman said to Miss Fontanez, when he had sat down again, 'I hope I'm not going to get you in bad trouble by doing this . . .'

'Well,' she said, 'I *am* a new member and I guess I am not supposed to get to sit at the top table next to the guest of honour *that* fast.'

'That's where life is so unfair,' he agreed with her, 'the pretty girl always gets ahead of the line. Think of it as helping me out.' And he added in a lower voice. 'The prospect of talking to Miss Cooper all evening was more than I could take, but I'm sorry if it means I'm getting you in trouble with your colleagues. If *you* would rather move . . .'

'No, no,' she said. 'It doesn't bother me. I don't care. I prefer to sit here with you.' She gave him a smile.

Hardtman had a sense of having won. Hettie Cooper was not a sufficiently tough adversary for her defeat to give him more than a slight frisson of satisfaction, but even so, he felt good. You might have thought that he had engaged in a bar-room brawl for possession of this girl. In order to make things easier for her, he now set out to make amends to Miss Cooper. He was a man who could be generous towards someone he had defeated.

He picked at the food. It was never a good thing to make a speech on a full stomach. He did, however, drink a little wine and, whether it was due to this, or to his victory over Miss Cooper, he was beginning to feel quite high, and he flirted with the girl. At one point she asked him what being an adviser to the President involved. He replied that it was akin to putting a message in a bottle and casting it upon the high seas, and she laughed warmly and disbelievingly at this, and said she could not believe that he could ever be subject to such storm-tossed helplessness.

'Really, what's he like?' she inquired earnestly.

'Very democratic. "Now this here is Joe, Your Royal Highness,"' Hardtman said doing a passable imitation of Truman's voice. '"Best darn chauffeur you can find, Your Highness. Never once got us one of them tickets you hear tell about . . ."' She let out a peal of appreciative laughter. It was necessary to encourage her evident responsiveness to him, since he was not at all sure about these other journalists and it would help to have one friend in the audience. Her flashing eyes, and quick attentiveness to whatever he said, would put him in the right frame of mind for his speech, make him more amusing. Since he tended to be very sober in his public manner, there was no harm in having another glass of wine. He was feeling very relaxed when it was time for him to get up and speak.

He made one or two mild jokes, which evoked no more than titters – the rest of the audience was not nearly so responsive to him as Joannie Fontanez – and then turned to his text. This began by describing the events that led up to Pearl Harbour. He told of the note that Secretary of State Hull had sent to the Japanese calling upon them to withdraw their forces from China and Indochina in return for a promise to unfreeze Japanese funds and resume trade. He summarized the Japanese reply which, in effect, by demanding US acquiescence in further Japanese conquests, amounted to a declaration of war. He described the scene in the White House when Roosevelt and Harry Hopkins together read the 13th part of the intercepted message to the Japanese Ambassador in Washington, and the events of the following morning when the 14th part of the message was intercepted, decoded and translated into English, and how several people saw the reference to a 1 p.m. Sunday delivery time as meaningful. But, and now he came to his thesis, no decisive action was taken in response to this clear warning. And he went on to describe the series of blunders that resulted in General George Marshall's warning cable being delivered two hours after the Japanese planes had released their bombs and torpedoes, and were heading back to base.

Having described the historical events from which his thesis had been derived, Hardtman next began to develop his own ideas. Some of the ideas were quite complex, and he felt a slackening of the audience's interest. As he expounded on the need for a profile of the enemy and a plurality of options, he saw people lighting cigarettes and looking around. But he stuck doggedly to his text, and pressed on into even more abstract territory. He was now describing the different stages of a crisis, and how they could be classified on an ascending scale of seriousness; he was showing that by the correct use of such a scale it was possible for Intelligence to determine how near a country was to war at a given time. On this basis, on the morning of December 7th, 1941, it should have been possible to see that all the options, for both sides, had run out, and that war was the inevitable next step.

Hardtman could see that he had lost his audience: they had drunk cocktails before dinner, wine with it, and liqueurs after, and they were in no mood for such theories. They were not exactly antagonistic, some were nodding in vague agreement, but their expressions were vacant. Julian had said that his speech could perhaps be more colourful, and here was the proof. The audience was bored. He saw himself momentarily through their eyes – a rather dry, remote, colourless State functionary, lacking the gift of communication that endeared a handful of his colleagues to the Press. These others gave reporters the stuff of their bread and butter, gave them stories, quotes, headlines. Whereas he gave them only colourless theories. He glanced towards Miss Fontanez, and caught her blinking rapidly as she felt his eyes upon her, altering her expression to one of deep attentiveness. But the truth was she had been bored, too. He had lost her as well. He continued reading from his prepared text, occasionally looking to her for a guideline; he could see he was over her head. He saw in Joannie Fontanez what he had also seen in his daughter: a sense of obligation to appear interested, when, of course, she was not. Something that had been high in him and rising before the speech craved the fascinated attention he had been able to evoke briefly in the eyes of this girl. He wanted to be colourful.

He looked up suddenly from his text, abandoning what was left of his theory. Nobody would realize, or care, that the argument had not been completed, the point not finally proven.

'Could be,' he said, 'that we are now, once more, in a brink of war situation. You hear talk of a nuclear Pearl Harbour.' The fidgeting in the audience ceased: he had their attention now. 'In some quarters,' he went on, 'it is seriously being propounded that this time we should become the perpetrators of a sneak attack. It now has fancier names. It is variously called "preventive war", a "pre-emptive first strike" or "getting it over with while we are ahead".' The journalists had put down their brandy glasses and were making notes on menus, the backs of envelopes, their gilt-edged invitation cards. Cigars had been put down on ashtrays or in the saucers of coffee cups.

'Of course, it does not escape my notice that we currently find ourselves in a dangerous situation in the world, and have to be ready for anything, but our being ready to defend ourselves is a very different thing from the proposition: let's smash 'em now before *they* are ready to attack

us. That kind of response has been called wargasm . . .'
They were all scribbling away now. A photographer had
come up to the top table and took a picture. Hardtman,
dazzled by the magnesium flash, turned his head and found
himself looking into the eyes of Miss Fontanez. She looked
flushed – an appropriate response to being so close to a
newsmaker. 'In the throes of such "wargasm" one has no
options – wild instinct prevails . . .' Miss Fontanez was
looking at him hard. The photographer took another
photograph. Oh, yes, this was being colourful. This was
copy.

'Now those who advocate this kind of war,' Hardtman
went on, 'justify it on the grounds that our system of values
is threatened and must be defended at all costs, or our
kind of society will disappear. What these people lose sight
of is that in waging such a "preventive war" we would
have become the new barbarians, and by our action would
already have destroyed all those values and principles in
defence of which we were purportedly taking up arms.'

Now he could see the headlines that he was in the course
of making:

PRESIDENT'S AIDE CONDEMNS PRE-EMPTIVE STRIKE AS
SNEAK ATTACK INCOMPATIBLE WITH AMERICAN IDEALS.

So this was all it took to be colourful, the utterance of a
few home truths, the abandonment of cautionary language,
a slight degree of over-simplification and over-statement.
If the Boss were to repudiate his speech it would sound like
an endorsement of preventive war, and so he would not be
able to do that.

As reporters left the room to phone over their stories,
he sat down to warm applause from those who remained.
Whatever the journalists might think of the substance of
what he had said, they approved of a man who was good
copy. Hardtman found himself the recipient of the kind of
attention that is accorded to somebody who has made
news: he was asked questions, by those gathered around
him, about his background, his private life, his views on a

variety of matters. He was considered newsworthy because he had used the word 'wargasm'.

After he had dealt with these supplementary questions, he said to Julian and Miss Fontanez, 'Why don't you come and have dinner with me?'

'Isn't that what we just did?' she asked.

'Well, you may have eaten, but I didn't,' Hardtman said.

'What we ate was not very good,' Julian said. 'Hotel food never is.'

'You'll join me? You could have some oysters.'

Julian was a night bird and so did not mind extending the evening, and Miss Fontanez it appeared did not mind either.

It had become a clear warm night. The town's energy could be felt. Seeing the great leaps of light all around, Hardtman thought undoubtedly this city was at its best at night, when you did not see the human loss, but only the electric illuminations.

When they were at the restaurant and seated, Hardtman said, 'The food is so good here, I am going to insist that you have something more than just oysters. This place really is an experience.' He studied the menu, which was written in mauve ink in an elaborate French hand, the majuscules all running to lavish curlicues. 'Now if you want something light you could have the *truite au bleu au pebre d'ase*. With a *quenelle de foie gras* to start. If I can tempt you to something more serious ...' His eye was making its knowledgeable way through great gastronomic intricacies. 'Well, a *demi-poulet farnese à la broche* ... or ... now this is really something ... *Ballotine de Lièvre* ...'

'What's that?' Miss Fontanez wanted to know.

'Hare.'

She turned up her nose at this.

'They marinade it in brandy and oil and spiced salt, cover it in game stuffing and chopped truffles. Add the hare's blood for thickening ...'

'Not for me,' she said, 'I am not that adventurous food-wise ...'

229

'You disappoint me,' Hardtman said. 'I'm going to have it. You sure I can't tempt you? ...' From the way her eyes rose responsively to his it seemed he could have tempted her to anything, had he but persisted; however, seeing her waver he said quickly, 'Don't let me force you. Have what you want.'

'Some oysters, I guess,' she said, 'since I have already eaten once tonight ...'

'A dozen bluepoints?'

Julian also chose oysters, and faced by such frugality, Hardtman felt compelled to resist the hare and to choose instead the quenelle, followed by the trout. The wine he ordered was a Meursault '46.

They sat on maroon plush, a welcome breeze came in through the open window, there were candles on the tables: Hardtman was in the ambience of his youth. He felt oddly free of ties and burdens, having become a risk-taker ... Where is your middle of the road now, faintly brushing thighs with this really very pretty girl that Julian had brought but, fortunately, did not appear to be at all possessive about? There was ample room in their corner for the proper separation of strangers, but she was making no effort to move away. When he spoke, she looked at Hardtman through a half curtain of dark hair and in her eyes he read the soft message of feminine compliance. She was going along with whatever he proposed; would have been ready, at a pinch, to eat hare cooked in its own blood ... She would resist nothing he suggested, he could see. Some time in the course of the evening, perhaps when she responded to his appeal and brought him a dry Martini and then asked those friendly questions, she had come to be with him. Just as well that Julian did not mind. But then he knew so many girls and was presumably not involved with all of them. There was certainly no indication that he objected to the intimacy that was clearly developing between her and Hardtman. Quite the contrary, he appeared amused – and even pleased. His sociability was gratified. He was always eager to bring people together.

They did indeed give the appearance of having taken to

each other very quickly, so quickly that Hardtman had scarcely been aware of its happening, and now there was no need to speak of it: the outcome seemed already a *fait accompli*. When he rested his hand lightly on her thigh, there was no question of an advance that might have been rejected. A little later, when he casually held her hand, it was on the basis of the tacit understanding that had already taken effect. He wondered, vaguely, how it had come about, this effortless seduction, and came to the conclusion that it was due to his speech – his colourful speech. That had clinched it. She had responded to the newsmaker. But was he really interested in her? He hardly knew. It was agreeable to have a pretty girl look into his eyes while he ate quenelle of fois gras, it was like having won a prize, a glittering prize. He was glad he did not need to resort to devices with her, since he detested devices, insincerities or pretences of every kind; he need say no more than he was saying – need not actually do anything to ensnare this girl into his bed, if that was where he wished to get her, for already her hand lay lightly in his lap, so intimately as to leave neither of them in any doubt about where all this was leading. Still, he was not at all sure he wanted to go through with it; but it was enjoyable to see how far this little adventure might go. Their knees in nudging rapport, hands and shoulders brushing, it was all very delightful, and spontaneous, and yet while this was going on no commitment had yet taken place; he could still withdraw, even at the last moment – he was a man who habitually asked for aisle seats in the theatre, so that he could leave early, if he wished. He was not a man of ungovernable passions – not an extremist – but with a hidden vein of sensuality that sometimes was at variance with his natural cautiousness. Tonight he was not himself, his head was turning and he had a sensation of falling: it was not a disagreeable fall now. Falling in love is also a fall of a sort. He did not believe that anything quite so significant was happening to him, or he might have taken flight, but it was a pleasant sensation and it was being experienced in the ambience of his youth. Nice to be able to let the weight of the world

231

drop away, and to feel free. Of course, he was a little drunk by now, not drunk enough to become irresponsible, but sufficiently drunk to feel his binding commitments eased . . . temporarily.

He spoke of himself; of his work; of his belief in a plurality of options, in stages and steps . . . and he felt, afterwards, that he had talked too much. He did not wish her – even if it was only a game – to see him as a lover. He tried to lighten the impression by saying, 'Ah but you must not believe everything I say. Like most men, I'm not entirely to be trusted where women are concerned.'

'Oh I know that,' she had said, in reply.

'Well, as long as you know that.' He was correcting any impression she might have got that he could be expected to behave in a gentlemanly way. That was not his plan.

She smiled unrebukingly – but not approvingly either. She gave away little of herself in words, however much she gave in implicit promises.

'Isn't there anything to which you feel committed?' she asked almost journalistically. He sensed some nuance of criticism in the question.

'Well,' he said, 'the truth is there are very few things I would be ready to die for. Yes, for one's children. That is one absolute commitment, isn't it? And for freedom – it's a word that has become a cliché – from over-use, but the right to exist as oneself is something one would have to defend at any cost, if it were ever threatened again, as it was by the Nazis. But I don't feel committed in any deep way to Harry S. Truman, or any political party, or stance, or to progressive over conservative doctrine, or *vice versa*, or to any of our hallowed institutions, or for that matter to "my country right or wrong". Perhaps because I have lived all over the world, I feel affection for different places, and loyalty: France, England – Italy. Oh many places where I have good friends. I have some good friends in Russia – or had. I don't feel particularly – or exclusively – American, you see . . .'

'A citizen of the world,' she said with that slight hint of

sharpness that he supposed was part of the cynicism of her profession.

He felt uncomfortable about having allowed himself to be drawn out to this degree; his inner thoughts were normally not so readily accessible; where his deepest loyalties lay was something he had not yet resolved for himself, and he regretted having been induced to reveal some aspect of his perplexity to this girl.

'The truth is,' he said, trying to extricate himself from being too serious, 'I am very fond of French cooking, Italian women, English literature, the American form of democratic government, the Staatsoper in Vienna, and the streets of Paris, Rome and New York, and if you found one country that combined all these things, I should gladly become a patriot for it, but failing that I have to be ... what I am.'

She did not take him up on any of this, whatever she may have thought; she had eyes of changeable colour, a wide mouth, a strong nose and ink on her fingers; she was a working girl, instinctive, no intellectual, and her response to him was evidently not based on his giving the right answers. Her hand had remained lightly in his while he was talking. She thought his view was based upon his class and position and wealth, but she did not say that; she let it pass with a light remark. 'You want to have it all, don't you?'

Again he felt he was being criticized, no matter how gently, though the pressure of her fingers could perhaps give a totally different meaning to her words.

'Yes,' he said, choosing this other meaning. She laughed up into his eyes while their conspiratorial fingers entwined upon the maroon plush, and the candle flame flickered inside its milky glass chimney.

'Now that's not such a bad thing, it's in the American tradition to want it all. Of course, I know it's not the Eastern view, but Julian is marvellously tactful at reconciling those sort of opposites.'

'Zen Buddhism tells you to reduce desires,' Julian replied in his most casually enigmatic way.

'I must say I haven't noticed *you* doing that, Julian.'

'Ah – you don't know what mine were like before,' he countered. 'I think it's a matter of keeping within reason . . . in all things . . . don't you?'

'I think I keep my desires within reason, being a reasonable man,' Hardtman said.

'Not *too* reasonable,' she said in the same playful vein.

'Why? Do you care to have *unreasonable* demands made of you?' To which she just responded with an intimate glance and a laugh. In the service of sexual arousal, entrenched positions are lightly sacrificed, and Joannie Fontanez was reasonable enough not to pursue the matter of his basic commitments, and he, for his part, chose not to go into what she had meant exactly by her original question.

He did, however, find out some things about her; that she lived – alone – in a walk-up between Central Park West and Columbus Avenue, in the Seventies; one of those large brownstones converted into apartments for bachelor living. She had formerly worked as a secretary and research-assistant to a successful journalist; had picked up the basic elements of her profession from him and from a night-school course in magazine writing; she lived precariously – but seemingly unpanicked – from assignment to assignment, filling in with research jobs when she couldn't get writing jobs. She was interested in Yoga, physical exercise, astrology, and the cinema.

'What sort of articles,' he asked her, 'do you write? The woman's angle?'

'Oh sometimes,' she said, 'if I need to, but mostly it's – crime.'

'Crime?'

'The man I used to work for, he had lots of those sort of connections, in the underworld. He had a line through to them, and I kind of got into that too.'

'Sounds like tough work.'

'Yes,' she conceded, 'but I like it. It's interesting and it sure beats covering hat shows.' She tossed her mass of full

234

dark hair with disdain for the aviary on the opposite side of the room.

'Isn't it dangerous?'

'I can take care of myself.'

She had a blend of toughness and sweetness. Her chosen profession had not yet started to turn her into a Hettie Cooper; so far she had not become hardened; at the same time she was no wilting violet – he recalled how she had got him off the hook at the dinner reception, taking over the questioning and not letting any of the men cut in. And he could imagine her in working clothes of slacks and boots and duffle coat and leather ear muffs, prowling around in snow and slush and bitter winds in the less salubrious areas of New York, making her pick-ups of information at Automats and street corners.

'What kind of crime stories?' he asked.

'Last one I did was about the inter-state white slave deal . . . Look, I don't always do things as tough as *that*,' she said quickly, playing herself down. 'Right now I'm putting together a piece about women spies . . . to tie in with Elizabeth Bentley? Well, you know, the Mata Haris and what they are about . . . I've got hold of a tame psychiatrist to say what it means to women being spies and using men in that kind of deceiving way . . .'

'And what are you about, Joannie?' he asked as she lit another cigarette; she had been smoking continuously, lighting up between courses.

'Me?' she said. 'I'm about living my life, that's all.'

'I think you smoke too much, Joannie.'

'Yes, I know.'

'You're a lovely girl.'

'Well, I'm not *that*, that's what I'm not about,' she said with the first show of sharpness he had found in her. 'I'm not a *girl*. That's so patronizing – "you're a lovely girl". That's such sugar. It's like calling an old Negro *boy*. I'm twenty-seven years old, I've been married – so don't call me a girl. *Please*.'

'What should I call you?'

235

'What do you think I *am*? Don't you think I'm a woman?'

'Well, you're a lovely woman, even when you get mad.'

He soothed her with his hand, which she had not removed from his during her outburst. It was not serious, only a kind of bargaining, a statement of what she would not give up for him: her womanhood. She would not be his little girl. He liked her for that. She had spirit, and strength. A broken marriage behind her. And she had not let this experience sour her.

'There's something very free about you,' he said.

'Oh, well, see, I was a troubadour in one of my previous lives.'

'How many have you had?'

'About eight.'

'Does that mean this is your last one?'

'Could be. But I hope not. So many other things I want to be – I'm *curious*.'

With his gift for making any occasion go, Julian adapted himself to the changing circumstances. He was there when he was wanted, and not, when he wasn't. He knew how to absent himself in their presence. He had a knack for tactful self-effacement, and for disappearing expeditiously at the right moment.

Outside the restaurant he waited with them for a cab, and only when they were already inside, did he suddenly say, 'I think I shall walk. It's such a splendid night. And the people I'm staying with don't live far from here. I'll telephone you tomorrow, Bill.' And with that, he walked off, fingers combing his hair back over the ears, patent leather shoes glittering through the garbage of the sidewalk.

Hardtman told the taxi driver: '59th and Fifth,' and then turning to Joannie asked quietly, 'Will you stay with me tonight?' Only when she had nodded her agreement, did he make the instructions more specific and say, 'The Plaza Hotel.'

'I didn't want you to think that I was taking anything for granted,' he explained.

236

'You're very correct,' she said, 'aren't you?'

He smiled in the darkness of the cab and she leaned her head against his shoulder.

As they headed uptown, he again had a sense of being in the ambience of his youth, with the night glitter of Manhattan all around him, like a perpetual Christmas tree for greedy hearts. At this moment something high in him reached out to this girl across the deep chasm of his pessimism, and touched her. It seemed, then, that good luck was possible after all.

He must by now have been fairly pickled, though showing little outward signs of it; there had been the drinks before lunch in the train, the wine with lunch, the dry Martini while shaving, the dry Martinis in the bar of the hotel, the dry Martinis before dinner at the Commodore, the wine with dinner, the brandy after, and then the wine and brandies with the second dinner at the French restaurant. Yet he was not in any sense incapable, only more concentrated in his immediate interests and concerns. He was aware of everything he needed to be aware of, but some things simply did not loom so large any longer.

Previously he had always had an apartment or house available to him – even tonight his own house was empty. But he felt he could not go there. Laurene might telephone him at the hotel, and also, adultery in the marital home, amid the dust sheets, seemed more serious than in the ambience of his youth. The desk clerk who handed him his key was, he could have sworn, the same one who had so conspicuously under-reacted when Hardtman had said that his daughter was going to stay the night. And now he was under-reacting again to the arrival on the scene of another 'daughter'. Imperturbability of that order had a collusive connotation.

Walking across the lobby to the lift, Hardtman had the impression, from their strenuously correct expressions, and their deferential 'good nights', that the entire staff of the Plaza Hotel were in league with him.

He did not tip any of them. Decided, instead, to tip

somewhat more handsomely than usual in the morning when his bags were brought down.

It seemed he had got the same expressionless lift boy who had taken him and Debbie up. No inkling of anything entered his unmoving eyes.

He did not switch on any lights as they came into his room; instead, went to the windows, drew back the curtains and opened the french doors to the balcony.

'Oh you have a terrace,' she cried. 'With a view. Isn't that fantastic. It's – *romantic*!'

A neon sign atop a distant roof informed them of the lateness of the hour: 2 a.m. The curve of lights around Central Park lay to their left, and behind were the set-back towers of 1930s apartment buildings, and high above up on the right the gargoyled steeple of the Sherry Netherlands. He stood, next to the girl, beset by a bewildering plurality of options, and let them rapidly diminish to one: took her in his arms and kissed her. After this first intimate contact, he stepped back from her a little and looked at her closely, and she said, smiling, 'Why are you doing this, Mr Hardtman?'

'You're a lovely . . . young *woman*,' he said. 'And I'm very attracted to you, you know.'

'Hmmm,' she mused as he came up close and ran his hand down the side of her linen skirt and then under it along smooth seamless nylon to the provocative bump of a suspender. His touch was light, light as a wish, and fast as wishful thinking he had slipped through all hindrances and in a moment was as sticky-fingered as a small boy in a blackberry bush.

'You been wanting to get in my pants from the moment you saw me,' she said. 'Hmm?'

'What sort of talk is that?' he said, a little breathless at having elicited such a quick and abundant passion with his darting fingers.

He had a sense of everything being possible, as he pulled her about, with a masculine deliberateness that might have been thought lacking in finesse by a young woman of less robust sexuality. But Joannie appeared quite undismayed as her linen skirt was yanked unceremoniously up, and the rest down.

'Oh you *have* got the hots for me,' she purred delighted, her eyes in the semi-dark glowing like a cat's, her buttocks squirming in his open hands.

He did not switch on any of the silk-shaded table lamps when she slipped out of his embrace to go to the bathroom, but waited for her in the dark. Some things were best done in the dark. Then there would be only that crossword puzzle of dark and lit windows as a background to their night's adventure. He wondered if he should undress, but the idea of himself as a naked satyr, pouncing upon her as she emerged from the bathroom, engaged his sense of the absurd, and he limited himself to untying his black bow tie and undoing the top button of his pleated dress shirt, and taking his jacket off.

She was in a slip of lustrous black rayon crepe beruffled with rayon lace at hem and bodice, and she had kept her stockings and suspender belt on, he was glad to see, since such things interested him as much as any man. He wanted to taste some extreme, something befitting a newsmaker and colourful character. And since she was so obedient to his wishes, he took her to the bed and made her kneel and draw up the slip, which she did not seem to mind at all, on the contrary, relished: the blunt language of love. The rayon crepe lay crinkled up on her back, the black elastic suspenders were taut against white thighs: he was enraptured by this bordello scene. She was looking over her shoulder to see how he was appreciating her, and he was moved to rub his face against all that bold flesh: he found her tangy as the English seaside in March, and slick to the tongue as a tasty oyster. Hurriedly he got out of his trousers.

He turned her around, having had his fill of bordello scenes, and came quickly and easily into her, almost without any sensation, and clearing away the tangled damp hair, discovered her face, all aglow and beautiful – with a hint of some exoticism in the curve of cheekbones, the changing deep greenness of the eyes: *un objet trouvé.*

239

'You're beautiful,' he told her with an air of surprise.

'You make me feel beautiful with what you are doing to me,' she said.

It felt to him like being out in soft warm rain that you can barely feel. He had to move very strongly to have any sensation at all – such was the embarrassment of riches that she gave forth. The amount he had drunk dulled his senses; at the same time he felt himself possessed of a ferocious potency. The air-conditioning was on, but even so their bodies sprang moisture wherever they touched and they were slipping and sliding all over each other like oiled wrestlers.

'Oh we're so sweaty,' she gasped, 'so *sweaty*, oh I love it.'

Below his considerable weight, which was not only a weight of pounds but also of years, and of weariness, her face was shining fresh. Some desire to penetrate her even more profoundly made him slip a hand round the back of her and find her there; with a slight quick spreading move-ment she granted him access, and then, with a little wriggle, that was a kind of self-impalement, entry. He had her in a pincer now: she was waiting for the death blow, mouth open, uttering deep, regular cries. *Oh! Oh! Oh!* He had her and was showing her his power. She wanted to touch this power and he came out to lie in the palm of her hand, and let her fingers make him out.

'Oh I love your cock,' she said drawing out the short word to make of it something exotic.

'Look in my eyes the whole time,' he told her. 'No, no, you mustn't look away.' He forced her head back from its twisting and turning so that he could see everything.

'You want to see it,' she said understandingly.

'Yes.'

Hardtman was tireless. He took his time, gorging him-self. There was something about her easy compliance that made every wildness possible. He had a feeling that she would permit anything: but there were some things that, after all, he would not permit himself, and her cries were beginning to worry him – people in the next room might

240

think somebody was being murdered, so he strove to bring her to her peak: it was not easy, at times he thought they were never going to get there. When he was finally successful, he almost at once dropped off.

'Did I fall asleep?' he asked, waking up to find himself still strong within her.

'Yes, for a minute.'

'I dreamt . . .'

'You did?'

'I dreamt I had met this lovely young woman with whom I clicked straight away, and she came back to my hotel with me . . .'

'Doesn't happen in real life,' she said.

'Oh I agree,' he said. 'It was a dream.'

'We make good chemistry together,' she said, reflectively.

All of a sudden she freed herself from him, jumped up off the bed and ran with wavy buttocks out on to the balcony, where she was clearly visible against all the lights stacked in the sky. He came after her, but stayed a little way back.

'Somebody might be looking out of their window,' he said.

'People have got better things to do at night,' she said, stretching. Anyway, so what! All they can see is a nude woman. They can't see your sperm running down my thigh. But I can feel it.'

She giggled and he kissed her neck.

The air was almost as sticky as her body: but now and then there was a sudden gust of cooling currents. She leaned over the coping.

'Wow,' she said, 'it's a long way down,' and turned to face him. Her hair was blowing all over her face on this high balcony. She held herself suddenly between her thighs, while looking at him very directly. She meant it to mean that she was holding him inside her a while longer. Having allowed herself an extra few moments of moist pleasure, and with her eyes still on him, she let her hand go, and gave

241

a little shrug. Then with a kiss to her glistening fingers, and a laugh, she went back inside, got into bed, and quickly was asleep.

He couldn't sleep. He had drunk too much and his stomach was beset by acidy turbulences. And the violence of this love-making, after all the alcohol, had made his heart beat excessively fast. He could not quieten it. But he felt good, exhilarated. He marvelled at Joannie's ability to go to sleep, so easily. He was too high for sleep, and could not come down that fast.

She was lying diagonally and occupying much of his side of the bed, and he kept pushing her more to her side and she kept rolling back, seeking him in her sleep. It seemed she would have liked to sleep in his arms, but it was too hot a night for that, as far as he was concerned. Despite the open french doors and the air conditioning their bodies were shiny with perspiration.

Unable to sleep and beset by a tremendous thirst he went to the pantry kitchen and emptied the ice-making tray into a jug and filled it up with water. He waited a few moments for the chilling to take full effect and when the outside of the jug had turned misty, drank deeply. He had drunk almost a jug of water before his enormous thirst was quenched.

Refreshed, he went to the bathroom and switched on the lights around the mirror and looked at himself. His hair was in disarray, but it was an attractive disarray – not the awkwardly flattened hair of a husband roused yawning from his bed, but the tousled head of the lover. Grey, true, but not unduly so, and not the greyness of middle-age so much as the greyness of the *boulevardier*. He had a self-satisfied look, he could not help noticing.

He would have to try and get some sleep. He took half a tablet of pheno-barbitone (which was not altogether wise after the amount he had drunk, but he was feeling perfectly sober now), and once more pushing Joannie to her side of the bed climbed in next to her and after a while fell asleep.

16

He woke as the sky was just beginning to lighten, rested, not even suffering from a hangover, and priapic – now he did not mind her rolling towards him, and seeking to entangle him, though she was still fast asleep and looked as though she could sleep through till noon. But not he. He was strongly aroused by her sprawling naked form, and eager to have her again – at once. Hoping to awaken her with a kiss, he pressed against her – she smiled faintly in her sleep, and with reflexes that he could not help considering wonderful, opened her legs, but did not wake up. Her position revealed the form of her sex – heavy as a Rouault outline. She had a slight belly, Blue Angel thighs, and miniature breasts. Strange. Part girl, a part woman. Though she wanted to be considered the latter.

He touched her and was rewarded with an immediate gooey flow: what a wonderful service of love she provided day and night, sleeping or awake. Even though she was moving sensuously in her sleep she was not, it seemed, going to wake up unless he did something more drastic, and since he was in the ambience of his youth, why not? Why not indeed! Awakened, finally, she observed with an air of neutrality what he was about; her body, though unmoving, was as fully involved as before, but her head was not, and as soon as he was through she kissed his nose and went back to sleep. Not he.

He went on to the balcony. It was just before dawn and a reddish light was coming out of the eastern sky, from behind the tall buildings. Watching the sunrise in the slow movement of light from place to place he had a curious sense of being no longer, in spirit at least, in the present. He felt himself to be in a scene from his past.

He saw the sun appear as a dark reflection in the black glass of a skyscraper, its light slanting like the struts of a

suspension bridge between the banks of the metrollops –
as he had once dubbed it with youthful punster's delight.
Ah! Memories of the metrollops. His other life. Before
becoming husband, father and solid citizen.

There was nothing for him to do for the moment, except
wait for Joannie to wake up, which could take forever. She
clearly did not have his restless need to be at the office
early. Being a freelance, she could presumably choose her
work hours, and was used to sleeping in the daytime.

In a sudden efflorescence, a section of the sun became
visible between the jostling East Side skyscrapers, as if
emerging from an eclipse, and a fierce blaze of direct light
abruptly struck down like something from a ray gun in a
comic book. He had to look the other way to regain his
sight. Sunlight trickling and cascading down the buildings
had formed pools in the still-dark crevice of 59th Street,
where litter and dust were briefly stirred by quickly expended puffs of air.

He watched the city come rosily into existence, its different parts emerging progressively out of the penumbra,
in a haphazard dispersal of dawn light. Slowly the parts
began to fit together, making larger parts – water towers,
sky signs, roof gardens, green rooftops and campaniles and
Gothic battlements and latticed attics and ugly chimney
stacks: the mixture as before. The final coming together
of the parts happened in fast-motion and there it all was.

It was time now to go back inside. He looked outside his
room to see if the *Times* was there, but it was still too early,
so he bathed and dressed while wistfully indulging in
memories of the metrollops. By the time he was ready the
paper was outside. His speech had been given front page
treatment – an account under a single column heading ran
for three or four inches on the front page, and continued
inside the paper. Bill Hardtman, the report said, was a man
who looked at an action not just in terms of the immediate
advantage to be gained, but from the standpoint of its
moral justification and ultimate value.

With mounting impatience he whiled away the remaining time until nine o'clock and then dialled room service and ordered breakfast; this was about as long as he was ready to delay the process of getting up. As the waiter came in and arranged the breakfast trolley he painstakingly avoided looking at the evidently naked young woman in the bed, minimally covered by the crumpled sheet that Hardtman had drawn over her just a moment earlier, but already somewhat dislodged: there was still enough bare back and mussed hair visible to suggest a wild night. Hardtman found it vaguely gratifying to be thought of by this waiter as a debaucher of young women: someone who takes a room for one and orders breakfast for two. He tipped him half a dollar (which was probably too much, but he could hardly have given a quarter in such sybaritic circumstances) and got back a slight nod that wasn't quite a bow from the downcast head.

Joannie was finally waking up, stretching, yawning, pushing sleep out of her eyes and pores and toes. Her limbs curled and twisted under the sheet, and finally pushed it off her. Her body gave off a rich warm smell that recalled the night. Dressed, shaved and lotioned for the day, he found this disturbing, a temptation to backsliding.

He said, 'I ordered breakfast for you.' He lifted silver lids. 'Poached eggs. Toast. And coffee.'

'Coffee,' she said. 'Lots of coffee.' She groped muzzily around for her cigarettes, eyes barely open. 'I need plenty of black coffee to get my eyes open in the morning. Christ, what time is it?'

'It's after nine,' he said.

'You mean it's only nine? You woke me up at nine a.m.?'

'I'm sorry.'

She had found her cigarettes; she lit one, drew the smoke deeply in, with need, coughed a little, and with the nicotine jolt to her system began to come back to life. He gave her the coffee and she gulped it down.

'You got to not mind me,' she said, 'I need a little time . . .'

245

He smiled, and told her to take all the time she needed, but dazed as she was she saw from his manner that there was a limit now to how much of it she could take.

'Your eggs,' he said. 'I hope this is how you like them.' He had finished breakfast and was dabbing his mouth with a napkin.

'I like them sunny-side up,' she said. 'Is there more coffee?'

'There's a little.'

'Not enough,' she said, seeing what was left. 'I've got to have more than that. Think you could ask them to send up another pot? – they never give you enough coffee in hotels.'

He had a vision of her waking up with other men in other hotel rooms and complaining about the insufficiency of the coffee. He dialled room service and told them to send up another large pot of coffee for two. While they waited for it to arrive she ate, soaking the cold toast in the cold poached eggs, sitting up naked on the edge of the bed, girlishly small above, but with broad womanly hips and an enticing little bulge of belly fat that added a touch of opulence to her lower body. He noted all this down in his mind, to add to his memories of the metrollops. This morning was different from last night – without the driving force of desire, he did not know quite what to say to her. Fortunately, her still half-asleep condition obviated the necessity of making continuous conversation.

When the room waiter knocked on the door, and Joannie either out of carelessness or forgetfulness made no move to cover herself, Hardtman went to the door and took the tray with the coffee. He poured her a large steamy cup and she gulped it down, and said: 'Thanks, saves my life.' She had stubbed out her first cigarette in a saucer and was now putting another in her mouth.

'You smoke too much,' he said.

'I think we already had that conversation.'

'When have you got to be at work, Joannie?'

'My time's my own . . .'

'Lucky for you . . .'

After another pause, during which she was compelled

246

to interpret his silence, she said, 'But your time of course isn't, I realize that. Are you in a terrific hurry . . .?'

'I have to be back in Washington today.'

'Won't take long to get myself put together – once I'm awake. And you've just woken me up. Give me a cigarette and coffee and I'm like Popeye after his spinach.'

He laughed. 'Please, Joannie. Don't feel I'm rushing you.'

She sent him an inquiring look across the distance since last night, and getting back no more than a wan morning-after smile, gave a slight shrug and went to the bathroom. Since she had not bothered to close the door, he could still see her as she showered and performed her toilette. Concentrating on that, she did not look at him. When she asked if she could borrow his toothbrush, she saw the moment of hesitation on his part; she laughed and started to say, 'Considering . . .' but did not press home the point, and used her finger instead of a brush. She then splashed after shave over herself, put on eye make-up and some foundation cream. Next she put on her suspender belt and stockings and he was back in his dream and could not resist going to her and running his hand (one last time) through her sprouting bush, redolent now of his after shave; this crude familiarity she let pass without a word or any kind of reaction. She had become very matter-of-fact, and practical, and even while he was fondling her in this way she was proceeding with powdering her face and applying lipstick.

'If you're all through,' she said, patting him away and picking up her panties and slipping them on. Bra, slip and shirtwaist followed, and then the skirt, and finally she stepped into high-heeled shoes and became three inches taller. After a final clinical look at herself in the mirror, and a little toss of her hair, which was again partly curtaining her face, she turned to him and said, 'See, didn't I say I was quick?'

He did not quite know what to say. He had a feeling of flatness, his emotions were muffled by lack of sleep and an incipient hangover.

247

'You really are a very lovely girl . . . sorry, woman,' he said.

'It's all right, say what you are used to, if you are used to "girls". It's no big deal.' She thought, and since this seemed to be the time for goodbyes she said, 'You're . . . well . . . not a *lovely* man exactly . . . but someone special and I'm really proud and happy I got to know you a little.'

'Oh come on,' he said, a little embarrassed by this.

'No, I mean it,' she said. 'I'm nobody. But you're . . . well . . .' She laughed. 'You know what they call you, some of the Press boys? The President's worrier.'

'What do they mean by it?'

'Like old-time emperors used to have food-tasters? Mr Truman never has a sleepless night by getting other people not sleeping. Like you. The President's worrier. It suits you – that's how I shall think of you. And what am I to you? If you don't mind me asking?'

'My adventure.'

'Oh I like that. You're my worrier and I'm your adventure.'

'You were a wonderful adventure,' he said. She noted the use of the past tense.

'Anything I can . . .' He stopped, not quite knowing how to finish. 'I would have liked to have given you something . . . as a memento of our . . adventure . . .' Again he broke off. There really was no way of ending this, whatever you chose to call it, without striking some regrettable notes. 'You know what I mean to say, Joannie.'

'Sort of.' They looked at each other. 'What time is your train?'

'There's one at eleven.'

'You should be able to make that.' She looked briskly around to see if she had left anything of hers, and then gathered up her large handbag and hung it over the crook of her arm. 'Looks like I'm all set . . .'

He came close to her.

'You're a really fantastic girl.'

'Oh I dunno about *really fantastic*, just *average fantastic* . . .'

248

Her eyes had the hard brightness of decorated enamel. They were all grey this morning, with no green at all. There was no plea in them whatsoever, no melting feminine appeal. Only a kind of camaraderie. We're both in this together, they said.

'Well, so long, Bill. See you.'

'Yes, so long, Joannie.'

He watched her go. Well, it was best this way. Like this there would be no complications – just a warm memory. He felt very warm towards Joannie Fontanez; he was full of admiration for her sturdy self-reliance, making out in such a competitive world as New York journalism. She had not sought to get anything out of him – not even the small advantage that she could perhaps gain in her profession by having access to the President's worrier.

She was going down the long corridor, doing her wavy high-heeled walk, and she did not glance back – though she must have sensed that he was still looking at her. At the lift she did half turn, it would have been unnatural to keep her back to him, and seeing him still at the door, she waved. That was all. He watched her get into the lift and then watched the lights of the floors flash on the down arrow.

He thought: I have let her go. I don't even have her address or telephone number. In a few moments she would be in the lobby and leaving the hotel and he'd never see her again. What a fool! What kind of self-punishing stupidity was it to let her go, just like that? Absurd not to have taken her phone number. He could presumably find her again through Julian, but how awkward to have to go through him. Why not take her phone number at least? There was no compulsion to use it. But it wouldn't be ending there and then, finally. He'd be leaving himself some options open. He believed in a plurality of options, didn't he?

Quickly, he went back in his room, picked up the phone and dialled for the bell captain. It seemed like ages before there was an answer.

'This is Mr Hardtman. There's a young lady just getting

out of the elevator, darkish hair . . . attractive, about twenty eight . . .'

'The young lady already left,' the bell captain said.

'You know who I'm talking about?'

'Yes sir. The young lady that was with you last night.' So despite their air of not noticing, of course they noticed everything.

'Yes.'

'She left a coupla minutes ago, Mr Hardtman.'

Hardtman didn't give himself time to think.

'She's probably at the entrance waiting for a cab. Or if she's outside, she can't have gone far. Ask her to come to the phone, will you . . . don't let her leave.' He spoke with enforced calm.

'Do my best for you, Mr Hardtman,' the bell captain said uncertainly.

'Do better than that,' Hardtman instructed, 'and there'll be something for you.'

Holding on to the phone, Hardtman felt undecided about where his true hopes lay: it'll be best if she has left, he told himself, much the best, but could not be sure that in telling himself this he wasn't just protecting himself against disappointment. The truth is – he also told himself, since he was not a man to shrink from giving himself contradictory advice – there is absolutely no reason (except Laurene! *Laurene!*) why I shouldn't see her again. What harm would it do Laurene? Joannie had demonstrated her emotional strength, had shown she could make a clean break without demur. Well, what if the clean break were to be tomorrow instead of today? That would give them another whole day, and night. And no harm done. And some happiness. Which, of course, was a classic piece of adulterer's sophistry, but so what?

'Hi, Bill.' Her voice was light. He kept his light too.

'I was afraid you might have gone,' he said.

'I was waiting for a taxi.'

He thought: I am forty-five years old, how many good years do I have left? Cautiousness is for the young, who can ruin their lives, or refrain from doing so. But I have

250

already had everything, what have I got to lose? He also told himself that this was just greediness, that he had known a dozen girls like Joannie Fontanez. Why did he need to know one more? *Because you have nothing to lose – except an experience you could have had and didn't. You are only worried about upsetting the status quo, but that will be upset in any case, sooner or later. Death is no respecter of the status quo.*

'I just had an idea,' he said lightly, very lightly, with all the lightness of a liar. 'What are you doing for lunch?'

There was a silence, as she thought about this. 'I guess,' she replied after a while, 'nothing I couldn't get out of, if I wanted to.'

'Want to!' he urged lightly, and waited breathless, his heart speeding again.

'Is that a good idea?'

'*I* think so.'

This time she was silent so long he thought she might have put the phone down and gone away.

'Hmm, Joannie?' he asked softly, after having given her all this time, pressuring her with the subtlest of intonations.

'I thought you had to be back in Washington?'

'They'll manage without me one more day.'

She was still far from certain.

'I guess I could make a phone call.'

'Make a phone call?'

'I'd have to get out of something.'

'Can you do that? I want to see you Joannie, I want to ... see you.'

'I think I could get out of it,' she said, without sounding too convinced.

'Will you?'

'Yes, I'll try.'

It was as near to a promise as he could get her to make.

'Where do you want to eat?' he asked her.

'Oh – anywhere.'

'How about "21"?'

'That's not *anywhere*, but I like it.' She hesitated. 'Isn't everybody going to see us there? Or doesn't that matter?'

'You're the Press,' he said, 'you're interviewing me. About my speech last night. All right?'

'Check,' she said with a laugh.

'Quarter to one?'

'Make it quarter past . . .'

'Check.'

As soon as he had hung up, some of his cautiousness returned. Would someone in his position give lunch to a reporter at '21'? A pretty female reporter. Being realistic, he had to recognize that she was simply not important enough, in her profession, to be given that sort of treatment, and people would jump to conclusions about why he was taking her to lunch. He was known at '21' – and so was Laurene. He was likely to run into people. He couldn't introduce her as Miss Fontanez of the *Times* or the *Post*. He'd have to say: this is Miss Fontanez, who is a freelance journalist and is interviewing me for – for what? It sounded defensive, put like that, whatever she was interviewing him for. *The Ladies Home Journal*? *Paris-Match*? Suppose somebody started speaking to her in French. What foolishness to have invited her to '21' – had he sought to overcome her hesitation with the name of an illustrious restaurant? Now he did not even know where he could get hold of her to change the venue. Sheer stupidity.

He telephoned Laurene.

'How did it go?' she asked.

'I think it went quite well,' he said.

'I read the report,' she said, 'in the *Washington Post*. I thought you were going to talk about Pearl Harbour. You did stick your neck out, didn't you?'

'Didn't you think my comments were appropriate, that they arose out of any historical consideration of Pearl Harbour?'

'I guess so, but is the Boss going to think they were appropriate?'

'I don't give a damn if he does or not. I was speaking as a private individual, I was expressing my own views. Actually, the Boss is broadly in agreement with the sentiments I expressed.'

'Bill, dear, I think what you said was great . . . I'm just a little worried that it might get you in trouble.'

'It's a risk I have to take.'

'Well, sure, sure . . . If that's how you feel. What train are you getting?'

'I'm staying another night,' he said. 'There has been some reaction to my speech, and one or two Press people want to talk to me, and I thought it might be best to clarify my position here and now – just to set the record straight. Rather than have to do it in Washington through official channels.'

'You think that's the way to do it, Bill?'

'I'll see how it goes. Telephone you later to tell you which train I'm getting.'

'All right, darling. And, sweetheart, don't work all the time. Have a little fun, too. How's Julian?'

'In good form. We're going to have lunch at "21". With one of his wowy girls.'

'Well, that sounds fun. Have a good lunch.'

After that he phoned Julian and informed him of the lunch arrangements.

'Joannie's also coming,' he said. 'She's – delightful.'

'Isn't she.'

'Don't be late,' Hardtman said, 'or I shall get a reputation for wining and dining lovely young women. That does no harm to a man of your Bohemian character, but in my position, things being what they are in Washington, and the Boss being who he is . . .'

'Not to worry, Bill. I shall take care that nobody gets any wrong ideas.'

After this conversation he sat still for a moment, marvelling briefly at his new-found capacity for duplicity. He was discovering unsuspected sides to his character.

Next he phoned his secretary in Washington, and asked if anybody had been trying to reach him this morning, in connection with his speech. No, she said, nobody. Well, it was a little early yet. It would take a while for a reaction to develop and harden.

'I have to stay on another night,' he told Mrs Taylor. 'I'll be leaving word with the hotel switchboard, where I am. I'll be lunching at "21".'

'Do you have the telephone number of that, sir?'

'Yes.' He looked in his book and gave her the number. Well, sometimes openness was the best possible cover.

Now all that remained was for him to book a table, and this done he found himself unexpectedly free until lunch, an unusual state of affairs for him. He had brought no work with him, since he had not expected to be staying. Had not even brought a book to read.

So having time to kill, he went down and bought the newspapers in the hotel bookstall and sat down in the Palm Court to read them. Most had given prominence to his speech. There was, of course, no editorial comment yet. Too early for that. The attacks and accusations – soft on Communism, a pinko, et cetera – would no doubt come soon enough. He was, in a way, quite amazed by what he had said. He had not planned to say anything controversial. Nor, of course, had he planned to be sitting in the Palm Court of the Plaza Hotel killing time until he could have lunch with his mistress.

When he had finished reading the papers, it was still only eleven. Two hours and fifteen minutes to kill. He decided to stroll down to the Museum of Modern Art and have a look at the Impressionists. This appealed to him more than the exhibition at the Metropolitan: 'the liberated collection of the Berlin Museum – rich in masterpieces of the German Gothic', it said. He was more in a mood for the Impressionists and they did not disappoint him. He arrived early at '21' and was given the usual extravagant welcome – that was part of what you paid for there. He sat at the bar while he waited for Joannie. Whom you were meeting was less noticeable in a crowded bar. He saw one or two people that he knew and exchanged a few words with them. He was congratulated on his speech. People tended to be congratulatory at '21'. After two dry Martinis, expecting Joannie any minute, he began to get a soaring feeling – which, after a third dry Martini and no Joannie, changed into a sinking feeling. It was this sinking feeling which informed him through a haze composed of dry Martinis and melting landscapes that he had lost one of his options: nonchalance. Stages and steps. If – with the amatory ruthlessness of the young – she simply did not turn up, it would end the adventure on a sour note of defeat. Well, she had only said she would try to make it. Perhaps she had not been able to get out of her other date. Almost half-past one. She had her own life to get on with. What if she had come to the sensible conclusion, reached by him earlier in the day, that it was best to end this thing before it could develop into anything. Perhaps he had been correct to let her go, and weak and foolish to call her back. He was preparing for disappointment, when he saw her come in, and it was the soaring feeling again, higher this time because of the violent turnabout from the sinking feeling of a moment before. He watched her look for him; did not immediately reveal his whereabouts: let her have a moment's apprehension that he had got tired of waiting and left. She was wearing a sharkskin two-piece that was light and summery and white, in tight at the waist and close fitting over the hips: the moulded look. With big satin-covered buttons running diagonally all the way down, suggesting, inevitably, that she could be unbuttoned from top to bottom. A marcasite brooch in the form of a posy of flowers glittered on her bodice. He was pleased by her moment of fear when she failed to see him. Then, as he was pointed out by the head waiter, she came weaving through the crush with a very wowy smile.

'Well, hi,' she said.

'You look lovely.'

'Thanks. So do you . . .'

He signalled to the bartender.

'Black Label on the rocks, two rocks . . .?' She nodded. 'Trouble getting out of your other date?'

'Some – but let's not talk about that.' She was searching in her handbag for a cigarette. He lit it for her with a '21' book match and snapped his fingers at the barman who had not yet responded to the gentler signal.

'What's this insistence on two rocks?' he asked her.

255

'One is not enough, and more than two takes the kick out of the whisky.'

'Well, that figures.'

'This is nice,' she said, giving him a secret hand squeeze and looking around. 'I'm glad you asked me to have lunch. And *here*.'

'Even though it meant standing up someone else?'

'Ah-huh.'

'Did he mind?'

'Yes.'

'Did you mind that he minded?'

'I can't help how people feel about me.'

'Is he someone you're involved with?'

'Sort of . . .'

'What does that mean? Are there others that you are sort of involved with?'

'Well, I'm involved with you now, aren't I?' She said it very matter-of-factly. He hadn't really been thinking as he talked, had been playing a game: inquiring about his rivals, indulging himself in vague emotional sensations. But her answer had cut through this sensuous fog, impressing upon him the concrete fact that games have consequences.

'Well,' he said immediately, his cautiousness re-asserting itself, 'that could be sort of unwise . . .'

'Don't you think I know that?' She laughed.

'I should tell you,' he said, feeling compelled to be honest (he was a man who was rarely brutal except sometimes in his insistence on honesty) 'I should tell you that there's nothing in this for you – you know, there can't be.'

'There's the same in it for me as there is for you,' she said. 'Quit worrying – you don't have to worry about me. Worry about the world. I look after myself fine. I never do anything I don't want to do.'

'I didn't mean what I said to sound . . .' He was again qualifying statements, adding clauses and sub-clauses, correcting impressions. 'The truth is I wanted to see you again. I know that was selfish of me . . .'

'You don't have to explain to me,' she said. 'Really. Let's just have a good time . . .'

256

Fortunately Julian arrived at this point, because Hardtman was addicted to explanations and would not have been able to desist from trying to make everything clear. Seeing him come in, he said quickly, 'I asked Julian to join us – I thought it was better . . .'

She understood at once, and smiled, and said, 'I like Julian a lot.'

After that everything became easier and lighter. He gave a sign for another Black Label on the rocks, two rocks, and another dry Martini for himself, and tomato juice for Julian, who was apologizing for his lateness, saying he had been out on a call – to a patient of his, a cinema actor suffering from *ennui*.

'I made him do some Yoga to revitalize his system and he would fall asleep standing on his head. I got him to talk about himself, and he must be the only actor of whom it could be said that he falls asleep while talking about himself. In the middle of relating how he and some dishy lady . . .'

Julian's stories made the lunch pass in an agreeable fog of allusiveness – if you could not be sure of whom he was talking, you could hazard a good guess most of the time.

Seated at their table, Julian was next to Joannie on the banquette, with Hardtman opposite them, maintaining a certain formal distance. He had little sense of time passing: he had become an afternoon idler as well as a morning idler, and a playful man, and could think of little else than making love to Joannie again.

When he saw that it was almost four o'clock, he became belatedly conscience-stricken. 'You both must have things to do.'

'Oh it's O.K.,' she said. 'The piece I'm working on isn't expected till end of the month, so I've got time.'

'And you're free and easy?'

'I don't know that I like being called *easy*,' she said laughing, 'but I'm free – yes.' She laughed again.

'A free spirit,' he agreed. 'Comes from having been a troubadour in one of your lives.'

'I think I was also a cat once, and cats they're very free creatures.'

'Unlike dogs,' Hardtman said. 'We men are the dogs, waiting for our mistresses. Whereas the cats – they take off ... Is that what you do, take off?'

'Sometimes.'

'Is that meant as a caution to us? Are we going to lose you?' He used the plural 'we' as a playful kind of disguise.

'Present company excepted,' she said looking around, 'there's nobody here I'm sold on exactly. If you don't count waiters.'

'And we don't, do we?' Hardtman said. 'Was it a good life being a cat?'

'You get a whole lot of cream.'

'I bet you do.'

'And what are your plans, Mr Hardtman? Remember, I'm interviewing you.'

'Ah yes. My plans. Well, since we have not been plagued with frantic telephone calls requiring my immediate presence in Washington, I guess I could stay another night.'

He awaited her response to this in a state of tingling suspense. She was looking directly into his eyes. She let a moment go by, during which he saw her turn things over in her mind. Nothing is a foregone conclusion where cats and troubadours are concerned. He sensed her changeability – from which he had benefited last night; somebody else might benefit today.

'Sounds like a good plan,' she said eventually with a laugh.

'You go along with it?' he inquired for the sake of getting things clear.

'Yes.'

'I have an even better plan,' Julian said suddenly. 'Why don't we all go to Fire Island? I have a cottage there. We could go for the weekend. I thoroughly recommend it, Bill. It's a good place to relax. Would do you the world of good. In any case, I shall go. I give some classes there during the summer.'

258

'Tempting though it is . . .' Hardtman was starting to say No.

'Oh I love Fire Island,' Joannie said.

'Well, come,' Julian said, 'you can stay at the cottage.'

'Ah, I think it is really out of the question for me,' Hardtman said. As he spoke he was beset by disturbing images of Joannie on Fire Island without him. How quickly one wished to curtail the troubadour spirit, when its freeness ran counter to one's immediate interests. It was just an elemental pang of jealousy, but it had the power to make him think again. Really he couldn't put off his return to Washington beyond tomorrow. There was too much to do. He had to be there to answer for his speech. To keep an eye on Walter Cole. There was Laurene. *There was Laurene.* He could not just take off for Fire Island – on a pleasure trip.

'As your medical adviser, Bill,' Julian said, 'I strongly advise it.'

'Well, of course, if my medical adviser orders it,' Hardtman said, and then became serious: it really was unthinkable – such a succumbing to pleasure. Unthinkable. But the unthinkable had to be thought, according to Sidney Myers. And so he thought of Fire Island and the hot sand and the ocean and Joannie.

They were now the only ones left in the restaurant.

'What do you think of Julian's idea?' he asked Joannie.

'If it means I get to have you another couple of days, I'm for it.'

Two days! What possibilities.

'It's really unfair to play around with the idea,' he said, 'because I don't see how I could possibly get out of going back tomorrow.' As they stood waiting outside the restaurant she leaned her head against his shoulder, so lightly that it was not noticeable to anyone other than him. When a taxi pulled up and the doorman opened the door for them, Hardtman turned to Julian and said: 'If by some chance it became possible for me to go to Fire Island, how would we get there? When would we have to leave?'

259

'There's a ferry boat from Babylon at 9.30 in the morning. That means getting a train at about 7.30 from Penn Station. If you were coming, I could pick you up from your hotel.'

'Well, let's check with each other later, Julian.'

The high feeling was beginning to give way to after-lunch torpor, accompanied by a vague sense of malaise. He was in need of replenishment. Had been working too hard. And if two days on Fire Island really would do him a world of good . . . But it was impossible. Wasn't it?

In his hotel room Joannie sprawled on the bed while he made his calls to Washington. He could not help but be aware of her all the time he was talking. There was still no reaction to his speech. No word from the Boss. About anything. Or from the Admiral. Walter Cole had telephoned – 'nothing urgent'. Several calls and memos relating to matters in the pipeline. But no deliveries of the kind he had to sign for personally and read while the courier waited in the outer office.

'Nothing much,' Mrs Taylor said.

'Surprisingly little.'

'I think everybody's already gone for the weekend,' Mrs Taylor said. 'It's so hot.'

'It's hot here too,' Hardtman said. The seasons had shifted: they were getting August heat in September . . .

He made a few more phone calls to various offices, sounding out if there was anything afoot. All he got were complaints about the heat. One or two casual references to his speech. 'Well, you sure stirred things up.' The situation in Berlin was much the same. There had been a further meeting in Moscow between Smith, Roberts, Chataigneau, and Molotov, the outcome of which was inconclusive. Stalin was undergoing medical treatment that could not be interrupted.

His last official call was to the Admiral. He was not available himself but his aide said there was nothing he knew of that required Hardtman's presence in Washington over the weekend. No mention of the speech.

'I'd appreciate it if you would double check. I was thinking of staying over in New York. Well, actually, outside New York . . . Fire Island.'

'Oh I hear that's a really nice place . . . sort of deserted, though.'

'That's the idea. To have a rest. I could do with it.'

'I see no problem, Mr Hardtman. Take it if you haven't heard from me in half an hour, it's O.K.'

'So,' Joannie said, when he had replaced the phone, 'will Western democracy as we know it last the weekend without you?'

'Seems like it will. Hard though that is to imagine.'

When after three quarters of an hour there had been no call from the Admiral's office, he phoned Laurene.

'Julian has suggested I go with him to Fire Island, for the weekend,' he told her.

'Are you going?'

'I'm sort of toying with the idea. Julian says it would do me good. Seems to think I'm tired.'

'I think Julian is right. Would do you a world of good to take a few days off. You never do that. I could come and join you tomorrow. We could have a long weekend, come back Monday.'

'It's so damned hot,' Hardtman said. 'I really don't feel like moving.'

'Well, you can swim. I'll bring your swim suit.'

'Okay, great,' Hardtman said. He hesitated. 'You really want to come all this way? Isn't it a drag for you? I mean, in this heat. I'd hate to get you all the way out here and then find we have to go back immediately because the Boss wants me.'

'What do they say?'

'They don't know. I have to stand by . . . things are critical.'

'I could take a plane, it's only an hour.'

'And another two or three hours to get out to the Island. To make the 9.30 a.m. boat, you'd have to leave Washington around 4 a.m.'

'I could get the flight tonight,' Laurene said.

'Yes,' Hardtman agreed, 'you could do that. You want to come tonight?'

'Well, let me think about it a minute. How was your lunch?'

'Oh, pleasant. Pleasant.'

'And the girl wowy?'

'Quite.'

'Is she going to Fire Island with Julian?'

'I have no idea. Perhaps he has other wowy girls there.'

'Knowing Julian, that's a fair guess.'

'Do you want to come?'

'Do you want me to come?'

'Sure, I'd like you to come, if *you* want to. But I don't want to make you spend hours on trains and boats in this kind of heat, if you'd rather stay where you are . . .'

He heard her hesitate. It was going to be a close thing.

'Tell you what,' he said. 'I don't even know that I'm going for sure. *If* I do go, I'll ring you from there, and then if you wanted to you could join me tomorrow. I believe there's a late afternoon boat, too – you could get that. If it looked as though I could stay. How about that?'

'All right,' she said uncertainly. 'You'll phone me tomorrow?'

'That's right – if I go. I'll phone you one way or the other. And if I can't – for any reason – well . . . you'll see me when you see me. O.K.? 'Bye, dear. Have to hang up, I'm waiting for a call from the Admiral. Talk to you.'

Yes, and my address is the forest. He was somewhat surprised, and impressed, by his newly found skill at dissembling.

'Well,' he said to Joannie, 'looks like it's all fixed.'

When Julian phoned, Hardtman said he had arranged things so that they could come to Fire Island. It had been difficult, he said, but he had managed it.

'Marvellous,' Julian said. 'Pick you up at seven.'

'Time for a drink,' he suggested to Joannie, when he had put down the phone, and she readily agreed. The mood that had been slipping steadily since lunch could be made to rise again with the onset of the cocktail hour. They went

262

down to the bar and sat in a dark booth of sleek black leather, with mirrors going all the way up to the ceiling. Across from them there was a shiny black piano, and a shiny black piano player seated at it playing a slow, smoky, romantic number, which he sang in lump-in-throat style.

Joannie took out a cigarette and lit it with a match from a silver-plated matchbox holder. Hardtman studied the large bar menu – the thousand and one ways of getting plastered. I have become a bar-fly, he thought, as he considered what he would have. Joannie was a creature of habit where drinking was concerned and was sticking to her usual Black Label on the rocks. Hardtman decided he would have a Pernod. When it came, he asked if she wanted to taste it, and she took a sip and was not sold on it.

'It's a French drink,' she said with a faint hint of disapproval. He said it was indeed: it amused him how American she was. She had never been outside the North American continent. Europe to her was a legend of long ago – Helvetia, Julius Caesar, the Romans. And her ideas of Europeans were based on stereotypes – there was French chic, English coldness, German brutality, and oh those Italian men! France was where you ate stuff like snails and frogs' legs and drank something that tasted like a medicine for ulcers.

'You like that drink,' she asked him when she had tasted it. 'To me it's got no kick.'

'Well, that's deceiving,' he promised her. 'It's rather well known for the way it destroys the mind. The road to perdition, by way of *pastis*, is an old familiar story in France. The chic French way.'

She laughed: she was very responsive to all his little quips.

The piano player was giving them a big nudging smile and singing to them; they were already known here, habitués after one night. Hardtman raised his glass and upon receiving another nudging smile felt obliged to buy the piano player a drink, which also afforded a suitable occasion for replenishing their own glasses. Across, in another booth, he spotted the furniture salesman from Hoboken with the girl in the see-through sleeves. Another pair of habitués. Like joining a club. The society of the King-size bed.

She said: 'If I'm staying the night with you, here, I ought to go back to my place and get a couple of things for tomorrow. Like, you know, a toothbrush.'

'We can go to your apartment right now and collect your things,' he said, 'and then go somewhere for dinner. I don't have anything else to do.'

'Suits me.'

She lived on the West Side, in the Seventies, just behind Central West Park. There was an enormous nineteenth-century apartment building on the corner, heavy with gables and bays and balconies, and at the back of it a row of brownstones with stone stoops going up to glass doors, through which rather dingy stairs could be seen. Hers was one of the better houses on the street. Next to it was an Italian restaurant, narrow and long, with candles in Chianti bottles on chequered tablecloths.

Hardtman was glancing around interestedly, since this was her area: he had a wish to place her, to picture her coming out of her apartment, going shopping, meeting friends. A few people were sitting out on their stoops, and one or two waved or called to her. A friendly neighbour-hood.

Her apartment was at the top of the house, and walking up to the fifth floor took all his breath.

'You're not going to die on me,' she said, 'are you?'

'These stairs must serve to dampen the ardour of some,' he said.

'Oh you'd be surprised.'

Her apartment had been economically but charmingly furnished with a lot of white-painted wicker garden chairs and a wicker settee, softened with an abundance of brightly coloured scatter cushions. Bare pine floorboards, sanded down and varnished with a clear varnish that brought out the grain of the timber. One pony skin. A gramophone; records. Bongo drums. Back numbers of magazines stacked under a window seat. A cast-iron Victorian garden table, painted white, covered with a slab of green marble. Slatted folding chairs. The kitchen was minute and looked as if it was not much used. The kitchen of a girl who ate out. Neat and tidy. As everything else was, too. Only the marble-top table was not: here the mounds of neatly typed work were toppling over, scattering pages over desk accoutrements, notes, shopping lists, newspaper clippings, source books sprouting markers, bills, photographs, scissors and paste, manilla folders. There was an ancient typewriter in the middle of all this: a machine of unusual construction, with the type bars arranged in a raised semi-circle above the platen, so that they would strike the paper in a downward movement. Curious about everything that was to do with her, he went to take a look at her books. Thurber. The *Collected Poems* of Keats, Shelly and Byron, in some classic book club edition. The *Collected Works* of Oscar Wilde, in a similar edition. The plays of Eugene O'Neill, William Saroyan. Thomas Woolf. John Dos Passos. Dreiser. An *Introduction to Freud, Jung and Adler*, which he felt was rather a tall order for such a thin book. Several Gunthers: *Inside Europe, Inside Asia, Inside Latin America, Inside U.S.A. Tobacco Road. The Loved One* by Evelyn Waugh. *The Naked and the Dead* by Norman Mailer. *Sexual Behaviour in the Human Male* by Kinsey and Pomeroy. Some Hemingway. Mystery stories in paperback. Ouspensky, *In Search of the Miraculous. The Collected Stories* of O. Henry. A book about Mata Hari. A few Olympia Press (Paris) volumes in green covers, including some Henry Millers. *War and Peace.* The plays of Shakespeare. And more, in this kind of mix.

The walls were hung with bullfight posters, travel posters, and one or two pieces of Mexican Indian art.

The next room was the bedroom: it was almost completely occupied by a huge bed consisting of mattresses placed on a raised wooden platform, covered with a beautiful patchwork quilt and many cushions. Over the bed had been pinned a cinema poster with the title in prominent lettering, ALL THIS AND HEAVEN TOO, which made him smile.

Part of the wall to the right of the sleeping area was covered with photographs. Mostly men.

'Boyfriends?' he asked.

'Yes – and no.'

'Is that highly evasive answer supposed to mean they are out of your past?'

Two of the men were in uniform: one an Air Force lieutenant, the other a sergeant in the Army Medical Corps.

'That one –' she pointed to the lieutenant, 'is the guy I was married to. For a while. A very short while. The other one is my father. And over there – the bathing belle – that's me. And the rest are none of your business. O.K.?'

'I was just wondering,' he said, starting to put one arm around her, but she pulled away.

'I thought we were going to have dinner.'

'Well,' he said, 'the one does not exclude the other. We could make it a late dinner.'

'I think dinner,' she said.

She appeared ill at ease in her apartment: was rapidly gathering together a few things and putting them all into a large Saks shopping bag. She did not offer him a drink, and seemed anxious to leave at once. Just as they were going out, the telephone rang; she said, 'I'm not going to answer,' and let it ring, and they heard the ringing continue as they went down the stairs. Whoever was ringing her was hanging on a long time: at the bottom of the stairs she frowned, and he thought she was going to go back up, but finally she decided to leave it, and he smiled, since presumably he had to count himself the beneficiary. Once more his spirits were rising. Her refusal to answer the phone (to whomever – but he guessed The Man in Her Life) gave him a renewed sense of conquest, of having carried her off; that he should be the cause and justification of such bad behaviour on her part – as he had to consider it – was exhilarating.

As they were carried joltingly along in a rickety old taxi, he had to recognize the vertiginous nature of this kind of life, with its sudden take-offs, as well as its equally sudden let-downs. The latter were emphasized by the taxi's proneness to descend, after every bump, to the lowest point of its wretchedly defective suspension. Nauseated and excited at the same time, he felt the seduction of lights coming on, as the high towers began to glow with electricity and glitter with reflections of the pink sunset. The *déjà vu* aspect of this nightly magic did not, on this occasion, lessen the power of the spell. Oh he knew this town to be a place of extravagant unfulfillable promises, like the world itself, but he could not, on this lovely evening, keep his expectations within the bounds of reason.

Which was only to say that Hardtman was forty-five years old, had seen his youth fade, his options diminish, and his future narrow down; that he had been driven almost out of his mind by the sheer intangibility of events in Washington, by evasions and double talk; that he did not know where he was any more, where his sympathies or hopes lay, whom to believe, whom to trust, did not know. And in contrast to all that – here was a girl, simple and straightforward, with healthy hungers and uncomplicated female warmth, in whose arms he had at least found some sense of his effectuality as a man. Men have fallen in love for less reasons.

He took her to another of his expensive little French restaurants; this one had booths enclosed by screens of misty patterned glass, purple walls, cacti in pots, Georgian silver on the buffet, and a lot of flambéing going on. They were not in the mood for the specialities of the *maison*. He let her order a steak, and chose an omelette *fines herbes* for himself. She was studying the menu, and seeing the price of the omelette said in a shocked tone, 'How can they charge that for a couple of eggs?'

'You pay for the ambience,' he told her, and thought; yes, the ambience of one's youth is worth the extra price, whatever it is. He realized he was beginning to feel protective towards her, and thinking of how she was going to make out. Well, she had done all right before he came along, and presumably would continue to do all right. As she kept saying, she could take care of herself. But she smoked too much, and drank too much probably, and

267

perhaps was a little too free-spirited for her own eventual good.

Seeing how she was wolfing down the *pommes frites*, after having just stubbed out her cigarette, he remarked jokingly: 'You do have a healthy appetite – for *everything*. You're going to have to watch yourself, or you'll get fat.'

She said nothing, and he saw a faint frown pass across her face. His jocularity had evidently not gone down too well.

'What is it?' he asked.

'Something funny happened,' she said flatly.

'What?'

'When you just said that, now.'

'That you could lose some weight?'

'I find,' she said with a peculiar kind of stiffness, 'that you saying that makes me not like you suddenly.' She was not joking. She was in deadly earnest, her face had become set in an oddly formal expression; the intimacy between them had gone in an instant. She had withdrawn from him.

'Oh but you're kidding. Oh really! Oh come on, Joannie! You're not serious. Because of what I said about losing weight? I really didn't mean anything by that, I think you're very lovely. I'm not too sold on skinny women anyway. It was just a remark, evidently careless and miscalculated, and I withdraw it.'

'You can't unsay something that's been said. That's so peculiar to think you can. See, I don't believe in apologies, what's done is done.'

He saw that she was really aggrieved and he could not understand it. She was white and tense with some long-held-down complaint against the world.

'What's got into you?' he demanded.

'O.K.,' she said. 'I know you go for me and you go for the way I look and you don't mind a few extra pounds, even though you made a crack about it, because right now a little extra flesh it's all right, it's all a plus in bed, isn't it? That's what they tell you. But I get the message, don't think I don't. A little extra around the hips and the ass and the belly is sexy when you're twenty-seven, right? But not so sexy when you're getting on for forty, that's when it gets to be blowsy, and Honey, you better watch yourself, and Baby, you're letting yourself go, and women let go fast when they let go, believe me, and either they have to half starve themselves to death, so they'll make the grade, or the guy turns to some young chick like me, I know, *like me* . . . that's what I get *now*, but I know the time'll come when I get to be forty . . .'

'Ah the unfairness of it all,' he said. He could not quite see what she was so resentful about. 'But why are you complaining now?'

'I'm twenty-nine,' she said. 'I lied when I told you I was twenty-seven.'

'O.K. Twenty-nine isn't exactly senility. What should I say, I'm forty-five?'

'It's all right for a man.'

'That's what you think. He's using up his time just as fast as a woman is: and usually he's got less of it . . .'

'O.K., but I'm not going to make myself over for anybody, not for any man, I like to eat – I have to eat – that's in my nature – and if it's not to somebody's liking, they can just forget it, because when I'm forty I'm going to have enough money to say the hell with it.'

'Good for you.'

'I'm not going to make myself dependent on anybody. See, that's why I'm ambitious . . .'

'It's as good a reason as any.'

'Don't put me down with smart repartee,' she snapped back. 'I'm off you.'

'But why? Why have you suddenly turned against me – because of an unfortunate remark? I was not to know . . .'

'There's something about your whole attitude,' she said. 'It's so . . . so . . .' She could not find the word for what it was. 'What am I *doing* here with you?' she suddenly demanded. 'I want my head examining.'

He concluded she was probably feeling guilty about the phone call she hadn't taken, the Man in Her Life she had stood up. And after all that, she had to sit there and be insulted, be told she was fat.

'Listen,' she said, 'you know I get enough trouble from men, as I am . . .'

'I believe you.'

'I used to be slimmer, I used to have a really slim body, like a model. Svelte.' She smiled briefly, delightedly, at this memory of herself. 'Didn't you see all those photos of me in the apartment? When I was younger, oh I can tell you, oh boy, oh boy – that was a time . . . I really looked fantastic then.'

'You look fantastic now.'

'I don't know what it is,' she said in some perplexity, 'but suddenly something just turned me off you, when you just said that, before, I don't know what it was, but I'm instinctive and I thought what am I doing here, *what am I doing here*?: I've got my ongoing life to get on with . . . instead of . . .'

He did not try to argue for himself.

'I was thinking along the same lines this morning, and remember I told you at lunch: there's nothing in this for you . . .'

'Yes, I know. But it's not *that*. I don't know what it is, but something just happened, first our chemistry was right and now it isn't.'

'You're really serious? Oh come on, you can't be that changeable.'

Hardtman ordered more drinks; he left half his omelette, and she left half her steak. He did not seek to woo her or win her round with promises and sweet talk. He was quite ready to end it all there and then, if she had suddenly realized the futility of the adventure. If the fizz had gone out of it, there was no point in going on. After all, he had wanted to end it that morning, had actually let her go. He could not blame her now for having the same idea.

He stayed silent for a while, then he said: 'There's a line of Auden's: "intimations of mortality like sounds of thunder at a picnic". I think what just happened is we heard the thunder. But we don't have to let it spoil things, you know. Everybody dies, and everything ends; but it doesn't have to be just yet.'

She looked up at this, and gave a laugh, and was back with him again, as quickly as that, a quick return, and he felt good at having found a way through to her.

She said, 'I'm sorry, Bill, oh I'm sorry. I don't know what got into me. Something you said got me mad, but it wasn't to do with you, not really, I'm sorry. I apologize for the tears. That's not me, as a rule.'

Only when she said this did he look at her fully and see the tears: while he had been staring into his Grand Marnier and quoting Auden, she had been weeping silently. And he hadn't even noticed. Well, he would have to go carefully; even someone as toughened by newspaper life as she, was vulnerable. But anyway she was back with him now, squeezing his hand, eyes shiny, and he thought no further ahead than the next day and Fire Island.

Later, when they were walking through the lobby of the Plaza, not talking and slightly apart so that they would not look too obviously together, it struck him – how thoughtful of her to have put her things in a Saks shopping bag, a most discreet way of travelling, it did not advertise that you were spending the night as a suitcase did, and at the same time was acceptable in the smartest places. That was his first thought. His second thought was – she has learned this from experience, she knows all about spending nights with men in good hotels.

He did not let this second thought weigh too heavily upon him, however. He was looking forward to Fire Island.

17

He was in a sort of mild mania, a state of elated sleepless-ness, after two wild nights in a row. Over-excitement of his nervous system shut out tiredness, and it was like the white nights of Riga again, when he had not been able to sleep for wonder and amazement. Except, of course, that he was no longer in his teens and indestructable.

He knew he would have to pay for this eventually, but for the moment he was feeling pretty good. He walked hand in hand (he had either become careless or was suffi-ciently confident that nobody would know him here) with Joannie along the Babylon waterfront in a bustling crowd of day-trippers, anglers, yachtsmen, surfers, spear-divers, all lugging their different gear along, making for the ferry boat ticket booth.

Julian, walking a little ahead of them, exchanged greet-ings with some of those in the crowd. He seemed to know quite a lot of these people. As they all waited in line to board the ferry, he was talking of the pros and cons of allowing a limited number of four-wheel drive vehicles on the beaches. Of the funnel effect of gulleys. Increasing wave velocity speeded the rate of erosion, he quite agreed. He had the capacity of easily becoming involved in other people's affairs, and of giving them his deep attention. He was quickly at home anywhere, and just as he interested himself in all the Washington rumours, whether personal or political, so he now wished to know about the fishing and the sailing and the various amorous arrangements among members of the island community. Such talk con-nected only with the periphery of Hardtman's conscious-ness. His mind was elsewhere – preoccupied with his own gaudy fancies.

Julian, in his baggy flannels, with his paisley silk scarf (in which the colours had begun to run), knotted inside his shirt, his old blue blazer draped around his shoulders, his hair in need of cutting, and blowing about his ears, had that air of slight shabbiness that eccentric upper-class Englishmen sometimes cultivate, dressing to look like their own gardeners.

Hardtman, by contrast, was somewhat embarrassingly over-dressed for the occasion in a grey lightweight suit, appropriate for summer wear in the city, but hardly for Fire Island. As a gesture in the direction of greater informality, he had refrained from wearing a tie that day. Joannie was in patched jeans and a man's open-neck shirt, and carrying her Saks bag with aplomb.

With others they scrambled along the gangway, and on the boat's upper deck managed to find room on wooden benches at the prow. All squashed tightly together – the boat was packed – Hardtman rested his head between Joannie's collar bone and an easeful small breast and slept for ten minutes. When he woke from this cat nap they were already far out in the bay and her hair was all over his face and she had, with her natural inclination towards bodily entanglement, crossed one of her thighs over his. He watched a strip of land float up out of the Atlantic swell and thought what a boy's adventure this was that he had got himself into; and demanding sternly of himself what he was doing here, could only reply, inadequate as such an answer must have been to Hardtman: having a good time.

'What a frown you have,' Joannie said. 'But I love it. I just love your frown.' She had been studying his face while he was ruminating. 'Oh your frown is the most terrifically sexy frown I've ever seen. It has such concern for the *whole wide world* in it.'

'No, no, not in the least,' he protested. 'If I was frowning right now, it was only in anticipation of delights I am not entitled to. The world couldn't be further from my mind. What do I care for the world when I have got wicked pleasures in store! Let the Boss drop the bomb on whomsoever he chooses – none of my damn business.'

'You tell great big lies.'

'What you have got to realize about me, young lady, is

that where women are concerned I am a compendium of Clausewitz, Metternich and Machiavelli ...'

'Just to get in my little ole pants.'

'Absolutely. Because,' – he whispered this in her ear – 'because your pants are the greatest pants to get into that I know of, and because I can't think of anything I want to do more, now, or for the rest of my life, other than to get in your pants ...'

She laughed delightedly at this declaration of his passion, which he had already proved in the course of two rumbustious nights.

As soon as the ferry boat docked, the passengers began to scramble off the boat as wildly as they had scrambled on, pouring out on to a narrow jetty, and then dispersing in all directions.

Julian led the way along a network of raised platforms which traversed the sand and scrub, connecting different places in the inhabited part of the island, and providing access to individual cottages, and the general store. Manmade amenities were at a minimum here, nature had not been much tampered with and the island remained bare and desolate – with no landscaping to improve upon the rough beauty of brush and sand and sea. The place was – blessedly – so the summer residents told you – without those comforts and conveniences of civilization that added up to being so burdensome just a couple of miles across the bay. Fire Island was devoid of cars, of petrol engines of any kind; motor yachts and motor boats there were in plenty, and even seaplanes – these were permitted because it was necessary to provide access to the island, but once there, everybody walked, and goods were transported by means of small pushcarts along the creaking gangways on piles. The cottages were also built on piles, to stand above the shifting sand. They were weathered clapboard constructions, and Julian's place was like most of the others. Inside, it consisted of a main living area, with a couple of bedrooms off it; sunlight poured through the large expanse of glass, burning the red cedarwood walls, bare except for a large fierce-looking stuffed marlin above the fireplace. There were fishing trophies on the mantelpiece.

'Who goes in for fishing?' Hardtman asked.

'The people who own this use it as a kind of fishing shack.'

At the end of the room, floor to ceiling sliding glass doors gave on to a sun-deck and beyond that you could see the ocean. There were no curtains to obstruct the all round view. Curtains were rather frowned upon on Fire Island; they belonged to the life of self-concealment on the mainland, but were felt to be unnecessary here, where people were so much more open with each other. There was something unnatural, it was thought, about curtains.

'You'll want breakfast,' Julian said. 'Why don't I get some things in while you and Joannie wander down to the beach. Have a swim. If the mood so takes you. There are swim suits in the bathroom. Meanwhile, I'll rustle up some bacon and eggs.' He looked in the fridge and seeing that it was quite empty said, 'Shall have to get coffee. Something for lunch and dinner. And booze . . . people tend to drop by.' He began to fumble, with sudden consternation, in his trouser pockets.

'Oh bloody hell. How very stupid of me. Came out without a dime, would you believe it.'

'Please, let me.' Hardtman said quickly, reaching in his pocket and producing a $20 bill.

'Oh thanks, Bill. I'll chalk it up. If that's all right with you, then, I'll leave you to find your own way around, while I get the groceries.'

'Need any help?'

'No, I can manage . . . You're here to relax, Bill. Doctor's orders.'

'O.K., doc.'

When Julian had left, Hardtman took Joannie out to the main sun-deck, and from there down some steps to the beach. They took their shoes off, and started to stroll towards the water. The sand was scorching on the soles of the feet, and the sun, almost overhead, beat down fiercely;

he was in a daze of temporary happiness. With sunlight flashing on the water, everything seemed wavy and slightly distorted. There was a shriek of violins in his ears.

He drew Joannie down on to the sand next to him.

'I'm enjoying this,' he said.

'So am I.'

The violins were shrill with forewarnings.

He looked around. White sand and sun . . . and boats in the distance. A shadowless scene. Why were the violins shrieking in his head? There was no danger here. Only pleasure.

He sighed. The daze he was in, part hangover, part happiness, prevented him from seeing anything too clearly.

'What is it?' she asked, seeing his look. 'Distant thunder?'

'This time, believe it or not, it's violins.'

'But violins are *nice*,' she said.

'Normally,' he said. 'Shall we walk?'

He helped her to her feet and they went down to the water's edge and walked along the line of the incoming tide, getting their feet wet.

'What is it?' she asked again.

'Oh I don't know. Delayed hangover, I should think.' He smiled broadly. 'No, really I'm enjoying this – enormously.'

'I can see that frown,' she accused. 'And this time it's not for the world.'

He said with a laugh, 'I was thinking somebody's going to have to pay for all this.'

'Why should anyone have to pay?'

'There have got to be rules,' he said. 'I believe in rules, there is a need for them, even if they are going to be circumvented or stretched, or secretly broken. But the rules have got to be there, rules of language, rules of conduct, of good manners – otherwise people don't know where they are, don't know what is expected of them. Impossible to live in a state of rulelessness. Except,' he smiled at her, 'for troubadours and cats – they're the exception to all the rules.' He was silent again while they walked on.

'Oh what are you doing here, what are you doing here?' she said mocking him ever so lightly.

He felt the age distance between them then.

'I just hope,' he said, 'that it's not going to be you who will have to pay for this.'

'I told you,' she said, 'don't worry about me. Let's have a swim.'

When they got back to the house, they found that Julian was already back and grinding the coffee.

'Who's for breakfast?' he asked. 'Everyone? Jolly good!'

The bar top was covered with shopping: brown paper cornets, cartons, cans, things wrapped in grease-proof paper, bottles. A large number of bottles. 'People tend to drop in,' Julian explained again. There was evidently no change from the $20.

'How many eggs?' Julian asked, putting a large pan on the range, unwrapping packages, getting plates and cups and saucers and cutlery out of cupboards.

'Three eggs,' Joannie said. 'And a lot of bacon, I'm hungry.' She shot a defiant look at Hardtman. 'I'm going to go on a diet tomorrow. But today I'm eating. O.K.?'

Watching him work and serve, Hardtman was impressed by Julian's deftness.

'Missed your vocation, Julian.'

'Oh I'm good with my hands,' he agreed. This was something Hardtman had noticed over a period of time. Julian never fumbled – except in his pockets for dollar bills that were not there. At all other times, he possessed great manual dexterity. Unfamiliar keys, locks, catches never gave him any trouble. He could open anything: jammed money boxes, peculiarly capped jars, unusual tubes, stuck windows, wine bottles (without a corkscrew – he used an ordinary screw and his powerful fingers), secret doors, rusty man-holes...

As he served the fried eggs with a neat flip of the spatula, sprinkled crispy bacon around, and poured coffee, he filled them in on Fire Island society.

Through one of the larger expanses of uncurtained glass,

they could see other weathered grey clapboard houses with similarly uncurtained windows. One of the people with whom Julian exchanged waved greetings was a young woman in an adjoining cottage; she was lying on her living room floor doing Yoga. Julian watched her. 'Good, good, very good,' he murmured. 'Oh well done, Katie. Katie is adorable,' he told them. 'And doing jolly well . . . she is going to get to the Fifth Stage in no time.' He applauded her, clapping his hands high in the air, and she smiled and waved back.

'Attractive young woman,' Hardtman said.

'Oh Katie is a real sweetie-pie, and a wonderful person,' Julian said. 'Married to Louis Kantzler – he's a big-shot attorney. Never comes here. Well, rarely. Occasionally takes the seaplane from the Battery. Likes to drop in unexpectedly, just to make sure . . .' Julian chuckled, 'Well, he is somewhat older than her, and she is a very pretty girl.'

'She a patient of yours?'

'I cured her of migraine. She'd been suffering all her life from dreadful incapacitating migraines. I put her on a gluten-free diet, and gave her some Yoga to do, and it was amazing: dramatic! She hasn't had a headache for thirteen months.'

'That is amazing,' Hardtman said.

After the late breakfast, Julian suggested a treatment and as soon as it began Hardtman felt the tiredness being drawn out of him. Julian's expert fingers seemed to gather it all togther and press it into a dense ball that turned into deep sleep.

When he woke up the sun had moved to a lower position in the sky and he heard voices from next door. People had begun to drop by, and, feeling refreshed after his sleep, Hardtman went to join them. The south wall of sliding glass had been rolled back, opening the living room on to the sun-deck, from which there were steps going down to the beach, and there was a good deal of coming and going. Julian was sitting in the Buddha position on the living room floor, with women around him, which was usual enough. They were listening to him talking, their faces rapt, and that was quite usual too.

On the sun-deck another woman, with a high proselytizing voice, and an avid mouth, was instructing a group of novices, presently holding themselves up in the candle position, legs floundering in the air. 'Higher, higher, higher,' the avid lady urged, as blood rushed to faces unaccustomed to such reversals of the norm.

Hardtman saw the girl from next door, the lovely Katie Kantzler, coming up the steps from the beach and step slinkily around the upended bodies on the sun-deck. Her precision of movement suggested some dance training. Her hair was upswept and she wore a silk turban and a kind of sarong of some gauzy material that showed off the small beach shorts she was wearing underneath, and as she walked on long legs made to look even longer by her high-heeled open sandals, the split skirt kept opening enticingly all the way up to the waist, revealing the startling curve of a buttock cheek that was like a ripe plum with the bloom still fresh on it. As she weaved past a couple of upside down men, red-faced in the candle position, they appeared to be having difficulties with their balance, they wavered and began to topple.

Coming into the living room she looked round to see who was there, looked at Hardtman, who was on the point of coming in from the other side, looked at the people around Julian, and then giving him a kiss on the cheek sat down next to him. Joannie, Hardtman saw, was in the group doing the exercises on the sun-deck.

'Oh, Bill,' Julian called, seeing him. 'Come and meet people. Help yourself to a drink first. *Help yourself*, I may say, is the house rule.'

Having taken a drink, Hardtman drew up a chair to where Julian was sitting, without actually joining the circle around him. The introductions were minimal: 'Bill, Katie, Bella, Harriet . . .' First names only, without embellishments. After this momentary digression, Julian lit another cigarette and continued with what he was saying.

279

'Christianity,' he was saying, 'has a lot to answer for. And the Jews of course, who started it all – needless to say. All this Messiah business. Heaven preserve us from Messiahs! Having an axe to grind – it most regrettably didn't, and we got Jesus Christ. Read Josephus on that subject, a damned sight more reliable than the Gospels, and considerably more readable. What wicked mischief the Church has done! If copulation were solely for the purpose of ensuring the continuation of the species, why would the Almighty so grossly overdo things as to give every man the capacity to reproduce himself fifteen thousand times. I don't believe the Almighty, whoever He is, would have been that wasteful. No, no: Reich has got it right – sex, nasty little word though it is, happens to be the biological life force. Well, of course, it's obvious, isn't it? Some dear old professor comes along and tells us what we actually do – *as if we didn't know* – and shock waves go around the world. All this stupid hypothetical denial of what we are is the fault of the Church, making each of us think that we are not only wicked but *uniquely* wicked and depraved; which, of course, gets everybody all tied-up in guilt, and is in the Church's interest, because it then can step in and offer to relieve us of guilt. At a price. The price of obedience to its commands. It's sheer bloody blackmail. They are crafty, of course, give you the semblance if not the reality. What they did with the old Roman festival of Saturnalia! When master and servant and men and women used to change roles and clothes and had the devil of a good time. Turned it into Christmas, the insipid celebration of sexless procreation.'

Katie Kantzler said, 'Hey, you just de-converted me. Anybody want to change clothes?'

'I doubt,' Julian said, 'if any of us has the figure for what you are wearing.' But all the same there were several offers, which Katie Kantzler promised to bear in mind.

Hardtman went out on to the sun-deck, and Joannie left off the exercise she was doing and went to him, earning a reproachful look from the class leader.

'How fine and *fresh* you look. Good as new,' Joannie said. They kissed as if they were seeing each other after a parting.

'Who are all the people?' he asked.

'I get the impression – mostly summer grass widows. Husbands slaving away in a hot office, making piles of dough. Now that Kantzler lady is quite some dish, I saw you looking.'

'Just looking.'

'Hmm?'

Julian, having disengaged himself from admiring women, came out to join them. They breathed the ocean air in unison, deeply.

'Nice place,' Hardtman said. 'Generous of somebody to lend it to you.'

'It's Dolly,' Julian said.

'Dolly Luessenhoep?'

'Yes. Belongs to the Luessenhoeps. They have been awfully good to me. They let me use it whenever I like. They hardly ever come here themselves. Arnold uses it as a fishing shack. But nowadays he fishes in North Carolina most of the time. They have got so many houses, they can't possibly use them all.'

'I had no idea there was such a sporting side to his character. I thought he was only interested in sponsoring Presidents.'

'Oh they both go very primitive when they come here. Dolly believes in Nature. To a fault. Dolly, dear Dolly, brings her own sheep – which she roasts on a spit, out there, when there's a night of full moon. The delicate hand that rules the *Morning Star* and the *Evening Sun* – or is it t'other way round? – carves great chunks of bloody mutton from the turning carcass, and serves them to her guests in white damask serviettes. But no knives and forks . . . Gourds of Nuits St George 1946 are left in strategic places all over the beach. Dear Dolly, I adore her. She handles Arnold superbly. What a secretary she must have been. They have a boat. All done up in washable rayon. The en-

281

tire decorative scheme is based on the motif of the stars and stripes, with the single exception of the flag, which is Panamanian, of course.'

Hardman laughed: Julian seemed to be in his most waspish form. He had evidently drunk a great deal of coffee. It affected him the way alcohol affects others: his eyes were brighter than usual, his words flowed more rapidly and with greater freeness, and he began to be indiscreet.

'You've never told us, Julian, how you came to be so close to the Luessenhoeps. What do you do for them?' Hardtman asked.

'Well, I keep him out of the loony bin. He hasn't been inside for eighteen months, which is something of a record for Arnold. Hasn't bought up any dying art magazines for ages or, what's more to the point, any thriving bordellos. He's very keen on buying bordellos and then turning them over to his own private use. Dolly decided that had to stop, and so I got him to take up fishing instead, which is a good deal less costly, even doing it on his rather grand scale, and moreover perfectly satisfies his violent urges. Well, naturally Dolly was very grateful. So was Arnold, as a matter of fact. He hates those loony-bins that Dolly keeps putting him in.'

'And what was it you did for Dolly?'

'That's another story—'

'Tell it, tell it,' Joannie insisted.

'Well, no names. I mention no names. A patient of mine who shall be nameless, hmm? A prominent Washington woman. But, mind, I am not saying who. Suffering, abominably, from hay fever . . .'

A slight smirk came over Julian's face. If it were not so well known that Julian didn't drink, you would have thought he was drunk. The sun was going down and casting long cool shadows across the white sand.

'Let me tell you, she had been doing extremely well, this lady who shall be nameless. A real gift for even the most difficult exercises. Great willingness. And readier than most to adopt the position of surrender, which is, of course, the great psychological stumbling block. I had her breathing out, *almost* unjerkily. And the predictable outcome was a re-commencement of bio-energy flow, with tingling.'

'With tingling huh?' Joannie said.

'Of course, she had massive armouring to overcome, but she persevered and with the help of deep massage of the nerves, she began finally to unblock. She described it rather graphically. It was like an unblocking of the ears in an aeroplane. But throughout her entire body. Only when she had recaptured her senses fully, did she realize the extent to which she had not been in possession of them before. You know, a long time ago, Fleiss had detected the reciprocal ebb and flow between the nasal passage and female genitalia. Well, with a lot of exercise, her bodily system began to flow again – and after a while she began to report streaming. This the treatment encouraged, and she began to feel the whole fireworks, as she put it. And the wonderful thing was once the deadness of the pelvis had been cured, lo and behold so had the hay fever.'

'Well, bravo,' Hardtman said. 'That does deserve congratulations. What a smart fellow you are, Julian. If I didn't have personal experience of your remarkable skill, I wouldn't believe half your stories.'

'Unbelievable, isn't it?' Julian agreed, with his knack for turning remarks to his advantage.

People were coming and going all the time. They dropped in to see who was there, had a look around, talked a little, helped themselves to booze, went out on the sundecks, talked, exchanged gossip, discussed where everybody was going to go later, and left. Or went to have an early evening swim. Young women with bare midriffs and strapless tops wiggled in a whirl of shoulder-length hair to the frenetic mechanical beat coming out of an old juke box.

She's mah candy,
An' Candy's always handy.
She's mah sugar,
An' sugar's what ahh'm sweet on.

Hardtman talked to a number of people, on a Bill/Joe/

Harry/Jane basis. Nobody was too interested in establishing precisely who anybody else was, and this conferred an agreeable kind of anonymity on everyone.

'What do you do, Bill?'

'I'm in government service . . .'

'Oh you mean like the post office?'

'You could say that.'

A middle-aged man with blue-rinsed hair, wearing wild silk blue dungarees, and gold snake bracelets on his wrists and ankles, lit two cigarettes at the same time, in the manner of Paul Henreid, and passed one to his companion, a younger man with very blue eyes. Katie Kantzler was slinking around wearing a bunch of gold razor blades around her neck, and several men asked her if they were expected to cut their throats in despair – and she'd say to them all, 'Don't despair *yet*,' and giggle wildly.

Julian, when Hardtman next came across him, was again in the Buddha position, which had induced one or two of the ladies to make use of his straight back to lean up against.

'Taken in 20–30 milligramme doses at intervals of thirty minutes,' he said, 'there is virtually no toxic reaction, no side-effects. Less harmful than alcohol.'

'What is?' someone asked.

'The much maligned leaf of the coca plant.'

'You talking about snow?'

'Exactly. The reason for the outcry against it is because it's said to inflame the passions – though why that should cause a *scare* is quite beyond me.'

'You use it?' a pretty girl wanted to know. 'What's it do for you?'

'Makes everything feel very much better,' he said.

'You mean it can feel better?' she asked.

'Try some,' he proposed.

A little later he was heard to say something about 'the sodding Empire'. Dear old England was in parlous shape.

'One of Coca-Cola's lesser outlets, I fear. The thing about us English, you see, is that we do insist upon going down the drain in our own way, and it's got to be our own drain, too. Of which, I may say, we have got a few to go down. There is of course the Josephus way out. If you can't beat 'em, join 'em. A time-honoured English custom. Well, Massada is not the way we do things in dear old England.'

The cutting edge in Julian's voice went largely unnoticed in the rising mood of tom-foolery. Of course, he didn't mean it, whatever it was he was saying. He was merely giving expression to some aberrant brainwave, to thoughts fished out of a mind seething from the over-stimulation of the medullary centre due to the excessive drinking of coffee. He must have been on his fortieth cup of the day by now. As he was quick to point out he might say what he meant without necessarily meaning what he said. No, he did not mean it. He never meant anything, when challenged.

A soft dusk like a sea mist was creeping inwards towards the shore. Just a short way out, it was already dark over the water, but on the white beach the twilight lingered on.

Julian announced: 'Time to do something about those dead pelvises, ladies. Who's for class?'

They all were, and eager, too, and with enthusiastic cries got up and followed Julian, picking their way through the jumping bodies around the juke box. Since there were people on the sun-deck, it was decided to hold the class down by the water's edge, a distance of three hundred yards. There it was quiet and still and almost private, with the constant passage of clouds dimming the halfmoon at frequent intervals.

Hardtman was looking for Joannie. He could not see her anywhere. Thinking that she might have joined the Yoga class, he went on to the sundeck and tried to make out the figures near the water. In the strange, almost sinister, light, it was difficult to distinguish forms, though he thought he saw Katie Kantzler there. When the moon was not covered, he saw an amorphous shimmer of movement, out of which the eye was presently able to construe more definite shapes. But it was difficult for the postures were not at all usual: heads and feet were in the oddest conjunctions.

285

Only Julian, a little apart from the others, stood out clearly. He appeared to have his blazer draped around his shoulders loosely, and his baggy flannels were fluttering in the breeze and his blown out long hair was like zig-zags of electricity. He was standing hands in pocket, calling out instructions in a dry voice, coaxing and commanding by turn.

'Very well done, *very* well. Let's do the Cat now. Nose along the ground . . . breathe in deeply as you rise, deep deep breaths, arch backs, and exhale. Exhale completely. Empty your lungs. Again, again! Get into the rhythm of it. Let us get rid of all that muscular armouring – hmm?'

Performing their feline crawls along the sand, arching their backs up at the moon, again and again, breathing in on the crawl and exhaling powerfully with the arching of the back, they *were* getting into a rhythm. After a while they did not need to think about the movements; having become cat-like, they simply gave expression to their natures.

Other exercises followed. They were commanded to kiss the sky. And to relax their lips. They were to smile until it hurt. Here and there he pulled out mouths by way of demonstration, into bigger smiles. 'Practise smiling,' he urged. 'Tight lips are for killers and politicians, not beautiful women.' After the smile, came the Lion, which involved turning their faces into roaring gargoyles, with tongues stuck out to their furthest extremity. They had to bend over backwards and grasp their ankles. This was said to help the adrenal gland and to stimulate the genital region.

'Must get rid of armouring,' Julian cried somewhat crossly. 'Armouring is the very devil, dams up bio-energy. You must let yourselves go, ladies . . .'

As far as Hardtman was able to tell, Joannie was not one of the class, and so he went back inside to look for her. None of the lamps had been switched on and the only light was the pale light coming from outside and the green, orange and pink colours shining through the illuminated juke box. Couples were dancing more closely, with deep amorous concentration.

Hardtman spotted Joannie. She was dancing, intimately,

with a large dark man, who despite his bulk was moving very energetically, and fast, to the swing beat. Joannie was being hurled outwards with quick flicks of the wrist and then reeled in like a fish, to be encompassed in a bear-like embrace, in the course of which the large man performed a great many violent hip movements that made her cry out half-protestingly. But he was determined, and sure of himself, and did not let her out of his grip, and despite her (perhaps only half-hearted) protests, he was persisting in his mock-copulatory movements. Hardtman felt a stab of jealous anger. He did not immediately know what to do. The impulse to rush over to them and pull them apart was clearly an unjustifiable reaction. What right had he to do that? She could dance with whom she wished. He lit a cigarette, and looking away as if he had not seen them at all, tried to decide how to handle this. He drew upon his capacity for distancing himself from any event for the sake of rationality and clarity of mind.

Allowing himself to look at the two of them again, Hardtman saw that the man's largeness was that of an athlete on the verge of going to fat, but still possesing verve and gusto and, presumably, strength. Joannie seemed to find him appealing, judging by the liberties she was permitting him. Could she not have waited a couple of days longer, until I am out of the way? Hardtman thought angrily. Does she have to do this in front of me? It was really embarrassing. The man's movements, if more symbolic than effectual, were explicit, and there could have been no doubt about the nature of the act he was parodying in this way. But she was docile to his purppose. Was she going to permit him to satisfy himself there and then? Hardtman's impulses were contradictory and managed to cancel each other out. On the one hand, he felt he wanted to rush up to them and punch this son of a bitch in his fat belly. Hardtman was amazed at the strength of this impulse in himself. It was, of course, impossible. Apart from the fact that the guy was far too big, doing such a thing would simply be a public admission of his relationship with the girl. Another option – and he was a man who cultivated his options –

was to break in on the two of them and say something so cutting as to shame Joannie and humiliate the man, but the trouble was that he could not for the life of him think of anything cutting enough to say. Only the obvious obscenities and scatological insults came into his mind. His third option was to ignore the whole thing, act as if he had seen nothing, go out and hope that when he came back in he would find them less intimately entangled. This seemed to be the best course of action, and so he went out on the sundeck again. Giving himself time to think at least.

It had got quite dark outside now, and the Yoga class had become even more indistinct: dark, stretching, striving, aspiring forms, seeking upwards and backwards and around.

Hardtman closed his eyes and tightly gripped the coping. To his great dismay, he felt close to weeping, out of hurt and anger and a sudden sense of hopelessness about everything, the whole lousy human situation: it all stank. His aptitude for clear analysis told him that he had no right whatsoever to any of these feelings. She was a free agent, not beholden to him. But still, even though there was no right or wrong about it, he just felt very cut up.

Julian's voice was distantly heard, drily urging his class to redoubled efforts.

'Now what about doing something about those dead pelvises, ladies?'

A discordant series of 'Yesses' came back and there were movements in the dark and the whole shape of the class seemed to be changing as it prepared itself for Julian's next words, while the regular beat of the tide subjected the supine forms to whiplashes of moonlight.

'Attitude of surrender,' Julian was calling out, 'relax into it, ladies, let all the tensions go, thighs wide, move from the pelvis . . .'

These exhortations appeared to Hardtman particularly aggravating in the state he was in, imagining how the big fellow with whom Joannie was dancing was perhaps even now enjoining her to a similar form of self-abandonment.

'Do not inhibit streaming,' Julian was instructing his

wide-thighed class. 'Permit it, let go, let go. Exhale . . . exhale . . . yes, yes, yes. Let all the breath out and permit streaming . . . do not resist it, we must get rid of those dead pelvises, mustn't we?'

Hardtman was reminded of an English clergyman drily reciting the phrases about the body and the blood of Christ, the resurrection and the life. Julian's words were having an untoward effect, or so it seemed to Hardtman, who may have been excessively susceptible to such imagery just then. It seemed to him, and as I say, perhaps he was just imagining it, it was dark, and one's eyes can play tricks in interpreting such indistinct movements: but it appeared to him that the dead pelvises were coming rumbustiously to life, seeking intercourse with the moon in their regular upward striving, and what he heard were not just the lapping sounds of the ocean, surely, but female gasps and cries and moans. Hardtman felt he must be hearing things – he was sometimes bothered by a ringing in the ears, and it was well known that at times of emotional stress the sense organs interpret information in a most biased way. These women appeared to be becoming delirious from the effect of their instructor's dry exhortations, and their armouring was clearly in an advanced stage of disavowal, and Julian was going on steadily, pleased with them. And now the sounds from the seashore were becoming, or so it seemed to Hardtman, perfectly orgiastic in their import.

He went back inside and the suddenness of his re-entry appeared to break the erotic spell in which Joannie had been held by her large dancing partner and she at once put a more decent distance between herself and him. She said something to him, and they stopped dancing, and both of them came over to Hardtman.

'Bill,' she said, 'I was looking for you. This is an old friend of mine, Peter. Peter, this is my friend, Bill.' As introductions went, under such circumstances, Hardtman thought that this one was a masterpiece of ambiguity.

'Is great pleasure know you, Bill,' Peter said, shouting over the boogie-woogie. 'Joannie tell me much about you. *Mes félicitations. Elle est adorable. Non? Is wonderrful woman*, Joannie.' He wagged a large warning finger at Hardtman. 'You will be good to her, or I kill you. Excuse me.' He gave a big laugh and threw massive arms around Hardtman's neck in a playful – but far from gentle – half-Nelson. 'Any time you don't want, I take back. O.K.? We make deal? Any time. Is fantastic woman, hmm? I love her. Am – excuse me – very jealous of you, Bill. You very lucky bugger, Bill. For two pins, I knock you down, huh?'

'Well, I have to say I sort of reciprocate that feeling, Peter,' Hardtman said.

'No, you don't need be jealous,' Peter said. 'Of me, *no*. I try but she give me big brosh-off. I am getting nowhere fast.'

'Didn't look as though you were getting nowhere fast.'

'Was for auld lang syne, like you say. We old friends, Joannie and me. Is not forever, I know. This is expectable and almost natural. I see you are swell guy so I wish you best of luck and remember, I take back any time, any time.' He chortled again at his own humorousness in making this offer. 'I wish you all best for you and go in peace my friend.' And with this he embraced Hardtman in a bear-like hug and kissed him upon each cheek, noisily, after which he kissed Joannie, and started to look around keenly. 'Is maybe something else for me here. I tell you I have big need for woman tonight. Have to have, you understand me?' He was searching out the field. 'One good thing, Julian always have plenty good-looking dames around. No? Excuse me.' He spread his hands eloquently and ambled off.

While her old friend Peter was talking, Joannie had kept quiet, partly because he had the sort of overwhelming manner of speaking that was not easy to interrupt, but also, Hardtman suspected, because she was furious at being handed over in quite such cavalier fashion.

The room was noisy and full of cigarette smoke, and Hardtman proposed that they go outside.

They walked along the raised gangway on piles, in the direction of the little harbour. He was angry with her.

'You know,' he said, 'I guess I have no right to ask anything of you, things being the way they are, but I do think it was – to say the least – a little vulgar of you to do that with your boyfriend in my presence.'

'We were just dancing.'

'You weren't just dancing, he was pawing you.'

She shrugged. 'I didn't notice.'

The transparency of this lie made Hardtman furious.

'You didn't notice!'

'That's how I am, I guess. He's an old friend, like I said.'

'Look,' he said, 'I don't ask very much – I'm not entitled to ask anything . . .'

'That's right, you're not. So don't ask.'

'While I'm with you, this short time, don't do anything, Joannie. It would be done to hurt. There couldn't be any other reason.'

'And afterwards . . . you don't mind what happens after?'

'I might mind,' he said, 'but *that* would be beyond the sphere of my expectations.'

'Oh I like that,' she said, ' "the sphere of your expectations". I like that a lot. What are they, as a matter of interest? In regard to me?'

'Just that you stay with me while we're together . . . why spoil it with little hurtful betrayals that can't mean anything to you? . . .'

'And what is this all supposed to mean to me? Huh? . . .'

'An adventure, Joannie . . . a perfect little adventure, with no hard feelings at the end. Isn't that the best?'

'Oh you do want everything your way.'

'Why not?'

'Yes, why not,' she agreed, and squeezed his hand suddenly, and said with a return of warmth. 'You got it wrong, Bill. I really wouldn't have done anything with Peter.'

'Not even for auld lang syne?'

'I already said that, didn't I?' And she kissed him deeply. It was like getting her back after having lost her and he held her tightly.

They were standing right in the middle of what was, though only three or four feet wide, one of the island's main thoroughfares, and seeing people approaching Hardt-man took Joannie's hand and together they jumped down from the raised gangway on to the rough scrub that grew out of the sand. They walked a few yards and stood kissing in the dark. They could be vaguely seen by everyone who passed, but he did not care. After a long time, they broke off, and he said: 'My! My! Kissing in public. At my age. How long since I've done that! Now there's a re-living of youth for you . . .'

'Not *re*-living,' she said softly. 'Living the part that's left.'

'Well, thanks for putting it like that. The truth is, and I suppose this is the old cliché, but I do feel younger being with you.'

She drew him towards her and offered very practically, 'You want to fool around?'

'You mean here?'

'Why not? There are going to be people at the cottage still – Christ knows when they'll leave. Over there, behind the bushes. Nobody'll see us, and who cares if they do?'

They found a spot to lie down. The sand was still warm. They could see people passing by on the raised gangway and even hear their conversations. She undid her jeans and slipped them off and then spread them out underneath her, and after that spread herself. He had to quieten her at one point, because of the sounds she was making. She was noisy in expressing her sensations, and being in a public place they could have been discovered by anyone who stepped off the gangway and walked half-a-dozen yards. But he hardly cared, carried away as he was by the re-living of his youth – or if she was right, by the living of what was left of it.

Afterwards they walked by the ocean, not returning to the cottage until after one a.m. It was very quiet when they came in. There were unwashed glasses and plates everywhere.

They couldn't hear any voices and concluded that everybody had left and that Julian had gone to sleep. Since no arrangements had been made about which room they were to have, Hardtman quietly opened one of the bedroom doors to see if it was occupied. It was, and Hardtman regretted his mistake. There was a smirk on Julian's face as the woman – it was one of the women from the Yoga class – lay across his lower body, her mouth busily working, while Katie Kantzler sat naked in the Buddha position, reading in a sonorous voice from a green-backed volume of pornography.

Julian did not seem unduly dismayed at being discovered; he made a mocking cross of benediction over the obeisant form, followed by a helpless kind of giggle, and a shrug of disapproval, which seemed to convey that whatever the stupid bitch was doing had nothing to do with him.

He did not even have the excuse of being drunk, Hardtman reflected, for his eyes had their usual late night cafeine-brightness.

What Hardtman had seen made him realize at once that he would have to leave the next day; in staying any longer he would be exposing himself to unforeseeable consequences.

18

In the morning he was awake early enough to see the sun rise. It appeared to come out of the ocean. His third morning waking up next to this girl. Now the *démon de midi*, as the French referred to these sexual compulsions of middle age, was quiet in him. Devoid of lust, he wondered what he was doing here: on Fire Island, in such dubious company. He was out of place here among these sort of people. And yet what he had seen and heard (or thought he had seen and heard) on the beach, and in the bedroom, while it had rather appalled him, in one way, had also – since he was a man who could always see the converse of any given point of view – posited the question: well, after all, why not? Was he to condemn somebody else's *démons*, whether of the *midi* or the *minuit*, simply because he – Hardtman – was not moved in that particular direction at that particular moment? Hardtman had to concede that whatever he may have felt last night he could not now treat Julian any differently. You could not repudiate your nighttime friends the next morning. But all the same he would have to leave before things got out of hand. Another night here might not find him as much in command of his *démon* as he was right now. There was something about Joannie, her easy persuadability, that made him fearful of his powers of persuasion.

He let her sleep until nine and then woke her, not with a kiss of passion this time, but with the news that he was going to have to leave this morning.

He saw that she resented being woken and told such things straight off. She, no doubt, preferred to say her goodbyes late at night, with drinks and music, and a bed to fall into, and perhaps somebody else already in it. Whereas he was one of these first-thing-in-the-morning fanatics, who had everything worked out before other people were even awake.

'I'm sorry,' he said.

'I'm not awake, yet, give me five minutes. I can't take things in until I've had coffee.'

'I'll make some,' he said getting out of bed. No passionate awakening this time.

When she'd had her morning coffee she did begin to comprehend what he was telling her. She did not protest. If that was how it was, well . . .

'What time do you want to leave?'

'We should get the morning boat.'

She looked at her watch.

'I guess we can just make that.'

There wasn't time to wash or shave, and he hadn't shaved yesterday either. Evidence of decline?

Julian emerged red-eyed and Hardtman said that he and Joannie were leaving on the morning boat. It took time for this to sink in. But as he gulped down his third cup of coffee, he at last appeared to regain consciousness.

'I'll come, too,' he said.

'Oh there's no need.'

'No,' Julian said, 'it is time I left.' He gave a slightly sheepish grin. 'One or two members of the class are getting to be a bit of a handful.'

'So I had noticed,' Hardtman said with a small smile, since he did not wish to give an impression of censoriousness.

'Yes, I think this is the best time to leave, before the rest are awake,' Julian said decisively.

'And your classes?'

'Oh well,' he said vaguely, 'I can only give them while I am here. If I am not here,' he shrugged, 'there are no classes – that's all there is to it.' He paused for a moment, and then added, 'Besides, I want to talk to you, Bill. I owe you an explanation.'

'Of course you don't.'

'No, but I would rather. I don't want you to think . . .'

'Really, Julian . . .' Hardtman gave a worldly grin. 'You have never exactly made a secret of your . . . bohemianism. I only regret that I opened the wrong door . . . that you hadn't had the foresight to lock it.'

'No locks,' Julian said. 'You see . . .'

'No, but really there's no need to explain, Julian, and besides we must be going if we are to get the morning boat. If we are travelling back to Washington together, then you can say anything you want to say to me on the train. There'll be plenty of time then.'

'All right, Bill.'

It was a rush to get to the boat in time, and they only just made it, and as it pulled out of the harbour they flopped out on wooden seats on the deck.

Hardtman, with Joannie dozing against his shoulder, watched Fire Island disappearing into the ocean in a great blaze of gold and orange like Sodom and Gomorrah being destroyed, he couldn't help thinking. Then he considered a return to reality – or at any rate, respectability. The first step would be saying goodbye to Joannie, and while she dozed he tried to work out how this could best be done.

When she opened her eyes, he said softly: 'What I thought we'd do is: have an early lunch together, and then I'll get a train immediately afterwards. We could eat at Penn Station. And I want to get you a present.'

'I don't want anything.'

'I want to get you something – some memento.'

'I don't believe in that. The only thing I want is – a photograph of you.'

'I don't have one.'

'Julian can take one of us. I'd like that. That's the only memento I'd like to have.'

'I haven't shaved for two days, I look like a hobo.'

'Oh I think you look lovely, and anyway this is how I know you and how I want to remember you.'

'All right—'

They told Julian what they wanted, and he took some photos of them as they stood against the boat rail looking at each other; the taking of the photographs seemed to mark the end of the adventure, and afterwards there was a glumness in the air. Joannie was quiet and Hardtman also could find little to say. As they were getting off the boat at Babylon, he suggested that they take a taxi back to New York, it would save waiting around for a train. They were on the quayside, in a crush of disembarking passengers, as he proposed this. Joannie looked up at him and said very quietly:

'Why don't you and Julian take the taxi and I'll wait for the train.'

'But,' he protested, 'we're having lunch ... at the station. Aren't we?'

'What's the point?' she said.

'I thought we had agreed on that?'

'A weepy lunch at Penn Station,' she said. 'All that'll happen is you'll get smashed, and I'll get smashed and it just drags out ...'

'Say goodbye here, in this crowd – just like that?'

'Yes, Bill.'

He was impressed by her strength in proposing this quick clean cut, but he was not ready, had not fully prepared himself for the final break, had been counting on lunch and the easing effect of alcohol.

'No,' he said, 'this isn't right, we can't say goodbye like this. Here. I would feel bad about it.'

'I'm going to say goodbye to you, Bill. Right now. It's better.'

He had lost her. He had lost his power to persuade her. She had already separated from him, inside herself, and was free of him.

'What will you do now?'

'I'll go back to my apartment.'

'I meant with your life.'

'I'll get on with it,' she said. 'Oh I'll go into hibernation for a couple of weeks, I expect.' She paused, and then looking at him said, 'I want you to know that I love you.' It was said flatly, a simple statement of fact, without strings. She started to walk away.

He was stunned. The combination of her saying this to

him, now, and at the same time walking away, made him confused. He let her go a few steps and then went after her and grabbed hold of her roughly.

'You're having lunch with me,' he said. 'Come on,' and he began to drag her in the direction in which Julian had been going.

For a moment it seemed as though she might resist, but he was holding her so tightly and there was such determination in his eyes that it was clear she would have to struggle to free herself, and so she gave a shrug, and went along with him.

Little was said by anyone during the taxi drive back into the city. For the first time Julian's presence was felt as an obstacle to their being able to talk; he sensed this, and at Penn Station when they had made their seat reservations, he left.

'Let me take you somewhere,' Hardtman began. He made an extravagant gesture of the hand to convey his generous impulse towards her.

'To buy my lacy lingerie?' she asked. 'I think it's sort of bad timing for anything like that, wouldn't you say?'

He had to agree that it was. 'There are other things.'

She thought a while and then said, 'The one thing I do want right now that I can't afford myself is a television.'

'Are they any good, those things?'

He seemed uninterested by this suggestion: a television set did not strike him as being a suitable parting gift.

'I want to give you something more . . . more personal,' he said. 'Well, anyway, let's think about it at lunch. Think of what you want.'

They were standing in the great vaulted space of the General Waiting Room, high light slanting down on them. Between massive Doric columns a double stairway rose to the train concourse and the station dining room.

'Should we eat here?'

'I'm not hungry.'

'Neither am I. We can have a drink.'

'That's what I was afraid of.'

But she laughed and was with him again.

Looking for a bar, they got lost in the vast Roman station, were carried along by jostling crowds of people possessed of departure hysteria, which each loudspeaker announcement brought to a new pitch. She had been right – there was something awful and weepy about railway station goodbyes. He remembered all the railway stations of his childhood: Vienna, Nice, Zürich, Berlin and the ache of leaving, the finality of it. No matter where you were going on to, you always left something behind that was irreplaceable, a piece of your lifetime. It was only a few days that he was leaving behind now, but they seemed as momentous as the whole of youth.

Not watching where they were going, preoccupied with themselves, they were swept along in sudden waves and eddies of rushing, overladen travellers, trailing distraught wives and screaming infants. Suddenly they were in an enormous greenhouse of dusty domed and vaulted glass and trains were leaving and people were waving and weeping.

'Christ,' Joannie said, 'I want a drink.'

'We can go to the Statler across the street.'

'I want one quicker than that.'

'They'll give us a drink at the restaurant, I expect.'

They went to the station Dining Room, though it was somewhat sombre, and a little too grand, with coffered ceiling and a long row of high arched windows, and Hardtman ordered a bottle of champagne and after the first couple of glasses everything eased up a little.

'We ought to eat something,' he proposed, 'or we *will* be smashed – we've had no breakfast.'

All they could face was an omelette, and they picked at that.

'I'm going to miss you like hell,' he told her.

'This isn't distant thunder any more,' she said. 'This is the whole fucking Warsaw Concerto. Check?'

'Yes.'

She pushed away the omelette.

'They say – somebody said, anyway . . .' Hardtman started.

'Like the man said . . . ?'

'. . . that the trick is, the trick of life is being happy in the full knowledge of loss, because in the end you've got to lose.' He laughed sharply.

'Yeah. That man wasn't kidding.'

'No, he wasn't.'

'What am I supposed to do about it?' she said.

'Nothing. There's no other way, that's all I'm saying.'

'If anybody ever invents another way, I sure want a piece of it.'

'Me too.'

'Get them to bring another bottle,' she said.

When they had drunk most of the second bottle, and were underwater swimmers together, gliding painlessly along in sad sentimental accord, he said, 'This really has been an adventure for me . . . uuuuph . . . excuse me. It's taken me out of myself. And I needed that. Uuuuph. There's something about me that doesn't take well to . . . uuuuph . . . pleasure . . .'

'Or champagne on an empty stomach.'

'Check. What I wanted to say . . . what did I want to say? Know I wanted to say *something*. Lost my train . . .'

'You've missed your train . . . Jesus Christ! Well, what is little wifey going to say? Naughty, naughty Billy boy. What have you been up to in the wicked city?'

'Joannie, I think you are drunk. Better eat something.'

'Who's calling who drunk? Talk for yourself, buddy.'

'What I'm doing. What do you say we have some caviar? My daughter, aged 15, loves caviar. Has become a goddam caviar connoisseur, aged 15. Now isn't that decadent?'

'O.K., I'll connoisseur some caviar, if you'll connoisseur us another bottle of champagne with it . . .'

'We've had rather a lot . . .'

'Can't have caviar without champagne.'

The caviar was brought in a small silver-rimmed dish sunk in a larger dish packed with ice.

The caviar made them thirsty and they quickly got through the champagne, after which, as a sop to the principle of self-restraint, he gave subsequent orders in half-bottles.

'Who said railway station lunches were no fun,' Joannie said.

'You did.'

'I did?'

'Yes. But what was *I* saying? Something . . . about . . . pleasure.'

'*What* about pleasure?'

'I'm not too good at it.'

'I'm good at it,' she said, giggling.

'I know. That's what I wanted to say. You're great at it. You're fantastic at it.'

'I am?'

'Yes, you've made me . . . lighter.'

'I *have*! Well, you've made me heavier.' She giggled again. 'No, no – I don't mean *heavier*. What do I mean? I mean deeper. You know, you probably changed my life.'

This last statement was made with a kind of drunken seriousness that had to be respected. 'I'll never forget you. I've never known anyone like you. Hey listen : don't forget to send me the pix . . .'

'You know what Kierkegaard says . . . ?'

'No, I don't know what Kierkegaard says . . .'

'Kierkegaard says that when you have given up the princess you regain her by virtue of the absurd.'

'Is that a fact? That's what Kierkegaard says. Well, hurray for Kiekegaard in that case. Good old Kierkegaard. Boy, is that like having your cake and eating it . . .'

'Yes, except that the eating is just a little bit abstract.'

'That's what I was afraid of. Abstract cake. Let 'em eat abstract cake like the lady said.'

Through a thick pink haze that was like the soft packing around breakable objects, he saw the hand of the station clock do one of its periodic convulsive jerks towards the Roman numeral IV.

'Jesus Christ,' he said, 'you see what time it is! I *am* going to miss my train.' He jumped up in some agitation.

She said, 'Don't forget to send the pix.' She kissed him. 'I love you,' she said.

'I love you,' he said formally, and then in sudden consternation remembered that he had not bought her a present. As he was writing a cheque to pay for the meal, he wrote a second one and pushed it into Joannie's jeans pocket. 'Take that,' he said, 'and get yourself whatever you want. I've made it out to Macy's – you can fill in the amount. Get a television, if you want to. Whatever. I want to give you something.'

'You've already given me something,' she said.

'Are you coming?' he asked now, urgently.

'No,' she said, 'I'm not coming to the train with you. Goodbye, Bill.'

'Goodbye, Joannie. You really are a lovely woman.'

As he was making his way hurriedly under the flying ribs of steel to the platform, he looked around and caught a glimpse of her making her way out, carrying her Saks carrier bag, a light traveller.

Julian was already in his seat when Hardtman came into the carriage and flopped down.

'You had lunch, I see,' Julian observed.

'A very liquid one,' Hardtman agreed.

He was only vaguely conscious of the train beginning to move, emerging from this dusty crystal palace into harsh sunshine, whose impact was merely visual in the air-conditioned car, and by lowering the blinds slightly that minor disturbance too could be eliminated.

The train seemed to be going in several directions at once, not only ahead, but also sideways and up and down, violently, like a roller coaster. Hell, I better try and sleep this off, he thought but when he closed his eyes it was worse: he was free-floating in space, without anchorage or sense of direction.

'I think coffee,' he said, opening his eyes and squinting at Julian. My God, how he must look. Unshaven, dishevelled, drunk.

Julian grinned. *He* was in one piece, all put together again after the events of last night.

Looking through the lower part of the car window, Hardtman saw the ground moving fast – he saw only the ground – the blind cut out the trees and buildings, and this ground that seemed to be shifting under his feet like a swamp into which he was sinking was strangely lifeless. He felt strange, not himself, as if he were not inside his own skin, as if he had a double, now this side of him, now that. A well-known phenomenon of drunkenness, he reminded himself, to see double, and who was to say that such tricks of vision must be confined to the way one saw others. Certainly, Julian did not have any of these mysterious appendages that Hardtman appeared to have acquired.

'Tell me, Julian,' he demanded, 'why I appear to have become double while you have remained resolutely single.'

'I am a great believer in citrus fruit and honey to counteract that effect,' Julian said with a grin.

'Well, I was brought up on the hair-of-the-dog school of thought,' Hardtman countered, summoning the steward. He ordered brandy. With the second one he began to recover, and after the third the unwelcome double had disappeared.

'I wanted to explain about last night,' Julian began. 'It was unfortunate that ...'

'Oh hell, Julian, it doesn't make any difference to me who you screw ... don't feel you have to explain to me ... anything. As you no doubt have concluded, I am hardly in a position or a state to pass moral judgment on anyone.'

'It is unfortunate that those rooms don't have locks on the doors ...'

'You could put some on,' Hardtman suggested helpfully. 'If you intend to go in for that sort of thing.'

Julian grinned back with complete understanding.

'On the whole,' he remarked, 'I think that the trip was a success, don't you? I haven't had a chance to say this before, but I do think that the speech went very well. You said some things that needed saying. I think you may have put a spoke in the wheel of some of the wilder people in Washington.'

'Well, I hope so. I hope so.'

Julian's brow ruffled up into an expression of deep concern. It indicated he was about to be helpful.

'You know,' he said, 'if you thought it might serve some useful purpose, Bill, I could get word to certain people on the other side – privately, you understand, indicating that in a crisis there was a line open, a line of reason and good sense. That the hot-heads aren't running the show . . .'

'Well, neither am I,' Hardtman said.

'Oh I know that. But at the same time, you are in a position where . . . well, there are avenues open to you. I happen to have a good friend who also happens to be a patient of mine . . .'

'Sometimes, Julian,' Hardtman said sharply, 'I think perhaps you have a few too many good friends in a few too many places.' Though he was packed safe as porcelain against rough handling, a couple of jolts were coming through all the protective cushioning, and he was feeling them. 'What I said in my speech, Julian, was a statement of my own personal views. I expressed my opinion, which you are permitted to do in this country, unlike in some. But I don't decide America's foreign policy, and though I am one of the people called upon to advise the President on some matters, whether or not he takes my advice is up to him, and it's not for me to get through to anyone else . . .'

'That's a cop-out, Bill, if I may say so. Isn't it?' For once Julian was not immediately backing down. 'If you don't mind my saying so, Bill, if there is no responsibility – or freedom of action – below the top, what are we doing at Nuremberg, hanging all those people who were just carrying out the Führer's orders?'

Hardtman did not feel in any condition to embark upon such a discussion, but the subject having been broached, he could not evade it.

'The case we were making at Nuremberg is that there are certain acts so patently immoral – that so obviously go counter to all standards of human decency – that even if

304

ordered to carry them out everybody has a superior duty to humanity, and himself, to disobey.'

'Don't you think that launching a preventive war against the Soviet Union comes in that category, Bill?'

'Yes, it might, it might. And if I knew it was going to happen I *might* feel I had to take action against my own government, and accept the consequences of doing that. But that is something I would have to decide at the time, consulting my own conscience. Anything I might do under such circumstances is not at all the same as informing a foreign power, in advance, that they can count on me. In case you don't realize it, Julian, doing *that* would constitute being an enemy agent.'

'Oh I think you are making rather heavy weather of this, Bill. I wasn't suggesting anything like that. Good heavens, you know me well enough. I was merely trying to be helpful . . . I thought it might be useful to correct any false impressions, and I just happen to know how that could be done on a confidential level . . .'

Hardtman felt he was falling . . . the ground whirling by outside gave him the impression he was falling horizontally into a deep pit. He was not feeling at all well.

'Anyone would think you were on their side, the way you sometimes talk,' Hardtman threw back at Julian. 'You're always defending the Soviets. For God's sake, Julian, can't you see that there is all the difference in the world between my making a public speech criticizing certain elements in my country, and doing the same thing by means of some private conduit to the other side? . . . That's what's called treason.'

'Oh you do exaggerate, Bill. You really do.'

'Maybe I do, maybe I do. I hope so, Julian.'

He suddenly saw Julian's face as he had glimpsed it on Fire Island; in that moment of accidental intrusion; the secret, gloating look, the heavy-lidded eyes. Oh those smitten women, helpless in his hands, under his influence: their cries. Getting them in the position of surrender, thighs wide, straining. Abasing themselves. Abusing themselves for a promise of freedom. Katie Kantzler reciting

305

filth. That other woman, worshipping at his loins. And catching again on Julian's face the look of having got away with it, Hardtman suddenly saw before him, admittedly only hazily, in view of the amount he had drunk, what he took to be an image of pure evil, evil such as the Communists represented, tyranny and orgy, the night call of the secret police. Hardtman saw Rasputin, no less: the mad monk and false healer, an incarnation of debauchery and malign influence and power. And then he knew he was going to be sick, that there was no holding back the swirling nausea within him, and he called the steward and said: 'I'm sorry to say I'm going to throw up. Will you please assist me to the men's room.'

Later, on the train, he recovered sufficiently to reassess his earlier views and categorize them as excessive. He was a fair-minded man, and when he had judged somebody unfairly he rectified his error. There was no reason to attribute such unworthy motives to Julian, there was nothing in his conduct, which had always been friendly and helpful, to make Hardtman think ill of him. Nothing. On the contrary, he had always gone out of his way to be helpful.

And his political urgings, taken in context, had surely been innocent enough, expressions of a wish that many people felt, to do *something*. Julian had not realized the way it sounded, and maybe it only sounded that way because everybody was so jittery at the moment, so obsessed with spies. Surely all he had meant to pass on was a message of peace.

19

To avoid a repetition of the incident when he had wandered around the streets unable to find a taxi, Hardtman had left his car with the doorman of the Commodore Hotel, which was just a short walk from Union Station.

So upon arriving in Washington he and Julian straight away went to the Commodore.

Hardtman was not in the best of shape; he had a heavy head, his legs were unsteady and it seemed to him as if everything that had happened in the past three days had happened to somebody else. It was all so unlike him: his wild sexual behaviour with the girl; his skilful lying to Laurene. And when he thought of the things he had seen on Fire Island, and of his conversation with Julian on the train, it seemed as if he might have imagined it all, or at any rate misconstrued the evidence of his eyes and ears in some basic way.

He was pacing impatiently as he waited for his car to be brought. The atmosphere was heavy and still: not a cool breeze anywhere in this whole swamp of a city. There was a lack of sharpness about everything. A Buick was standing at the end of the hotel's drive, not moving, with people in it, and it annoyed him. Why were they not getting out, or driving off? Why were they just sitting there? Watching him? Was that what they were doing? He walked up to the car and stared at the couple inside, through the windscreen. They were kissing – they had the air of illicit lovers. As a matter of fact, the man, though his face was obscured by the woman's passionate caresses, looked a bit like the furniture salesman from Hoboken, the fellow bar-fly of the Plaza Hotel. Beginning to see furniture salesmen from Hoboken everywhere. A bad sign.

His car finally arrived; Julian offered to drive, but Hardtman rejected the offer a touch disdainfully.

'I am perfectly capable of driving, Julian.'

'Of course.'

As he drove off, fast, it felt as if the wheels were not making contact with the ground; the Lincoln's steering was light, but this was like driving a paper dart. He was sealed inside thick protective glass, and feeling nothing. Nothing. He put his foot down on the accelerator pedal and made the car leap forward – just to get a shot of adrenalin flowing through his system. It was a clear stretch, and the Lincoln's rapid acceleration took him up to 60 m.p.h. in seconds. In the mirror he saw the Buick Roadmaster coming up fast behind him, getting up to 60 too. Wasn't that the car from the Commodore Hotel drive? With the illicit lovers. The Hokoben furniture salesman and the passé secretary in the see-through sleeves . . . Ha, ha, ha. He was getting to be like Walter Cole, seeing conspiracies everywhere. The lights ahead were just changing and his speed would have carried him through comfortably, but he slammed on his brakes and came to a screeching halt and watched the Buick do the same. It pulled up with its bumper practically touching Hardtman's, that close. Adjusting his mirror, Hardtman tried to get a good look at the occupants of the car behind him, but they were kissing again. Evidently couldn't leave each other alone even for a moment at a red light, such was the intensity of their passion.

'Sit tight,' Hardtman told Julian. 'I believe we're being tailed.'

He put his foot down hard, and the big limousine shot off from the light, with a great forward leap of power, and the Buick, in its more modest way, followed suit.

'Copy cat,' Hardtman murmured darkly, keeping his foot flat on the floor. 'Let's see you follow this, whoever in hell you are.' He was over the railway bridge, getting to the seedy part of town. Out of the corner of his eye he saw an ancient black drunk sliding down a billboard-plastered wall, sinking slowly, head turning in all directions in his delirium.

The two cars, virtually in tandem, went through two

changing lights together. What the hell was this? They were in an area of abandoned houses and pawnshops. People were out on their stoops. Some were on the iron fire escapes, bedded down for the night. It was a hot night again. A Baptist church, low and old and crumbling. The dark hulks of tenements. Heads were turning, and shaking, as the two cars whooshed by. Parking lots. A violent domestic scene framed in a lit window. Hardtman took the view that you were not required to talk to everyone at a party, and likewise you could not become involved in all aspects of life. Some aspects you just whizzed through in a fast car. One chose one's areas of involvement. And he was not involved with these people here. Just driving through, followed by a Buick. Hardtman was a man who subscribed to the philosophic concept that character is destiny, and if this was so, since he was a man of careful character, nothing untoward should have occurred in his life – barring a brick on the head. But bricks do fall on even the most careful of heads ...

The light ahead was red, but the streets looked clear, and Hardtman was determined to test the illicit lovers in the Buick, and he shot through the light. From his right a taxi cab moved off prematurely from stop, not waiting for the green, and Hardtman had to swerve out to avoid hitting it ... he saw the cabby's furious face at the window, a shaking fist, and he saw the Buick also going through the red light, and the taxi spin round like a whipped top to get out of the way.

Past the light, Hardtman slowed down a little to see what the Buick would do, and it slowed down too.

'What is this?' Julian asked.

'I don't know, but I'm going to find out,' Hardtman said.

He was slowing down, with the intention of stopping and confronting these 'lovers' and demanding an explanation, but now the taxi cab had caught up with them, and the cabby was hurling abuse:

'Fuckin' crazy madman ... what are you? Speed-kings? Huh?' And in his frustration and rage, he suddenly twisted his steering wheel sideways as if he was going to run

309

right into the side of the glittering and polished Lincoln, as if to batter its shapely bodywork with his cab, which looked as though it had battered one or two cars lately – it's grille was like an open jaw from the loss of vertical chrome bars, and its exhaust pipe was loose and banging against the ground regularly, and the lid of the boot was loose and making a clatter as it bounced up and down, and the hood was tied down with string and shaking and clattering, too. Trying to keep up with the Lincoln in order to get his foul thoughts across, the cab driver was causing his engine to emit a screaming whine. It was like being hounded by some clanking African witch doctor hung about with pots and pans. Hardtman kept having to swerve away to avoid being hit by the cab. This was absurd. He was being abused with a degree of violence out of proportion to what had happened . . . evidently this taxi driver had some grudge against people in large Lincolns. 'It's guys like you,' he shouted through his open window, 'stink up the air. You think you own the streets, you think you own everything, huh. Do what you like, huh? Big guys! Huh? Big guy. Big car. Big asshole! That's what you are. Big fuckin' assholes.' Hardtman thought: it appears to be my fate to be persecuted by taxi drivers. Even when I try to avoid having any dealings with them, they somehow catch up with me. Such was the unavoidable nature of one's fate. This was really crazy. He was not going to start arguing with this oaf. Since one could not stop to argue with everyone. So he put his foot down on the accelerator and pulled ahead. It got the taxi driver even madder, and with head stuck out of his window he kept after the Lincoln, filling the night with his obscene shouts. The Buick, attempting to follow, was on the taxi driver's tail, making it a sort of procession. The cab was being pushed way beyond its capacity: it was emitting a death rattle of all its loose parts. When Hardtman went through a changing light, the taxi followed, even though by then the light was red. There was a sky-blue roadster coming from the right. To avoid it, the taxi driver swung to his left and went into the oncoming lane of crossways traffic. It was all coming straight at him, and he could

310

only go up on the pavement. He hit the kerb with the side of his wheel, and instead of mounting the pavement was bounced back into the oncoming traffic. A Ford coupé went into his tail, causing him to spin like a whirligig. Coming out of the spin, he did, now, mount the pavement; hit a lamp-post; came off that and with a sudden bursting open of his loose hood went right into a hardware store window.

On the iron fire escapes all around, black faces were shaking with a silent sort of knowingness.

Hardtman had pulled to a halt. He saw the messy pile up on the other side of the road, and he saw the Buick, hemmed in by other stopped cars now, and he ran to it and wrenched open the driver's door.

'What the hell are you . . .'

He stopped short in amazement. It *was* the furniture salesman from Hoboken. No question. The bald pass between the high peaks of hair either side of his scalp. The seducer's knowing air. Only the girl was different. Another thirty-seven-year-old secretary trying to look twenty-nine in see-through sleeves.

'You sure do get around,' Hardtman said.

'What?'

'Why are you following me?'

'You're crazy, Mister. I'm not following you. What gives you that idea?'

'I've seen you twice at the Plaza Hotel, and now you've been tailing me ever since I left the station . . .'

'You're crazy,' he said. 'Crazy guy,' he said to the girl at his side, and pulling his door shut, and locking it, performed a quick manoeuvre in the traffic pile up and threaded his way out. Hardtman was looking to see where he was going, noting the car's number, and about to take off in pursuit when he suddenly found himself grabbed by the red-faced taxi driver whose face was even redder now that there was blood running down it from his skull and nose. Hardtman felt himself gripped at the neck . . . and he ducked in time to avoid the worst of the blow, which none the less connected with the side of his face, bruising him

311

and stunning him. Julian, with the help of another man, managed to grab the taxi driver's arms and hold him.

Arms held, he was reduced to words again, and he vowed: 'You are going to pay for this, asshole. Oh you are going to pay for this, assface.'

I shouldn't be surprised, Hardtman thought. One always paid for one's pleasures and such dues were not always collected by people with the best of manners.

The police were soon there. He heard their sirens converging from several directions, and then overlap.

'Let's go back to the car,' Hardtman said to Julian. He waited there without talking until the accident officer came over.

'You the other party involved?'

'Well, I wouldn't really say I was involved, but I more or less saw what happened. Something got into that taxi driver ... I don't know what.'

'You O.K., sir?' the cop asked, seeing the mark on Hardtman's face from the fist blow, and that he was in a Lincoln.

'He took a swipe at me, for some reason.'

'Claims you were going like crazy, sir. That you nearly went into him.'

'He came after me ...'

'What sort of speed were you doing, sir?'

'I don't know. I'd like to talk to the lieutenant.' He felt in his breast pocket and took out his White House pass which he showed the accident officer.

Cops were lighting accident flares and putting up detour barriers and directing the traffic around the pile-up. Others were on their knees in the road, measuring skid marks.

The police lieutenant arrived within a couple of minutes. He was very respectful. An ambulance had arrived and the taxi driver was being escorted to it, despite his protests.

'Is he all right?' Hardtman asked.

'Oh yeah, seems to be. It's amazing, looking at that pile of scrap metal, but he just seems to be shook up, that's all, and some small cuts. Lucky. He was lucky.'

He paused and then said hesitantly, 'You want to say

now why you were exceeding the speed limit, sir?' He shot a glance to the skid marks made by the Lincoln as it pulled up. 'I think they're going to show,' he said with a practised eye, 'that you were doing around 50.'

'I was being tailed,' Hardtman said. 'I don't know by whom, or for what purpose. But since my job is connected with national security, it seemed necessary that (a) I should establish that I was being followed, and (b) to get the hell out of it, since there was no knowing what the man's purpose might be . . .'

'And this person who followed you, I take it he didn't stay around?'

'No, he didn't.'

'All right, Mr Hardtman. We may need to ask you and Dr Blake some more questions but we can leave that for another time. In view of your pressing obligations, I won't keep you here.'

He was glad to have been let go. He did not feel in any condition to answer more questions. Perhaps in the morning he would be more capable of making sense of things.

He was evasive with Laurene when he got home, telling her only the barest details of the accident. He was exhausted and wished to rest, he said.

'Wasn't Fire Island restful?' she asked.

'I'll tell you about it tomorrow,' he said. 'I want to try and get some sleep. My jaw is hurting. Hope that maniac hasn't broken my jaw bone . . .'

'You want me to call Dr Davies?'

'No. I just want to sleep.'

But he slept little, and badly, and dreamt he was driving a car around blind corners without being able to see where he was going.

20

Next morning, at the office, he waded through a pile of papers. The situation in Germany was worsening. Stalin, according to the latest reports, was saying that as long as Germany was treated as a whole, the presence of allied occupation troops in Berlin, as the capital, was natural; but as a result of the London conference, a separate state had been created in Western Germany, a state that was once more raising the spectre of German aggression, and it had its own capital, Frankfurt. Two capitals now existed. Berlin was the centre of the Soviet zone. If Germany was divided, and the Western state was becoming an outpost of Western imperialism, and a base for assaults upon the East, then the right of Western powers to maintain troops in Berlin had lost its juridical basis. There were more of the usual charges. The West had broken international agreements concerning the dismantling of German armaments industries. American bankers and monopolists were making the former patrons of Hitler the vassals of American imperialism, and promoting sabotage and sowing the seeds of future war.

Hardtman phoned Cole.

'Yes,' Cole said, 'they're trying to build up a legal pretext for military interference in Berlin. Their aim is to apply so much pressure that our position there will become untenable. They want to bamboozle us into agreeing to a so-called Democratic Central Government for the whole of Germany, which they would allow to continue as long as they saw fit. And then they'll seize control of the whole of Germany by means of a *coup d'état*, as they've done in Czechoslovakia. We're not buying that, Bill. At least, I hope we're not buying that.'

'You making sure, Walter?'

'I do what I can.'

'I bet.'

'Sorry to hear about your little accident, Bill.'

'Oh you heard about that – you hear everything, Walter.'

'Only what I need to hear. Ho-ho-ho.'

'How does it happen that you needed to hear that?'

'We have an arrangement with the metropolitan police that we're informed if any of our people get into any scrapes.'

'I'm not one of your people.'

'Those hairline distinctions are lost on them. Anything I can do?'

'What d'you mean *can do*?'

'Well, we can't have the local cops poke their nose into things that are none of their business, Bill. I trust they are not being a nuisance. If they are, just let me know, and I'll take care of it.'

'You can do that?'

'Oh surely.'

'I don't think that's going to be necessary . . . I think they are being reasonable.'

'About the speed thing?'

'You have a detailed report, then?'

'The relevant details.'

'About that speed thing, and the reason why I was speeding, I think I should talk to you about that, and not on the phone.'

'Meet me at the Jefferson Memorial,' Cole said. 'You can usually park there. Say 12.30? By the way, congratulations on your speech.'

'Yes? You approved?'

'Sure.'

'Never quite know with you, Walter, where you stand.'

'Bill, the Madman's Advantage is a stratagem for external consumption. You and I are not obliged to be crazy, you know.'

'I'm glad to hear that. With all your bluffs and double-bluffs and feints, I wasn't sure.'

'You know I stand firm on the basics.'

'What are they?'

315

'Bill, I don't have to tell you that. I stand where I've always stood. That's where I stand. Where you stand. And I stand behind you. Remember that, Bill.'

'O.K., and we're not going to take this lying down, right?'

'Ho-ho-ho-ho. Right, Bill. Right.'

He met Cole at the foot of the Jefferson. Swarms of tourists were toiling up the high steps to look at the great figure in bronze and read the self-evident truths inscribed in white marble. The sky was a glowing grey, like hot metal, with no sign of the sun. Walter Cole was wearing a Panama hat. They started to walk around the Tidal Basin.

'Well, Bill, what's on your mind?'

'I'm being followed, Walter.'

Cole said nothing.

'What happened last night is that somebody was following me in a Buick; I was trying to throw him off, and that's how the whole thing occurred. The thing is I got a look at the guy who was following me, and it's somebody I spotted a few days ago in New York, and also once before.'

'Yes, I know,' Cole said.

'You know . . . you *knew* I was being followed?'

Cole nodded.

'By whom?'

'FBI.'

'How d'you know that?'

'I know. The FBI is supposed to let us see their files. They are somewhat remiss in this regard, but we have our own way of remedying their defaults.'

'Are they tapping my phone as well?'

'Yes.'

'Why?'

'You are very friendly with the British, and there is a leak in the British Embassy.'

'That means they know all my moves, where I go? What I do? Everything?'

'Yes.'

'And you know, too?'

'Yes.' And he added by way of clarification. 'Yes, I know

about Miss Fontanez. Now don't be . . . upset about that. Your secret is as safe with me as if I were your priest.'

'It's illegal for them to tap my phone.'

'I shouldn't be surprised. It's also illegal for us to tap their telephones, but we do all the same. Only way of getting certain information out of the Bureau.'

'What has earned me their special attention?'

'Well, Bill, I can see from their point of view that there is a greater-than-usual degree of rationality in their action. With all these spies everywhere, that we read about, and the Bureau not having been able to find them, what else can they do but leave no stone unturned? You do see a great deal of Dr Blake.'

'What has that got to do with anything?'

'Don't be ingenuous. Dr Blake is, to say the least, a dubious figure. I'm interested in him myself.'

'What are you implying?'

Cole looked back across the flat expanse of water to the neo-Grecian temple at its edge.

'He knows everyone . . . and he moves around. Doesn't he move around! You see him everywhere. At British receptions, Polish receptions, Russian receptions . . . Takes his patients with total impartiality from both sides of the fence. Now the reason it didn't click with me sooner is because we've all been thinking of Homer as one person. But when you examine the evidence, there's no reason to suppose that the sources all refer to one and the same man. If we postulate a source inside the Embassy, and somebody outside acting as a conduit for passing the messages to the other side, you can see what a perfect role the latter would be for Dr Blake.'

Hardtman began to feel an insistent tap tap on the protective glass that surrounded him, remembering Julian's proposition on the train: that he go to people on the other side . . . a line open to reason . . .

'What's the matter, Bill? You're not looking well.'

'Since you know everything about me, Walter,' Hardtman snapped back, 'I don't suppose I have to tell you that I had rather too much to drink yesterday.'

'Yes, all that champagne at the railway station.' Cole shuddered. 'Personally, I'm not that fond of the stuff. But I suppose it is *the* drink for certain kinds of occasions. You can see, can't you, Bill, that Dr Blake is the perfect conduit? His patients are protected by the secrecy of the consulting room. And there would be nothing inherently suspicious in the fact that he saw somebody from the British Embassy at nine and from the Soviet Embassy at ten. Note the fact of his carelessness about bills, which you may have experienced. Bills usually give the dates of consultations and names, which might establish a pattern of links. But since he rarely sends bills, and when he does just tends to write "for services rendered", it would be impossible to establish links.'

'Is that the sum total of what you have on him?'

'There's also the way he cultivates you, and others.'

'Other people do that, too.'

'Perhaps not quite to the same degree. Taking you to New York . . . introducing you to that girl.'

'What are you suggesting?' Hardtman said touchily.

'He has photographs of you and this girl, which could indicate an intention . . . at some future stage . . .'

'I asked him to take those photographs. They're perfectly innocent. He gave them to me. The negatives as well. It was the girl who wanted it. A memento.'

'Foolish, no? No matter how innocent, a man looking into a young girl's eyes, like that . . .'

'A boatdeck snapshot, that's all.'

'You underestimate his skill as a photographer and your own expressiveness. That is another thing. Useful hobby photography. Takes his camera into important people's houses to do portraits of them . . . who knows what papers are lying about? While he's administering one of his relaxing massages . . .'

'All this is sheer speculation, Walter. Not one hard fact there.'

'I agree. But in this business we can never get much closer than to establish a strong likelihood. There are all sorts of things about Dr Blake that point to him. For me the most persuasive, is his character. Remember what I said once, and you agreed with me, about the sort of person it would have to be. A sarcastic bastard. Someone secretly contemptuous of the whole society that he was moving in, and slyly sending it all up.'

'Yes, I thought that was a good theory.'

'Well, you know what he gets those women to do – as part of his treatment. Gets them to practise self-abuse. All that stuff about streaming and energy flow . . . self-abuse. Now that, I would say, is a pretty savage joke, wouldn't you? Quite worthy of Homer.'

They had completed their circle and were back at the car park.

'What are you going to do?'

'As you know, I'm prohibited by statute from taking any action, but I guess the Bureau are capable of watching him, they're quite good at that sort of thing.'

'I'll watch him, too,' Hardtman said.

When Julian came in the evening, he said he had been questioned by the police about the accident.

'Oh, what did they want to know?'

'How much you'd been drinking.'

'What did you say?'

'I said I prescribed a medicinal dose of brandy.'

'They buy that?'

'I don't know. They kept asking a lot of very odd questions, and there were others there who didn't look like cops.'

'What sort of questions?'

'They asked me if I knew someone called Helga and someone called David and somebody else called Helmut *or* Gerhardt . . .'

'Did you know them?'

Julian laughed. 'I told them most of my friends were the sort of people who have two names.'

'What they say to that?'

'They were *quite* pleasant. No third-degree stuff, anyway. Wanted to know about Fire Island and . . . Joannie.

319

I'm afraid they seem to have got on to that, Bill. But they were very reassuring. Said there was an established old principle in Washington. That booze and dames are a man's own business. They kept quoting that to me, and asking me about Joannie. So I said if it was a man's own business they ought not to ask so many questions, and anyway they ought to ask you, I didn't know. They seemed to think because I'd introduced you to her . . .'

'Yes, they get funny ideas,' Hardtman said lightly.

Julian's fingers were working at the base of Hardtman's skull, bringing relief and relaxation. No, it was really impossible to believe that Julian, with his great capacity for easing the mind, could be . . .

'They want me to take a lie test,' Julian said quietly.

'Whatever for?'

'They say people take them all the time . . . saves having to dig around needlessly.'

'What do they want to give you the lie test on?'

'I thought it was unusual, in connection with a road accident.'

'Are you going to take it?'

'Oh I might,' Julian said easily. 'You know the advice of Sir Isaac Newton to a friend setting off on his travels? "Observe the humours of the natives",' he said. ' "The purpose of travel is to learn, not to teach." I shall try to bear that in mind.'

'These are peculiar times, Julian,' Hardtman said, 'people get strange suspicions in their heads, sometimes. However outlandish they are, it's best to clear them up. Observe their humours, as you say. I'm sure you'll have no difficulty . . .'

The massage was relaxing all the tensions in Hardtman's body.

'I feel a lot better,' he said.

'I'm glad I've been of some help.'

'Help? You're a damn marvel, as well as a good friend.'

'I hope you will always think that.'

'What an odd thing to say, Julian.'

'Oh I just have a feeling, Bill. I have a feeling that the buggers are out to get me. For some reason.'

Hardtman was at the stage of total relaxation, and the effect was almost like a drug – it made all dangers, and all forms of unpleasantness, seem remote and unlikely, and he decided that he would ask Julian tomorrow what he meant exactly.

The phone call came at 10.30 while Hardtman was drafting a memorandum to the Admiral. Walter Cole on the line.

'Well, I was wrong, Bill.'

'That's a highly unusual admission for you, Walter.'

There was no laughter.

'The FBI were not that great at handling it. Our bird has flown.'

'What are you talking about?'

'Packed his bags and gone – Dr Blake.'

'I can't believe it.'

'Threw off his tails, which I can tell you requires some professional expertise.'

'It's incredible . . . You're sure he hasn't just taken off for a day or two?'

'It doesn't look that way. The FBI are at the Institute, taking it apart. I suggest we both get over there. In case they find anything we ought to know about.'

In the waiting room a big cop, feet up on the desk, was watching over three of Julian's patients. They had been found on the landing, outside the Institute's locked doors, and were being held for questioning, in case they could shed any light on Dr Blake's disappearance. They were an old Negress with a bad hip, a little boy with a trembling lower lip, and a long, bent man with a domed head who winked continuously at the fat detective, first with one eye, then with the other, and as Hardtman and Cole came in, winked at them, too, several times, after which he turned away and winked at the wall – which was now quite bare, with only dust frames where the signed photographs of the royal, the distinguished, and the famous had formerly hung.

The cop glared at Cole and Hardtman. He didn't take his feet off the desk.

'And who may you be? What you want?'

'Go in there and tell Mr Vaux that it's Walter Cole.'

Slowly the cop took his big feet off the desk and got up; he walked heavily to the door of the adjoining room.

'Somebody called Walter Cole?' he said with a lot of doubt in his voice.

Vaux came out after a while. He resembled one of those lead-weighted toys that always stand up again when they are knocked down. His cheeks were full and very smooth, and pink with high blood pressure. His hair was a narrow mat lying on a round polished skull. He had his jacket off, and one thumb inside the armhole of his waistcoat as he came out to greet Walter Cole.

'Well, if it isn't Mr Cole.'

'Well, if it isn't Mr Vaux.'

'Here on business, Mr Cole?'

'That's right, Mr Vaux.'

'This is clearly an internal matter,' Vaux said, out of a thicket of cigar smoke.

'Has obvious external ramifications, Phil,' Cole said. Vaux considered this for a while. He had the slow manner of a man who's been told by his doctors to take it easy, not to rush, not to get too excited. 'Want me to spell it out?'

'No, no,' Vaux decided. 'You can stay, if you want. Just don't remove anything . . .'

'This is Mr Hardtman,' Cole said.

'Glad to know you, son.' And then the penny dropped, and he said, 'Oh yeah, Hardtman. *Yeah.*'

'Find anything, Phil?'

'Bills, mostly bills.'

'What sort of bills?'

'Unpaid bills,' Vaux said. 'You're gonna have to excuse me,' he said. 'I got things to do.' He indicated the next room with his polished head.

'Invite us in, Phil.'

'All in good time, Walt.'

'You don't mind us taking a look round the rest of the place?'

'Be my guest. Just keep your hands off the silver, huh?'

Wandering through the other rooms, where mattresses had been ripped open, floorboards prised up, and sections of wall dug out in the search for hiding places, Hardtman had difficulty in picturing Laurene here: she who could not stand dirt, and would sometimes embark on a surprise tour of inspection of restaurant kitchens to ensure that they were up to her standards of spotlessness. Julian's magic must have been potent indeed for Laurene to have failed to notice the seediness of this place. Its walls were in need of painting, its windows grimy, its window sills and radiators undusted.

The door to Julian's office opened and two of Vaux's assistants with files under their arms came out.

'They leaving with all that stuff?' Cole called to Vaux.

'Just going to put it away somewhere safe,' Vaux called back.

'That's what I was afraid of, Phil,' Cole said, and reaching under one assistant's arm pulled out a red appointments' book.

'Mind if I take a look?' Cole asked and without waiting for an answer began to leaf through the pages rapidly. Vaux's lips moved tentatively, he stroked his smooth cheeks slowly – he was not going to give way to unhealthy emotions that could raise his blood pressure.

'Take the rest,' he told his assistants and they left hurriedly, before Cole could grab anything else.

'He wasn't doing so well,' Cole said, going through the appointments' book.

'Who knows. Maybe he had other sources of income,' Vaux said.

Cole was turning pages. 'Appointments fell off in the summer.' He shook his head. 'July, August were pretty bad months by the look of it.'

'Yeah, the city dies July, August,' Vaux said.

'Everybody goes out of town,' Cole agreed. He was continuing to turn the pages. 'Yes, a real falling off. Even Mrs Luessenhoep, who was coming two or three times a week in January, February, March, April, May, June, came only twice in July, not at all in August and September.' He turned to the back of the appointments' book, where there was a ledger section and spent a few moments studying the entries. 'Her donations came to an end, too,' he said.

'Yes,' Vaux said, 'and so did Mrs Hardtman's.' Seeing Hardtman's reaction, he said quickly: 'You didn't know, Mr Hardtman, that your wife was making donations to the Institute? Two thousand bucks in April, two thousand in May, fifteen hundred in June – and then nothing.'

Cole handed the appointments' book to Hardtman and pointed to the figures in the ledger section.

'My wife makes donations to a number of charities and foundations. I don't concern myself with these matters. There are trustees and advisers that she consults, if she needs to . . .'

'Yes, I know of Mrs Hardtman's charitable work,' Vaux said. 'These payments were not made through any of the Blum foundations. They were personal cheques, drawn on her private bank account.'

'There's no doubt some reason for that,' Hardtman said. 'She might do that, for instance, if the trust funds are all committed . . . in a certain period.'

'Must be a complicated business,' Vaux said, chuckling, 'giving money away. Problem I never had to deal with . . . Well, everybody must have been getting low in funds in July . . . *all* the donations stopped. Which accounts for the number of unpaid bills.'

Hardtman turned the pages of the appointments' book. At the beginning of the year, Laurene's name appeared frequently. Perhaps three or four times a week. Later, her appointments dropped to one or two a month, at which point Hardtman's appointments became more frequent, eventually rising to one a day. He was surprised by the number of blank pages in the diary. Could it be that Julian sometimes did not have any patients for three or four days? Of course, he saw a lot of his patients at odd hours. And perhaps, considering his casualness in such matters, he did not always remember to keep a record of his appointments.

'You have to wonder,' Vaux said, 'what Dr Blake was doing all those days when he didn't have patients. Pursuing his hobby – maybe. Hear he is a keen photographer.'

Hardtman turned to that day's page in the diary. It was blank. He turned back one page. Here there were three or four names. The appointment with Hardtman was not recorded.

'Doesn't look as though he could have written down all his appointments,' Vaux said. 'Didn't write down the appointments with you, Mr Hardtman. For instance.'

'But, of course, since you were having him tailed, you know what appointments he had.'

'That's right.'

'*Did* he see anyone who could throw any light on his disappearance?'

'No – unless you could, Mr Hardtman.'

'I don't think there's any explanation I can offer at this time.'

'Perhaps Mrs Hardtman has some idea. Since she was one of the patrons of the Institute.'

'If she had known he was packing up and getting out, she would surely have told me. Did you speak to Mrs Luessenhoep? Does she have any idea what may have happened?'

'Nope,' Vaux said. 'No idea. Mrs Luessenhoep was a bit abrupt, to tell you the truth. Didn't seem to want to talk about it. Said she had not seen Dr Blake lately. And that she no longer had any connection with the Institute. Oh she was real definite about that. You'd almost think it was sort of an embarrassment to her.'

'I don't understand it,' Hardtman said.

He went into the next room. Venetian blinds, their mechanism jammed, hung askew half way down one window. In the bathroom there was a tube of Kolynos toothpaste that had been cut open and its contents examined. The bedroom was as stark as a monk's cell. Julian had left little more than a few books and magazines and gramophone records.

Hardtman was not sure what he was looking for. Something that would explain what had happened. A letter, perhaps – a letter of explanation. But there was no such letter. Or it had already been removed by the Bureau. They were thorough.

There was a stack of old *Tatlers* on the floor. Some of the issues, Hardtman found, were from before the war. He wondered why Julian had kept them. Idly, he began to turn the pages. Inane-looking young men in white ties and wing collars. Others in dress uniform. Precisely parted hair, brushed and shiny. The girls bare-shouldered, in pearls and taffeta. Lt.-Cdr. Aldridge and Miss Audrey Hall-Whyte enjoying a pause during the strenuous programme of dances . . . The attractions of ice-cream being discovered by Major Sir Reginald Carpenter and Miss de Lisle Winnington-Ingrams. Mr Arnold Kemble and Miss Hazel Bartley escaping the heat of the ballroom on the croquet lawn. Why had Julian kept these old *Tatlers*? Hardtman flicked through them rapidly. A sepia picture taken at the Chelsea Flower Show. 'In a brief gleam of sunlight, Miss Elliott, Miss Lethbridge, Lady Patricia Lucas-Scudmore and Lady Broughton make a charming Arcadian group in the eighteenth-century formal garden. They represent Autumn, Summer, Spring and Winter.'

A world that Hardtman had once known was evoked by these pictures – pre-war England, formidable ladies in Liberty print frocks, the orchestra on the lawn, tea under the marquee, rock cakes, cucumber sandwiches, jam tarts. England. The Boat Race, seen from Hammersmith Bridge. Blue-blazered men in open Allards whizzing down to Maidenhead, for what was called, with British disapproval of such concentration on the carnal, a dirty weekend. It all came back. He was still flicking through the *Tatlers*. 'Miss Caroline Worthington, only daughter of the late Mr Greville Worthington, and the late Lady Diana Worthington, and a niece of the Earl of Faversham . . .', he said. 'Miss Mary Plunkett-Ernle-Erle-Drax, of Charborough Park,

Wareham, Dorset . . .', he read. 'Miss Shirley Rachel Askew, only daughter of Mr H. Royston Askew, of Aubrey Walk, London, W, and of the late Mrs Askew, who is to marry next month Capt. Innes Arundel du Sautoy Watson, R.A., only son of Lt.-Col. R. H. M. Watson, D.S.O., R.A. (retd.) and . . .'

Why on earth had Julian kept these old magazines? Was he nostalgic for England, the Chelsea Arts Ball, racing at Ascot, the Boat Race? Julian, with his ironical tone of voice, secretly cherishing such memories?

Pressed between the glossy pages of one issue there was an old clipping from the *Washington Post* social section. There was a photograph of Laurene, and an item which began:

Laurene Hardtman comes from the ruling dynasty of Blums. Her father is the grandson of Adolph Blum, who founded the business from which the Howard & Blum retailing chain grew. The wife of William C. Hardtman, who is advising the President on special national security matters, she is one of Washington's prettiest hostesses.

Apart from taking a keen interest in her husband's government work, Mrs Hardtman is also very much involved in the running of various Blum trusts and foundations, whose activities range from tree-planting projects in Palestine to the funding of medical and scientific research projects.

This last paragraph had been underlined.

Hardtman dropped the *Tatler* with this clipping back on to the pile, and slowly stood up.

Vaux was coming into the room, holding something in his hand. There was a look of contained triumph on his big face. Dramatically, he flourished his find: a tie, a little crumpled but of good silk, a blue tie, the colours possessing the richness of hand-blocked squares. As Vaux came closer Hardtman saw that it had light blue diagonals against a dark blue background.

'You know what this is?' Vaux demanded. 'I'll bet you

327

dollars to doughnuts what this is is an Eton old school tie.'

Hardtman examined it. There was a Herbert Johnson, Bond Street, label sewn into the inside.

'Yes, that's what it is,' Hardtman agreed.

'You realize,' Vaux declared, holding down dangerous excitement with a struggle, 'that you-know-who went to Eton?'

'So did one or two others,' Hardtman pointed out.

'One or two others didn't take a powder last night, throwing off some o' my best surveillance personnel. He used all the pro techniques. No stop lights on his car . . . which is a well-known technique . . .'

Hardtman took the tie thoughtfully.

'He never mentioned to me that he had been to Eton, and that was the sort of thing he was inclined to mention.'

Cole came in and took the tie from Hardtman, and also examined it. He seemed impressed by this latest piece of evidence.

'For Christ's sake, Walter,' Hardtman said. 'It's only a tie. What the hell does a tie prove?'

21

When he got home, Laurene was on the phone, in her study, with the door open; one of her long telephone calls. Her innumerable interests, business or otherwise, sometimes kept her on the phone for hours at a time. She was talking in Spanish. A language he did not know. They had taught her something in that fancy Swiss finishing school. Whom could she be talking to in Spanish?

He fixed himself a drink in the library, leaving the door open so he would hear when she had finished her Spanish telephone call.

Laurene seemed surprised to see him when she finally came down the stairs.

'Who were you talking to so long in Spanish?'

'Oh – only the lawyer.'

'You have a Spanish lawyer?'

'I have an Argentinian lawyer, who looks after one or two things for me in Buenos Aires.'

There were a hell of a lot of lawyers in her life. She appeared to have a different lawyer for every occasion. He was a lawyer himself. Rich women have need of lawyers to implement their wishes.

'Doesn't he speak English, this lawyer?'

'Yes, he speaks English. But since I speak Spanish, I speak to him in Spanish. Keeps me in practice.'

'That's true. Also – wise. If you don't want everyone to know your business. Since our phone is tapped.'

'Our phone is being tapped?'

'Security.'

'Are they allowed to do that?'

'I don't know if they're allowed, but they're doing it.'

'Why? What do they think . . .?'

'Julian has gone.'

'Gone where?'

'Blown. Vamoosed, as you may or may not say in Spanish.'

'I don't get it.'

'Neither do I. I don't think we are meant to get it – Turns out Julian is not quite what – or who – he seemed to be.'

'You know, I had this flash about him. There was something that didn't quite hang together. What do they think?'

'Seems he got money out of various people.'

'Well, I told you he borrowed money . . ,'

'He got money out of you, Laurene.'

'Yeah, until I got wise to him.'

'You never told me. You never told me that. You spoke of him borrowing the odd five dollars. You didn't tell me you were making two-thousand-dollar donations to the Institute.'

'At the time, I thought the work was valuable and that he ought to get support for what he was doing. Dolly was helping him too, so were others. He had a whole lot of clinic patients who couldn't've afforded to pay any fees. It seemed worthwhile to help him continue.'

'What changed your mind?'

'I don't understand you.'

'You suddenly stopped your contributions some time in July.'

'I'd had enough, I wanted out. I told you at the time, remember? I had a funny feeling about him. I had this flash – he was always borrowing money. Big or small, I didn't like it. I thought, something fishy going on.'

'You mean you found out that he was sleeping with the women who gave him money, like Dolly. Why did she also stop *her* contributions? Did she think she was the only one, and get riled when she discovered that he had other patronesses?'

'I don't know why Dolly withdrew her support,' Laurene said flatly.

'Well, I can guess that someone like Dolly might have got a kick out of being his mentor, and bedmate, but that finding out she was one of many . . .'

330

'I don't know what sort of dirty crack that's meant to be, all I can say is that in *my* case he was someone I thought deserved support, and then I didn't like the way he did things, so I stopped. There was no proper accounting of the money . . . you didn't know what it went on. His book-keeping was non-existent.'

'I suppose if he understood, and thought the women understood, that the money was being given to him for his own use, and making donations to the Institute was understood to be a polite euphemism, he wouldn't expect to have to account for the money . . .'

'Whatever anyone else understood, that sure wasn't what I understood. And there was no basis for *him* to have understood that.' Her voice became angry. 'What is this cross-examination?'

'There are questions I have to ask you Laurene. In normal circumstances, I think there are some things in a marriage that the other person doesn't need to know about, O.K. But in this case . . .'

'Oh is that so?' She became tense and pale. 'You mean like I . . . don't need to know about your mistress in New York?' She had come out with it in a sudden rush of words.

He gave himself time to think before replying. He pursed his lips slightly and rumpled his brow into an expression of pained interest, while she waited shrunken, hands tightly clenched, for his answer.

'I think,' he said slowly, deliberately as a chess player who has carefully thought out his move and is now making it, 'that is called a diversionary tactic. The reason we are talking about Julian is that he has disappeared and questions of national security arise. Otherwise I wouldn't be asking these things. Other things can be talked about at other times . . . if need be. When it will be easier for you to see that you are jumping to all sorts of unwarranted conclusions. You're interpreting shadows, Laurene, shadows. And that's notoriously tricky. People tend to see whatever has been put in their head.'

'I see what's in my head, do I? Do I?' Her voice was hitting all sorts of wrong notes. Abruptly, she turned around and tore out of the room and he heard her going upstairs, fast, and through their bedroom. Had she gone to throw herself sobbing on the bed, or what? She was behaving most unusually. Laurene was not the type to run away from anything. She confronted situations head on. He poured himself a drink, and was just raising the glass to his mouth when Laurene stormed back into the room, white and dramatic as a Kabuki player, and threw the photographs at him.

'Where did you get these?' he asked sternly.

'From your safe, from your goddamn safe.'

'You . . . you go to my safe? You can open my safe?'

'I have a key.'

'You gave me both keys.'

'They provided three.'

'You shouldn't have kept a key, Laurene.'

'I always have a key to our safe.'

'Secret papers are kept in that safe, you should not have had a key.'

'I didn't look at your damn secret papers. I'm not interested in your big secrets . . . just in *that*.' And she moved the scattered photographs with the point of her shoe. 'Who is she? Who's that girl whose eyes you're peering into?'

'You're being ridiculous, Laurene. Those are' – he looked down – 'holiday snapshots. The girl is a friend of Julian's. He posed us. Under those circumstances, you do tend to look into the other person's eyes, out of common politeness.'

'If what I see in your eyes is common politeness, that's some politeness! And if those pictures are so innocent, why lock them in your big secrets safe?'

'They were just put together with some other papers from my briefcase.'

'It's a lie,' she hurled at him. 'Why would there just be photographs of you and this girl, and of nobody else? You think I can't see? I can see what's in your eyes, and in her eyes.'

Looking down at the photographs on the floor, he was

reminded of what he had given up and he spoke harshly. 'I am suggesting to you, Laurene, that it is perfectly possible for you to accept my explanation, and save yourself a lot of pain going into things that there is no need to go into, that I can assure you there is no need to go into, but if you *want* to pursue your suspicions . . .' He shrugged, 'Well, suit yourself.'

'All right,' she said steelily, . . . 'if they're just snapshots, like you say, tell me to tear them up, tell me to burn them. Prove to me how little these "snapshots" mean to you, by telling me to tear them all up.'

She had got on to her knees and was violently gathering up all the photographs, making a pile of them, and was waiting for a sign or word from him to authorize the burning.

'The significance,' Hardtman said in a level voice, 'lies in the fact that you want to burn them.'

'They hold sweet memories for you, do they? You want to look at them and remember how you looked into her eyes?'

'If that's what you need to do,' he said, 'you must do it. But don't ask my permission. I'm not going to give you permission to destroy those pictures. But you can, of course, do what you want. I shan't get on the floor and fight with you over a few photographs.'

'Then I can burn them?'

He laughed harshly: people invariably read everything to mean what they wanted it to mean, but he said nothing as she picked up the photographs and in a silent frenzy began to tear them into tiny pieces, watching his expression all the time, watching for any sign of wincing on his part, and then she put all the bits in the fireplace and put a match to them. She continued to watch him as he stared into the flames; the glossy photographic paper was curling and bending into contorted black shapes before becoming stiff ash.

'If that's all finished then,' he said, 'perhaps we can now get back to what I, unfortunately, have to ask *you* about.'

333

She was sullen; burning the photographs had appeased something in her, but not satisfied her.

'I have got to know,' Hardtman said, 'exactly what sort of pitch Julian gave you to get the money. And I have to know if – in whatever circumstances – he ever asked for anything else. Or was getting round to asking. No, wait,' he cautioned, seeing she was going to deny everything. 'Listen to me, Laurene. We're in an area where nothing's clear-cut, that's their way of operating, so we are obliged to play it their way, to read the signs; spies don't come out in the open and ask outright, they protect themselves. If the response isn't right, they didn't mean what you thought they meant. He asked me, once, if I wanted to be put in touch with people on the other side . . . the next minute he denied it. I have got to know what really went on between you and him, awkward as that may be to talk about, but it has now become a matter of national security.'

'He once asked me to have a drink with him in his private rooms, and we sat on the floor together, only there wasn't anything much to drink – he'd run out of pretty well everything – and he was all the time building up to something, I could see, and I thought it was what you are suggesting, only what he was building up to was a touch . . . Trying to get me to be a patron of the Institute. Fishing for money.'

'And so you gave him those sums of money? Twice, two thousand dollars, once fifteen hundred. I don't know how much else.'

'It was eight thousand dollars altogether. He had a lot of debts.'

'Did he ever try to get information from you, or try to get you to introduce him to people?'

'He was always trying to get one to introduce him to people, you know that. He was very keen to meet important and influential people.'

'I mean people in sensitive positions.'

'He wanted to meet that man who works in the Defence Department, whom I hardly know . . . what's his name . . . Wild . . .?'

'Wildmore. Leonard Wildmore?'

'Yes. He was very interested in him. Said he had a very pretty wife. He'd ask to be seated next to certain people at dinner . . . you know the way he has of asking things like that.'

'Laurene . . . is it even remotely possible that he may have thought you were in love with him? Think clearly. The reason I ask is because it's a well-known ploy of . . . of foreign agents . . . to place prominent people in compromising positions . . . and then they ask them for special favours. It's a technique that's used. It's called entrapment. They manipulate these people, progressively stepping up the demands. First, it's just a harmless introduction. Then carrying a message. They involve you in mild conspiracies, which become more complex . . . until it's too late to get out. I don't know what stage he had reached with you . . .'

'The answer is he had reached no stage with me.'

'You did a hell of a lot for someone who had got nowhere with you. Gave him eight thousand dollars. Introduced him to people, kept asking him to the house . . .'

'You were the one who kept asking him to the house . . . I tried to stop you.'

'That was later.'

'Maybe it was *you* he was "entrapping".'

'Sure, I'm forced to consider that, too, except that he wasn't getting anywhere with me . . .'

'Wasn't getting anywhere with you . . . you were completely dependent on him! You couldn't sleep without his coming to give you a massage. Did he introduce you to that girl?'

'What are you implying by that remark, Laurene?'

'Because that's the kind of thing he does.'

'What is the kind of thing he does?'

'Introduces men to girls . . . so I've heard, anyway. That was something else that finally put me off him.'

Hardtman gave a hard laugh. 'Well, frankly, Laurene, I consider that pretty contemptible of you, to make that suggestion. Do you think I'm the sort of man who has to have girls provided for him?'

'No, you're not,' she admitted, but she wasn't backing down.

'I think it's pretty vulgar of you to suggest it then.'

'Even more vulgar to do it.'

'Well, if that's what you think of me . . .'

'What you were suggesting about me wasn't exactly that flattering . . .'

'There is some evidence to indicate that you behaved foolishly where Julian is concerned.'

'And you didn't behave foolishly? Where Julian is concerned?' she added, mimicking him viciously. 'Did he introduce you to that girl or didn't he? She just happened to be with him, and was available? Is that the story?'

'She wasn't so available. There was someone in her life.'

'So – so, even more of a thrill, taking her away from someone else. Your chemistry just happened to be right? Hey-ho, and off to the races we go. Boy, that's some capacity for self-deception you've got there. *Listen*, I wasn't born yesterday. You think she didn't have any angle? Just did it like the free spirit moved her? *Shit!* I know what that you-can-have-me-anytime-look means.' She gave a contemptuous toss of her head towards the fireplace, where the burnt photographs were still smouldering. 'It means you can have me any time, at a price.'

'That's really low of you, Laurene. You have all the low suspicions of the very rich, and it's one of your least attractive qualities. You think that money – your damn money – is what everybody wants, because *you're* so in love with it.'

'You're quite a catch even without my money,' she said quietly.

But he would not be appeased now. She had gone too far. Hurt him to the quick in some area of his male pride. 'You flatter me,' he said, 'only in order to flatter yourself. Well, let me tell you something. Since you seem determined to get it out of me – though I wanted to spare you this. Yes, there was something about that girl in New York. It was more than just . . . a one or two night thing. Shall I tell you what it was about her? It was the fact that she could

336

say goodbye to me . . . she could let me go, no clinging. No staking out her claim. I wasn't a desirable piece of property for her to possess. Just someone with whom to experience something honestly, without angles, and then let go without regrets, with a little pain, but without all that holding on, holding on . . . you kill me with your holding on. I can't live like that.'

'What!' Her voice had hit an entirely different note now, making a new sound in their quarrel, the sound of someone in pain.

He saw this immediately, and realized that their quarrel had changed, had gone beyond the immediate and into a more fundamental area of their differences.

He said, 'Let's just stop and give ourselves time to know what we are saying.'

For he was a man who believed in control, and he realized he was at a point of not being able to control what he was saying. Things were coming out uncontrolledly.

But she said in her new, anguished voice, 'I don't have to think about it, because there is nothing for me to think about: I know. You're all I want. I've never wanted anybody else since I've known you. I love *you*, and that's all there is for me. You and Debbie. I'm very happy with my life, and I don't want anything to come along and mess it up.'

He felt uncomfortable about this declaration of love from his wife; he loved her, too, perhaps not quite so vehemently, so defiantly, so exclusively, but loved her dearly, and part of him wanted to believe her unquestioningly, and to respond to the passionate sincerity in her voice and face; but at the same time he felt he could not afford to be unquestioning. In some way, Julian's disappearance had put everything in question.

He tried to take a reasonable attitude towards what Laurene had said. It could be true. It sounded true. Only he couldn't be sure. What could you be sure of? Only the Walter Coles of this world could be sure. He forced himself to be coldly rational on the subject of Laurene's involvement with Julian.

'Look,' he said, 'since it is extraordinarily difficult to prove a negative, it is not going to be possible to prove you never . . .'

'Don't you *believe* me?' she cried. 'Oh Bill. Oh Bill. Oh Bill, I'm scared. I'm scared. If you don't *believe* me . . .'

He felt that she was doubting him in the matter of his most basic human capacity: to be able to sense and respond to the truthfulness of another person. He was angered and hurt, the more so since this was a capacity of his that he was himself beginning to doubt.

'How do I know this isn't an act he put you up to? – He seems to have been very good at taking people in. How do I know that kind of ability doesn't get passed on by contact?' he demanded bitterly.

'Why can't you *believe* me?' she asked, as if he were refusing her some simple act of humanity.

'Laurene, you only see your side of it. The problem is that if Julian is what they think he is . . .'

'A spy . . .'

'Yes, a spy. Then it is all going to come out, his relationship with me, with you, and it is going to be relevant – embarrassingly relevant – if he was sleeping with the wife of one of the President's national security advisers. Especially since this same wife had a key to the safe in which her husband was keeping secret papers. You must see that. If I say: I asked my wife if she had had an affair with him, and she said, "No," and I believed her, you think that will convince anyone? Especially if it comes out that he was sleeping with Dolly Luessenhoep and all the other women who gave him money for the Institute. On what basis do I then prove that you were the exception?'

'I'm not interested in what other people think. I'm interested in what you believe.'

'I don't know what to believe.'

If you were feeling your way in the dark, you had to learn to interpret the meaning of shadows. He was peering hard, striving to see what they meant.

Surely Laurene was unlikely to have given Julian money if she was having an affair with him; in those circumstances her highly developed guard would have become activated. She had been schooled from the cradle about gentleman adventurers. It could be, therefore, that she was telling the truth. But he could not be sure.

If Julian were a spy, that postulated a lot of people having been taken in, in various ways, and Laurene might have been one of them. But there could be several other explanations of Julian's disappearance. People saw spies everywhere. Well, spies *were* everywhere. Though not necessarily where they were thought to be.

She said, 'Bill, I'm scared I'm going to lose you . . .'

'I've told you that you have nothing to worry about.'

'I don't know if I can believe you. *Can* I believe you?'

'Yes.'

She was wringing her hands and walking about in great consternation, no longer knowing if she could believe him or not.

'I don't know, I don't know, I just suddenly feel . . . unsafe. I've always felt safe, and now I don't. Everything seems to be threatened. Oh God, I feel awful.' She turned on him. 'Why, why? Why have you spoilt things for us?'

'That's a stupidly naïve question.'

'Have I failed you in some way?'

'You want to pin-point something that can't be pinpointed.'

'If I don't know, if I don't know what I've done wrong, I can't ever feel secure again. Can I?'

'What d'you want? A renewal of the till-death-us-do-part vow? What good would that do you? People break their vows if they want to, or need to. There are no promises that you can hold anyone to. Don't you know that?'

'What are you saying? Are you saying I *do* have to be afraid?'

'Oh, I think being afraid is the natural condition of being alive.'

'Are you saying that you don't love me?'

'I do love you,' he insisted, 'but at the same time, it seems, it seems, I have other needs as well. So it would seem.'

'Isn't that every man's excuse?'

'Yes, I guess.'

'You want your freedom?'

'That's a conventional phrase – meaning what exactly? Who doesn't want their freedom? That's not the question, is it? . . . The question is: at what price? It has a price, I know. The price is betrayal. It's ironical, isn't it? That our capacity for freedom should be linked to our ability to betray. But it is so. That's why so often betrayals are motivated by love – oh, of one sort or another. There has to be something strong enough to make us ready to betray . . .' He shrugged. 'Some force majeure.'

'Was that how it was with you and her?'

'You keep talking about her, and I've told you that's past. I'm talking about general things.'

'Young girls, right? Those are your "general things",' she said bitterly.

'They are included in the generality, yes. What do you want me to do, Laurene? Lie to you. Say I am not attracted by young girls when it is quite obvious that I am. Since we seem to be facing up to some home truths, at last, I don't see how we can avoid that one.'

'At last? You mean we weren't before?'

'Let's say that like most "happily married couples" we have learned to steer around dangerous shoals. The need-to-know principle. Saves us from a lot of brutal truths. Doesn't it? Doesn't it? *Think.*'

She was silent.

'I think it's best,' he said, 'the truth is too tough to face all the time.'

'You want to sweep it all under the carpet? You want to be free to go to bed with whomever you like, and no questions asked.'

'Laurene, you can safely leave me to my own sense of guilt, it's more than adequate.'

'You don't think you have a duty – to me and Debbie? Oh I know this is the great age of finding your own happiness and to hell with everybody else's. But we do exist as well. We have rights.'

'I am not unaware of your rights.'

He was shocked by her bitterness.

'Well, I'm not letting you do what you like. I don't buy that. That may be very un-modern of me but I happen to believe in certain things, the family, and duty and cherishing somebody.'

'I believe in all that, too.'

'I'm holding you to your promises to me.'

'Laurene,' he said gently, 'nobody can hold somebody who doesn't want to be held: it's tough, but that's life.'

Her eyes had become large and bitter and censorious.

'I won't put up with it, Bill,' she said grandly. 'I won't. You have a duty to me. Duty is something I don't take lightly. I am not going to pretend and pass it off and be modern about it, I do feel betrayed, I do feel betrayed . . .' She began to sob. She emerged from the fit of sobbing with her resoluteness enhanced. 'I have the right to my moral absolutes. You are the one who was always talking about moral duty . . .'

This was true. He had to admit it was true. He tended to make rules. Not long ago, he would have agreed with the point of view that she now so passionately proclaimed. Perhaps she had even got it from him, since he often talked of moral imperatives, and he could be a persuasive talker. But he realized now, with only mild surprise, that there were things he had thought he believed in that he did not believe in after all.

That night Hardtman could not fall asleep. Finally, he gave up trying, and wandered around the house. He had still not got used to the quietness. In this silence all your secret thoughts made themselves loudly known.

As soon as it was light he called Walter Cole.

They met, as they had often done, half way between their two offices, in the park of the Ellipse, and walked towards the reflecting pool. There was a chill in the early morning air, a feeling of the end of summer. The sky was bright but unclear, and the sun was like a cataracted eye, a distorted red blob, with surrounding white matter.

Walter Cole took one look at Hardtman and said, 'You look terrible.'

'I feel it. Walter, are we seeing things that don't exist? I no longer know.'

They were walking along the length of the reflecting pool. Its mood today was sullen. Its opaque surface gave back no glimmering to Washington or Lincoln. All it reflected was the covered sky.

Cole said: 'Peter Volniakov left last night – recalled to Moscow. Very suddenly. For a cultural attaché, he knew remarkably little about the ballet. Of course, we know what he was doing. He was Number Two in their espionage set-up. He also – in case you didn't know this, Bill – enjoyed the favours of Miss Fontanez, and guess who brought them together. Our cupid-playing Dr Blake.'

'Is Volniakov a man of about thirty-four or five, beginning to go to fat?'

'That sounds like him.'

'Big, boisterous, a bit overpowering. Dances in a sort of exhibitionistic way ...'

'Personally, I've never danced with him, but I would say the description fits. You've met him?'

'Yes, I've met him.'

'I can see how it would appeal to Homer's sense of humour – getting you and Volniakov fixed up with the same gal.'

'I think "fixed up" is uncalled for.'

'Is it? I don't wish to hurt your self-esteem, Bill, but facts are facts. Dr Blake did go in for that sort of thing, you know. Discreetly of course. He has a light touch.'

'In this case, it would be a mistake to take that interpretation of it ...'

'You paid her four hundred dollars.'

'That's an absolute fabri ...' He stopped in the middle of his denial. 'I gave her a present. Or rather, I didn't have time to buy her a present, and so I gave her a cheque and asked her to buy herself something. It was made out to Macy's. The amount was not filled in.'

'Yes, well, whatever the actual mechanics of it, she evidently considered four hundred dollars an appropriate sum . . .'

'It's the price of a television. That was what she wanted.'

'The fact is she cashed the cheque and did not buy a television.'

'Believe me, however it looks, I am quite sure that . . .'

'The whole matter is of absolutely no consequence, Bill. Except for the light it throws on Dr Blake's use of such girls, for his own ends. These introductions he seems to have effected, quite frequently, were undoubtedly a source of his popularity among certain prominent Washington figures. A time was going to come, presumably, when he was going to draw on the credit he had built up . . . with you and others.'

'You are saying I was set up.'

'Incidentally, she also has been a member of the Young Communist League, so perhaps there is a little ideology thrown in.'

'If that were true – that I was set up . . .'

'The facts speak for themselves. She cashed your cheque. And she was brought to you by Dr Blake, in exactly the same way that he brought her to Volniakov . . . it is all part of a clearly emerging pattern.'

'You are saying Blake was just ruthlessly setting me up so he could . . .'

'It's the way they work. Look, let's not forget that Homer is capable of being completely ruthless. Every time he has come close to being identified, the people capable of identifying him have ended up with their throat cut, or their brains blown out, or recalled to Moscow for new duties in the vicinity of Siberia.'

'Well, if you're right about that, what's needed of me, quite clearly, is my resignation. I'll go and see the Admiral this morning.'

It was definitely the end of summer. The flags around the Washington Monument were flapping in the wind, and some of the tourists climbing the steps to the Jefferson Memorial were carrying light raincoats.

As Walter Cole said, facts were facts, and when placed

against sentimental fancies the former had to be considered the superior currency.

'If you want my advice, Bill, I would not be too hasty in resigning,' Cole said.

'What else is there for me to do? When all this comes out, what a mess it's going to be! God, what a mess! I think what I regret the most is the effect on Debbie. She has sort of an idealized picture of her father.'

'What daughter hasn't?'

'Now she's going to read her father was set up by enemy agents with a prostitute. And her mother placed, to say the least, in a compromising position with a man who used the women he slept with to finance a whole network of . . . of . . .' His voice petered out; he was shaking and could not finish. 'It rankles, Walter. It rankles,' he said, when he had recovered sufficiently to be able to speak again.

'I know it does, Bill. I know it does. But I don't think you should let yourself be driven into acting prematurely. Listen, Bill . . . Bill, those of us who were in OSS together, we're the living piece that has carried over from the war up to today; we're the human link, and there aren't that many of us left from the old days, and those that are I think need to stand by each other, because there was something valuable we had then. Hell! We did some fantastic things during the war. Allen in Berne. Frank. Ray. Some of the things I did. Things you did. What we did is not blazoned in the public prints. That's the nature of our business. But we know, among ourselves, and we know we did what had to be done, and that we did a darned good job, for no personal glory or gain. We know how covert actions have to be handled; that you can't keep running home and asking for instructions, because if you do, sure as anything you are going to get the wrong instructions from people who just don't know, just don't know *what we know*. Am I right? Now suppose Hoover gets his way, gets his greasy hands on the entire operation. That's going to be a Gestapo. And believe me, he will use anything, anything, to discredit us, and you are part of us, in the sense that you are part of the mechanism for making this all work, and it's going to hurt us for you to resign and let this stuff come out.'

'I don't see any alternative. I'm sorry if it messes up your grand design...'

'Now wait a minute. I agree you may have to resign. But only if it becomes necessary. That is if they catch Blake, and everything comes out. But there are other ways it could go. Supposing he's not caught. Supposing he has got away, and is in Moscow. Does us no harm. The leak has stopped. He's no more use to them. Now in those circumstances, you can deny everything with complete credibility. If anything comes out in the Press, you sue. You say – supposing he hasn't got away. Well, let's consider another scenario. When the FBI start digging, they leave holes, and sometimes people fall into them. Frankly, that's the best thing that could happen.'

'It'd have to be a very deep hole, Walter. The kind you don't come out of ever.'

'Yes, yes,' Cole agreed.

'We can't count on that,' Hardtman said. He looked at Cole and realized that his expression had not changed throughout the whole of their conversation; nothing ever altered in his face, no matter what the subject matter.

Hardtman laughed and said, '... and since that's something we can't count on ... such a fortuitous eventuality...'

'There's no reason to *discount* it. I'm only saying, don't act prematurely. There is no need to resign yet. Wait. I was taught: "Offer the sacrifice of righteousness, and put your trust in the Lord." I was brought up to believe in the efficacy of prayer.'

'I was never a praying man myself.'

'Oh don't write it off. A word in the right ear never comes amiss.' He gave a little laugh, his moustache rising like a flag being run up.

'I wonder why it is, Walter, that when you talk of God, I get the shivers?'

'It's getting chilly,' Cole said. 'I felt it myself this morning. It's the end of the summer.'

22

That the FBI's endeavours to find Julian Blake were so in-effectual does not say very much for their vaunted dragnet, considering that he made his escape in a pre-war Bentley, of which there could not have been that many in the United States – a lovely motor-car, it was, of clean, elegant upright lines; it must have stood out a mile among all those chrome-encrusted American cars of the period.

But perhaps they were not trying all that hard to find him. Or – another explanation – did not need to search because they knew where he was and were just waiting to see what moves he would make. They must have argued that if he were Homer, having been made to run had brought his usefulness to the Russians to an end, and that in his attempts to escape he was bound to involve others in the underground *apparat*. It is fairly standard procedure of counter-espionage to let a running man run, to see where he goes.

The big crackdown didn't come until 1950, following Fuchs's arrest. Meanwhile, a great many suspects remained at liberty for lack of solid evidence, and also, of course, because the arrest of one would have alerted all the others.

I speculate, since the FBI files of the period are not avail-able to me. But one has to ask was it really carelessness that made them omit to search Harry Gold's cellar in 1947, where they would have found masses of incriminating evidence?

There are other aspects of this whole affair that also in-vite speculation. For example, what led to the sudden eas-ing of the Berlin crisis towards the end of September, after the brink-of-war feeling at the beginning of the month?

I have heard it suggested that Homer may have played some part in averting disaster by letting the Russians know how reluctant many highly-placed Americans were to embark upon a war in defence of Germans. As Ambassador Smith put it at a secret Washington briefing, 'I would have been considered a hero three-and-a-half years ago if I had succeeded in exterminating those same Germans.'

The Americans – through their spies – also had a pretty good idea of Russian intentions; Smith, at the same briefing, was so confident the Russians would not deliberately attack any American military installation that he offered to go and sit in the field at Wiesbaden amid all the weaponry.

Another highly relevant piece of military Intelligence that Homer passed on to the Russians was that the B29s – the atom bomb carriers – now based in threatening numbers in Britain and Germany had not been adapted to carry the A-bomb. The people of Britain, very conscious of being in the front line, would no doubt have been glad to know this, and perhaps had reason to thank Homer for letting the Russians know. At least such information may have served to counteract some of Clay's wilder statements, to the effect that he would not hesitate to atom bomb Moscow and Leningrad.

Spy for the Russians though he was, Homer may not have been entirely without some form of patriotism for the country of his birth.

Of course, spying is a wicked business and Bill Hardtman, at this time, was feeling personally betrayed, and was under great strain. He was expecting any day to learn of Julian's arrest, and with that would come all the sensational revelations about his and Laurene's and other people's intimate connections with the spy.

The news that resolved at least one of his uncertainties came in a phone call from Vaux in New York.

'Well, we found Blake.'

'Where is he?'

'He had a fall. Out the window.'

'Hurt badly?'

'Hurt to death. It was a seventeenth-storey window.'

'He's dead? Blake is dead?'

'That's right, son. Theory is he jumped. Which would

347

fit. Lot of defenestration going on. As the net closes, they jump . . . shows we were on the right track.'

He was behind thick glass again, protected, senses dulled. In his blocked ears there was a high tuning-fork vibration, a scream reduced to a single plaintive note.

'Was there a suicide note?' he asked.

'There was,' Vaux said. 'It was addressed to you. I took the liberty of opening it. Want me to read it to you?'

'Yes, will you?'

He began to read in his matter-of-fact cop's voice:

' "Dear Bill, Looks like the buggers have got me by the balls. Exit lines are called for. I hate goodbyes, if you need to say them it's too late, and if not you might as well save your breath. So I will confine myself to practicalities. The Bentley is of no further use to me, and I'd like you to have it. It's in the hotel garage, there will be a garaging bill to pay, and I'm afraid I'm a little short. The stop lights will need to be fixed, and the engine has got low on oil, but otherwise the car is in fairly good condition . . ." It ends there, the letter ends there. It's not signed.'

'Isn't exactly a confession,' Hardtman said.

'I guess the confession is what we swept up from the sidewalk.'

'You're letting it rest there?'

'No, son, we don't let things rest. We've treated it as jumped or fell. And we're making inquiries. We leave no stone unturned, son. That's the way we work.'

After he had put down the phone, Hardtman gave himself five minutes to adjust to the news and decide how he felt. He was shocked, but at the same time detached, curiously detached, almost admiring of the aplomb with which Julian had cheated the buggers. He had once remarked, apropos somebody's endless complaints, 'I sincerely hope that when my life becomes as boring as that I shall have the courage to end it – instantly.' Was that what he had done? Coolly decided to end it? Because it had become too boring. Julian was always pragmatic, played everything by ear. And if his ear had told him it was all over? That being so, you left – unfussily. With positive dash, you might say: from a seventeenth-storey window. 'Exit lines are called for.' But no goodbyes. Why hadn't he finished the letter? Unless it was not a suicide note at all. He spoke not of killing himself, but of 'exit lines'. Perhaps he was merely leaving the country. In which case, one would have to postulate outside interference with his plans. Was it feasible that Julian would have thrown away his life so casually? Jumped or fell. How could he have fallen if he had not jumped? By accident? Julian was very lithe on his feet; his sense of balance was remarkable – and he didn't drink. Impossible to imagine him falling accidentally out of a seventeenth-storey window. What other possibilities did that leave?

He telephoned Laurene and told her what had happened, preparing her first. She took it with apparent calm. Of course, he told himself, she would have to stay calm so as not to incriminate herself: he did not want her to incriminate herself, and so gave her every chance to dissemble. Giving her the news on the phone was a way of enabling her to hide her feelings, should she need to. Perhaps it was also a way of not having to look her in the eyes as he told her: 'Julian is dead.'

'You know, I sort of expected this,' she said.

'That he would kill himself?'

'Oh he didn't kill himself. Julian did not kill himself. He always had an answer. He could wriggle out of anything.'

'Then what do you figure happened?'

'They were out to get him.'

'*Who* was out to get him?'

'I don't know exactly. But I always had the feeling there were things . . . that he didn't talk about, because he couldn't.'

After talking to Laurene, Hardtman thought for about thirty seconds and then called Vaux in New York.

'You didn't tell me when this happened.'

'Last night. Around 10 p.m.'

'Took you some time to get the information out.'

'We were making inquiries, son.'

'O.K., I'm coming out. I'm getting the first plane to New York. I want to look into this.'

'Well, this is an FBI investigation, I . . .'

'You want me to get an executive order? You're supposed to co-operate, Vaux.'

'We'll co-operate, son. Keep your shirt on. We don't keep anything from the White House. Tell me what flight you're coming in on, and I'll send a car to pick you up, how about that for co-operation?'

'It's a start.'

The police car came right on to the tarmac at La Guardia, and Hardtman was let off first from the plane. They drove into town in the soft autumn dusk.

Vaux was going to be co-operative. He was in shirt-sleeves, his large beer-belly straining against Sea Island poplin, cigar in mouth, when Hardtman was shown in.

'Now that's terrific time you made,' Vaux said, looking at his watch. 'My, that was going it. Well . . . take the weight off your feet, son. Cigar?'

'No thanks.'

'Drop o' something?'

'No, no, not right now.'

The office walls were densely covered with framed photographs of Phil Vaux with the famous. There he was, hugging his near double Edward G. Robinson. Another of him and Joe Louis. Phil Vaux with President Roosevelt Phil Vaux with President Truman. And countless lesser luminaries, restaurateurs, barbers, football players, baseball players. Phil Vaux with Walter Winchell. Vaux with Jack Benny. An exclusive all-male mutual admiration society. Who wouldn't want to be friendly with Phil Vaux? One of Hoover's chief lieutenants. You could never know when you might need him. Some of the other framed pictures in the room were of magazine covers. There was one from an old issue of *Life* which showed Vaux on the running board of a 1929 Buick sedan, cradling a Thomson sub-machine gun with canister magazine.

350

Seeing Hardtman's eyes going around the walls, Vaux grinned and said, 'Friends of mine.'

'You have a lot of friends.'

'I have friends everywhere, son,' Vaux said. 'Now, what's on your mind?'

'First, fill me in on the details. Where'd it happen?'

'Place called the Aragon, over on the Upper West Side.'

'What sort of place?'

'Used to be a real swanky place one time, oh I guess back in the Twenties, Thirties. Now it's mostly guys from out of town, visiting their lady-friends. It's not a joint, but they don't ask too many questions. So, inevitably, it also attracts a certain clientele that don't like to have too many questions asked.'

'How long had he been staying there?'

'Eleven days.'

'He paid the bill?'

'He was on a weekly basis, he paid the first week's ...'

'What did the autopsy show?'

'Consistent with a high fall.'

'No other marks on him? Throat, face ... to suggest a struggle?'

'Hard to say, the condition he was in.'

'Anyone see the fall?'

'It was night time.'

'And nobody heard anything – a scream?'

'Nobody heard a scream.'

'He have any visitors around that time?'

'The desk clerk says no. But the fact is, it's the kind of hotel where once you checked in they aren't too careful about who goes up to your room.'

'Any signs of his door having been forced?'

'No. And there's a double lock on it. And a chain. If you let go the door it slams shut and you need a key to get in. All the maids have keys with which they can get in all the rooms. But from inside, and only from the inside, if you turn the knob the door is double locked and there's only one key that will open the door then. It's on a big brass collar and the bell captain, or an assistant manager, are the only ones allowed to use it. And the door *was* double-locked from the inside.'

'Any spare keys?'

'One. Kept in the manager's safe.'

'All of which points to him having jumped or fallen, without outside help.'

'Right.'

'In fact, you're saying, it would have been impossible for a visitor to have left the room and then double-locked it from outside.'

'Check.'

'You'd say it looks pretty conclusive then that he – jumped or fell?'

'Pretty.'

'In that case, why go asking questions?'

'So nobody can say we didn't.'

'What was found in the room?'

'Personal things. Clothes. Toiletry articles. Et cetera. Not much . . .'

'He take his meals out, or at the hotel?'

'Out. Or sometimes he just bought delis and ate in his room. There's a little kitchenette. He made himself toast, boiled an egg. Made coffee.'

'He'd have to have coffee, that was his drug.'

'Yeah, there was a whole Thermos of coffee in his room.'

'A Thermos of coffee?'

'Yeah.'

'The window. Could somebody have fallen out of it accidentally?'

'He'd have to have been standing on a stool by an open window.'

'I want to have a look at the room. Will you fix that?'

'Sure. I can fix that. When you wanna go?'

'Who are the people you interviewed?'

'We interviewed around twenty people – to check out where they were last night, around ten. Which was when it happened. Just to see how they'd take the news.'

'How'd they take it?'

'They all said they never heard of him.'

'Who were they, these twenty?'

'Mostly they're people we think are part of the Communist underground *apparat*.'

'So you'd expect them to know about Blake, if he was who we think he was?'

'Not necessarily. A, they know each other by code-names. And, B, they use a lot of compartmentalization, and they wouldn't necessarily know about somebody they didn't need to know about. Also, they could be lying when they say they never heard of him.'

'I'd like to see the agents' reports of the interviews.'

Vaux hesitated only for a moment before saying, 'Sure.' His secretary had left and so he got the reports himself from a steel filing cabinet with a combination-number lock.

Seated at the secretary's desk in the outer office, Hardtman read the accounts of the questioning. In one or two cases, there were verbatim transcripts of questions and answers. They were a rather ordinary bunch, these suspected spies. A chemist from Philadelphia. The husband and wife owners of a radio repair shop in Brooklyn. A Lower East Side matzoh manufacturer. An ex-technical sergeant in the army. A stenographer. A chemical engineer. People of that sort.

Hardtman leafed rapidly through one or two of the interrogations.

Question: Do you know a Dr Julian Blake?

Answer: No, I don't think so.

Q: You never heard of him? A practitioner of unorthodox medicine. Nerve massage and so on.

A: No, I never heard of him.

Q: You know Don Finer?

A: Yeah, I know Don.

Q: Finer was one of Blake's patients. You didn't know that?

A: Was he? I didn't know. You say he's a massage man. This doctor. Massages the nerves – never heard of that. A faith-healer, perhaps. What would I want with faith-healers? I'm an atheist.

Q: What did Finer need with a faith-healer?

A: How should I know? How do I know what Don Finer needs? Don's a hypochondriac. His nerves *need* massaging.

Q: Do you know that Dr Blake fell out of a seventeenth-storey window last night?

A: I don't even know him, how should I know he fell out of a window? I'm sorry to hear it. What can I say? Don Finer'll have to find himself another masseur to massage his nerves. What sort of faith-healer is it that jumps out of a seventeenth-storey window, tell me?

Most of the interrogations were no more revealing than that. Was it pure coincidence that a man known to be a Communist agent knew a man – a hypochondriac – called Don Finer, who had been a patient of Julian's at one time? As he continued to read, Hardtman found himself being led into a web of such tenuous connections.

He went back into Vaux's room, and asked him about each of the people interviewed.

'Now the fellow with the bad feet, for example . . .'

'You mean Tiviello?'

Hardtman flicked back through pages of transcript until he came to this section:

Q: You were back at Oscar's Piano on West 72nd Street before 9.15?

A: You got it, my friend.

Q: It took you less than four minutes?

A: I took a cab.

Q: It's only one block and you took a cab?

A: Yeah. You know I got bad feet. You know, fallen arches.

Q: Kept you out of the Services, didn't it? Your flat feet.

A: That's right, that's right. My bad feet. Can't walk too far.

Q: You can run pretty good?

A: Yeah, I'm on my toes, see. Don't run on my arches.

Q: You were seen near the Aragon last night, Tiviello. You saying you weren't around there at all?

A: The guy must have made a mistake. I was at Oscar's Piano all night.

'The one with the bad feet,' Hardtman said.

'Yeah, that's Tiviello.'

'Is he a Communist agent? – He sounds like a hood.'

'He is a hood. Used to be Frankie Picarelli's strong arm. Till they fell out. Over a broad. The boss had been fooling with Tiviello's broad, and Tiviello wasn't having any of that *droit de seigneur* stuff, so he quit and set up for himself. Hires himself out. So much per hour. Or per job. Takes messages. Does protection work. That sort of thing.'

'Why were you questioning him?'

'Well, he's been known to deliver drop dead messages, too.'

'You mean Blake could have been pushed out of the window?'

'Could have been.'

'Tell me about Oscar's Piano.'

'That's the joint he protects . . . meaning if they don't pay him to protect 'em he smashes up the place. We might be able to work on that alibi a little. See how watertight it is.'

'I'd like to talk to Tiviello. Where do I find him?'

'Not that easy. You'll find him at Oscar's sometimes, or at his parents' place. There are one or two spots he frequents. No fixed address.'

'Give me his parents' address.'

'Wouldn't advise you to see him on your own. He can act agreeable if it suits him, but he'll also break your neck if it suits him. He's been up for attempted murder three times, and four times for murder, and got off each time. Witnesses disappear or have a cardiac arrest or change their evidence. I tell you *I* wouldn't go and see him alone, and I have maybe more experience of looking after myself.'

'Just to talk to, Vaux.'

'Well, it's your funeral, son.'

He scribbled something on a scrap of paper.

'His parents' address, and the address of Oscar's and one or two of his other hang-outs. And I'll arrange for you to see the room in the Aragon. Now don't let Walter Cole tell you we don't co-operate.'

Vaux took him along the corridor to the elevator. As they waited for it to come up, Vaux said:

'You carry a gun?'

'No.'

'Let me arrange something, if you're going to go looking for Tiviello.'

'Come on, Vaux. You've already arranged something. Your people have been following me for months.'

'A guy across the road – sometimes that can be too late.'

'I'll risk it.'

Vaux shrugged. 'Do me a favour, give me back that piece of paper I just gave you. Don't want my handwriting found on your body.'

Hardtman looked at the addresses and memorized them, and returned the piece of paper to Vaux.

'So long, son,' Vaux said. 'Give my regards to Bobby Tiviello.'

23

He started with Tiviello's hang-outs. He went into bars and sat facing pyramids of inverted glasses on mirrored shelves, and drank whisky while juke boxes blared. He was treated warily as soon as he mentioned Bobby Tiviello. The barmen evidently were accustomed to people looking for him. And they said they'd tell him when they saw him.

In the third bar that Hardtman went to, the barman said, 'Yeah, heard you was lookin' for Tiviello. I ain't seen 'im today but I'll tell 'im when I see 'im.' The word was being passed along. Try Mike's place, somebody said. And at Mike's place they said, try Sadie's, which turned out to be a whorehouse. But Tiviello wasn't there either. The day was heavy. Garbage overflowed the gutters and the air was full of flying litter, and the asphalt gave off its stored-up heat.

A bar-room door flew open, there was the sound of breaking glass, and he saw in grainy snapshot overlapping shapes fusing into a single dismal mass beneath the rotating blades of a large ceiling fan. Fitful music accompanied him as he walked. At the end of a dark corridor a thin old man sat in a yellow light under a sign saying 'Rooms'. He was totally enclosed by glass. A self-protective measure with which Hardtman could sympathize. One sometimes did not wish to enter into too close contact with one's fellow man. There were people from whom to keep one's distance. The Bobby Tiviellos of the world. A warm damp laundry smell came out of an open doorway, and clung to him like body odour. In a luncheonette a man knocked over a glass, spilling beer on the plastic table top and started shoving a woman with henna'd hair and thin plucked eyebrows, shoving her with force and anger towards the door.

Hardtman observed this scene with the same detachment that he observed himself going about his business, whatever that might be. The air was thick and warm and heavy with a hint of thunder. Something was going to have to break. Soon. Perhaps his mind, which had been subjected to some mind-breaking experiences lately, and presumably could not forever retain its under-glass, Ivy League poise. There must come a time when even civilized Hardtman turned baleful in a corner. What was he doing here, and what was the use of looking for Bobby Tiviello? He was playing detective. A stubborn man, Hardtman. He had to find out. Why could he not have left well alone? There were times when I was dismayed by his actions. He did not know *what* he wanted to know, only that there was something worse than these low streets: the abdication of not knowing. He had to know the worst there was to know, or else everything was just a dream. You could not live always under glass.

The streets were divided into sunny side and shadowed. He preferred the shadowed. From where he stood Sixth Avenue stretched ahead, changing in character several times within the eye's span, before making its sudden rise at Rockefeller Centre. In New York you could stand in one spot and see your whole life schematically laid out. A matter of moving up or down one or other avenue. He had spent most of his life moving up; now he was coming down.

His image in dusty silhouette flickered on-off, on-off, on-off in shop windows. Trusses and belts; corsets for grossly distended abdomens; skin lotions and balms for the horrifically depicted ravages of acne; toupees on the heads of faceless dummies; skeletal feet shod by Dr Scholl; wheelchairs, crutches . . . A window full of eye-glasses returned his glassy stare. This side street seemed to have made a corner for itself in the body's failings. Everything for the crippled. He cut down another street where Chinese laundries alternated with restaurants of many nationalities and walk-ups providing a variety of personal services: tattooing, palm-reading, chiropody, massage, and French lessons under a red light.

A man of elephantine girth wobbled by carrying his belly before him, supported by a harness of belts and straps. A

358

legless beggar propelled himself along the pavement by means of roller skates attached to thighs and forearms. Hardtman paused to observe his ingenious form of self-propulsion. First he rolled forward on his arms until he was fully extended, and then he pulled his stumps after him. In this way he could move with considerable speed, making a snake-like hissing with his little metal wheels. Men stupefied by alcohol stood against walls of tattered billboards in postures that strove in vain towards the upright. One had already quit the losing battle to maintain the standing up position, and lay in a foul bundle of rags in the middle of the pavement, a trickling pattern of his own body fluids oozing from him. A large, spruce Negro in a broad-brimmed black hat of rich velour lounged against this same wall, shining the points of his two-tone shoes against the backs of his trousers while at the same time manicuring his nails.

Hardtman felt cloaked in dust, rendered anonymous by dirt and dismalness. The neighbourhood disguised him. This was no place for a man who believed in the *via media*. This was a place for men with guns in their pockets and illicit gain on their minds. He was unknown here, to others and to himself. He had a sense of being in a ruleless universe. What you chose to do made you what you were. Choice, again. Options. His dusty image in shop windows made him look as desperate as everybody else : a man aiming to get himself killed? It was remarkable how unperturbed he felt in himself – this was either the courage of last resort or great folly. Or the indifference of being under glass.

For a moment he paused to consider where he was going : stupid just to go from bar to bar in this way. He was feeling light-headed from the heat and not having eaten, though he had had quite a few drinks. The alcohol seemed not to have affected him. He was burning it up as pure energy.

He decided to pay a visit to the Aragon, since he was having no success tracking down Tiviello.

It was situated on the Upper West Side in an area of

large old hotels and apartment buildings. Coming in through the revolving doors the eye was drawn to a castle on a hill, a *trompe l'oeil* effect that made the small lobby seem larger. There were little tables with brass lamps and tasselled silk lampshades, and lots of mirrors in ornate gilt frames. Those walls which did not afford views of distant castles, were of mock château stone. The front desk was made of dark wood. Hardtman went over to it and said who he was and that he believed they had been told he was coming. The receptionist gave him a cute look, and said, 'Everybody wants to see that room.'

'Oh do they?'

'I'm not suggesting you, natch,' the desk clerk said, 'but people do have morbid minds, they really do, well, don't they?' He gave Hardtman the key to the room. 'Can you manage on your own, sir?' he asked cutely. 'Gives me the creeps. Just thinking . . . oh my, oh my. Gives me palpitations just to think about it. There's nobody in there, so you just go right on in. White House, is it? What was his connection then . . .?'

The maroon carpet in the lift was badly worn in places and the rosewood panelling, with its borders of golden *fleurs de lis*, had been deliberately marked with a penknife.

Hardtman let himself into the room. It was small and very full of things, and airless. You could smell the dust. The double bed occupied almost the whole of what was in size a single room. A *bureau de dame*, its drawers ascending like the steps of an Aztec temple to a mirrored plateau, provided the only table surface. There was hotel notepaper in the little drawers, and it was presumably here that Julian had sat writing his suicide note. In a lemonwood veneer wardrobe hung a couple of Julian's suits, and the fitted drawers down one side held shirts and socks. There was an armchair, and a baggage stand piled with suitcases, and the room was full, quite full. A man of any girth would have had a job squeezing between the foot of the bed and the wardrobe to get to the window. But the bed was large and comfortable-looking, and that was presumably what mattered. This was not a room in which the occupants were expected to spend much time out of bed.

One reason for the smallness of the room was that part of it had been partitioned off to make a bathroom and a pantry kitchen. On the drainer board stood a chrome Thermos bottle. Hardtman opened it and smelled. Coffee. Almost full. He wet his lips with a drop of it. Still warm.

He went back into the room and pulled open the drapes, bringing down a cloud of dust on himself. The view was spectacular. He stood looking out. The converging and intersecting light paths of so many man-made marvels gave him the feeling of being at the centre of some great energy source, pulsating with a powerful brightness. He could see to the right, the curve of the Hudson river: a large ship, all lit up, was coming into dock. The whole town seemed to be ablaze, the continuous interplay of moving lights creating a night battle effect, with tracers of light flying between the set-back towers. Hardtman could not help feeling a touch of patriotic pride for a country that had so concretized aspiration. This wonderful achievement: America. How it crowded space with its wealth of creativity! America was a place where the rewards heaped upon you were very great, but to fail was to die: death, too, was an option among the many options, and perhaps, after all, Julian had had good reason to choose it. Perhaps it was wrong to see murder plots when a simpler explanation sufficed: failure.

Hardtman suddenly felt extremely weary. It was late, and he had not yet checked into a hotel. Might as well stay here, he thought, and tomorrow decide what to do next, whether to give up this foolish playing at detectives and return to Washington, or go on looking for Tiviello. He called the desk and asked if they had a room for him for the night. High up, preferably. He might as well have the view. Yes, they said, they could give him a room on the sixteenth floor.

It turned out to be just as small as the one Julian had occupied, and as overfilled and dusty.

He lay down on the bed. The coverlet was not very

clean and he drew it down. The sheets were purple. Well, that might appeal to some. He rose and went to the window and watched the way the cars seemed to be climbing straight up into the sky. There was ambition for you. Later, he had difficulty in getting to sleep. He was trying to imagine what might have occurred in the last ten days of Julian's life to make him decide to kill himself.

He thought, surely there must be some place cool and restorative where he and Laurene and Debbie could go to retrench, and stem the outflow of their fast-wasting resources before they were all expended, before there was nothing left any more of love and loyalty and truthfulness. The lower forms of life had the capacity to regenerate lost past, severed limbs – to re-grow them good as new. But beings of mind and heart had lost that primal skill, and could do no more than knit together wounds, and that only if they were not too deep, not too wide.

He wondered if it was already too late for him to find his way back to what once had been – before the great expectancy engendered by the Presidential summons. Such thoughts kept him awake; finally, he took a sleeping draught.

In the morning there was a fog and the skyline in the fuzzy light was a haphazard jumble of chimney stacks and warehouse roofs and dockside derricks and factory smoke and advertising signs.

He resumed his search for Tiviello. It was another heavy hot day and it was exhausting trudging through the scabrous West Forties. He spent the whole morning going round the places he had been to last night. No, Tiviello hadn't shown up. Maybe he was doing a job. Blowing somebody away. Sometimes when he was doing a job nobody saw him for days. While the heat was on. Hid out somewhere.

Hardtman left the phone number of his hotel at all the dives. Just as well he hadn't stayed at the Plaza. Even the perpetual imperturbability of its staff might have been strained if a few of these lower-depths characters came asking for him.

On this second round of the places frequented by Tiviello, some of the faces were already familiar, and he was remembered from last night. 'You'se the one that was lookin' for Bobby Tiviello, tha's right.' He had an identity, he was the guy looking for Tiviello. Which made him all right. He was accepted. At Sadie's place he was propositioned by one of the whores, a half-caste they called Brown Sugar. 'Don'tcher wann spen' a little time with me, while youse waitin' for Bobby? Spen' a little time with me. C'mmon. Won't cost you much, and I'm real good. Promise you. You never been with a Lady of the Night that's as good as me. They call me Brown Sugar 'cause I'se so *sweet*.'

He said it was a little early in the day for him, but offered to buy her a drink. She had large eyes that seemed to take up most of her face. Her expression of deep sadness was pushed aside every few seconds by a great big smile, no matter what she was saying at the time. It wasn't faked – it was something achieved.

'What you want with Bobby Tiviello?' she asked astutely. 'You don't look the type.'

'What type do I look?'

'Oh I dunno. Business man?'

'I'm an attorney.'

'O.K., that figures. You wouldn't be Bobby Tiviello's mouthpiece, would you?'

'No, no, I'm not. Does he have a mouthpiece?'

'Oh sure, Bobby's very big. He handles big stuff. Oh he's in with very big people. Carriage trade. You sure, Jack, you wouldn't like to make pretend it's a little later in the day and sort of have a little female company? I'll give you a real good time.'

'Buy you another drink before I go?' he offered.

'Sure, what else have I got to do?'

He left her cuddling the drink against her cheek. Brown Sugar. His world had become bounded by half-a-dozen sleazy bars, populated by prostitutes and pimps and fences, and professional criminals of various kinds, one or two of whom were ready to hire themselves out for any kind of work.

He suddenly decided he would go to the place where Tiviello's parents lived. He remembered the address. His street orientation had quite gone, though, and he had to keep asking directions. But he carried on determinedly, in the grip of some necessity. Why would he not give up, and leave Tiviello to the FBI? Something forced him to go on. Hardtman was no detective but he had been an interrogator of Nazi war criminals – so the ghastlier reaches of the human spirit were not unknown to him, nor was he inexperienced in questioning guilty men. Having questioned Dr Kaltenbrunner, among others, he could surely deal with a petty murderer like Tiviello.

He had at last found the place: an old tenement building, mouldering and damp-smelling and seemingly held up only by its iron brace of fire escapes. Hardtman went in through an entrance smelling of dog piss, and made his way along a dank corridor until he had found the number. He banged on the door and it was so quickly opened by a smiling young man that Hardtman felt bound to ask, 'You were expecting me?'

'That's right, Bill.'

'Tiviello?'

'That's right.'

He was big, Bobby Tiviello, but not especially big, considering his profession. A little under six foot, with lustrous black hair, that underwent a series of deep waves from front to back. He had pale skin, and large white regular teeth, and a warm huckster's smile. He was selling himself, from the moment he opened the door.

He was dressed in blue gaberdine trousers and wearing a waistcoat – what Americans call a vest. The jacket, with the wide padded shoulders of the day, hung from a shaped wooden coat hanger. His shirt was deep blue and he wore cufflinks of diamond-studded dice. The top button of his shirt was undone and his Miami beach tie hung loose around his neck. His shoes were suede, midnight blue, their pile upright. The tops of Havana cigars in metal canisters protuded from his waistcoat pocket. His eyes were darkly eager and his breath was a curious mixture of garlic and chewing gum and cigars.

'Come right on in, Bill. Heard you was lookin' for me.'

'Who'd you hear that from?'

'I got my sources,' he said laughing. He stuck out a big hand. Very friendly. 'Glad to know you, Bill.'

'Well – I don't know how glad you're going to be,' Hardtman said. 'I don't know what your sources have told you.'

'Oh that don't worry me none,' he said generously, laughing. 'Always ready to listen to any proposition, always ready to listen. Take your weight off your feet, Bill. Sorry about this place. This is my folks' place.' The most noticeable piece of furniture was a mirrored cocktail cabinet, fully open to display the rich interior, which was like a *Saturday Evening Post* advertisement come true. There was a range of mostly unopened many-coloured drink bottles lined up around an array of unused Venetian glass goblets. Presumably the gift of a loving son to parents who don't drink.

'What's your poison?' Tiviello inquired.

'Nothing.'

'Mind if I do?' He proceeded to make himself a white lady. He had all the equipment in this emporium of a cocktail cabinet. He dropped crushed ice into the cocktail shaker, and poured on precisely $4\frac{1}{2}$ jiggers of gin.

'Where are your folks?' Hardtman asked.

'They're out,' Tiviello said. 'They go out, meet their friends. They're out a lot. Got nothing else to do, have they? What else should they do? They're retired, you know.' He added $1\frac{1}{2}$ jiggers of lemon juice to the shaker. 'I don't see too much of 'em when I'm workin',' he admitted. 'You don't wanna bring trouble home, do yuh? I see 'em when things are quiet, like right now . . .'

'Things are quiet, are they?'

'Oh there's not much doing, I can tell you.' He added a jigger of Cointreau, and two egg whites, and replacing the

365

cap commenced a vigorous shaking movement of the cock-tail shaker.

'You do that very expertly,' Hardtman said.

'I been a bar-tender, see.'

'You wouldn't have done a little job night before last by any chance?' Hardtman said.

'Nawhhh, didn't do nothin' night before last.' He removed the cap of the shaker and taking a frosted glass from the fridge, poured out the drink, using a silver strainer.

'You not gonna join me in one – I made it for both?'

'No thanks.'

'Nawwwh,' Tiviello continued, casting his mind back, 'night before last – yeah that was the night, that's right, went down to Oscar's Piano over on Second. That's what I did . . .' He gave his disarming smile, full of peace of mind, the result of much striving towards self-improvement. He took a small sip of white lady and mimed approval. 'Very good, Bobby,' he congratulated himself. He laughed. 'That job,' he said confidentially, 'it ain't my style, you know. Out a window – huh? That ain't me. Don't like heights. So you can count me out far as the other night's concerned. Besides, you know I got an alibi for that night.'

'Oscar's Piano, isn't that the place?'

'That's it. The waiter'll swear I was there all night.'

'Isn't that the place you protect?'

'I look after them,' Tiviello admitted with a grin.

'And they look after you?'

'Nawwwh,' Tiviello said, after a delay, as if it had taken him a moment or so to catch the insinuation, 'that'd be perjury, wouldn't it.'

'Tell you what,' Hardtman said, 'why don't we go to Oscar's Piano. I'd like to see it.'

'O.K., O.K., I'm easy,' Tiviello said. 'Anything you say, Bill. They'll tell you I was there. You'll see, they don't lie none.'

Tiviello finished his white lady extra fast, took his jacket off the hanger and put it on, did up his collar button and tied his Miami beach tie. Hardtman could not tell if there was a gun in the breast pocket or not. There was no bulge, but the jacket had a loose-fitting cut.

They took a cab to Second Avenue. Oscar's Piano had a smart black-and-white awning and a logo consisting of a piano keyboard. The doorman had black-and-white striped trousers, and the ironwork over the glass doors repeated the motif.

'Oh hi there, Mr Tiviello,' the doorman called out when he saw who it was. 'How's things, Mr Tiviello?'

'Great, great,' Tiviello murmured, giving the doorman a friendly punch in the stomach.

Inside, on the bar, stood a shiny pewter vase holding shiny pewter flowers, each gittering petal of which was hollowed out to form ashtrays. Behind the bar, a rainbow traversed a pyramid of drinks, while the sun shone down fine rays of neon light. A bar waiter in black-and-white livery immediately welcomed them and took them to a corner booth overhung by an octahedral black glass ceiling light, emitting from its smoked interior a single white beam that made a pool of light on the shiny black table top. The mirrors which surrounded them were of smoked glass, and gave you back a darkened and improved image of yourself. There was even a piano, and a pianist playing.

'A little different from your other hang-outs, this,' Hardtman said.

'Oh this is a swell place,' he agreed. He ordered a white lady, and Hardtman a dry Martini.

'Level with me,' Hardtman said as coaxingly as to a girl; indeed there was a feeling, due to Tiviello's acquiescent eyes, that he *could* be coaxed, could be coaxed to do almost anything.

Tiviello took a cigar out of a metal canister and pierced it with a silver piercer. And surrounded himself with the expensive aroma of Havana. His smile was deep and sincere; he grinned with a large majority of his perfect white teeth.

'O.K., Bill. Shoot. What's on your mind, my friend?'

'Want you to answer some questions.'

Tiviello laughed in his most friendly manner. 'Lot's of

things I do, Bill. But answerin' questions ain't exactly what I'm famous for.'

'Try it,' Hardtman said.

'What's there in it for me?'

'I'll pay for your time. Your usual rate.'

'See, Billy, it's like my fee depends on the job. I can give somebody a bloody nose, or I can do a job that'll need stitches. Or a priest.'

'Your fee for talking.'

'Talking ain't what I'm good at, like I said . . .'

'I'm not the FBI. I want to know for my own information. Two nights ago, when it happened, you were reported seen in the neighbourhood of the Aragon.'

'Must 'ave been mistaken identity, Bill, 'cause I got an alibi for that night. I was here the whole time. The boys'll verify it.' He grinned broadly and made a hand gesture at the waiters, like an MC introducing a favourite act.

'You ever work for the Communist party?'

'Listen, Bill.' His voice became confidential, and sonorous with good advice. 'You oughtn't ever to ask me that, because talking about a client ain't done. It's the unwritten law. If I talk I'm dead so quick it ain't even funny. So that's where I can't help you, Bill. Besides, you're on the wrong track with that . . .'

'Then why are you talking to me?'

'Because you wanted to talk to me. People want to talk to me, I talk to them.'

'All right, let's talk. Tell me about yourself. How'd you get into this line of business?'

In the cool soft dimness of the bar Tiviello's smile was like an automatic 'Welcome' sign lighting up. He certainly knew how to sell himself. Hardtman reflected what a good public relations man he would have made – or a salesman for self-improvement courses.

'First time I hit somebody in the head, I was fifteen. That was the advantage. They couldn't burn you. Under age. One day this guy comes to me and says how'd you like to make two grand fast. That was a good price in those days. I say, You name it. O.K., he says. I want this guy to be

368

found floating. So I said, O.K., I'd do it. How else was I going to make 2Gs, aged fifteen? It was fantastic! I said to myself, Right, Bobby, this is your big chance, your chance to be somebody, because I know, like you know, if you can do something like that it gets you in big. Nothing gets you more respect than if you can do the big job. The ones can do that are the *crème de la crème*.'

'What you sleep like after the first time?'

'Fantastic.'

'What'd he done?'

'I dunno. I didn't ask. It wasn't none of my business.'

'How'd you do it?'

'I walked up behind him as he was coming out of his girlfriend's place, 3 a.m. in the morning. I reckoned at least he had a good time beforehand. I give it to him in the back of the head. He didn't know nothing about it. Used a .38 with a silencer. Plop! That's all there was to it.' He tapped his loose-draped jacket. 'It's a good cannon, a nice piece of machinery.'

'How many have you done?'

'I've done twenty-six on contract, three for myself, for my own personal satisfaction. I don't mind saying that. What the hell. It's been said in the papers, and I didn't take out no libel action, did I?'

'The ones for your personal satisfaction, why did you do those?'

'Somebody does me dirt, I don't forget.'

Tiviello's smile was as thin as the first crack on the surface of a frozen pond.

'Are you giving me good advice?'

'Naaww, I'm not threatenin' you, Bill. What would I want to do that for? We're havin' a friendly discussion. You look at my record, the people I give it to – they all had it coming, some way. Bad guys like me. I don't mess with anybody that's straight. But somebody does me harm, that I haven't done nothin' to . . .'

'Yes? What happens?'

'If you'd ever hit somebody in the head with a long .22 you'd know what it does – it goes in some and then it scrambles their brains. That's what I use when I want to make sure they know who hit 'em and what hit 'em.'

'That's when you're not doing it from behind.'

Tiviello's mouth closed tight, extinguishing the Welcome sign. There was a thin line going down from his lips, fine as the mechanism of a hair trigger. Then he grinned again.

'If you got your back to me,' he said, 'I give it you in the back. If I'm looking at you, it's the front of the head.'

'I thought maybe you didn't like to look in their eyes.'

'Don't bother me none.'

'One day they'll catch up with you.'

'Oh sure. You think I don't know that?'

'Perhaps sooner than you think.'

'Nobody oughtta get the idea it's gonna be easy, catching up with Bobby Tiviello. The cops have tried. Even people think they've seen you somewhere, turns out they was mistaken, or they have an accident, fall off the end of a pier.'

'Or out of a seventeenth-storey window.'

'That can happen, too.'

'If he's got it coming. Did you know Dr Blake? Maybe you went to him about your bad feet. Or was it to do with a woman? What was the connection?'

'You're just guessing in the dark, Billy.'

'I'm impressed by the coincidence that you were in the area when he fell.'

'It was a mistake, whoever saw me. He made a mistake. What'd your friend done? Why'd he take a leaper?'

'I'm not sure what he'd done. He played around with other people's women, and he got mixed up in things . . .'

'They say in the papers he was a spy.'

'That's what some people think.'

'Maybe he had it coming.' He blew out cigar smoke easily.

'Sometimes, you know, it's difficult to remember that technically you come within the category of what is called the human race.'

'Listen, my friend, I'm within the human race. Remember one thing, people like me wouldn't exist if people like you didn't need us.'

'I thought you confined yourself to fellow hoods.'

'No, I said I give it to them that's got it coming. Baddies.'

'And when you don't know who it is? When you hit them from behind?'

'Friend, a brick can fall on somebody's head, too. And the brick don't know either if the guy has got it coming or not.'

'That's supposed to be the difference between bricks and people.'

'O.K., Hardtman, lay it out. I'm getting pissed off with you, friend.' His eyes were as changeable as the sea.

'If somebody had wanted Dr Blake blown away, whom would they have gone to?'

'They might have gone to me,' Tiviello said, 'I'm the best. But they didn't, see.'

'But if they had wanted to, how would they have approached you?'

'Same way you did. Ask around. They find me in the end, after I've checked them out.'

'Then what?'

'Like the way you did. Invite me for a drink. We talk a little. I give you my credentials, I show you you can trust me. A confidential relationship. Me, I got to make sure you're O.K. I got to have good recommendations.'

'What were mine like?'

'The best. Or I wouldn't be talking to you, would I? Now the other thing is my fee. I get paid in advance.'

'Who told you I wanted a job done?'

Tiviello grinned with deep professional understanding. 'Why else you come looking for me, and I know I'm not easy to find?' He laughed. 'People are bashful at first. Don't like to come out with it. Ask you a lot of questions. That's normal. It takes a little time – a few drinks. Till they get more relaxed, before they'll say what's on their mind.'

'Let's have another drink, Tiviello. At my hotel. More private there.'

'Whatever you say, Bill.'

Hardtman called over the bar waiter.

'Night before last,' he said. 'Did you see Mr Tiviello here?'

'Oh sure,' the waiter said, 'I see him here all night long. And if you wanna know, mister, all the other guys see him here all night long too.'

'From when to when?'

'From . . .' He spread his arms as if to say, take your choice. 'From seven o'clock, maybe earlier, to midnight, maybe later. Okay?' He shot a look at Tiviello, who grinned and nodded.

'O.K.,' Hardtman said, 'how much is this?'

'It's on the house,' Tiviello said.

'On the house,' the waiter echoed. 'Sure, sure.'

Hardtman put down a five-dollar bill on the table and got up.

From a bunch of fives, Tiviello peeled off one and gave it to the waiter, and on the way out shook hands with all the other waiters, pressing fivers into their hands. At the cash register he stopped, made a sign and the cashier rang up a minus sum, took out a packet of notes and handed them to Tiviello, who took a fiver off the top and gave it to her, and pocketed the remainder.

24

'Nice day again,' the desk clerk at the Aragon said, giving Hardtman his room key and messages. 'Quite an Indian summer we're having.' He glanced up at Tiviello waiting by the lifts.

'I want the keys of the other rooms as well,' Hardtman said. 'The ones I saw yesterday.'

'Oh yes, I know, I know.' Again the desk clerk shot a look at Tiviello.

'Have you seen that man before?'

'Not that I know,' said the desk clerk, and then with a coy giggle intimated, 'Wouldn't mind seeing him again.' He gave Hardtman a secret smile.

Going up in the lift, Hardtman asked Tiviello, 'What you think of the hotel?'

'Nice place. What was your friend doing here?'

'I don't know. Tell me, you ever refuse a job, Tiviello?'

'Sure. The Picarelli brothers told me to give it to the "Bird" Rollo. I said: That's ridiculous. Bird Rollo, what's he done? The Bird don't have it comin'. I refused. Like I never give it to a guy in front of his family. Or in a house of worship.'

Hardtman watched Tiviello closely as they went along the corridor to the room that had been occupied by Julian. Murderers, at the scene of the crime, were supposed to give themselves away.

By the door, Tiviello placed a hand on Hardtman's arm. 'See, I'm a hood, I'm an all round bad 'un, right? But to me – to me, I think really I'm sort of an O.K. guy, too. I don't feel too bad about myself.' He gave Hardtman his most deeply sincere look. 'I'm not bullshitting you. You know, it's a dumb thing to be what I am – what's the future in it? I know. But what could I do? You know what I wanted to be when I was a kid in the streets? An artist. A fuckin'

artist. I could draw pretty good. I wanted to be a fuckin'
artist like Constable. He's dead now. Now he could paint a
picture. You oughta see them. They got them in all the art
museums. You should of seen those trees – you could of
lied down under them trees, they're so real-lookin'. Now if
I'd of had brains like this Constable, would I have to be a
baddie . . . ?'

'Life's not fair, is it?' Hardtman said.

'I tell you somethin', you're right there.'

Hardtman let them into the room, and looked around.

'This where it was?' Tiviello asked. He went over to the
window, opened it and looked down. 'Yeah, it sure is a
long way down . . .'

'You once put Johnny Bigsby in the hospital for three
weeks?'

'That's right,' Tiviello agreed, with pride. 'And you
know what he was! He was light heavyweight champ of the
world.'

'I expect you had a little advantage over him – like a gun
in your pocket?'

'No, I didn't have no cannon. I don't even carry a cannon
for that kind o' job. I'm fit. I keep fit. I work out every day
– part of my business, keepin' fit. Don't drink too much.
Don't hardly smoke, except for cigars. I live a clean life. I
box . . .' He delivered a sudden punch into air, and followed it with a hand and foot movement too quick to follow. 'Speed of the hand deceives the eye,' he said grinning.
'And I'm a Judo black-belt. To get to my position with the
Picarelli brothers, you got to have good diplomas, I tell
you.'

'So it would have been no problem for you bundling
somebody out of that window?'

'No problem,' Tiviello agreed. 'If I'd done it, which I
didn't, like I been tellin' you. The word is he jumped, ain't
that it?'

'That's the theory.'

Hardtman went to the pantry kitchen. He picked up the
Thermos of coffee, took the cap off and sipped a small
amount.

Julian needed caffeine to keep his brain alive and sharp.

Hardtman said: 'Why would anyone want to keep coffee hot if he was about to throw himself out the window?'

'People do dumb things,' Tiviello agreed.

'Now on the other hand, if he had no intention of doing anything of the sort, but somebody knocked at the door . . .'

'Why'd he let him in?' Tiviello asked.

'Perhaps he was someone he was expecting, someone bringing him money, say . . .'

'Didn't I hear the door was double locked from inside?'

'Oh you heard that?'

'They already been over all this . . .'

'Yes, they leave no stone unturned,' Hardtman said. 'There's a fire escape within three feet of the bathroom window. From there to the stairs would be no problem for somebody who keeps fit.'

'That so?' Tiviello mused.

Hardtman was watching him closely all the time.

'All right, Tiviello. Want you to see something else.'

He took him to the lift and they went down a floor and walked along the corridor to Room 169. It had not yet been made up. A certain laxness clearly existed at this hotel: the dust, the frayed carpets, the easy-going attitude where night-time visitors were concerned.

'Smells as though somebody was smoking quite a few cigars in here,' Hardtman said. 'Good cigars. Havanas, wouldn't you say? You ought to know the smell. They're what you smoke.'

'That's right,' Tiviello agreed easily.

'Neat fellow,' Hardtman commented. 'Didn't leave any stubs, emptied all his ashtrays.' He went to the bathroom, lifted the toilet seat flap. There were traces of cigar ash all around the pan, and a single stub was floating in the water.

'Now why'd someone bother to flush his cigar stubs down the toilet, do you suppose? You think he might have heard about saliva tests?'

Tiviello laughed. 'That's good thinking,' he said.

'The person who was occupying this room,' Hardtman said, 'checked out the night Blake fell. Well, others did, too. This hotel is very popular with people who don't stay the whole night. But usually the ones who check out like that are couples. This one was a single. The only *single* who didn't occupy the room the whole night.'

'It's an interesting idea,' Tiviello said, 'but like I told you before, I got an alibi for that whole night, and besides none of this sort of stuff is what they call evidence, nobody could go to a jury with it.'

'I don't need to go to a jury,' Hardtman said. 'I just have to be reasonably sure – in my own mind.'

He was pushing Tiviello hard, trying to scare him, trying to get some reaction out of him, however momentary, that would confirm the wild notion that was growing in his mind.

'I heard about that,' Tiviello said, 'I heard about the free hand you get in national security. But you're knocking at the wrong door, my friend.'

Hardtman thought, if he has done this, could he be so untroubled-looking, so at peace with himself, would there not be some glimpse of the killer? Perhaps, after all, Julian had killed himself. He thought of Julian's lithe body at the open window, his hair blown about by the wind, as it had been that night on Fire Island. Hardtman thought of the fall, like a fall in a dream from which you did not wake up. Hardtman thought: a time can come when all one's options have run out, and then perhaps there is nothing else to be done.

Hardtman went to the window and opened it and looked out. The dusk was less kind to New York than the dark. Ugly water towers and waterside warehouses marred the cross-river view. He turned round, resting his weight on the window sill, open space behind him. It was a gesture of his contempt for this hood and killer, this sincere psychopath. He would show him how little he was impressed with his brute strength, his boxing prowess, his black belt. He would demonstrate the superiority of strength of character. Hardtman often could not help feeling superior to others, since he so clearly was. And now, with an almost palpable sensation of empty space behind him, and the intoxication of too much adrenalin in his bloodstream, he said:

'All right, Tiviello, I'm going to tell you what is going to happen to you. First, I'm going to break your alibi. Five-dollar alibis stand up to only a certain amount of pressure. I'm going to have the FBI go over those waiters till one breaks, and when that happens, the others will follow. And with a little work on the desk clerks here, I should think one of them'd remember you. There's also the register you must have signed. Even if you disguised your handwriting, an expert can almost certainly attribute it. Then: finger-prints. It was hot. You couldn't have worn gloves all the time. All the time you were waiting in this room, smoking your Havanas. Your story won't stand up, Tiviello.'

He had come very close to Hardtman, who was feeling the headiness of tempting fate when you have guilt to dis-charge and debts to pay. But Tiviello was not coming to push him out of the window. He was shuddering.

'You mind,' he said, 'I can't stand to see that,' and he winced. 'Heights give me the willies. Besides, I don't wanna be blamed for you like falling out the window, by accident.'

Hardtman stayed where he was by the open window, staring out this crass hoodlum.

Tiviello was evidently turning over in his mind what Hardtman had been saying. His thought processes, unlike his reflexes, were slow, and it was some time before he had worked out what he was going to say. 'You know, Bill,' he said at last, 'I think you got this all wrong. Maybe you got some things right, but you got other things wrong, see. O.K., now this is what you do.' Tiviello's voice was full of friendly helpfulness. 'What you do is, go talk to my lawyer, he'll put you straight. Yuh, that's the thing to do, go and talk to Mr Kantzler.'

'Louis Kantzler?'

'That's right.'

'Louis Kantzler is your attorney?' Hardtman said in astonishment.

'O.K., you got it, Bill.'

377

Hardtman was shaken. He slipped down from the sill, his feet seeking firm support for the sake of feeling something solid beneath him.

'That's a pretty high class attorney for you to have, Tiviello.'

'Yeah,' he agreed, 'they say he's pretty good. Now you talk to him, Bill. That's what you do. He'll put you right. No hard feelings. No offence. I know it's, like, your job. Only you ain't got it right, and so for my protection and yours, you go and talk to Mr Kantzler and he'll put you right.'

Kantzler's apartment overlooked the East river, at the end of a cul-de-sac. As you were admitted to the building a bell started ringing and did not stop until the doorman had punched out the correct code de-activating the alarm, something he did not do until he had elicited the caller's name and checked it against a list to determine if he was expected. Having found Hardtman's name on the list, he stopped the bell, and said, 'Fourth lobby, Mr Hardtman. Take the elevator to the tenth floor,' and picked up the house phone to announce the visitor.

Hardtman walked along a vaulted arcade and took the elevator up. The elevator doors did not open automatically upon arrival, but remained shut until they were opened from within the apartment by a manservant. Hardtman found himself in a circular hall, with broadly curving open-tread stairs soaring like some aeronautical symbol to the galleried upper storey of the duplex.

The manservant led the way across deep white carpet overhung by many-faceted long, glass lanterns. The walls were white-washed brick hung with Babangi masks from the French Congo. There was a great deal of tubular steel furniture. The tables had ivory tops and the chests had ivory knobs. The area around the floor-to-ceiling windows was an indoor jungle of potted cacti and rubber plants and Brazilian palm trees.

At this point there was a door connecting the living room

and the den, and here Kantzler was waiting to receive Hardtman. He led him inside.

'Come in, Mr Hardtman. Glad to see you, Mr Hardtman,' he declared with the quiet fervour of a man taking an oath. He seated himself on a kidney-shaped green silk sofa, offering a green leather wing chair to his guest.

'Can I fix you a drink, Mr Hardtman?'

'No thanks.'

'I think I will have one.' He pressed a bell for the manservant who appeared at once, and told him: 'An old-fashioned, Hank. You sure you won't take something, Mr Hardtman?'

'Sure, thank you.'

'Cigarette?'

He offered a box made of Brazilian onyx, and Hardtman took a cigarette. It was lit for him by Kantzler pressing back on a polished brass nude, who thereupon divided at the waist and gave out flame from her innards. Hardtman lit his cigarette in the fiery lady, and sat back. Beyond the floor-to-ceiling windows there was the continuous night traffic of the river.

Kantzler said, 'There are always boats going by, so you have a permanent sense of movement, which I find helps my thought processes. You find movement soothing to the mind, Mr Hardtman?'

'Do I find movement soothing to the mind?' Hardtman asked himself. 'Yes, I expect I do, I expect I do, Mr Kantzler.'

The manservant had gone to the end of the room where the wall consisted of floor-to-ceiling mirror panels. They folded back at a touch to reveal a bar, softly lit, amply stocked. As Hank prepared the drink, Kantzler said:

'I love this place. Right bang in the middle of Manhattan – and just get a load of that peacefulness!' He shook his head in quiet astonishment at the privileges he was capable of commanding. 'Isn't that something, hmm?'

'Quite something,' Hardtman agreed looking at a painting of a lady in a voluptuous Italian car showing the white's of her eyes in some kind of ecstatic transport of driving.

'Well, Mr Hardtman, what exactly is the problem?'

'I presume your client has filled you in.'

'I expect I will get it more clearly from you,' Kantzler said.

'Anyway, you've got Tiviello's story?'

'Yes, I have.'

'And it's good?'

'It's a hundred per cent.'

'A hundred per cent what?'

'Watertight.'

'Yes, I bet. Tiviello is pretty smart for a dumb hood. Especially smart of him to have a smart lawyer like you, Mr Kantzler.'

Kantzler smiled modestly. He had a soft manner: unassertive. His shoulders were rounded, and his powdery grey hair lay thinly spread across his skull. His forehead was high and much crossed by the lines of his cares.

'As you say,' he smiled, 'a hood. Yet you know, I rather take to him. Nothing to be said in his favour – a thoroughgoing rascal. But he does have the courage of his villainy. He's honest in his own way. In any case, you'd agree, even a hood is entitled to legal representation and justice.'

'Yes, that's what it says in the book.'

'I enjoy the work,' Kantzler said, 'surprising as that may seem. I started out in criminal practice . . .'

'So did I.'

'Oh did you? . . . Well, I have a certain *nostalgie de la boue* for all that . . .'

'Amply satisfied I should have thought with clients of Tiviello's ilk.'

'I do a great deal of very dull corporation law. The few criminal cases I take help keep my hand in. Keeps you in touch with the real world. Otherwise you can get lost in big numbers. Up there on Wall Street, away from the raw human material . . .'

'Some pretty raw human material there, too,' Hardtman said.

Kantzler smiled; his smile was very good – knowing, but not condemning. He was a man who had seen everything, the worst that life could do, and was still unshocked. Hadn't lost heart.

'Human beings there are everywhere,' he agreed. 'Everywhere. Even, as you say, on Wall Street. Though sometimes I take leave to doubt it . . .' He gave a slight self-deprecating laugh at this little touch of cynicism. 'But it's more concealed there, human nature. Under glass, if you know what I mean. Am I right? But you get out into the stinking melting pot where the Tiviellos of this world hang out and you see life without cosmetics.'

'Yes, I saw where his parents live. I also saw the bar he protects. Oscar's Piano. Now that's not too bad – if you don't mind mirrors you can't see yourself in.'

Kantzler laughed.

'Your client kill Dr Blake?' Hardtman asked.

'My client was questioned by the FBI,' Kantzler said carefully, 'and they appear to have been satisfied that he is in the clear.'

'That doesn't answer my question.'

'What a question for one lawyer to expect another lawyer to answer. If you don't mind my saying so. What kind of lawyer would I be – even if I thought he had done it – issuing confessions on his behalf?'

'Not as smart as you are reputed to be, anyhow.'

Kantzler again smiled modestly.

'You got him off three attempted homicide charges and four murder charges.'

Another modest smile, of agreement.

'You know I went to the hotel, I had a look over it. My guess is that if the FBI wanted to take that place apart they'd find that your client's fingerprints in the register are identifiable; and that the desk clerks could be got to identify him, and the waiters at the Oscar's Piano to withdraw their alibi.'

'Well, I wonder. Anyway that's your theory, and you are entitled to it. But let me point out that even if it were established that Tiviello had, by chance, occupied a room in that hotel on the day of Blake's fall, this would still not be evidence that he'd had anything to do with the guy's death.'

'Quite some coincidence. For a professional killer to be in the same hotel the day somebody falls or jumps from the seventeenth floor.'

'Life is full of bizarre coincidences – but there you are.'

'What was he doing there?'

'I didn't say he was there. I said, even if it turned out that he was, there could be another explanation. He does a lot of escort work. Somebody might have been staying there who needed protection.'

'I know the kind of protection that Tiviello provides.'

Kantzler laughed.

'Well, we all know the sort of person he is. Nobody makes any bones about that. He is a baddie, no question. We don't deny it. Still, we should bear in mind that those with whose extinction legend links his name were a pretty bad lot, too.' His words became even softer, almost inaudible, achieving thereby an inverse emphasis. 'Scum, frankly. The lowest of the low. Who can say they didn't have it coming?'

'Did Dr Blake have it coming, too?'

'There are those who do say,' Kantzler conceded, 'that he was a very dubious character. I believe it is being suggested he may have been a spy – isn't that so? Well, I wouldn't know. That's more your department, isn't it? But there are a lot of people around who'd say he was an unscrupulous womanizer, and I think there are maybe several prominent men – and women – today, good people, people who have made solid contributions to the State, who will not exactly lament his passing.'

'Might one of these solid citizens have seen fit to send him a message. A drop dead message? Through Tiviello?'

'Everything is possible. But proof, that's another thing.'

'Why don't we stop playing legalistic games. I want to short-cut this, Kantzler. I'm not basically interested in Tiviello, if you can get him off – it's no skin off my nose.

But I am interested in getting at the truth, and if there is something behind Blake's fall, I want to know.'

A look of bewilderment spread slowly over Kantzler's face; he did not seem able to grasp what Hardtman wanted exactly. He had the bemused expression of someone who has been side-tracked and has somehow lost the continuity of his thoughts.

'I don't think I quite know what you want me to say, Mr Hardtman.'

'Level with me, Kantzler. That's all I ask.'

Kantzler gave his worldly-wise world-weary laugh, as if to say: that's *all* he wants.

'Why come to me?'

'Tiviello sent me to you.'

'But *you* got on to Tiviello – as far as I can make out by means of some wild guesswork. I understand,' he said, trying to explain it to himself, 'that in your position it behoves you to make inquiries to satisfy yourself that everything is being done to get to the bottom of this. Yes, yes, understood. But surely you have amply satisfied such requirements, and there can be no iota of blame attached to you if you now leave the inquiry to the FBI to handle?'

'But I haven't satisfied myself that everything is being done, that's exactly . . .'

'So it seems, so it seems,' Kantzler said more bewildered than ever.

'Look, Kantzler, let's stop playing around. There are just too many coincidences. The coincidence that Tiviello was in the same hotel the day of Blake's fall. The coincidence that Tiviello's lawyer is someone who knew Blake . . .'

'Slightly, very slightly,' Kantzler said.

'Your wife knew him,' Hardtman said. 'Katie. She was in his Yoga class out on Fire Island . . .'

'So I believe,' Kantzler said. 'I understand your wife also knew him. Yoga classes too?'

'You'll agree it's straining credulity to assume that it's pure coincidence that the hit man, who happens to be in the same hotel at the time of Blake's fall, should have for

383

his attorney somebody who knew Blake, and whose wife was possibly involved with him . . .'

'That could be said of rather a large number of wives, including yours, Mr Hardtman,' Kantzler pointed out mildly.

'But Tiviello is your client. Or are you his?'

Kantzler was unable to pass off this aspersion, it was too direct, too much of an accusation to be ignored. He got up, swirling his drink noisily, drained it and then went to the bar to fix himself another, with his own hands this time. He took several calming sips before replying.

'Let me say this,' he said, eventually. 'There are aspects of your visit here that I find pretty damn puzzling. But I can imagine that for reasons I do not know – it not being given to me to know everything – it was necessary for you to come here and make these insinuations. Though God knows why. I can only conclude that some essential piece of knowledge has been denied me, and without it, as you can see, I am not able to be very helpful.'

'Well, let me help you then, Kantzler, by spelling it out. Here you are with your Heriz rugs and your sexy cigarette lighters and your white carpets and your air of great decorum, and you and I know perfectly that you are among other things a front man for the mobs. That you represent their interest, not just when one of their best boys is up on a murder charge, but in the upper levels of Wall Street . . .'

Even Kantzler's supreme patience was beginning to run out, and he permitted himself a touch of anger.

'Let me tell you something, Mr Hardtman. You are talking crap. You have got hold of a few facts and strung them together to make up your own crazy story which, I may say, bears more resemblance to the ravings of paranoid lunatics than to anything else. It shouldn't be necessary for me to teach you a lesson in national security, nor to fill you in on how things are done, but since you come here accusing me of all sorts of things, we had better bear in mind what you know as well as I, that one of the "mobs" that I work for is the government of the United States.'

384

'No, I didn't know that . . . I really didn't,' Hardtman said. 'What sort of work?'

'Frankly, you've lost me, Mr Hardtman. I can't read the action any more. Whatever is going on, it beats me. If this is some kind of internal dog fight between you and Cole and the FBI, I beg to be left out of it. Look – talk to Walter Cole . . . Work it out with him . . .'

'What has Walter Cole got to do with it?'

'What?'

'Where's the connection . . .?'

'I didn't say there was a connection . . . what I said was . . .' He seemed to have wearied of these proliferating confusions. 'The fact is, Mr Hardtman, I'm going to have to ask you to excuse me . . . I have people coming to dinner . . . I suggest you ask him.'

'You work for Central Intelligence?'

'Come now, Mr Hardtman, please don't play games with me.' He walked to the door and called, 'Hank, would you show Mr Hardtman out. You didn't have a hat, did you Mr Hardtman?'

Walter Cole was in New York but tied up.

'I know you're busy, Walter. But this is urgent,' Hardtman said on the phone.

'All right, I'll try and grab ten minutes. Why don't you get over here soon as you can, and I'll try to get out to you?'

This was next morning. Hardtman took a taxi to the hotel and having announced his presence on the house phone, waited in the lobby for Cole to come down. It was another fine warm autumn day, and it was going to get warmer. The heat was already building up and in midtown Manhattan there was an oppressive sense of confinement, of being able to move only within narrow limits. There was hardly room to pace as Hardtman waited. It was half an hour before Cole came down.

'Sorry,' he said, 'but I just couldn't get out to you sooner.'

'What's the feeling in there?'

'High,' Cole said. 'Very high, as you'd expect.'

'In there' referred to Dewey's election offices in the hotel.
'I'd like to get out of here – this is a little cramped.'

'I have a lunch, Bill, otherwise . . .'

'I understand, Walter. Let's just walk outside, hmm?'

It was worse outside, hotter and dustier, and Madison
Avenue was a living torrent in which you could easily go
under without anybody noticing. Hordes of people swirled,
indifferent as an ocean, around the shivering black buildings.

On Park Avenue there was more space. They walked towards Grand Central. The corbelled tower rising above the
station was one of the more calming landmarks of the city,
telling you clearly where you were among the otherwise
undifferentiated masses all around, providing a graspable
scale with which the eye could measure distance. Hardtman
found himself thinking that what America lacked was any
sense of scale – in its desire for bigness, and greatness, in
its restless strivings, it had discarded all the rules of proportion, permitted itself every enormity.

Cole said, as they walked, 'Kantzler has been on the
phone to me for the last quarter of an hour. Very upset.
You really put the poor guy in a sweat. You accuse him of
being the front man for the mobs?'

'Isn't he?'

'I've heard it said,' he conceded. 'But people say a lot of
things.'

'Kantzler says he works for the government – specifically
for you.'

'He has done, yes. He's a useful man. He knows a lot of
people who can be useful.'

'Like Bobby Tiviello?'

'That doesn't surprise me. He has underworld connections. We used him during the war when we needed some
things done in Italy . . . Well, you were in on that, weren't
you?'

'I knew about it.'

'There are risks, of course, in using people like the
Lucky Lucianos of this world . . . their patriotism is sort of

386

a transferable commodity. But there are times when you've got no choice.'

Hardtman put a hand on Cole's arm and stopped him: they stood at the kerb facing a red light.

'Walter, I'm pretty sure Tiviello was in the hotel the night Blake "fell or jumped"—'

'Yes, that *is* a coincidence,' Cole agreed. The light had changed to green, but Hardtman detained Cole where they were on the street corner.

'Futhermore, Walter, do you realize that Katie Kantzler was involved with Blake . . .'

'Yes, I heard that rumour, too. But you know how vicious – and unfounded – rumours can be. I heard the same rumour about Laurene. You tell me, and you should know, that there was nothing in that. Well, I'm just pointing out to you how different things can look, depending on your point of view.'

'I do know there was something going on between Blake and Katie Kantzler. I saw with my own eyes . . .'

Cole stopped him.

'Let's cross,' he said taking his arm, hurrying him as the light began to change.

They stopped on the grassed central traffic island, halted between the two solid rivers of cars.

'Bill,' Cole said, 'I don't have a great deal of time. Look, I want to let you in on something. You know who was in there with the Governor and Foster? Allen. Allen Dulles. If Tom Dewey gets in, next month, Foster is going to be Secretary of State, and Allen will head CIA. The Admirals will go. Both Foster and Allen have a very high regard for you, Bill. Of course, Allen knows all about your OSS work during the war. We all think the President ought to have a national security adviser who's a pro. And at the same time commands the respect of – what shall we say? – more conservative elements in the country. Who better than you, Bill? Hmm?'

'Walter, right now that job – desirable as it may be, and much as I might like to have it under different circumstances – is not my first interest.'

'I understand, I understand what's been worrying you. But there's no problem now. Allen and the Governor and Foster know of the little trouble you had – for heaven's sake, they're men of the world. They don't see anything in the situation, as it has evolved, that would count against you.'

'We're talking at cross-purposes, Walter. I am telling you something and you're not listening. First, there is a circumstantial link between Blake and Tiviello, and now we find that Tiviello has a lawyer whose playful wife . . .'

They had missed the light, and were again stuck upon their narrow island between the two-way flow . . . From the blocked vista at Grand Central, Park Avenue was an undulating serpent flashing its shiny chrome scales all the way to Harlem. Hardtman saw that Cole had become impatient. It was the same expression that had been on Kantzler's face – the bemused look of someone who has missed the point, lost the drift. Hardtman wondered if he were talking incoherently. It was true he was not feeling very well, that he was suffering from dizziness again, that his head was full of wild notions and tortuous unravellings. But it seemed to him that he was at last beginning to make sense of some things; that the various pieces were beginning to fit together to suggest at least the vague general outline of the truth. Even if, in parts, that truth was still obscured there was now a feeling that it was only a matter of time and patience before the picture was completed.

Cole had turned round, abandoning any intention of crossing over to the eastern side of the avenue; he was turning to go back.

'I have to get back, Bill,' he said looking at his watch. 'They're waiting for me.'

'Walter, you haven't answered me . . . it seems to me that you have evaded everything I have said to you.'

'Bill,' Cole said as if addressing an uncomprehending child who requires gentle re-direction, 'I think we're talking about details, and frankly I don't have the time. I have to delegate the details to others to deal with – you follow me? All I can hope to do is give a general sense of direction to their endeavours. Let me just say this – the FBI is the proper investigative agency to inquire into Blake's death, and they appear satisfied that it was suicide. Now let's not fool ourselves – Blake's fall is kind of heaven-sent to us. Why look a gift-horse in the mouth? I seem to remember you uttering a *cri de coeur* : Who will rid me of this pestilential priest? Your prayer seems to have been answered. Why complain?'

The light had changed to green and the tide of traffic stopped abruptly to let them pass, and Cole taking Hardtman's arm led him across.

'You all right, Bill?'

'I'm all right,' he said, allowing himself to be brought further on to the pavement. But he was not all right. His eyes had become tightly screwed up, and from them shatter lines spread outwards across his face.

Walking by the reflecting pool with Walter Cole, had he meant *that*? A moment of wild wishful thinking, yes. But he had not meant *that*. Surely he had not meant *that*. He had not meant Julian to be murdered.

'Do I understand you to say, Walter . . .?' he began.

'Bill, you always understand a darned sight too much,' Cole said with an easy, evasive chuckle and a kind of humorous agitation of his silver moustache. It was clear he was not going to be more explicit. Words could mean anything. Had he meant Julian to die? In that moment of profound bitterness, by the reflecting pool. Seeing the shame and disgrace that Julian would bring upon him, seeing his marriage undermined, his career crumbling, Debbie's precious idealization of him lost. There *are* moments when one could kill somebody – and if the means are at hand . . . could he have known how close at hand the means were . . . Walter Cole? A word in the right ear and no sooner said than done. But no, he still could not believe it, he was over-interpreting. Cole could not possibly mean that.

'Well, I'm going to grab a taxi back to the Roosevelt,' Cole said. 'I said I'd only be ten minutes.'

'O.K., Walter.'

He had got a taxi to pull up by the kerb and was opening the door. He patted Hardtman's arm.

'Relax, Bill. Your problems are over. Phone me any time, hmm?'

Hardtman walked on for a time without any sense of where he was headed. All around him people were streaming out of high buildings, fighting to get from point A to point B, in the grip of some sort of panic as they beat against the sticky air as futilely as flies stuck to fly paper, and he was part of that vain attempt to escape. He was moving vaguely in the direction of Grand Central where, if he could stay on his feet, there were trains out, that would take him somewhere else. A taxi pulled up at the kerb, discharging its fare, and without thinking Hardtman got in.

'Where to, Mac?'

25

He had no idea where he wanted to go.

'Where to, Mac?'

Hardtman gave Joannie's address. It was just to tell him somewhere to go. He could not, at that moment, think of anywhere else.

When Joannie opened the door and saw him, she seemed amazed. He must have broken one of her fundamental rules by arriving unannounced. The free-and-easy life depends on people not intruding into it at the wrong times. This clearly was a wrong time. Perhaps there was somebody with her . . .

'What are you doing here?' she said, and he remembered her using the same phrase on Fire Island.

'I was in New York and I thought . . .' he began, trying to make light of it. But he did not have the appearance to carry off lightness, he knew that, and he saw from the way that she was looking at him that she realized something was wrong.

'Are you sick?' she asked with the faint note of distaste that she showed for any kind of infirmity of heart or body. He was very out of breath from the climb to the top floor, and hot. He gave a hoarse laugh, full of street dust.

'No, I'm all right,' he said. 'I was near here . . .'

'Why didn't you buzz me?'

'Didn't have time. Is it awkward?'

'I'm expecting someone.'

'How soon?'

'Any moment.'

Well, if the new love of her life was due any moment, an old love, as he knew from his own Fire Island experience, could be an embarrassment.

'Ask me in for a drink, Joannie,' he insisted, since he was still standing in the doorway.

He watched her pour him a Scotch, what was left in the bottle, which wasn't much; he drank it at a gulp, counting on its restorative effect.

'It's a shame we haven't got longer,' she said, just to make it quite clear that he was expected to leave after having finished off the last of her whisky. Her manner wasn't exactly welcoming, he thought; he saw her emotional toughness – it was, in a way, what had attracted him in the first place, but now it seemed less enticing.

'Well,' he said, 'you have evidently come out of your period of hibernation . . .'

'I told you that was how it'd be . . .'

'Yes, you did – how remarkably you've kept on schedule.'

'Is this a friendly visit?' she asked a little sharply.

This forced him to think about why he had come here.

'I'd hoped,' he said, 'that it was going to be a lot more friendly than it looks like being. Right now.'

'That's the way it is,' she said.

'When something is over for you, it sure is over.'

'What d'you expect? You expect me to sit home moping? You have your dandy little adventure. Then you go back to wifey, and one day the mood takes you to to stop by, and I'm supposed to drop everything? Fade out on long clinch? Well, I tell you. I learned something a long time ago, and that was how to cut off.'

'I suspected,' he said, 'that you had hidden strengths.'

'What kind of crack is that supposed to be?'

He stood up, finished the Scotch, and walked to the shelf where the liquor bottles were. He bent low, examining them.

'You're out of everything,' he reported.

'Yeah.'

'What do you say we go and have a drink somewhere?'

'I told you, I'm expecting someone.'

'Ah – yes.'

He was playing for time, now that he had finished his drink and had no further excuse for staying. He went to the window. Sudden rain beat against the pane.

'Do you suppose it's going to let up?' he asked. 'I didn't bring an umbrella.'

'You can usually pick up a cab on the corner.'

'In the rain?'

She made a little gesture of not knowing, and not caring.

'Perhaps you could call one for me?' That might give him a little more time, but she was not going to go along.

'If I wasn't expecting someone,' she said.

'Sure.'

He was completing a small circle, passing the open bedroom door. He glanced inside. There was a new photograph pinned directly above her platform bed – he could make out a mass of thick curly grey hair. She went for older men. No sign of the photographs Julian had taken on the ferry. Destroyed? Or consigned to the gallery of ex-lovers? She kept her records of the past. He was looking around to see if she had kept any of the photographs of them together. She had wanted so much to have them and they had caused him such a lot of trouble.

'What are you looking for?'

'You were so insistent that Julian take pictures of us on the boat, and you haven't even kept them.'

'Sure I kept them.'

She opened the bedroom door wider, and showed him where she had put his photograph, on the wall with the other men in her past.

He acknowledged his position with a slight nod. Quite close by he saw some new photographs of her – they were nude studies, shadowy, but touched by a fresh new sensuousness.

'Is he a photographer?'

'I'm not talking about it.'

'Married?'

'Isn't everybody?' she snapped back, looking crossly at her watch.

'He's late, huh? Well, that's how it goes. Married men – not to be relied on. Hmm?'

'I wish you'd get the hell out of here.'

She went to the window and looked in both directions, through the rain spattered glass.

'No sign of him? Maybe he isn't coming. Maybe his wife found out.' He hesitated. 'You heard about Julian?'

'Yeah. What a lousy thing to happen to him.'

'Yes. You liked Julian, didn't you.'

'Yeah, I liked him. Whatever they say about him, he didn't deserve ending up like that – a mess on the sidewalk. It was a terrific shock to me when I heard about it.'

Though she said she had been upset, she clearly had got over that, too. Like the end of love, death was something she took in her stride and was not excessively awed by.

'There were all sorts of stories about Julian,' Hardtman said.

'I know.'

She was looking out of the window again, a touch anxiously. He couldn't be sure how much attention she was paying. She was a girl who concentrated on one thing at a time: this gave her a certain quality of whole-heartedness when you were with her, but when you were not with her she got on with the next episode of her life. Well, he could not blame her for that.

He said, 'You've heard the rumours, then?'

'You mean that he was a spy? Oh sure.' She laughed. She was still looking out of the window. 'Is that what you think, too?'

'There are things that would seem to point to it,' he said cautiously. He was talking to her unresponsive back. He could sense the impatience in her – a girl waiting for her new love, filled with eager anticipation of his caresses. She had no time for things that were past. Him. Julian.

She turned round abruptly.

'Well, since you've drunk all my booze, you can buy me a drink.'

'What about *him*?'

'He'll wait around, I guess.'

As they came down into the street, the rain suddenly stopped and rainbows appeared linking the ziggurat castles in the air; half the sky was black, and the other half glowed with an intense aquamarine light. She took him along her street, past the back of the Dakota apartments, to a dark bar where a jukebox glowed like a cathedral window, with musicians jiggling their instruments under moving clouds inside a domed console. A record tumbled in slow motion under the needle, and a warm thick female voice told of the deceptiveness of love. They sat at the bar. Joannie was known here: there was in the barman's attitude towards her an implied familiarity with at least some of the details of her presumably complicated love life. Without a word he prepared her drink, putting the right amount of ice in the glass, and then raised a questioning eyebrow at Hardtman.

'The same.'

They could see themselves in the bar mirror. She was very responsive to the visual, and the sight of them together brought her closer to him.

'Well,' he said, 'to old times. How've you been, Joannie? The truth.'

'Fine.'

'You're a girl of robust constitution. Take things in your stride.'

'Right. And you? How've you been, Bill?'

'Oh not so fine. I don't get over things as fast as you. I suddenly realize . . .' He hesitated. '. . . I want to see you again. I didn't come here to say that. It just came out.'

'You know the way I am. I move around. But if I'm with somebody that's who I'm with.'

'For how long?'

'I don't go in for reading palms.' She laughed, and watched herself and him in the bar mirror. 'We do look kind of good together though,' she admitted. She took out a cigarette and lit it and surrounded herself with smoke. They exchanged long looks in the mirror.

She laughed, and then said: 'I'm sorry I snapped your head off before. I was sort of nervous for some reason.'

'I'd like to see you, Joannie.'

'Next time you're in New York, call me. In advance. Nobody's ever been shot for asking.' He put his hand over

395

hers on the bar top. The barman stopped busily wiping in their immediate vicinity and went on wiping further away. She had not forced Hardtman's hand away. No wonder barmen were cynics, with what they saw.

'Joannie . . .?'

He watched her face closely in the mirror; she was looking down; he thought of the nude photos on her wall. The record in the jukebox slid aside and a new one tumbled smoothly into its place.

'. . . that time, at the boat, when you said . . .'

'That I loved you?'

'That's what you said. You said it again later, but then you were drunk. We both were.'

'Boy! What a head I had next day! I didn't think you could get that drunk on champagne.'

'Joannie . . .'

'I meant what I said, both times.'

'Still you can say you are fine.'

'I told you I can cut off.'

'You must have learned in a very tough school.'

'I did, and I learned good. O.K.? Remember, I was married when I was eighteen. He was charming but he didn't believe in, like, paying the rent. So I had to fend for myself.'

'Strong.'

'Oh, I can be strong.'

He thought she looked very lovely in all her strength, and he could not help thinking how her eyes showed everything she was feeling when she looked unflinchingly up into his as they were making love.

'Joannie, did you spy for the Communist Party . . .?'

'You're a shit,' she said softly. 'You're a real shit.'

'I have to know.'

'Fuck you.' She had slipped off the bar stool and was leaving. Anger changed her, the way the seasons change things. She was wintry now. He saw the barman's eyes flicker towards them in his deadpan face as he polished glasses. Hardtman's hand shot out and caught her wrist and held her fast, preventing her from leaving.

'Let's not have a ruckus,' she said, pulling, but unable to free herself.

'I agree. Sit down, Joannie.'

Seeing she had no alternative, other than make a scene, she sat again, but only on the edge of the bar stool.

'Let's go sit down in the back,' he proposed. 'More private.'

She accepted the necessity for this gloomily.

'Why does it upset you so much, what I asked you?' he said when they were seated in the back.

'I thought you said it was a friendly visit. I was already grilled about all that by the FBI.'

'About what?'

'Having been a member of the Communist Party.'

'So you were?'

'Yes. It's no secret.'

'And did you do any undercover work for them, I'm not trying to trap you, I'm not the FBI. But there are some things I have got to get clear.'

'Undercover work?'

'Secret work.'

'Oh sure – it was all dead secret. You can imagine schoolgirls! Passing secret notes. Holding secret meetings. Secret meetings in the john . . . oh boy! Bill, I was sixteen at that time. That's when I was a member of the Communist Party. Following year I fell in love with a boy who worked for De Beers in London, and I decided there was more to be said for diamonds.'

'You were only a member for one year?'

'One year. Maybe I didn't actually resign at the end of the year, but that's when I quit in my head.'

'Why did you join in the first place?'

'They were standing up against Fascism, while the rest of the world sat on its ass.'

'What exactly did you do for the Communist Party while you were a member?'

'I collected dues. Recruited new members.'

'I'm sure you were good at that.'

397

'Yeah, I was. Not many guys put the phone down on me, or shut the door in my face.'

'What else did you do for them?'

'Let me think. Oh we distributed literature – spilled the beans about how everything was fixed by the capitalists to give the bosses the whip hand and keep the workers under.'

'What else?'

'What do you mean what else?'

'I mean did you report back to anyone, with information you had got hold of.'

'Oh sure. We had our little cell. The head of the cell I think was called Elspeth. For some reason. It wasn't her real name. I told her everything – you can imagine what that was. I gave her the low-down on all the bloated capitalist fathers of the other girls, and we decided, come the revolution, which of 'em'd be allowed to lick our boots, and which of 'em we would send down the salt mines.'

He was silent; he shook his head several times; catching sight of himself in a mirror, he saw the lines spread out from his screwed-up eyes, in continuous corrugations across his face – as when a single stone had disturbed the entire surface of a pond.

'Yes,' he said, 'it begins like that. Sometimes they will keep people gathering trivia for years and years, and reporting back, routinely, getting them used to the discipline. And then, one day, they ask you to do something that isn't so trivial, and by then it doesn't seem any different from a hundred other little things you've done.'

'What are you talking about?'

'In the light of what's happened, I have to ask myself: what was Julian's angle in bringing us together. You and me.'

'His angle?'

'He also brought you and Peter Volniakov together.'

'That's right. He introduced us.'

'You know who Peter Volniakov is?'

'Sure. I know he worked at the Russian Embassy. There's no law that says you can't speak to them, because they're Russian.'

398

'He was the Number Two in their espionage set-up here. He was running agents. He left the country the morning after Julian's disappearance became known.'

'I didn't know that. I didn't know any of that.'

'You're lying, Joannie.'

'I thought you said this was going to be friendly.'

'Considering that you'd had a close relationship with somebody high up – let's leave out for the moment what precisely he was – somebody high up in the Russian Embassy, didn't it occur to you how . . . how suspicious it would look . . . to go from him to me, and perhaps back again? Taking into account my position . . .'

She hesitated a fraction.

'When I met you it was all over with Peter. Was I supposed to put myself in quarantine because I'd once known some Russian? Anyway, how was I supposed to know anything would happen with us? It just happened, didn't it?'

'Did it? Did it just happen?'

'What the hell are you trying to suggest?'

He was looking directly at her. Her face softened into a smile of sensuous recollection, spanning the distance between their time together and now. 'You know how it happened,' she said, 'we just sort of clicked, didn't we?'

'Our chemistry was right?' he parodied her. 'Was that what is was? Or had Julian arranged it?'

'You think I'm a hooker or something, you think I can be arranged? Is that what you think?'

'The cheque I gave you. You cashed it.'

'You gave it to me.'

'I gave it to you . . . to buy yourself a present. It was made out to the store. They cashed it for you.'

'I was broke. Seemed crazy to buy a four-hundred-dollar television when I didn't have money for the rent.'

'That's one way of looking at it. Another way is to say I gave you four hundred dollars for services rendered. Cheap at the price.'

It looked as though she was going to hit him; his hand tightened on hers in semblance of a lover's squeeze.

'What a lousy shit you are,' she said in a low voice.

'Julian must have considered it a terrific joke. A Russian espionage chief and a Presidential security assistant sharing the same mistress.'

'That's presuming he laid me on for you.'

'Well, even if he didn't. Maybe he didn't need to actually suggest it to you. Knowing you as well as he did, and he did know you very well, didn't he? Knowing you, and that you had been a troubadour in one of your previous lives, he could presumably count on your chemistry being right. Volniakov was a lonely Russian, always looking for women, so that was a safe bet. And I . . . well, I was a married man of a certain age . . . a safe bet, too.'

'Jesus Christ! What was I supposed to do? If I *was* laid on for you as you so insultingly suggest, what was I supposed to get out of you?'

'Placing somebody like myself in a compromising position . . . vulnerable to blackmail, or pressures . . . it's a familiar technique.'

'Jeez. You can believe that the whole thing with us was set up?'

'I found it very difficult and painful to believe . . .'

'But now you find it easier?'

'When things fit, you are obliged to come to certain conclusions, painful as they may be.'

'Things can be made to fit, if that's how you want to see them.'

'Julian was trying to get something out of me,' he insisted.

'I agree. Sure . . .'

'You admit that?'

'Julian was trying to get something out of everybody.'

'Yes, yes, perhaps . . . but I wasn't exactly everybody. He must have been after something very special, in my case – somebody working for the President.'

'That's right, that's right.' She seemed to remember something suddenly, something that made her lips curl in a slow secret smile. 'I remember now. He told me once. He told me what he wanted from you.'

'He told you?'

'Oh Julian didn't do anything for nothing, see. He was always doing people favours, but it was for a reason and the reason was that one day he was going to ask for something in return, and sure he was going to ask you for something, when the time was right. What he wanted from you was . . .' She had to laugh; she couldn't help it, her eyes filling up with a lovely cynical kind of amusement, that was not harsh, just knowing, and at the same time excusing, she was not too hard on people, she knew all about their inordinate appetites . . . 'What he wanted from you was an introduction to Mr Truman. Wanted you to sort of recommend him. He wanted to be the President's . . . physician. Well, you know the kind of thing he did. Massages. He knew the President likes a rubdown at night to help him sleep. And he thought that if he could start with that . . . it was a way in. Julian was always thinking about ways in. He thought if he got in with the President, he'd be made. See, the thing to understand about Julian – poor old Julian – is that he was on the make. Like everybody else. All that reduce desires stuff – bullshit! Julian wanted the lot.'

It was necessary for Hardtman to think about this explanation. Events were open to so many different interpretations, when you were engaged in secret work. You had to go by the ring of truth. For you rarely were in the position of having absolute proof of anything. You were all the time listening hard. But even so you did not hear some things.

'What was it about Julian?' he asked now. 'Why did all the women fall for him? Including you.'

'Oh he had some nice ways. Always made you feel good. Unlike some people I could name.' She gave him a look, but it was already somewhat softened by forgiveness. 'Being with Julian gave you a lift. I don't know why really . . . there were always things happening, and you felt he could make all sorts of things happen for you. He could do all these things, and knew so many people . . . there was nothing that was out of his reach. It seemed. And he took those terrific pix. That made you look so good, better than you ever dreamed you looked in your vainest moment. Add then another thing, whatever it was, an argument, or a

401

game, he'd let you win. Well, for a while. It was all so he could win in the end. He didn't make it, did he?'

'Not many people do.'

'I've got to go,' she said. 'Will I see you again?'

'I don't know, Joannie.'

'You do believe I've been telling you the truth?' she said looking at him directly.

'I don't know,' he said. 'I don't know what to believe.'

26

The truth is that Julian did not fit the Homer profile at all. He had never been to Eton or Oxford, it turned out, or to any public school or university. The nearest he came to Eton was when, for a time, he was a pupil at the Windsor Boys' Grammar School. It was on the other side of the river from Eton, and he used to see the Eton boys all the time in their shiny tailcoats and grubby top hats. They must have left some kind of permanent impression on the twelve-year-old clergyman's son from Virginia Water. They must have conveyed a sense of being superior and privileged young persons of a most enviable sort. I suppose we did give ourselves grand airs in those pre-war days. We tended to be very dismissive of grammar school boys. The clergyman's son from Virginia Water would not have needed to be hyper-sensitive to realize that we did not consider him good enough to mix with us.

In the shops along the High Street, Julian would have seen the automatic deference with which some snotty-nosed top-hatted nine-year-old was treated by the shopkeepers, and this must have given him ideas.

One cannot help to some extent admiring the verve with which he practised his deception, the skill with which he mimicked our ways. If people can be so easily taken in by an accent, a tone of voice, a manner, a tie bought for a few shillings at Herbert and Johnson, then they deserve to be deceived. Yes, I admire his cheek and lament his sad end. When you come to think of it, the brilliance in our blood often was passed on by the likes of him. We all have our skeletons in the cupboard.

It was, of course, the Americans, with their deeply suppressed class-consciousness, who were, to use their own expressive terminology, the real suckers. What a stroke of genius it was on his part to go to America in 1938. It was not Eton and Oxford that nurtured him, but the School of Osteopathy in De Moines, Iowa, and it was there he discovered that he had a gift – a gift of the fingers. He was never a pupil of Felix Kersten's in Amsterdam or of Dr Ko's in Berlin, nor did he train with Master Kodo Sawaki in Yokohama, and he never had any connection with Wilhelm Reich. But he was a quick and catholic reader, and he had a knack of selection, and he took what was best – or most readily adaptable to his purposes – from each of his unwitting masters. From Kersten he took the idea of nerve massage, and a certain mysteriousness of technique, which helped to elevate what he did above the level of a Turkish Bath attendant's rubdown; from Yoga he took the rediscovery of the body and the idea of the attainability of grace; from Kneipp he took the healing power of natural things, water, plants, snow, earth, berries, balms; and from Reich he took the therapy of sexual freedom. He put all this together with what he had learned at the School of Osteopathy in De Moines, and added his own intuitive understanding of some things, and it worked. For a time. There is no question that he brought people relief from pain, that he helped them to sleep, that he eased their backaches and their headaches, and taught them to breathe, to move better, and cured them of some inhibitions.

About the signed photographs in his waiting room. They were genuine. He really did know famous people. He had a great talent for socializing and was in addition a rather good photographer, at any rate his photographs were highly flattering. He had the ability to catch the best in people. Through one of his connections he had got a commission to do a series of portraits for the *Tatler and Bystander*. This gave him an entrée to society, and he used it to good effect. His subjects were usually quite willing to autograph the charming photographs he took of them. It was in this way that he obtained signed photographs of Winston Churchill, King Peter of Yugoslavia, and all the rest. The implied suggestion that these famous people were his patients was not necessarily untrue. Often he would contrive to combine a photography session with a little massage. The one led naturally enough to the other. He might ask in the course of posing his subject, did he happen to suffer from backache, did his shoe heels wear away on the outside rather than on the inside, and from such casually-elicited information he would offer some general theory about the tendency of a certain kind of work – such as writing – to produce a lowering of one shoulder and a curvature of the spine. If the subject inquired what he could do about his condition, Julian was quick to offer his services. With an unrefusable, 'May I?' he would apply some deft pressure to neck or skull or spinal cord, and this often had an immediate beneficial effect. Sometimes this led to a full-scale massage there and then, sometimes not. Occasionally it led to the photographic subject becoming Julian's patient. But whether this happened or not, Julian would send his more eminent sitters a complimentary portfolio of photographs he had taken, and few of these people were so churlish as to refuse to return one picture appropriately autographed (he always included a stamped and addressed envelope).

It is really amazing, when you come to think of it, how readily one gives one's autograph to a complete stranger. A signature is a most powerful symbol of legitimacy, it is what seals a contract, enforces a marriage vow, certifies a death, and is the means by which great fortunes are passed on, and yet one does sign some things, such as photos of oneself, very casually, without a thought about the use to which one's signature may eventually be put.

The name-dropping anecdotes that Julian told also had some basis in actuality. Julian encouraged his sitters to converse while they were being photographed, he said it made them 'more themselves'. People will open up amazingly to someone who has a professional pretext for asking questions, and Julian – great flatterer that he was – knew always to leave the best role and the best lines to others. And people came away from him feeling in much better shape.

It was perhaps not totally ridiculous to suppose he might have been a spy. In Washington he had access to many people who were in possession of secrets; socially and professionally, he must have picked up a great deal of information that could have been useful to a foreign power. He may even have repeated some of this gossip to his friends on the other side. It was an aspect of his sense of humour that he enjoyed hobnobbing with the capitalist hyenas as well as with their implacable class enemy. He no doubt enjoyed enormously the joke of Joannie Fontanez going from the bed of the Soviet spy chief Volniakov into the arms of one of the President's national security assistants. For Julian contriving such a Schnitzlerian roundabout of love must have been no end of a lark. Of course, he miscalculated how seriously his lark would be taken by the people entrusted with the defence of the Republic at a time of nation-wide suspicion and fear.

He was not to know how closely his assumed background – Eton, Oxford, Villiers blood in his veins, closeness to the right people – corresponded with the profile of the spy. I fear he was too clever by half. If only his mimicry had been less good, if his accent had had some middle-class intonations to give him away; if only he had said mirror instead of looking glass, or toilet instead of lavatory, or asked his host for *a* whisky (as if he were in a saloon bar) instead of whisky – if only he had committed any such solecism, it might have saved him. There would have been no need for anyone to bump off a clergyman's son from Virginia Water, upstart though he was, and too attractive to women for his own good.

After leaving Joannie's apartment, Hardtman took a taxi to the Roosevelt and demanded to see Cole. He was still in conference with the Governor and the Dulles brothers, but he came out immediately when he read Hardtman's scrawled message. He was in shirtsleeves, glasses pushed up on to his moist, statesmanlike and tense forehead. Solicitously he walked Hardtman up and down the hotel corridor, saying nothing at first, wrenching his thoughts from the great schemes of the Governor's suite to the practicalities that had to be faced here in the corridor.

'Bill, you're crazy,' he said finally. 'You're crazy to resign. There's no need. I realize that you are troubled by certain nagging questions. I realize that. You may be right. Mistakes are sometimes made. But let us keep our mistakes in the family – hmm?'

Hardtman said, 'I can't be sure of course, but I don't think that Julian Blake was a spy. And I don't think Julian would have filled a Thermos with hot coffee and then thrown himself out the window. I also think he would have finished his letter to me . . . I could be wrong. The thing is, I intend to find out. *I need to know, Walter*. I'm going to the D.A.'s office and I'm going to tell them what I know and I'm going to ask them to look into it, sparing nobody.'

'You'll be dragged through the mud,' Cole said.

'Can't be helped.'

'Damn crazy foolishness, Bill. There is no need, there is no need. It's all been settled . . .'

'That's what I thought. Walter, I was brought in to keep an eye on you, and I can tell you that's a tough job the way you move around, left hand not knowing what the right is doing. I don't know how seriously I was expected to watch you, and up to now I never could put my finger on anything specific enough. But this is specific enough. I want to find out how something like this can happen. Blake's death, I mean. No matter who gets hurt. Because, if nothing else, it may show up what's wrong with the way you've got it worked out. And that is – as I interpret it – what my job is about. So if I can just get this going before I resign, I will feel it points the way at least towards what needs to be done.'

Cole had listened to this quietly, but now he seemed to have lost patience. 'Bill, you were always a stubborn cuss, with that peculiar sense of honour of yours. I really think you'd have been more comfortable living in the eighteenth century. Looks like it may be necessary to cut our losses, yes, yes . . .' He made a small hand gesture like a monarch waving to a crowd, and turned away and went back to his conference.

*

The inquiries that followed did not establish Julian's innocence with any certitude, though they did show that the assumption of his guilt had been based on very flimsy evidence and a total misconception about his origins. Even so, people continued to believe that he probably had been involved in dubious dealings with the Russians, or else why would he have thrown himself out of a seventeenth-storey window? As one Congressman put it, 'Our proof that they are Communist agents is when they jump out of windows.' The notion that Julian had been murdered was given little credence. The FBI had not been able to get enough evidence to charge Tiviello, and to most people the idea of a murder plot involving a hired killer, acting on behalf of unknown people, seemed too far fetched at that time.

As Walter Cole had predicted, the effect of the investigations was to drag Hardtman's name through the mud . . . what did not come up at Congressional hearings, the Press dug out, and since national security was involved, the readers were spared no spicy detail of how a government figure had compromised himself with a girl of dubious connections and Russian lovers.

Those who knew Hardtman well understood how hurt he was by the scandal, especially because of what he thought might be its effect on his family. But in this respect he was lucky: Laurene and Debbie stood by him staunchly. Others, who had suffered his acerbities, got satisfaction from seeing him brought down.

Hardtman at least could say that before resigning he had drawn the President's attention to the great danger of letting the clandestine service act as an executive arm of government policy.

27

When the inquiries had come to an end and all the fuss had died down and Hardtman was back in private life in New York, he still went on trying to clear Julian's name. He was determined to keep the case open. Clearing Julian was part of the process of clearing himself. To this end he was constantly going over all the events, searching for clues to the real identity of Homer. Hardtman examined the material with me again and again, and presently I began to perceive a certain purpose in his confidences. They were of a kind to encourage similar confidences in his listener. He was seeking to draw me out.

He went over the events with me, step by step. Who was present on such and such a day when this or that was said? Who, in the Embassy, or in SIS, would have had access to a particular piece of information? I was the obvious person to help him. One day he asked me how many people had known of Truman's promise, once the elections were over, to review the question of the custody of the atomic bomb.

I reminded him that I had myself given him this particular piece of information. He had telephoned me from New York to check the *Herald Tribune* story, and I had told him everything I knew.

'It would be interesting,' he said, 'to know who told you, because whoever it was knew something that nobody else knew until many weeks later.'

'Is that so? In that case, I must try and remember who it was. If it's important. I do believe it was Graham Forster . . . he had very good connections everywhere, and always seemed to know what was going on.'

On another occasion, he suddenly remarked, 'It was really pretty damn unfortunate that you did not get to Starkov in time. If you had, we would have known who

Homer was, and a lot of things might never have happened.'

'Yes,' I said, 'it was a real balls-up. We waited for him for hours, Medlicott and I. Finally there came a point when we got sick of waiting and decided to go home. There was that terrible snowstorm, and we assumed that this had delayed him. We thought he would come the following day. Of course, I had no idea that the duty officer was quite so dim.'

'He says he was not told that someone important was expected.'

'He was new, and I don't think he paid much attention to what was said to him.'

'Odd to have left such a raw new man in charge, that night especially.'

'Well, he only had to lift the phone and call one of us. I suppose Medlicott assumed that even Corporal Brown was capable of that.'

'From the way he acted, he would seem not to have had a clue that the Russian was someone who was expected. And important.'

'Yes, it is strange. There was a school of thought that Medlicott – who died in somewhat strange circumstances, if you recall, about eight months later, when there was that fuss about what had happened – that Medlicott might have been got at by the Russians. I blame myself now for not having insisted on staying that night. One doesn't like to pull rank on the local man, and I thought the purely procedural aspect was something he could handle.'

It had become clear to me, by this time, that Hardtman's questions and his enlisting my help in the elaborate reconstruction of events, had a definite purpose. He was conducting a methodical process of elimination, and by this time his list must have been narrowed down to a handful, at most.

My presence in Berlin at the time of Starkov's death, of course gave me a key role in these reconstructed events. I had been sent there to question Starkov and satisfy myself about him: to make sure he was not an MGB plant. He had made it known to us that he could identify Homer, and I was supposed to determine if he was telling the truth. To lose a source is always an embarrassment to a professional Intelligence man, but it is something that can happen to the best of us. However, Hardtman, in his slow methodical elimination of one alternative after another, finally, I saw, was coming to other conclusions.

He knew that I had been sent to Berlin to bring Starkov in, and that I was considered the best man for this delicate job. But at the same time he was making various connections in his mind that others did not make until much later.

Seeing what was going on in his thoughts, I decided it was time for me to leave. It was obvious that it would not be long before he had the whole sequence of events worked out. And I was not going to wait for that to happen.

It had taken me only a short time, sitting in the abandoned car, already half buried in snow, to establish that Starkov's information was genuine, for after a certain amount of bargaining he told me Homer's identity, and I was in a position to know that he was not fabricating.

Fortunately, the only photographs he had seen of Homer were ten or twelve years old, and did not look at all like me. So he suspected nothing. In any case, it was dark in the car. I knew that I would have to kill him immediately. I could not permit him to repeat what he had just told me. I was prepared for this contingency; after the MGB boys bungled things, I realized I might have to take care of Starkov myself. In my briefcase I had my toiletry bag, and in that there was an old fashioned cut-throat razor. I complained of there being no air in the car, and leaned across him to wind down a window on his side, and as I drew back again I did it with one stroke across his throat. The razor was so sharp and my hand so fast that I don't believe he realized his throat had been cut until he saw the blood spurting out of his body.

Not a pleasant business, but soon over (though he continued to twitch, distressingly, for some time after he was dead); I cannot say that I felt any moral compunction. Elimination is one of the standard expedients of our profession and he had used it himself, often enough, and unhesitatingly. Besides, I have no sympathy for a man who will sell his country for money. The deal he had demanded in the car had included a substantial financial remuneration for betraying me. So I could tell myself I was acting in self-defence.

Hardtman, in his questions, kept returning to what had happened in Berlin that night. He understood that for me to have gone home when expecting an important defector was out of character. There were some who might have done that – but not I. He knew me to be too conscientious about my work. I would have waited all night long, and the next day, and the next night. I would not have left the handling of such a big catch to a dim-witted duty officer.

Hardtman was careful in our conversations not to let me know how much he knew, or had guessed. He did not want to scare me off before he had all the pieces. I deduced from his manner towards me that he probably did not yet have enough solid evidence to go to the FBI. After all the mistakes that had been made he would be very careful. To accuse me, and not be able to prove his case, would backfire on him. Also, there must still have been an element of doubt in his mind. And I knew that the way to reinforce that doubt was not to make any precipitate moves that would confirm his conjectures. I was not going to make the same mistake that Julian made. And so I continued to see Hardtman, from time to time, and let him try to panic me into doing something that would give me away. As part of his game-plan he was progressively making his suspicions clearer to me; as part of mine, I was refusing to react. I do not panic easily, and as a matter of fact I was rather enjoying the sense of danger engendered during our civilized little lunches.

One lunchtime he said to me, 'You know what gives the spy away in the end – the core of secrecy in his being. It does not permit him any indiscretions, and ordinary human beings are sometimes indiscreet, among friends, anyway. Now you never are, I know, but that's unusual. You are an unusual fellow, we have known each other for several years, and whereas you, of course, know a great deal about me, I feel I know little of your deeper feelings and pre-occupations.'

'Put it down to British reticence,' I said.

'Is that what it is?'

'I expect so. And an English public school education. One is taught early on to hide what one truly feels, on pain of mockery and derision.'

'It must be lonely,' he mused out loud, and added quickly, 'the spy's life . . .'

'Oh I don't know,' I said, 'he gets to meet lots of interesting people, and to hear their secrets.'

'Yes, but nobody with whom he can share his true feelings. They say that in prison even men of the strongest character are able to take solitary confinement only for a certain length of time before a psychological deterioration begins to set in. There seems to be a fundamental need to communicate with others on a level of truthfulness. The spy must suffer terribly from the denial of that.'

'Not only the spy,' I pointed out.

I saw it was time for me to pack my bags and leave. And so I now activated the recall to London that I had been carefully engineering for the past few months, ever since I began to realize that Hardtman was on to me. Fortunately, for me, he was at that time the only one who had found me out, and since his credibility had been consider-ably impaired by events, I had enough time to make a graceful departure. If he presented his suspicions to the FBI and the counter-Intelligence boys of CIA, they did not act on them. I called on all my American colleagues at both agencies, bade them farewell, and was given a warm send-off.

Soon after my return to London I was able to effect a plausible change of career for myself that immediately took me abroad, and I have not returned since. I have not disappeared exactly, since I write to old friends and even meet some of them when they come to my part of the world, but on the other hand I am not easy to find if I do not wish to be found.

413

On the question of why I did it – ah! the endless Freudian search for a hidden motive: I have little taste for that sort of exercise. My principle in life has been: never apologize, never explain, let the facts speak for themselves. And as I said at the beginning, this is Hardtman's story not mine. The reader must infer what he can about my nature. He will have observed, by now, that I have a certain taste for secrecy, as he has perhaps, too, in some areas. There are compulsions at work in all our lives. It is not only fatal women who sweep men off their feet and drive them to extremes of behaviour at variance with their apparent characters. Ideas can be similarly seductive, powerful, deceiving, and finally fatal. And so it was with me.

But that is another story.